THIS
MOURNABLE
BODY

Also by Tsitsi Dangarembga

THIS MOURNABLE BODY

A Novel

TSITSI DANGAREMBGA

Graywolf Press

This publication is made possible, in part, by the voters of Minnesota through a Minnesota State Arts Board Operating Support grant, thanks to a legislative appropriation from the arts and cultural heritage fund, and a grant from the Wells Fargo Foundation. Significant support has also been provided by the National Endowment for the Arts, Target, the McKnight Foundation, the Lannan Foundation, the Amazon Literary Partnership, and other generous contributions from foundations, corporations, and individuals. To these organizations and individuals we offer our heartfelt thanks.

Published by Graywolf Press
250 Third Avenue North, Suite 600
Minneapolis, Minnesota 55401

www.graywolfpress.org

Published in the United States of America

ISBN 978-1-55597-812-9

2 4 6 8 9 7 5 3 1
First Graywolf Printing, 2018

Library of Congress Control Number: 2017953356

Cover design: Kimberly Glyder Design

Cover art: Shutterstock

This book is dedicated to my children,
Tonderai, Chadamoyo, and Masimba

There is always something left to love.
—Lorraine Hansberry, *A Raisin in the Sun*

THIS
MOURNABLE
BODY

PART 1
EBBING

CHAPTER 1

There is a fish in the mirror. The mirror is above the washbasin in the corner of your hostel room. The tap, cold only in the rooms, is dripping. Still in bed, you roll onto your back and stare at the ceiling. Realizing your arm has gone to sleep, you move it back and forth with your working hand until pain bursts through in a blitz of pins and needles. It is the day of the interview. You should be up. You lift your head and fall back onto the pillow. Finally, though, you are at the sink.

There, the fish stares back at you out of purplish eye sockets, its mouth gaping, cheeks drooping as though under the weight of monstrous scales. You cannot look at yourself. The dripping tap annoys you, so you tighten it before you turn it on again. A perverse action. Your gut heaves with a dull satisfaction.

"Go-go-go!"

It is a woman knocking at your door.

"Tambudzai," she says. "Are you coming?"

It is one of your hostelmates, Gertrude.

"Tambudzai," she calls again. "Breakfast?"

Footsteps tap away. You imagine her sighing, feeling at least a little low, because you did not answer.

"Isabel," the woman calls now, turning her attention to another hostel dweller.

"Yes, Gertrude," Isabel answers.

A crash tells you you have not paid sufficient attention. Your elbow nudged the mirror as you brushed your teeth. Or did it? You are not sure.

You did not feel it. More precisely, you cannot afford definite conclusions, for certainty convicts you. You strive to obey the hostel's rules, yet they just laugh at you. Mrs. May, the hostel matron, has reminded you frequently how you have broken the rule of age. Now the mirror has again slipped off the crooked nail in the wall and fallen into the basin below, resulting in a new crack. The next fall will shake all the pieces from the frame. You lift it out gently to keep the broken fragments in place, thinking up an excuse to tell the matron.

"Now then, what were you doing with it?" Mrs. May will demand. "You know you're not meant to meddle with the appointments."

The matron is fighting for you, she says. She tells you often how the board of trustees is complaining. Not about you as such, but about your age, she says. The city council will revoke the hostel's licence if they find out women of such antiquity reside there, women who are well beyond the years allowed in the Twiss Hostel's statutes.

You hate that board of bitches.

A triangle falls out of the looking glass, onto your foot, then slides to the floor, leaving a spot of dark red. The concrete floor is the grey-green of a dirty lake. You expect to see the rest of the fragments fall onto it, but they hold.

Outside in the hall, Gertrude and Isabel reassure each other that each has slept long and well. Several other hostel women join them and they begin their never-ending chatter.

The floor out in the hall is shiny, though it is made of cement and not of cow dung. You wrote tourist brochures at the advertising agency you walked out of many months ago. The tourist brochures you composed said your country's village women rub their cow pat floors until they shine like the cement floor. The brochures lied. There is no shine in your memory. Your mother's floors never shone with anything. Nothing ever glittered or sparkled.

You pad away from the washbasin to pull your wardrobe door open. The fish bloats to the size of a hippopotamus in the oily white paint that covers the wardrobe's wooden panelling. You turn away, not wanting to see the lumbering shadow that is your reflection.

At the back of the cupboard, you find your interview skirt, the one you bought when you had cash to purchase an approximation of the fashion spreads you mulled over in magazines. You loved the pencil skirt with its matching top. Now squeezing into it is a major assault on the pachyderm. The zip bites at your skin with treacherous teeth. Matron May has organized this interview that you are dressing up for. It is with a white woman who lives up in Borrowdale. You are concerned there will be blood on your skirt. But it clots quickly, like the line of red on the top of your foot.

Gertrude and company clatter down the corridor. You wait until the babble of young women going to breakfast dies away before you step into the hall.

"You people! Yes, you," the cleaning woman mutters, just loud enough for you to hear. "Always coming down to make more mud before this floor's dry." She curves out of your way and her bucket clangs against the wall. Filthy froth slops out.

"Has my bucket done anything to you?" she hisses under her breath at your back.

"Good morning, Mrs. May," you call.

Your matron, at the reception desk in the hall, is pink and powdered; she looks like a large fluffy cocoon.

"Good morning, Tahmboodzahee," she answers, looking up from the crossword in the *Zimbabwe Clarion*, which lies in front of her on the desk.

She smiles as you respond, "How are you this morning, Matron? I hope you slept well. And thank you for everything."

"Today's the day, isn't it?" she says, good humour deepening at the thought of a life without battling the board on your account. "Well, good luck! Remember to mention me to Mabel Riley," she goes on. "I haven't seen her properly since she left school and then we both went off and got married and got busy with our families. Do tell her I said hello. I spoke to her daughter and she was quite sure you'll work something out about the cottage."

You recoil from the matron's enthusiasm. She leans in, mistaking the gleam in your eye for appreciation. You feel it, yet you are not sure yourself what this glow means, whether it is proper, or whether it is something that you are daring.

"I'm sure everything will go very well," Matron May whispers. "Mabs Riley was a wonderful head-girl. I was just a little junior but she was absolutely lovely."

Specks of powder flutter from her trembling cheeks.

"Thank you, Mrs. May," you mumble.

The "yesterday, today, and tomorrow" bush in the hostel garden throbs purple, white, and lilac. Bees wade through air to push proboscises into the splashes of light, lighter, lightest.

You stop by the shrub in midstride, to avoid squashing a daring lucky beetle. Beyond it the hibiscus hedge rages scarlet. Years ago, you don't want to remember how many, you blew the fat-bottomed beetles out of their sandy pits with laughter and careless puffs. When the insect was exposed, you dropped ants into the hole and watched the tiny gladiators fight and perish in the mandibles of their tormentor.

You turn onto Herbert Chitepo Avenue. The urchins mistake you for a madam and whine for donations.

"Tambu! Tambu!" a voice calls.

You know the voice. You wish you had crushed the beetle.

Gertrude wobbles up in her stilettos, Isabel in her wake.

"We are going the same way," says Gertrude, who calls herself Gertie. "So now we have a chance to say good morning and find out how you slept, after all. Isabel and I are going to Sam Levy's."

"Good morning," you mutter, keeping distance.

They settle beside you like police constables, one on either side. The spring in their step irritates you.

"Oh, I didn't know," Isabel rushes on, as though, for her, speech need not be preceded by thought. This affords you some amusement, so you smile. The young woman is encouraged.

"You're going to Sam Levy's, too. You love the sales, just like us. I didn't know old people like fashion."

The girls' breasts jut out as they pull their shoulders back to make the most of their chests.

"I am not going to Sam Levy's," you say. Their eyes look past you, examining the cars on the road and the middle-aged men who drive them.

"My aunt lives there," you declare. "I am going to her house in Borrowdale."

The young women turn their attention back to you.

"Borrowdale," says Gertrude. You are not sure whether her astonishment is due to your having an aunt or to the fact that a relative of yours might live in Borrowdale. Nevertheless, gratified for the first time that morning, you allow a smile to inch up as far as your eyes.

"So is there anything amazing in that?" Isabel shrugs. She adjusts a red bra strap that has slipped down her arm. "My babamunini, my father's brother, had a house up there. But he lost it because he couldn't pay for it. They said it was the rates or something. So he went to Mozambique, with diamonds, I think." She wiggles her nose. "Now he's in jail there. It's only people like that who go to Borrowdale. Elderly!"

"So who is this relative, Tambudzai?" Gertrude asks.

"I don't mean ones like you, Sisi Tambu," Isabel interrupts. "I mean those really old ones."

There is a crowd right up to the curb at the corner of Borrowdale Road and Seventh Street.

"Vabereki, vabereki," a young man bellows from a combi's dented door.

The vehicle swerves toward the curb. You all draw in arms, feet, and heads. You lurch back with the crowd. A moment later you surge forward with everyone else, using your elbows to nudge back sharply as many people as possible. But it is a false alarm.

"Parents, we aren't taking you," the youthful combi conductor shouts, with a smirk. "We're full. Did you get that? Full."

The driver is grinning. Crows zigzag out of the flamboyant trees up the road. They screech away from the cloud of soot that belches from the combi's belly.

In a little while everyone lurches forward once more. Steel and rubber scream as the driver of another minibus stamps on the brakes. Wheels bump against the curb. Young men elbow past and jump up. You duck under arms and in between torsos.

"Parents, get in. Get in, get in, parents!" the new conductor shouts.

He makes a shield with his body to hold in half a dozen school-children who are packed on the engine hub. You squeeze past, your thigh brushing his privates, the contact making you feel ashamed. He grins.

"Ow, Mai! My mother!" a child squeals.

You have trodden on her toe with the two-tone Lady Di heels of real European leather shoes that were a present received some years ago from your cousin who travelled abroad to study.

Tears trickle out of the child's eyes. When she bends over to nurse her toe, her head bumps into the conductor's bottom.

"Ha, you people, vana hwindi," your hostelmate Gertrude drawls. One of her feet is on the combi step. Her voice is mellow and confident.

"Those are just little children. Weren't you ever a child yourself? We call them kids, but our children are not the same as those of goats," she says in the same languid tones.

"If you've come to look after children, that's all right, but don't do it here. Do you want to make us late?" a man in the back of the bus shouts.

"Ah, did she say anything to any of you?" says Isabel, who has clambered in after you.

Offended passengers murmur about your companions.

"Girls who don't know what they're talking about."

"Youngsters who don't have a clue about anything. They don't know God gave them a mind for thinking and keeping the mouth quiet."

Glad to have wedged yourself into a seat, you say nothing at first.

"Maybe our young women are asking for something," the man in the back says. "Asking for something to be taught to them. If they are not careful, someone will teach it and they will have to learn it."

"Those children should draw their feet in," you say moments later. For you are part of this mass of being in the combi.

Isabel doesn't speak again and finds a seat. Gertrude too stops fighting for the children and levers herself up. She pats the little girl on the head as she takes the last place opposite the conductor.

"She's the best," the schoolboy seated beside the girl tells Gertrude.

"She is going to run at the school sports day. When she's all right we always win."

He looks down in disappointment.

Everything is uncomfortable. There are too many people in the combi, too tightly packed. The engine boils under the children's bums. The smell of hot oil seeps into the air. Sweat runs down from your armpits.

In a few moments the conductor is collecting money and shouting out stops: "Tongogara Avenue. Air Force. The robots."

"Change," a woman pleads at Churchill Avenue. "I gave you a dollar." She has a chest like a mattress, is the kind of woman that men themselves do not dare to start with.

"Fifty cents," the woman begs, looking over at the young conductor. She is one of the people who laughed at the young men's banter.

The youth scowls. "Where can I get change from, Mother?"

"Is there no one with fifty cents in that combi?" the woman continues pleading as she climbs out. "I can't leave my fifty cents here." But the conductor has banged on the roof and the combi is moving. The woman disappears in a burst of black fumes.

"Ah-ah! Didn't she hear there isn't any change?" the man at the back says. His mouth is a crescent moon of amusement.

Your hostelmates climb out at Borrowdale shops.

You go on to Borrowdale Police and make your way between the BP and Total service stations. By the side of the road, you peel off your Lady Dis. You pull out black Bata plimsolls and push the pumps into your bag.

You dread the people of the fine suburb seeing you in canvas shoes, especially as you carry a much better pair hidden away. So it is a relief when you arrive at 9 Walsh Road where Widow Riley lives without bumping into any acquaintances. You sit down on the drain bridge by the fence to squash your feet back into your pumps.

Lips are all you see to begin with and you are terrified. Swollen feet wedged into your Lady Dis, you leap up. The lips are arranged in a snarl around yellow teeth. They belong to a small shaggy-haired terrier.

"Yau! Yau!" the dog yelps, outraged at your presence.

"Who are you?" a high-pitched voice trembles through the morning air. "Ndiwe ani?" the woman repeats. She uses the singular, familiar form to address you. Since a person worth something is plural, where your value is concerned, this woman agrees with the dog.

"Don't even think of moving or coming closer," she warns. "If it reaches you it will eat you, truly. Stay there!"

Her words drive the canine's tail into the air. It gallops up and down beside the fence. Its snout is speckled with foam. Its tongue hangs out and it dashes off at intervals to circle the speaker who approaches from the house.

Well-fleshed and egg-shaped, the woman emerges from behind a prickly pear bush. She waddles down the brick path.

"Just stay there, like I told you," she says.

She unties the straps of her cotton maid's apron and ties them up tighter as she nears you. The terrier trains one eye on her, the other on you, and subsides into guttural growling.

"What do you want?" the woman demands, looking at you through the fence.

"Ask those garden boys around these streets," she goes on without allowing you to answer. "If you do, you'll find out that I am not being bad to you. I am warning you for your own good. If you ask the garden boys, you will find out how many of them have had pieces torn out, because of this little animal."

She continues to examine you. You do not look back at her. Her air is so imposing that you have become a country girl again, before a mambo or headman in the village.

The woman is mollified by your silence.

"Even me, it's gripped me, nga, just like that, as if it wanted to eat me," she tells you more kindly.

"Now, what do you want? Madam Mbuya Riley, she said someone was coming. Have you been sent by Grandmother Riley's daughter?"

You nod, your spirits rising.

"The widow does not get on with her daughter," the woman says. "That Madam Daughter Edie is always lying. We are all right, Madam

Mbuya Riley and me. I am the one who works here and we do not need anyone."

You pull from your handbag the smalls advertisement that Mrs. May gave you.

"I am here for an interview," you explain. "I have a recommendation."

"But there is no work here," the woman says. A spark of suspicion flashes in her eye. "So there is no interview. Try down the road. They're hiring for a market garden. Potatoes, or maybe sweet ones. And on the other side someone is farming chickens."

It is your turn to be outraged. "I am not here for a job like that. I have an appointment," you spell out slowly.

"What is an interview for?" the woman smirks. "It is for a job, isn't it? You won't get in here with your lying."

The dog growls.

"If only you would just walk on," the woman says. "Because this dog is mad. Every dog Madam Mbuya has had has been like that, ever since the war. And Mbuya Riley up there is just like the dog here, if not even madder. So now, be walking!"

Snakes, the ones your grandmother used to tell you about when you were small and asked her the things you could not ask your mother, the snakes that hold your womb inside you open their jaws at the mention of war. The contents of your abdomen slide toward the ground, as though the snakes let everything loose when their mouths opened. Your womb dissolves to water. You stand there and your strength is finished.

A hole opens in a mesh of ivy vines that strangle the building at the top of the drive. The woman who is talking to you takes a step forward. She grips the fence rails tightly. Anxiety seeps out of her, as strong as an ancestor's spirit.

Widow Riley, the woman you have come to meet, approaches. Her back is humped. Both bone and skin are fragile, brittle and translucent as shells. She totters over the uneven brick paving.

The dog gives a yelp and bounds to meet its mistress.

"Now what will I say to the madam?" the woman before you whispers. She speaks intimately now, as though to a friend.

"See! She's already thinking you're a relative. One of mine. We're not allowed, not at all, not even when we've gone off. And now is the worst time because my off isn't until this weekend."

"An interview. For accommodation," you whisper back. "Somewhere to live." You are so desperate your voice climbs high into the back of your throat.

"She'll cry," Mbuya Riley's help hisses. "She'll say I'm bringing my relatives here to kill her. When her daughter comes they talk like that. It's been like that since the war. That is the one thing they agree on."

"There is a cottage," you say. "The matron said she fixed something. It is not expensive."

"Are you hearing what I am saying?" Mbuya Riley's help goes on. "It's impossible when she cries. I have to feed her or else she shuts her mouth and won't take the food. Just like a baby! You go now."

The dog yelps up at the top of the drive. The frail white woman sinks to the ground. Her head, with its halo of soft white hair, rests on the paving like a giant dandelion. She stretches her arm out toward you and the woman in uniform.

"There!" complains the maid. "Now I'm going to have to be bending over and carrying her, even when my own back is breaking."

She hurries up the path, throwing accusations back at you over her shoulder.

"Go away from this number 9. Because if you don't, I'll open the gate and if you manage to shake this one off it won't help because I'll unlock the big one."

The woman bends down to her mistress. The little terrier whimpers, licks the widow's arm.

CHAPTER 2

The man turns from the window to talk to you.

"Ha, Father, I did not mean to disturb you."

You kept the leather Lady Dis on when you trekked from Widow Riley's. You walked quickly, unsure why speed was essential. The asphalt was hot. Your feet are bloated and blistered. You peel the Lady Dis off in the combi that is returning you to the hostel. You search for your plimsolls. You nudge the man next to you several times, once mortifyingly close to his groin.

"You will have to wait," he says. "It is better to just sit, whatever it is. Like everyone else."

"These shoes," you say, as obliquely. "They are European. Not like the ones here. They won't stretch just like that. I should have put on some local stuff when I left my house."

It is the answer he deserves. The passenger droops his head and shoulder against the window. He is not a man, you think: he is already finished.

"So the place you are coming from, is it yours?" the man asks. His voice quivers with a new interest that he strives to hide.

"Yes," you lie.

"The plots there," the man says. "When you stand at one end, you can't see the other boundary. It's not just anybody who can find places like that."

You smile agreement.

"Are you doing market gardening?" he asks.

"I am," you reply, nodding firmly.

"It is good," the man sighs again. "Since the government started giving people land in places we thought were for Europeans only."

"It was my aunt's place," you say. "She was given it by her employer. He went to Australia."

The man clasps his hands in his lap and looks at them. "So what do you cultivate?" he asks.

"I am in dahlias," you say proudly. "I am the only one who can do it. She could not manage things like that, my aunt; things that need brains and telling people what to do," you add. "So our family said, Tambudzai, you have studied, you take the plot before that one has a stroke or something, before she goes where no one can follow."

"Ah, horticulture," your companion says. His voice is wistful with an admiration he is now comfortable showing. "One day I will do that too," he promises with a small splutter of energy. "Fruit for me. People always need to fill their stomachs, so filling theirs will also fill yours."

"Yellow ones," you put in. "And roses. The ones that are called tea roses."

"Oh-ho!" your companion nods. "I once worked in a nursery. There were tea roses. I sprayed them."

"Blue," you say. "The roses I have are blue."

"Blue," the man repeats. His energy drains away once more. He slumps against the window again. "Roses like that! I've never seen them."

"Sweden," you say. You are relieved to inject a fact into the nonsense you are dishing out. You lapped up a moment of glory at the advertising agency when you created a campaign for a Swedish company that produced agricultural machinery. "I have a lot of customers in Sweden. For yellow and blue. Those are that country's colours. I send them over there by air," you conclude, imagining that what you are saying will one day be true.

"I could be a gardener," the man says. "Do you still have any place for anyone?"

"Ah, I will remember you," you say. "These days there are already too many."

"If it weren't for that El Niño," sighs the man. "That water and wind haven't left anything to live off, for most of us."

Your companion asks for a pen. He scribbles his neighbour's telephone number on the corner of an old receipt he pulls out of his pocket. You take the scrap.

"Pano! Armadale!" he says.

"Here! Armadale," the conductor relays to the driver.

Disembarking, the man hunches his shoulders and ambles off.

You drop the note under the seat. People climb in. You slide into the would-be gardener's place, lean against the window. The combi stops at the hostel corner. You allow it to carry you onward.

The Market Square is the combi's last stop. The ground between the stalls is covered in banana peels and oily potato chip packets. Plastic sachets swell like drunkards' bellies. Orange peels curl on broken paving.

An urchin sucks at a sachet as at a mother's nipple. A second boy grabs the bag. The first sinks down and stays on the crumbling pavement. The sleeve of his jacket is a frayed rag. It flutters in the gutter. Beneath the cloth little dams of used condoms and cigarette butts build thick puddles of charcoal-coloured water.

There is a row of combis. Yours swerves to a triumphant stop. The windows disgorge sweet potato peels and sweet wrappers. Men and women grumble angrily and scatter. As passengers scramble to get out, a woman remarks, "Couldn't they see our vehicle coming? So why did they just stand there? Why didn't they get out of the way?"

Those in line waiting to descend bend double. The people in the queue waiting to enter start bickering.

The conductor asks where you want to go. You shrug and he reminds you, "Helensville."

You snigger silently. With your education, you know the suburb is called Helensvale. Helen's Valley.

"Helensville," the conductor says, without showing the impatience he must feel. "That's where this one is going back to."

He jumps out to bellow at the passengers, "Parents! Whoever's going, all I can tell you is get in. It's only who's going who goes."

You slide toward the vehicle's open door. Changing your mind, you slide back up against the window. You change your mind again and end up in the middle of the seat; halfway here and halfway there, where there is no necessity, neither for decision nor for action.

A couple of passengers climb in.

"This one for the shops and the police station," the conductor shouts.

A woman turns round and hisses at a man to stop pressing himself up against her. The man laughs.

Another combi arrives, spewing fumes. Everyone splutters and when the air clears again you all gape at a young woman who is threading her way through the stalls of fruit and vegetables toward the combis.

She is elegant on sky-high heels in spite of the rubble and the cracks in the paving. She pushes out every bit of her body that can protrude—lips, hips, breasts, and buttocks—to greatest effect. Her hands end in pointed black and gold nails. She holds several carrier bags that shout "NEON" and other boutique names in huge jagged letters. She sways the bags languidly, as she does her body.

You gape as much as anyone else, recognition stirring. The young woman sashays over to a combi. Fasha-fasha she goes, like that, all her parts moving with the assurance of a woman who knows she is beautiful. The crowd shifts and regroups. Men inside and outside combis exhale sharply. Windows mist. You stir, too. Your breath stops in your throat as you finally identify the newcomer. It is your hostelmate Gertrude.

She grasps the iron seat frame inside a combi to pull herself into the vehicle. Practised, she swings her bags behind her buttocks to prevent unwanted sightings. When her grip slips, she clutches at the cheap material that covers the vehicle's seat. The upholstery rips, disgorging fountains of foam rubber as she teeters backward.

"Knees! Knees!" a hoarse voice yells at your hostelmate. "Keep them closed."

Laughter hoots.

"There's a little fish. It's going to show its mouth hole, just like it does when it's out of water," a man shouts.

Gertrude pretends she isn't tugging her dress down as she lands back on the ground. But beneath the carrier bags, she's doing so for all she's worth. In her other hand is clutched, as though for safety, a fistful of cushion stuffing.

The crowd ripples and fidgets, hums and buzzes with amusement. Energy swirls out from this mirth. It slides you from your seat to the ground and into the throng. The crowd guffaws. You do too. As you do, you grow and grow until you believe you are much bigger than yourself and this is wonderful.

The woman rubs her arms and slides her weight from one leg to the other in discomfort.

"Hey, you driver," a man shouts. "Use your eyes to find out what she's doing to your vehicle."

The man raps the windscreen and claps his hands to the sides of his head in exaggerated indignation. You laugh with everyone else at this performance.

"Just move, mhani, move. These ones are a problem," screams a young woman draped in red and green, the garb of the Passover Apostolic sect. "A problem," the young woman repeats, pushing past everyone to a combi.

"A problem! A problem!"

The crowd takes up the idea and spits it out from deep in the gut. It is like the relief of vomiting when what is pent up rushes out. The crowd pushes forward in its unexpected new freedom.

"Someone open those thighs for her," a man says. "Do it for her if she won't!"

The crowd picks up the new refrain. You fling it at Gertrude and out over the market: "Open! Open!"

An urchin grabs a mealie cob from the rubbish in the gutter. The cob curves through the air like a scythe. Satisfaction opens up in everyone's stomachs as the missile hurtles past Gertrude's head, taking strands of her one hundred percent Brazilian hair weave with it.

Gertrude lunges forward and finds a foothold on the combi step. Now, without a thought for the length of her skirt, she scrambles forward.

Everyone laughs and the combi driver sneers, "What's the matter with you? Since when are naked people allowed to come into vehicles?"

A gang of workmen nearby lounge against scaffolding and adjust the hard hats on their heads, observing. Their laughter is without menace and without joy, without hate, without desire. The chuckling says anything at all could spring from their depths.

The single voice made up of many lets out a howl of anticipation.

The noise whips up the driver's desire to see something more happen.

"Move, move! My car wants to go," he shouts at the woman from your hostel. "With self-respecting people! How can it now, if it's packed with naked women?"

Tension spurts out of you and out of the crowd. Your laughter hangs above you. Up there where it is no one's, it snaps and crackles like arcs of lightning.

"Ja!" the driver brags. He examines Gertrude. "Who told you my combi's a bedroom?"

The people are hollering now about holes in her woman's body. They compose a list of what objects have been or shall be inserted there, and the dimensions of such cavities belonging to their hostage's female relatives. A shrill voice declares your hostelmate is squandering blood by bringing shame to the liberation struggle, in which people's children fought and fell.

The urchin bends to the gutter again. Sunlight flares from the bottle he throws.

"Who does she think she is? Let her have it," the malnourished boy bawls.

The bottle's arc exerts a magnetic force. The power picks you up. You are triumphant. You reach the crest of the missile's trajectory as you would the summit of a mountain. The crowd at the Market Square ascends, moaning, to that high place with you. It is a miracle that has brought everyone together.

Your hostelmate whips her head from side to side. She is frantic for escape.

The workmen stroll toward Gertrude. Those standing massage their flies surreptitiously, behind women's backs, as the builders pass. Hunger moves, wafts like mist over everything. You clutch your handbag to be sure you hold on to your Lady Dis.

You heave toward your hostelmate with the crowd. She jerks her beautiful legs and fights to enter the combi. The conductor splays his arms and legs to the four corners of the door to prevent her. The driver clenches and unclenches his jaw nervously. He wants any vandalizing done outside his vehicle.

"Help me!" Gertrude screams. "I beg, someone, please, please help!"

"Helping is what we are doing, ehe," a woman jeers back.

A builder walks up to Gertrude. He stretches out an arm to rip her skirt from her hips. The desperate young woman reels, is suspended in the combi's mouth for an eternal moment. Everyone sighs in irritation when she winds her arms around the conductor.

The young man writhes at the touch. He wants to dislodge her but dares not loosen his grasp on the door frame in case the crowd surges forward.

Hands lift Gertrude from the combi's running board. They throw her onto the ground where she sags with shock. The crowd draws in a preparatory breath. The sight of your beautiful hostelmate fills you with an emptiness that hurts. You do not shrink back as one mind in your head wishes. Instead you obey the other, push forward. You want to see the shape of pain, to trace out its arteries and veins, to rip out the pattern of its capillaries from the body. The mass of people moves forward. You reach for a stone. It is in your hand. Your arm rises in slow motion.

The crowd groans again. Now it is a moan of disappointment. A man stands beside Gertrude and throws a frayed denim jacket over her buttocks. It is a driver from one of the other combis. The sun reflects from his teeth as well as from his sunglasses. He turns to the crowd with an air of understanding. Gertrude gazes up at him. Her eyes are wide, and much too white. Appearing to feel this, she looks away.

"Tambu," she whispers, singling you out.

Her mouth is a pit. She is pulling you in. You do not want her to entomb you. You drop your gaze but do not walk off because on the one hand you are hemmed in by the crowd. On the other, if you return to solitude, you will fall back inside yourself where there is no place to hide.

"Help me," Gertrude pleads.

Still smiling gently, the young driver whispers to Gertrude. He removes his T-shirt to use it as a curtain. Gertrude pulls the pieces of her skirt from the mud and knots it about her body. She puts on the jacket and closes it to cover her breasts.

The crowd is enraged once more, this time at the gentleness of it. The urchin launches a Coke can. It catches the young man's back and rolls away but the young man appears not to feel it. He stretches his hand out to Gertrude.

"Young man, can't you find a decent one? Well turned out as you are, yes, you can find one," a woman screeches like an ominous spirit.

"Or else keep your whores at home," a builder says.

"And just make sure she doesn't delay people who don't want to see anything, who just want to go where they're going," a man grumbles.

"Yes, I'll tell her. I'll make sure she hears everything." The young man smiles, keeping your hostelmate's hand in his.

"Sisi, you have heard them, haven't you?" he tells her.

When Gertrude stands shivering, head bowed, and does not answer, a builder calls in a voice loud with disgust, "Now that you're decent, why don't you go in?"

Grief mounts Gertrude's face. Another urchin lobs a plastic bottle at the combi in a halfhearted gesture, as Gertrude clambers into it.

"Iwe! Do you know whose combi this is? What I'll do if I catch you?" the driver hollers at the youngster.

The boy darts away, teeth shining, holding the loops that bob from his ragged shorts away from his knees. The stone rolls out of your hand.

CHAPTER 3

That evening it is as though the hostel has folded its arms more tightly against you. You feel this the minute you walk into the dining room and see Gertrude. She is sitting at her group's table, where the young women talk about the latest lipsticks and vie with each other to be the best loved of or worst abused by their respective boyfriends. You never sit at their table.

Gertrude's face is like the relief maps you pored over at school in geography classes. Hills and riverbeds are carved out of gashes and bruises, the imprints of feet, some bare, some shod, some booted. Evening light drips shadows onto her skin, thickening the knots of swelling, deepening lacerations.

Isabel passes the back of a finger across Gertrude's cheek, delicately, with such care that surely she touches only the hairs on the other woman's face. Gertrude winces and grasps Isabel's wrists; even this gentle touch is too much. They sit for a while, hand in hand. The five forget pale yellow custard dripping over rich brown pudding in dishes before them.

Your people say: you don't lose your appetite over another person's problems. Knowing this, you are impatient to sit down to your meal. You edge toward the white girls who sit further in, closer to the buffet tables. They chatter amongst themselves. They dribble stock cube gravy over slices of pot roast beef and boiled potatoes. Your hostelmate and her companions lift their chins at you as you pass, tilting their heads to one side as though they are a single woman.

When you are several steps away they turn to each other. They suck air in through their teeth in harsh hisses.

Five.

This is your thought.

Against a market. Five. Against a city, a nation. A planet. Women. Five. What do they think they can achieve? They can hiss as much as they wish.

Ten eyes stare you down as you walk back past, your tray laden with food. You sit alone, letting them see your profile to prove their eyes cannot touch you. When they leave, you return to the buffet table, making sure to walk slowly. Onto your plate you load more meat and potatoes, and another double portion of pudding. You pass your hostelmates' empty table. There are smears of blood where Gertrude's arm rested.

Chew and swallow; chew and swallow. You do this until the bell rings for the end of dinner. Waiters in khaki overalls cover up chafing dishes. They stack plates and haul them away. A young man stands sentry beside the hall door to let the last diners out and stop late arrivals from entering. You smile at the youth briefly, then work a piece of gristle stuck between your teeth back and forth with your tongue.

"Manheru! Good evening, good evening, Auntie," he nods respectfully, holding the door wide for you.

"And greet your family, too. Everyone at home," you say, wishing him a peaceful evening.

The youth's smile widens, as he promises to deliver the message.

You tread gently across the foyer in order not to disturb Mrs. May. You sigh with relief when her head remains bent over her crossword puzzle.

"Is that what you do," you say, stopping outside your room.

You don't bother to put a question mark into your voice. Why should you put a question mark anywhere? So many things have happened today and no one has asked you anything. Besides, what you know is this: you did not want to do what you did at the market. You did not want all that to happen, nor did anyone else. No one wanted it. It is just something that took place like that, like a moment of madness.

"So now you're standing here to ambush me," you say to Isabel.

She is waiting for you in the shadow of a pillar. Your lips part in a parody of a smile. You like the fact that the young woman wants something from you. This grants you two powers. Your first power arises from her desire. You can laugh at a woman who wants something, as you watch her run here and there to obtain it. The other power, which trickles down from the first, is your right to refuse her.

"We could report you," Isabel says in a low, trembling voice. "She is in so much pain. Groaning! This isn't nothing-nothing. You must pay for a taxi. We are taking her to the hospital."

Down the hall, Gertrude opens her door. She calls to Isabel to leave it.

"If anything happens, when her relatives come asking, you'll have to pay much more. In damages," Isabel threatens.

"It's all right now. Leave that one, Bella. Rachel gave me Panadol," Gertrude says.

"Hm-hm!" you sniff, pulling your door key from your pocket. "What's wrong with you? Get away! Why are you standing there like that, as if there's anything to speak of? Who told you I am responsible?"

The following day you apologize to Mrs. May for having bungled the interview with Widow Riley. You ask the matron to save you each day's *Clarion* so that you can search through the smalls for a room.

The matron agrees. She pushes the rolled up paper into the corner of the reception desk every evening. You make sure you find it quickly to prevent other inhabitants from taking it.

"Big room with God-fearing widow."

The announcement drifts into focus a few days later.

"In large, attractive, well-kept house. For sober, single, God-fearing young gentleman."

You propose a bargain concerning your gender to God and call it praying.

In the phone booth you throw the fact that you are unemployed and the number of decades you have walked the earth into your plea as you dial the number given.

"I have relatives who speak like you," the widow says after a couple of minutes of conversation. With that, she asks where you come from.

"From the mountains," you say. "Manicaland. Mutare." It is the truth and for once the truth seems to be the right answer.

On the day of the meeting you find the property and rattle the gate. It is a long time before the widow comes out. Even then, the first thing you register is her voice.

"Mwakanaka! Mwakanaka, Mambo Jesu! You are good, you are good, King Jesus," roars a ferocious alto.

The sun glares at you off what looks like millions of teeth. They are too large and too pointed. You smile, smothering an instinct to flee. The widow swings the gate open and gestures you in.

"Good afternoon! I am so glad, so glad so glad you like my house," your prospective landlady declares.

Her eyes slide to the bare fingers at the end of your handshake. You twist them together behind your back, wishing you'd had the foresight to purchase a fake wedding ring down at the market.

The woman bends down to slide the bolt of the tall wrought iron gate back into the earth. It is her second exertion in a few minutes. When she straightens up, sweat pops out on her nose and slides from beneath her green and purple Nigerian-style headdress. She fans herself. A herd of rhinoceroses lumber round her index finger on a thick gold band. Beside it, on the middle digit, a cumbrous emerald glitters. A two-ring matrimonial set bulges large but dull from the fourth finger of her other hand. Crud is caked in the crevices of her jewellery. All of it needs cleaning.

"Yes, this is so wonderful, that you telephoned and now you are here," the widow says. She sails up the drive. "I have to talk to people carefully on the phone and I have to know where they come from. You cannot trust anything anyone says today."

She moves slowly on fragile-looking pointed sandals, the fashion dictated by Nollywood television. You realize you are in danger of overtaking her. You adjust your stride to keep yourself half a pace behind.

"You have heard, haven't you, these are the End Days," your prospective landlady remarks. "All the big prophets are saying it. Yes, the time has come, because now, these dreadful days we are living, do you receive when you give? Never. You lose everything. You are left with nothing after the giving."

You open your mouth and close it again, understanding with some relief that your response is irrelevant.

"And me, even though I am my husband's widow," your companion jabbers on, "you can't imagine what people come here saying. That they want to work or want somewhere to live. Just so they can find out what I have and make a plan to steal it. These people are using the intelligence God gave them not to multiply, but to reduce the little bit VaManyanga left me. I am trying to multiply, to make it bigger, just as the Bible says it must be when the master leaves. But those, they want everything I have to be smaller."

By now your breathing is shallow. You swallow saliva, suddenly bitter. You realize you are afraid of her. You do not know why. You laugh silently at yourself for indulging such timidity.

"But you say you have been living in Harare for some time," she forges ahead. "Miss Sigauke, I did not want to inquire over the phone. No matter how many things the white people brought, some things can't be said like that. But now you are here, that is good. Tell me, are you working?"

You are sure something has given you away. This in spite of the Lady Dis your cousin sent, paired once more with the skirt and matching top from your past that you wear again to this new interview.

"Working? Of course, yes. I am not one of those who just sits. I'm a worker, a real one," you respond with only slight hesitation. "Work is something I have known from the time that I was little."

"That is good," the widow says.

"After the fields as a child, I was teaching—temporary. But now I have a job at the advertising agency Steers, D'Arcy and MacPedius. You know it. 'Down in Honey Valley where the finest fresh foods grow.' That is one of mine. The whole of Zimbabwe knows it."

You hum the jingle from the old account and wonder who is writing their copy now.

"Oh, you are going there?" your prospective landlady exclaims, recognizing the tune after a moment's reflection.

"I am between the teaching and something better," you assure her, as it is clear this is the kind of thing she wants to hear.

"A big company! What will you do there?" the widow inquires. "Will you be doing the singing?"

You smooth the edge off your voice. "The words," you explain.

"Oh, you sing the words! Like me. At church, I am one of the best leaders in the Praise and Worship team."

As you approach her house, the widow interrogates you about your morals: Are you married by common law, or any other, or thinking of it? Do you associate with male friends or have one who might wish to visit for some time? This is not permitted. For, contrary to what you will hear from the neighbours, she does not run a brothel.

You mumble something about not going to church much, preferring to pray privately.

Widow Manyanga responds she is a prayer warrior and gives a litany of the people she has healed, the miracles she has wrought. You walk up chipped stone steps, past a rusting security door into a dim verandah.

"Welcome, Miss Sigauke," the widow says, holding the inner door open. "You have come to the house of a God-fearing family.

"Do you see that, there?" She inclines her head toward the adjacent wall. Pushed up against the bubbled paint is a row of desks. A telephone sits on each desktop.

"That," the widow begins. She stops with one hand supporting her on a desk, to gather a coil of cable up from the floor. "That is the harvest of revelation."

Dust crawls up your nostrils. You sneeze, and apologize for your allergy.

"That revelation did not come to me," the widow goes on. "It was given to VaManyanga. My husband. The late. But it came while I was praying with him. So it was because of me that he had this revelation."

You nod as you examine your surroundings, and succeed in looking appreciative, since the widow's circumstances, though dubious, are very much preferable to your own.

"Those phones you are seeing," volunteers Mrs. Manyanga, "are one of the many things my husband was working on when he left me.

VaManyanga was not like other men, never! He did things like this for the university students because after he had the revelation that he was called to do something for someone, he did not know which people to do what thing for. And so I decided to help him. I said, VaManyanga, there are more and more students because the government is educating young people. So isn't this thing that you have to do, isn't it something we can do for them? Yes, it was me. I said it!"

You stand in a dim, stuffy hall while your companion searches for the right key on a metal ring the size of a small tambourine, which she removes from the drapes of her West African robe.

The first key sticks.

"Don't worry," she says. "Don't worry about anything. All the doors are perfect. VaManyanga wanted things like that. Everything perfect. That's what he wanted."

She inserts another key after a brief hunt. The lock clunks. The heavy teak door swings open.

"I thank God," your prospective landlady announces, proceeding. Once inside, she pauses to take her bearings. The living room has been locked up for a long time. The air is musty.

"Yes, I do, I thank God," she declares, "for the gift I had, of a perfect husband."

The room is crammed with bits and pieces like a secondhand shop: with occasional tables and coffee tables of Tonga, Cape Dutch, Pioneer, and Colonial Railway sleeper origin, as well as a couple of the sort you can purchase by the roadside from vendors and weavers; and on them are all sorts of figurines. Heavy armchairs and sofas, and kudu skin pouffées fill the leftover spaces. Your prospective landlady steadies herself with a hand on a chair back as she threads her way forward.

She motions you to an armchair. The seat emits a mist of dust at contact.

"Yes, it was clear to anyone who has the correct spirit to listen to divine instruction, Miss Sigauke, that something was needed for our young people at the university. How many of them have cars? Most of them don't. So isn't it most of them are suffering? Isn't that the way things are happening?"

The widow lowers herself onto a sofa. You lean toward her; now she has your attention. Suffering! Of those who are no longer children but are not yet old: the widow has defined your own quandary. It is soothing, though at the same time alarming, to have your situation scrutinized, turned this way and that and dissected by someone you do not know.

"Yes, Miss Sigauke, you see," says the widow, encouraged by your engagement. "Look at yourself. You have a degree." With that she reverts to the students, encouraging you to consider them in a Christian manner. "Now think about those poor young people. When we go to the Women's Fellowship meetings it breaks our hearts to hear how many of those girls at the university are just giving in these days. I am sure it was not like that during your time."

You nod. You believe you are still a virgin, although there are a few incidents you are not sure of: does it count if, overtaken by circumstances, you had inserted a tampon to make sure you did not get pregnant?

"But now," the widow proceeds with passion, "the young ones at these colleges are lying down all the time, with anyone. So therefore, because the university is just over there, where those girls are, I said to VaManyanga when he had his revelation, I am going to be like a mother to those distressed students. I said, yes, I am going to treat them well."

Over the course of the interview, you learn that VaManyanga, being involved with many other business interests at the time, wished to begin to act on the revelation slowly. On the other hand, Mai Manyanga, who had a few months before been elevated from executive secretary to spouse, did not want to lose a moment. Overflowing with enthusiasm, she immediately put down a concrete slab at the back of the two-hectare property. A bit of corrugated iron nailed onto a short pole was still in the back garden, proclaiming how the concrete slab was destined to become the "SaManyanga Students Village." At the same time as termite poison was poured into the boarding rooms' foundations, to ensure that her future tenants could communicate freely, Mai Manyanga began the pay-phone venture, the investment that now lay scrambled in the verandah.

"Ah, those poor students." Your prospective landlady shakes her head and stares into her recollections.

"What a dreadful blow for them! Did they know my husband was going to be grabbed from them, like that? When there was no problem. None. With anything. We were even going to take the women students. Women like you would have benefited, Miss Sigauke. And they were going to be safe. VaManyanga never ran here, there with anything that lies down! No, that is not what VaManyanga did, like other men, so there was no problem with taking the women students."

Your palms are now clammy. You are anxious for the interview either to begin properly, or to be over. Your armpits are dripping in the tight costume, yet at the same time you want the widow to go on talking, flinging further and further into the future the moment of decision as to whether you are or are not adequate.

"Ah, yes, you have recognized them," crows Mai Manyanga.

You dodge outright denial: "It is a beautiful picture."

The photograph, which you happen to have glanced at, is placed grandly at the centre of the widow's display cabinet. Around it are half spheres filled with water containing small white flakes and models of the towers found in several European cities.

"Don't you see it? The resemblance? You must," the widow says. She waves her jewelled hand to cool herself. "I am sure you see who they are."

When you produce a gentle, silent smile, so as not to chance an inopportune answer, the widow heaves herself out of her sofa, past bronze, brass, and copper figures that stand on her little tables.

The cabinet's glass doors shake in protest, but after some rattling obey the widow. She removes two thick china cups and their saucers, part of a set that occupies the upper shelf along with a silver tea service turned copper with tarnish. Below the squat teapot, in a green-flecked frame of old Kamativi tin, stands the photograph the widow commands you to recognize.

He is clean shaven, light skinned, of medium height, and his immaculate dress includes a buttonhole as well as a handkerchief in his breast pocket. He holds a briefcase higher than normal for a standing man. His grip is two handed as though he had first sat, then was requested to stand, but decided to keep the bag at its previous elevation. His grasp is tight enough to bring out tendons on the back of his hand.

She, however, dimples coquettishly at the lens. A plump hand lingers on the arm that holds the briefcase. The other rests lightly on the back of a wooden chair on which a well-polished mock-python handbag gleams. She is wearing platform shoes and a shift dress, whose colour is uncertain in the black-and-white snapshot. Keeping the picture company on either flank, and on the shelves below, crowd various other ornaments: a cat of pink quartz that has lost an ear, a lone thick mug from a place called the Kings Arms. There are copper plaques depicting proteas, springboks, and blazing flame lilies, the blossom of Rhodesia, as well as shields proclaiming the year, location, and purpose of the many conferences Mr. Manyanga attended.

The widow walks past a grandfather clock whose pendulum swings heavily but does not keep time. Placing her cups on a large mahogany dining table, she announces she will make you tea. She likes you. In spite of your searing need to be favoured, your heart sinks. The snakes in your belly yawn. You feel as though your womb twitches. You are growing suspicious at being liked by this woman, knowing there is nothing about yourself that counts as amiable. Contempt for everything floods you. It lurks just under your expression as you regard this woman who likes you. At the same time, your fascination with her and the life she had fashioned for herself increases, so that you smile away your befuddlement.

"Those men of mine didn't get round to breaking them," the widow says when she returns to set on the table a fraying raffia tray loaded with an enamel teapot, sugar bowl, and milk jug. She pours your refreshment and nods at the lowest shelf, which displays six matching, painted drinking glasses that sparkle with regular dusting.

"They are all there. Not a single one of them was broken," she says with pride. "Even though we used them on all of our big family celebrations. These days I only use them when my sons come. But do they come here often enough? No! Just like sons. That's what boys do these days. They don't ever come to see their mother!"

You heap half a dozen teaspoons of sugar into the cup the widow hands you. Energy pours into your body and you know you will manage the journey back to the hostel.

You want another cup of the hot, sweet tea. As soon as you set your cup down, however, the widow begins a tour of the house. She pulls open thick drapes of imported purple satin to present the disused gorge of a swimming pool, its tiles black with mould.

"Now the boys are gone, it is no longer used," she says. "Of course, we taught our boys to swim in it."

The kitchen must have been, fairly recently, beautiful. You learn it had been initially renovated under Mr. Manyanga's supervision. He could abide tiles from one location only: Italy, in one colour only: golden ochre. But since his passing, squares have fallen off. The grout followed. Colonies of cockroaches reside in the grungy cracks. A gecko scampers across a crust of blackened cooking oil. You itch to attack everything violently with detergents.

"This one," the widow informs you as you stare into a room mustier and more airless than the one you have left, "was going to be the first room that I rented out to the university students. I agreed with my husband when he said that to do the business properly we must do a pilot first. I did not want to disagree with him and his revelation. I said, I do not know about a pilot, but God knows. I just told my mother's heart to be still. You know that heart inside a woman? It just wanted to do much more for all those students."

The widow walks briskly about the tiny compartment, pointing out the window, a corner of which gives a view of the yard, although most of it opens onto the garage. She admires an old coffee table whose back edge is propped up on piles of *Parade* magazine, and points out a clothes rail hidden by yellowing curtains of pink satin, behind which drift clouds of cobwebs.

The widow apologizes for having made you wait at the bottom of the garden.

"Doing that," she says, indignant on your behalf. "Even when I employ a gardener. And I pay him every time. On time! There isn't a single month when I don't. I knew it anyway as I was interviewing him," she confides. "But what could I do with this heart, the one of a woman?

Every woman is a mother at heart, Miss Sigauke. And every mother is also a woman. That's why I said, come, I will pay you, when he was nothing but a vagrant."

You remain silent, renewing your bargain with God and also invoking your ancestors.

"I told him this morning, go when she comes, I'm expecting a someone. But he leaves me to walk all that way down to open the gate and goes away early because it's Saturday. I said wait for Miss Sigauke. I should have told him there were also some men coming for this interview."

You smile more widely, relieved to know there are not any. Mai Manyanga, however, sounds regretful.

"That's why I always say please, please, someone from the rural areas. A person from those barren places without any rain. Those people know when God has given them something good. Because those people really know suffering."

The widow has gauged you well. She is aware of it. You accept her terms immediately, as there is no question of your returning to the family homestead in your father's village.

She offers to have one of the telephones from the verandah connected, and is pleased that finally God will bring to fulfilment VaManyanga's revelation. The rent is already too high, having been calculated against a young professional man's salary. You decline the connection, even though the widow points out communication at that rate is a bargain. You assure yourself, as you trudge back to the main road, that one day, somehow, anyhow, you will enjoy the luxury of a telephone by your bedside. By the time you flag a combi down, you have promised yourself three telephones, in the kitchen, living room, and bedroom of your future home. Sitting in the minibus, you mull over a fourth for the bathroom.

CHAPTER 4

Moving to the widow's is a great mistake. When you arrive, your room smells worse than before.

Mrs. Manyanga hovers around. She says to your wrinkled nose, "Yes, Miss Sigauke, your God favours you. You are home now. Only, isn't it the greater favour for me, a poor widow, to bless someone like this?"

A leak in the roof has dripped onto the mattress, causing fungus to fuzz the cloth and ceiling. Has your landlady not seen it?

"Everything is nice and fresh now," she says. Stretching an arm behind the clothes rail, the widow pulls down a few filaments of spiderweb.

"There was just a little hole, one like that up there in the roof. Just tiles that had moved like that because of the wind but as soon as I decided and I knew someone was coming to sleep in this room, you can see I fixed it," she says, dusting her palms.

"You know, Miss Sigauke," she goes on, "I am still looking for a girl. A decent one to ask to do this and that for me in my cottage. But that's over in my cottage. That's the only place I want someone to assist. Here I aired this room. All the windows were opened every day since you stood in that doorway. And I came in to close them myself each night, because you know when you have something that is good, all the time people are thinking of stealing it."

Your landlady proudly informs you how she removed the satin curtains and washed them with her own hands.

"You see, God is good. I am a widow and my sons have left too. But

35

I receive so much power. Not for myself but for someone else. God still pours down His strength!"

You cannot decide whether you are happy or not to be left alone when she departs.

"Makanaka, Mambo Jesu," you hear her singing as she crosses the yard to her cottage.

Packing your things in grimy drawers, you swear that when the time comes to move away, you will not go down the widow's drive the way you walked up it—with nothing.

You spend most of your time sitting on your bed, brooding over your new misjudgement, contemplating how much you detest the place already. At other times, you wonder how you can suppress your growing feelings of doom. You endeavour to put together a plausible excuse for not going out to the job you said you had, in case the widow asks.

Your three housemates do not raise your morale. They all have jobs. It is better not to get to know them. By which you mean they should not become overly acquainted with you. You devise ways of avoiding contact, especially with the man in the bedroom next to yours who changes girlfriends more frequently than he does his trousers. The quiet woman gets up first, usually before the cocks crow, to make sure she has hot water. She takes a long time bathing. The big woman follows her. The man in the main bedroom gets up last because he has his own en suite bathroom. Their preparations wake you; when they go off to catch their combis you cannot fall asleep again for thinking of their offices, their contracts and monthly salaries.

You venture out infrequently for air in the garden or to sit on the humped roots of the jacaranda by the gate. When you are at the gate, you make an effort. For once, your village upbringing is an asset.

"Hello, how has your day been? How is everything, is all well where you are from?" you greet passersby.

Speaking so seldom, you are startled by the sound of your voice so that you don't smile. Neither do the people. Sometimes they do not answer.

Once a week you go shopping at a tiny supermarket as depressed in its appearance as you are. Leaving the yard, you force a spring into your step in order to walk like a woman with lots of dollar bills lying in the bottom of her bag. Inside the shop, pretence suffocates you, as though you are wearing a too-tight corset. Completing your purchases, you do not want to go out again, because your bag bulges with budget-pack plastic bottles, smallest-size sachets, and minute boxes. Cooking oil, glycerine for your skin, candles for power outages, matches—everything broadcasts your poverty.

You keep your supplies in a corner of the kitchen cupboard, away from the other residents' belongings. Hoarding your food the way you hoard your savings from the advertising agency in your building-society account, your principle is "less is more": less eating is less spending, leaving more cash in your balance. More money on your monthly statements is more time to sort out life. Breakfast is a slush of mealie meal porridge you can hardly eat as the widow's stove neither simmers nor boils anything properly. In the afternoon you stir the same mealie meal thicker for your sadza. You begin taking vegetables for relish, a few leaves a day, from the widow's garden.

The rest of the time you sit by your window, staring past the once baby pink, now yellowing material onto your landlady's patchy lawn. When this grows unbearably tedious, you shift a bit to face the slab Mr. and Mrs. Manyanga put down for the student housing. Sometimes, beyond the concrete, you see the widow's shadowy form waft to and fro in her living room.

You are concerned you will start thinking of ending it all, having nothing to carry on for: no home, no job, no sustaining family bonds. Thinking this induces a morass of guilt. You have failed to make anything at all of yourself, yet your mother endures even more bitter circumstances than yours, entombed in your destitute village. How, with all your education, do you come to be more needy than your mother? End up less than a woman so dashed down by life that she tried to lean on her second daughter—a daughter who requires support herself, after losing a leg in the war, and now fends for two liberation struggle babies, your nieces, seen only once when they were toddlers. Your uncle, who intervened to keep you from your mother's fate by sending you to school, is in a wheelchair, made a casualty of Independence by a stray bullet from a twenty-one-gun salute that burrowed into the delicate membranes beside his spinal cord during the first celebrations. You force yourself not to spare a thought for your father, the very idea of whom fills you with despair. The only person who might help with your and your family's predicament is your cousin Nyasha. But she has emigrated overseas. You last heard of her when she sent the shoes, propitiously at a time when the post office was still forwarding packages rather than pilfering them. You cannot remember whose turn it is to contact whom, or even if you sent a letter to thank her.

You have shed friends in the years since university because you could not keep up with their lifestyle and didn't want to be laughed at. Years later, after your abrupt departure, you drifted apart from your colleagues at the advertising agency. You torture yourself, in the early days of your stay at Mai Manyanga's, with the idea that you have no one but yourself to blame for leaving your copywriting position. You should have endured the white men who put their names to your taglines and rhyming couplets. You spend much time regretting digging your own grave over a matter of mere principle. Your age prevents you from obtaining another job in the field, for the creative departments are now occupied by young people with Mohawk haircuts and rings in eyebrows, tongues, and navels.

Distraction from your dismal preoccupation arises on a Sunday, some weeks after your arrival, when a battered blue Toyota crunches over the widow's gravel.

In a cloud of exhaust, the vehicle stops in front of the multiple carport, in precisely the spot to prevent any other from entering.

You look up from the magazine you brought with you from the advertising agency, which you are reading for the hundredth time, to see a sinewy leg slide out of the driver's door. A long muscular arm snakes out and fumbles at the rear handle until it opens.

Half a dozen children leap out.

"Mbuya!" they holler.

They do their best not to destroy the widow's vegetable garden. But ridges crumble as they jump. Vines snap.

"Hey, you watch it! Wait until somebody sees what you've done," their father yells, quickly emerging from the car. "You'll get the thrashing of your life. If your grandmother doesn't want to, you can be sure I shall do it."

The children giggle and shriek and charge off faster to hammer fists on the widow's door. "Mbuya!" they shout again when the door opens and the widow invites them inside.

This arrival is a gift, bringing you a man to consider. It is a stepping stone to another life you crave, away from this nowhere and the days that gape empty behind you. You do not think of love, being obsessed only with what the gentleman can do for you, how the widow's son will be insurance against your absolute downfall.

You suck the saliva out of your mouth, like a person biting into a lemon, when a woman descends from the passenger seat. "I am not staying in this car," the woman says. "I'm telling you, I won't do it."

The man's limbs are too long. They roll like a conveyor belt, as if his cartilage and ligaments are several sizes too large for his bones. He plants enormous feet on the gravel as he takes a few paces, before rubbing his palms on his wrinkled shirt. He leans against the car, sulkily lighting a cigarette.

"Today I am going to meet her," the woman insists. "Whatever you say, today, I am going to do it."

You scoop from your depths the scorn that had punished you in the weeks since you came to the widow's. The man's derision becomes poignant and satisfying as yours drains out of you and mingles with his, and the whole of it pours onto the woman.

A moment later, there is a shout down at the gate. Bolts clank and a long, low Volkswagen Passat shudders toward the house.

The man and woman are shaken out of their dissatisfactions. Smiles gash their faces as they turn to the approaching vehicle.

"Larky!" the man with the too-long limbs calls out to the new arrival. He steps forward and flicks his cigarette away.

The woman folds her arms moodily and leans her denim-bound buttocks against the Toyota.

Larky rolls down his window and shows all his teeth in greeting.

"Yah, Praise!" he grins, nodding at the blue Cressida. "So that's it! That's the winner you told me about?"

The other man grins also. But anxiety pulls his lips too far apart.

"A new one," Larky says, stepping out of his car, his smile still wide. "Garbage, brother! Why waste your money importing this Japanese scrap metal?"

The woman's shoulders droop. Larky holds out a hand. The two brothers bump shoulders.

"Me, I'm fine, bro," says Larky, turning to make sure his voice carries. "You know, I bought another one, number three. For a spare when the others break down. Mother of the children drives the Mercedes. I'm using the BMW. But not at weekends. No more Japanese," he brags. "Just the real ones. German."

"Japan's just as good," says Praise. "Even better. They understand the way we do things."

"How are you, Babamunini?" throws in the woman.

"But you're going in the right direction," Praise acknowledges more loudly, to drown her out. "I hope I'll see that number three of yours, if it's as good as you say it is."

"Come! Come and see it," Larky laughs. "Don't stay away too long. We'll roast some meat. You must bring the children."

The men make a double fist. They wave the club of it back and forth, laughing.

"Sharp, mupfanha," says Praise. Showing all his teeth again, he turns toward the woman.

"Babamunini! Babamunini, I have to tell you something," she begins.

The fingers of each hand scratch the opposite bicep. She hunches her shoulders because she is a hopeless woman, the kind who reports her man to his younger brother.

"Mbuya, here, here! Me, me!" the children's voices ring out. The cries grow louder as the widow's door opens and they rush onto the stoep.

"*Mwakanaka*! *Mwakanaka*! You are good, King Jesus!" The widow's voice threads through the afternoon.

"Mai, don't let that herd trample you to pieces. We're coming," Larky says. He steps forward and dimples dramatically. You push the curtain tentatively aside.

"Is that what you do?" the widow says. "What about coming to greet me now, you Praise and Larky? At least these children know how to do things properly, greeting their grandmother."

"We're coming, Mai. Right now," the men promise. "Aren't we here? It means we want to see you."

"Now, children, guess what I've got?" the widow says.

She holds something. It is small, a packet.

"Sausages!" a child squeals.

"Red ones!" shouts another.

"Which of you wants a sausage?" the widow sings in a full voice as though she were at Praise and Worship.

"Ini! Me, me," the grandchildren answer.

The noise dies away as the children concentrate on biting and chewing.

"How's everyone? How is Maiguru?" Larky pays his respects to his brother. In the near-quiet, he goes on, "What about that boy? Did you tell Ignore we want to see him?"

"Fine and what about with your everybody?" Praise scratches his head. "Our young one? Yes, where is he? Didn't you call him?"

Larky hitches neon-hued Bermuda shorts up over his boxer's belly.

"Why me? It's that youngster Ignore you should be asking why he isn't here. Why are you questioning me as if you're not the eldest, the one who should be organizing?" he says, an edge to his voice.

Praise pulls another menthol cigarette out of his pack. Smoke drifts from his mouth as he looks about the disintegrating property.

"Anyway, what's Ignore doing that stopped him?" Larky says.

Praise scratches the top of his head again before offering his brother a smoke. Larky accepts. Blue coils float up.

"So now you're behaving?" Praise yells at the children. "That's what you're doing now. Didn't I tell you to?"

The men draw together to wave and make fatherly faces at the group on the step.

Inserting herself into the men's distraction cleanly, like a knife, the woman in jeans slides away from Praise's Toyota.

"Just watch me, Praise," she says when she has moved far enough for the widow to see her. "Today it is too much, I don't care. Even if she's ignoring me, I know it's only because you've told her something. Just now she will know she has another muroora, another daughter-in-law. This afternoon, I'm meeting your mother."

Widow Manyanga turns her back, a resolute gesture, on the group by the garage.

"I told you, not today." Praise turns to the woman.

"Liar!" the woman hisses.

She raises a finger, lets it sway. Her body takes up the rhythm, balancing in stilettos.

"You are lying to me and you know it, Praise Manyanga. Only I don't know why you want to do it. Why were you lying like that to me, you Praise? When you said next time? But now in front of your brother and in front of your mother and in front of your children, also, you want to make me look stupid.

"Next time, next time, next time, next time," she repeats in a high-pitched crescendo. "Are you going to lie again and deny it? All the time, you told me lies. That's why now your family ignores me!"

"Mainini, I am glad to see you here. I was happy to see my biggas, that's all," says Larky.

He spreads his arms for an embrace.

"Come on, is this what you really want?" he says. "To be unhappy like that? When my elder has done well and gathered us all for this visit?"

"To be like what?" the woman says, dipping her head like a bull about to charge, but then leashing herself up again.

"What are you saying I shouldn't be like? Am I the one who shouldn't be like something?"

She lengthens her lip, and when it will not descend any lower, she allows Larky to give her a hug. He manipulates her into his Passat and once they are in his vehicle she allows him to pat her back. The engine throbs. You smile faintly, judging that this woman will not be strong competition.

"Who wants what I've got?" Mai Manyanga calls out to the children, another packet of Viennas clenched in one hand. A short knife is in the other.

"And Praise, what about it? Didn't you tell Ignore?" asks your landlady, turning from the children, in a church choir voice loud enough to be heard in the next yard.

"Ask Larky," Praise says.

The widow stabs the knife into the new packet of sausages, ripping it open.

"Don't tell me you didn't tell that son of mine?" she begins anew when she has done feeding the grandchildren.

"Don't worry, Mbuya Manyanga! We want to eat all the good things you've prepared too," Praise says, folding his arms. "As soon as that one you are talking about arrives."

You listen, daydreaming about how, when you have made your move, you will be a member of this family.

In the end, Larky's Volkswagen does not leave with the unhappy "small house" woman his brother keeps because a tawny-coloured car, flat like a frog, crawls toward the carport. You realize that this last is the best of the three vehicles, for the noise in the yard hardly changes when it stops, nudging the Passat's bumper.

"Hey mhani, Ignore, behave like a person," Larky says, his head out of the window.

"There's no problem! Is there a problem, Larky? Praise?" the third man shrugs, stepping out of his vehicle and smiling. The other men look at the car with longing.

Ignore nods at his mother's cottage, but Praise links an arm with him and pulls him forward until their foreheads touch.

The children wave their sausages, or try to take bites out of each other's.

"I will bring more," Widow Manyanga says. As she disappears clutching the empty pack she shouts, "And are you still not coming to greet your mother, now that Ignore is here?"

43

"I am coming," Ignore calls.

The children run into the cottage after the widow. Larky gets out of his car. The men huddle, nodding their heads.

The woman is shunted from the Passat into the Porsche. Ignore climbs back in, to return a few minutes later—to your great satisfaction—without his passenger.

"Big brother," Ignore says as he steps out of his car for the second time, "tell me which dustbin you picked that woman of yours out of."

"Which big brother?" snaps Praise. "Why are you talking about dustbins?"

"You have to examine it, where the fish are," Ignore shrugs. "That way you can taste all the waters. But examining doesn't mean eating. Biggas, what is it? Are you examining, or are you eating?"

Praise scratches his head.

"How is she?" asks Ignore, looking at the widow's cottage.

"Happy," says Larky. "First she fed her grandchildren. Now you're here."

From the back of his car Larky hauls out a cardboard box. Praise drags crates of Coke, Fanta, and Stoney Ginger Beer from his. The Manyanga sons sit on the slab looking over the widow's vegetable garden. They lift bottles and drink and when the level of liquid in the bottles sinks, they top their drinks up with spirits.

Larky asks Ignore about a lawyer.

Ignore pours shots and says, "Kamuriwo."

They talk about the lawyer. Your mind drifts to the two-year-old magazine from the advertising agency that lies on your lap.

"Estate agent?" Larky says. You weigh your current company, an oil-stained magazine, against these men who have already inherited once and are set to do so again in the future.

Outside, Ignore shifts, but does not volunteer an answer.

Larky stands up, drink in hand. He studies the slab, the sinking fence, the progress to ruin.

"That's the trouble," he says. "I told you when Baba died, didn't I? I said we have to start managing this place so it doesn't rot. So there's something to get out of it."

There is sorrow in his demeanour as he talks about his mother's house. His speech is punctuated by words like *kitchen* and *wasted money*. In a little while, Ignore starts laughing. Praise shakes his head, perplexed.

"And that black granite they wanted in the swimming pool." Larky goes on, his voice rising and shaking. "I told them, I said, Mai, Baba, start with lessons. For swimming. Not with a pool! That's how to start. But these parents of ours, do they listen? How many times did I fix it? I'm sick of maintaining this place when she can't do anything for herself!"

"After the accident I did my bit with the car repairs," says Praise. "Larky, it's not right for you to say you are doing everything."

"The estate," says Ignore, still amused. He talks about knowing people and expediting signing of papers.

"If she doesn't sign now, what's next?" inquires Praise. He scratches the back of his head.

"This son here," Larky nods at Ignore. "Like he said, his connections will make it happen."

"Buyer?" Praise uncoils and stretches.

"When we have the buyer," says Ignore, "Praise, what are you going to do with her?"

The children, who have assembled on the porch once more, finish their cold drinks. They throw the cans at a guava tree.

"Maybe we can think again," Praise says. "She's rented out the little room. The woman there didn't want the telephone option, but at least she put down three months' deposit."

Your breath catches in your throat as you realize you are the woman spoken of. You are suspended between one thought and the unformed one that follows. The throb in your chest accelerates, with one beat for hope and the other for more disenchantment. You wish it was all the same, that none of it mattered.

"Let's get rid of the telephones," Ignore is saying. "They'll raise some money. I'll find someone who'll take them."

"She's still talking about the pay-phone business," Praise objects, with a frustrated click of his tongue. "She wants to bring a relative over to help her manage a business with them."

"Sell," repeats Larky firmly. "Otherwise we're all going to be in ruins."

You inhale and exhale slowly. You have decided it is of no consequence to you who buys the house. The jeans-clad woman is done with, leaving the Manyanga sons available and desirable for your newly hatched project of ending life's downward spiral. Their wives are not in sight, which means either that the men do not value their women highly, or that the wives have little time for their husbands. It is going to be easy to challenge that sort of woman. Life has been kind to you at last. It has deposited you in the right family. You choose Larky as your first target because he is the most powerful.

Oblivious to what you have in store for them, the men finish their discussion. The children shout greetings as their father and uncles leave the slab to go to their mother's cottage.

You slip into the bathroom, where there is a better view of the widow's place. But the front door closes as you peer out, and after that there are only shadows passing in different gaits and rhythms behind the curtained windows.

You wait, as days extend into weeks, for an opportunity to ensnare your landlady's son. When this does not arise, lying on your bed with the sagging mattress in the pink frilly room, you reconsider your options and devise a wiser system to maximize your chances of success by working through each heir, starting with the eldest. You dream of the house you will live in then, in which there will be neither pink frills nor yellow kitchen. You train your heart and mind on the black granite swimming pool, to make sure it will be waiting for you. Finally you will make good the lie you told your colleagues when you left the advertising agency, saying someone had whispered "You!" and you were getting married.

CHAPTER 5

The energy that had animated your landlady seeps away after the visit. She emerges from her cottage less often in the weeks following her appointment with her sons. She avoids the sitting room that she displayed so grandly before. She speaks of her sons less frequently when she happens on you in the yard or hallway.

When she does attempt to yell a hymn, her voice is weak. The tunes trickle out of her like the tired flow of a silted river. In the middle of the night she is an upright shadow in her front room, as though she cannot bear the pain of sitting, and when all her lights are turned off her attempts at song give way to silence or quiet groaning. After some weeks she carries a bandaged arm in a sling. You avert your eyes. No one in the house talks of it but when you see it, you shiver.

In her new silence, the widow surprises you in the garden on several occasions. You explain why you are harvesting her vegetables. She hardly listens, her eyes trained on the slab where her sons sat, but when you have finished, she gathers a handful of yellowish leaves from a plant's thick base. These she hands to you, encouraging you, as gently as she is able, to pick a bundle now and again before the gardener neglects everything completely and turns her yard to jungle.

"Now and then" soon becomes every day. You continue to help yourself to your landlady's crop with decreasing compunction until the day you hear two voices quarrelling in the cottage. By this time the widow has not inspected her property for more than a week, nor sat in the sun on her porch. The arguing rises and soars like a song, a happy one as though the quarrellers are elated at the opportunity to tear each other apart, to broadcast their rage in savage voices across the neighbourhood.

"Those phones are out of date," insists your landlady's adversary.

"So what? Are you here to tell me about my things? A phone is a phone. Where did you see an expiry date written?"

"I'm not here because you asked me," the visitor says. "And it's not because I want to be. The people who sent me said go to look after her. They didn't say go and make sure she loses everything her husband left her. Because of all the foolish things she is doing!"

"Wouldn't you love me to lose everything," the widow says. "I'm not going to. Those are my things. I worked for them also." The viciousness in her voice cracks through the air, insisting on submission. "When you are here, you do as I tell you. Otherwise go back to that village you came from."

Fear, your recurrent dread that you have not made enough progress toward security and a decent living, prickles like pins and needles at the mention of "village." You have dodged this fear for too long—all your conscious life. Now even here at Mai Manyanga's, you are trapped by it. You scold yourself for not having made a move toward Praise, putting into action your strategy to start with the eldest. Because of your inertia, the Manyanga sons might sell the house before you have positioned yourself properly, exposing you to eviction. You cheer yourself up by disparaging your prospective mother-in-law. You vow not to be overawed by a grandmother whose presence is dwindling away before your eyes. As evidence of this decline, you were easily able to filch her vegetables, to boil them on her own stove and consume them in her kitchen for a long while without her knowledge. For your plans to come to fruition, you must become wary of the newcomer instead. She could influence the widow in any number of ways, wreaking havoc with your project to become reputable.

"I'm not going back. That topic's finished," the newcomer says, in a quieter tone. "Yes, at least coming here has brought me out of the village. I'll see what I can find to do until the matters are sorted out. But don't waste your time telling me to: I won't touch any of those telephones."

You meet your landlady's companion that afternoon.

"Mwakanaka, Mambo Jesu!" You hear the widow approach while you are cooking the greens you collected in the morning.

"Vasikana! Girls!" Mai Manyanga calls her tenants loudly, once she is in the hall. "And Brother Shine too. Today I want to see all of you."

You do not hear the other tenants reply, and so you decide to remain silent also.

The landlady appears energized by her bout with the woman.

"I am sure all four of them are in," she remarks to her companion. "That is why we agreed for you to come on Saturday. Bertha! Mako!" she calls again, her voice soaring in frustration at having to shout so many times when presenting a visitor.

Their footsteps stop at a door in the hall. There is knocking that goes unanswered.

Your landlady and her companion start back down the hall, allowing you to slip out of the kitchen.

"Good afternoon, Mai Manyanga," you call, voice sweetened in the way you used to speak to the matron at the hostel. "Is there something you wanted?"

"Ah, Tambudzai," Mai Manyanga replies. "You must have been making a racket in the kitchen with the pots since you did not hear me come in."

The landlady indicates the woman beside her. "I have brought my relative, to introduce her. I don't want anyone getting frightened of anything and calling police. Saying there is a strange person here. Who is doing this and that. So everyone must come and say hello to her."

The lodger Bertha, the large woman who washes later than the other, timid housemate, opens her door halfway. She squeezes through the narrow opening to make sure Mai Manyanga does not enter.

"This is Christine, my brother's child," your landlady announces, emphasizing the word *brother* with pride. "The one who was the first in our family. She is his daughter. Yes, daughter of the firstborn of my parents. Her father was killed when we thought God had been merciful, bringing him through the war when so many were dying, being killed either by the soldiers or by the comrades. She is called Kiri."

The landlady is still for a moment, like a woman who has departed to sit beside her sibling. Her words open up a void, out of which troop your own wounded and dead. You regard your memories from afar, and finally turn away from them.

"Yes," the widow says after a while. A tremor runs through her body. "Even though my brother survived the war, the monster that walks around was only lying down. It stood up again and chewed on him down there in Bulawayo."

After another moment, Christine shakes hands with everybody. Everyone engages in the pleasantries.

"Is that it, Tete?" Christine asks, when the greetings are finished. "Saying here is someone, but only talking about her father. And of things that nobody can talk about sanely in this country."

An awkward silence follows, for you are all members of a peace-loving nation. You do not talk about how citizens dissented and how their ghastly crushing cast bodies into disused mine shafts and swept them into railway carriages like debris dropped by a whirlwind.

"Are you saying it is not true, that there is no one that I called brother, Kiri?" your landlady says in a tone that stops everyone thinking anything at all. "Yes, if it weren't for that cyclone down where those Ndebeles come from, there would still be someone for me to turn to in these times that are so bad nobody can say it. Yourself, Kiri, wouldn't you be a different woman, one who has a father?"

Then Mai Manyanga remembers the reason for the gathering in the hall and remarks in an offended voice, "Now, where is that other girl, Mako?"

Even though the widow says "Mako" loudly and you all expect a response, there is none.

"What's going on now?" your landlady asks. "I heard her move in there when I knocked and I thought, ah, that is the young woman with manners. She is standing up, getting ready to join us."

"What about Shine?" says Bertha, who still stands so as to block her doorway. "Mai Manyanga, has that young man been called also?"

"You know me," says Mai Manyanga grandly, ignoring Bertha. "I don't talk much. But everyone calls me a prayer warrior. If there is something wrong, this Mako should say so. That is all. Only that. And my knees will bend down for her."

Bertha is strong, of a size that thinking men run from should she be displeased with them; a woman who often says she is hardened past femininity by too many things to talk about. She gives a shallow chuckle.

"We want Shine to know there's someone else here," she goes on. The next laugh is shallower and emptier. "He needs to know. We don't want anything you don't want, Mai Manyanga."

Your housemate's bosom heaves up and down. You wonder whether to laugh with her, but decide against it.

Mai Manyanga proceeds back up the hall.

"Ah, now we can meet Mako," she says as Mako's door creaks. The widow smiles, for your landlady rates her fourth tenant highly. Mako is the kind of occupant everyone with a contract should be—she pays her rent on time, never leaves a light or tap on, nor does she play loud music.

When Mako still does not emerge, the landlady wonders why. Bertha wades forward, past the widow and her visitor.

Your lip rose in disdain when you met the housemate Mako. It was a few days after you arrived at the widow's. She must have applied to live at Widow Manyanga's during happier times, for the very air in the room now reeked of incessant adversity and failure.

"Makomborero," the woman said to you at the introduction. "Makomborero. You know what that means, don't you? So just call me Blessings."

"I am Tambudzai. How are you, Blessing?" you said.

The quiet tenant shook her head, emphasizing, "Blessing-*ssss*!"

"Tambudzai, I hope you and Mako will understand each other nicely. Mako works at the Ministry of Justice as a legal secretary," said Mai Manyanga.

"As long as people don't say a legal fool, Auntie," said your co-tenant, with a shrug. "As long as it's not that, I can't complain. Aren't we all fools, staying there, working at that ministry?"

The sound of scratching and gnawing emerged from a corner. Small clawed feet scampered across the ceiling.

"If you can call it working," Mako shrugged once more, the last traces of vitality ebbing from her voice and paying no attention to the vermin. "What is work? If it's work it should pay you something. So isn't it just foolishness keeping on there, when the pay is as good as nothing? That's why people say it anyway. Legal fool. We who work there know, even if they don't say it while we can hear it."

As she spoke, a grey rat bolted from beneath a plastic bag concealed in a corner. Its claws trailed streaks of soiled cotton wool, at which it had been gnawing. Falling over, the bag deposited a red, clotted mass on the floor. Disgust stopped your breath as you realized why the young woman's room smelt even worse than yours.

"I keep it there to burn it," your housemate said dispassionately.

"Yes, that is something else for you to know," your landlady nodded, turning to you. "There is more to pay if any one of my toilets stops working."

After that introduction, you ignored Mako's request to be called Blessings, as does everyone else in the house. She herself exudes defeat in suffocating waves as dreadful as the rank odour.

Now, several months after that introduction, Mako uses both her hands to close the door once everyone has entered. The second it clicks shut, the legal secretary starts weeping. Down onto the floor she crumples. There her short, thin body curls up, forehead buried in the crook of her arm. Her fingers clench a wad of tissue. She is like a zongororo prodded by curious children.

"Get up!" commands Bertha roughly, her face without expression.

"What are you doing, going pfiku-pfiku, sniff-sniff, like that?" your housemate says harshly. "It's enough now. Iwe, get up and tell us."

Your landlady breathes deeply as though she is about to sing. Bertha changes her mind quickly and smoothly.

"Don't mind. Don't mind anything," she says, bending over the broken secretary. She hauls the young woman up.

"No, I just want to die now. That's all I want," your housemate insists and cannot stop weeping. "What can I do?" she goes on, trying to slide from Bertha's grip, back onto the floor.

Bertha grasps her firmly.

"There is nothing else," the young woman sobs.

"Shine!" Bertha exclaims. Her voice flies past outrage to hover half-way between disgust and amusement.

"Hi-hi! Hi-hi!" Mako weeps ever more loudly, confirming Bertha's suspicion.

The new woman watches intently, although she does not speak.

"Shine is not here," the landlady says. "He didn't come when I called him."

After that your landlady joins Bertha in advising Mako to wipe her face.

The good advice accomplishes nothing. Mako keeps choking on mucous and tears. The widow tells Christine, "This is the one called Makomborero."

Christine nods without response. The widow taps the newcomer's shoulder to prod her to leave. Apart from walking a little more quickly than usual, Mai Manyanga departs calmly as though nothing extraordinary has happened.

The door clicks shut again. You, Bertha, and Mako are alone. It is a different time of the month. The pall of putridity you experienced at your first visit is somewhat diminished.

"Shine," Bertha says again in a hollow voice.

Mako wails and slips back onto the floor.

Bertha stands over her and tells her to stop falling down and to pull herself together.

You move to the door. Bertha turns to go as well, looking quite ill at the sight of Mako's fragility.

"The lavatory," Mako sobs to make sure you do not leave her alone.

You halt, your hand on the doorknob.

"The brush scrapes so loud. Then you have to flush it and keep brushing, so I didn't hear anything," gasps Mako. "I didn't hear him coming."

Bertha returns to the bed and pulls Mako up onto it once more.

The legal secretary's shoulders shudder. Her voice quivers. She can hardly tell you that Shine sidled out of his bedroom.

"Oh, why am I so foolish? Why didn't I hear him?" she wails, savaging herself with self-accusation. "I thought he was just going out. Why didn't I do something?"

Your housemate weeps that her dying started right there, with her error of judgement. While she leaned over, brushing inside the bowl, Shine heaved in and wedged his knee between her buttocks. She says no more than this, telling it to you again and again, varying her anguished account of the incident only to inform you she knows her agony will go on forever because now that this has happened, she does not know how to stop either the dying or the housemate who caused it.

You had put the episode at the market firmly behind you when you came to Mai Manyanga's. Now, though, you think of Gertrude. Mako is wearing baggy sweats and a long-sleeved T-shirt for cleaning. You have never caught her in a miniskirt or tight leggings. With Gertrude, the reason for what happened was clear for all to see. Yet something similar has happened to Mako. Your heart beats faster. You are a woman alone. Your room is next to Shine's. After this attack on Mako, will your age and general unattractiveness prevent him coming for you? Hoping so, you move away from your housemate, wanting distance between yourself and the woeful young woman.

"Did anything happen?" Bertha asks when Mako is calmer.

"I told you what happened," Mako says. "He enjoyed himself behind me. And I thought only let him finish. Let it be finished. Let him go. So I kept quiet."

"Only that? Then why are you crying?" Bertha demands. "He didn't threaten you? He didn't say he will find you again? Mako, if you ask all women at your workplace, in fact all women, maybe just not Tambudzai over there, then you will know it's what nearly every one of them puts up with."

Bertha's forehead creases with uncertainty when your housemate sobs more loudly at these words. At much the same moment you realize there is nothing you can do or say since it is already done. Mako's noise does not undo anything. As neither you nor Bertha wants to continue considering the cause of her grief, you say goodbye, telling Mako you will see her when she has herself under control. For one reason or another, however, you fail to leave.

Mako throws herself across her bed and pushes her face into her thin pillow. You do not talk and now even Bertha is silenced. She stretches out an arm and pulls up Mako's tracksuit bottom, which has slid half-way down her buttocks.

That evening, when it is dark, after you have finished up your hidden food, because another's grief is no reason to lose your own appetite, as your people say, and also because it is better to be out of your room this evening, beyond the range of sighs and groans from Shine's bedroom, you forage for the next day's vegetables in the widow's garden.

"I have your parcel," your landlady's niece says softly from the cottage porch. She sits so still you only notice her when she wishes.

"Mealie meal," she continues. "Your people at home are thinking of you."

Your saliva turns bitter.

"Your mother walked all that way to bring it herself to our homestead. She said make sure you bring it right to where my daughter is. And a letter. That she wrote. They do not see you, but they are thinking of you. Your mother told me to tell you."

You are quiet for a long time. Christine retreats, although she does not move, her presence merely melting back into the shadows.

"Your aunt is a wonderful woman," you say in the end. "She is so kind, so full of love. She allows me to take the vegetables."

"I can bring it now?" Christine says. She does not sound as though she wants to move, the question a formality.

"There is no need," you say. "Why should you worry yourself? I'll come over in the morning."

You leave the garden carrying a smaller bunch of covo leaves than you intended.

"I'll tell my aunt you say thank you," says Christine.

"Thank you?"

"For the vegetables," Christine says.

CHAPTER 6

The next day, you decide not to collect your mother's parcel from Christine. Knocking on your landlady's door, being offered a seat, engaging in the conversation that is part of a visit will associate you too explicitly with the homestead. Then you will grow quiet and surly. Or you will talk and divulge too much concerning your family's circumstances. Mai Manyanga will learn firsthand the extent of your family's privation. She will put two and two together and realize that while you are educated, you have nevertheless become a failure. A notice letter might well follow, as you still do not have a job.

You spend the morning writing a letter to your cousin Nyasha, who has become a filmmaker in Germany, in which you ask for advice concerning leaving Zimbabwe. You want nothing more than to break away from the implacable terror of every day you spend in your country—where you can no longer afford the odd dab of peanut butter to liven up the vegetables from Mai Manyanga's garden or the petty comfort of perfumed soap—by going away and becoming a European. You do not post the letter. Instead, you tear it up and laugh bitterly at yourself: If you cannot build a life in your own country, how will you do so in another? Were you not offered an escape from penury and its accompanying dereliction of dreams through many years of education provided by your babamukuru, your uncle, first at his mission, then at a highly respected convent? All this you threw away with your wilful resignation from Steers et al. advertising agency. You wonder whether after all it is your fate to become as indigent as your father. To nurture whatever esteem your landlady might have for you, built on quite a few half truths and many small lies, you stay away from her cottage.

Naturally, as you have forbidden yourself association with her, Mai Manyanga's niece becomes fascinating. Admiring the determination that brought her to a more prosperous life with the widow, despising her affection for her home—buried as deep in her heart as both of your umbilical cords are interred in the earth of your villages—you succumb to an agitated obsession.

You spy on her from the bathroom window. The newcomer spends most of her time in your landlady's yard, doing the work the gardener doesn't. She stops from time to time, looks up at the little window as though she can see you, and then resumes her work. At times you indulge yourself by imagining a kinship with this woman who confronted Mai Manyanga sober, a feat managed before only by Bertha.

Your heart taps your ribs anxiously whenever you meet her, but, to your relief, Christine does not mention the gift again. As time goes on, however, her silence grows into wordless condemnation.

She becomes an undulating presence moving in and out of your orbit. When you think she is in agreement with you, she is a sun giving off warmth and strange, invisible sustenance; when not, she seems too brilliant and strong, a bolt of lightning waiting to strike. She works around the yard with the same fluid quietness with which she moves and appears and disappears wherever she wishes. She connects the hose and jets of rainbow drops spray out along its length. Her expression does not change as she searches in the garage. She emerges testing a couple of catapults. You watch the expertise of her fingers enviously as she strips off lengths of black rubber, repairing the hosepipe from her bounty. Deftly, she lays the hose spout at the highest point of a seedling bed while she swings a hoe. She waters the sweet peas around the widow's cottage. She sweeps the students' slab. She replants a patch of grass under the guava tree. She is a woman who is good at what she does. And this is intriguing.

The new woman does not sweat, nor do you see her out of breath. She is too calm at every task as though her core has fled to a distant place disconnected from her body. Her look, hidden under her bland expression, travels far beyond the widow's cottage. She stares down the shaft of her gaze as though when the time comes she will weave herself into it to slide away to a place where vision coincides with a deep wanting. You have seen this manner before, this being where the body is and not being there, in your sister Netsai, who went to war, who lost a leg, and who said to you when they said there was peace, "Yes, I went and I am here but I never came back. Most of the time I'm still out there wandering through the grass and sand, looking for my leg."

You grow thinner, and do not know whether to be pleased about this or not. There is a dullness to your skin, like a thin membrane enveloping despair. It tells people you have collided with your limit; you do not want them to know this. The vegetables become too disgusting to eat, as first cooking oil then salt fall off your shopping list, and you do not have the heart to drain a portion every day from Bertha's or Mako's bottle. Every minute of each twenty-four hours taunts you with what you are reduced to. Although it seems they cannot be, the nights are yet more horrendous since your housemate Shine takes a different woman into his room practically every day of the week.

The encounters in the next room grow more strident from one night to the next, as though Shine measures the noise level from his women to set some kind of standard. You struggle to find sleep and when you do you are woken up again almost immediately. You try to read or resort to covering your head with your blanket. Finally, rest being as futile as everything else, you climb out of bed to stare over the yard, into the knowledge that you do not have the courage for anything you want—neither emigration, nor ensnaring one of your landlady's sons.

One evening, several weeks after Christine's arrival, you hear Shine's bedroom door open earlier than usual. Footsteps pass by your room, toward the entrance. Gratified at the prospect of peace, you put away your disintegrating magazines and climb into bed.

"You will call me?" your housemate's woman wheedles, out in the hall.

"I will," Shine assures her.

"What if you don't? Can I get you here? On the number you gave me?" the voice continues with plaintive longing.

"Are you afraid I will forget you?" Shine chuckles.

"Don't do that. I'm sure you can't, after tonight," the woman says with the hint of a giggle.

"Don't worry." Shine's voice is dark and slow like treacle. "You're not someone a man wants to forget."

You tie your nightscarf tightly over your ears and bury your head beneath your pillow.

The front door closes. Shine's feet pad back into his room and across to his bathroom. A few seconds later his shower trickles, spurting occasionally, under the city council's irregular pressure.

You have finally fallen asleep when your door handle turns and rattles.

"Tambudzai! Tambudzai!" your housemate whispers.

You hold your breath and do not answer, glad the door is locked.

"Tambudzai. Don't worry, let's just spend some time chatting," Shine's voice drips between door and frame.

Your mouth dry and gravelly, heart jarring against your ribs, you do not move.

"Bitch," Shine breathes into the quiet.

You do not answer.

"Missing one like you is missing nothing," he decides.

He pads back to his room. Silence returns like a punch. Then his footsteps are in the corridor once more. He leaves the house and returns several hours later with a raucous partner.

It is later still when a tentative inquiring sound startles you back from the brink of sleep.

Ta-ta-ta. Fingernails tap at your window.

"Do you hear me?" a hushed voice asks.

A staring eye gleams in the moonlight.

"Which one is in there?" the woman who surrounds that eye whispers. Mottled and shadowy through the pink curtains, her drooping figure hunches toward the window.

"Is there a key? I want the door open now. You must let me in there," she says.

Knowing she can see in through the gap between them, you pull the curtains back, revealing a cloven face, one side silver, the other ebony.

"You know me, don't you?" the woman says.

You stare at her.

"It was last week when I was here," she rushes on. "With Shine, don't you remember?"

She knocks again, harder. You open your window.

The woman relaxes slightly. "Are all of them like this?" she asks, nodding her head at the burglar bars.

Now you nod, and add, "Except for the toilet. But that one is tiny."

"So open for me," she begs.

"Try there," you gesture toward Bertha's and Mako's windows. "Because my key is missing!" you volunteer when she opens her mouth to insist.

Smh, your visitor sucks her teeth. She slides along the wall, trampling the nasturtiums that Christine has been diligently watering. Soon there is more knocking.

Minutes pass as you lie back beneath your cover wondering whether it is better to have your housemate's women in his bed or outside your window. You squeeze your eyes tight as a giggle from Shine's room is quickly stifled and you realize you are dealing with both options. After a few moments of thick silence from your housemate's room there is unintelligible murmuring, followed by a spate of curt whispering. A few minutes later a dull thump tells you someone is clumsily trying to open the small bathroom window.

Doors squeak down the hall as your other housemates hurry into the passage.

"Chi'i? What's going on?" Mako's voice filters under your door.

"These ones! Disturbing us to be bitten by what they've dug up," Bertha whispers.

"Maybe she's gone?" Mako hopes timidly.

"Ah! Going away from where she followed herself," scoffs Bertha.

"Iwe, Mako, what kind of woman does that? If you have any, tell me where have you put your senses."

"You were disturbed?" whispers Mako, appeasing Bertha with sympathy. "She tapped at my window also."

"Why else would I come out?" the big woman snaps. "I told that girl, stop knocking, as if it is your window. And I said, don't you know it's not your husband's window either? Now look at her, thinking sugar isn't bought in shops with your own money, but with Shine's foolish organs."

"Running after that one," agrees Mako in a thin wavering voice.

Bertha chortles nastily, as is her habit when savouring other people's misfortunes.

"Ha, I bet his mother is crying, because she is looking after half a dozen, if not a dozen children. If I were Shine's mother, I'd have swallowed him down. I'd have passed him out like shit and that would've been the end of everything," she says.

"Shh," cautions Makomborero. "What if he hears you?"

"Then we'll see!" Bertha cackles.

While your housemates talk, a medley of shrieks begins in your landlady's front garden.

You stumble out of bed, feet groping for plimsolls. Although you do not want anything to do with the commotion, you know you must be informed in order to ensure your own safety. Deciding not to be seen in your fraying nightdress with its missing buttons, you drag on jeans and a T-shirt.

Bertha is pulling the front door open when you walk into the hall. She strides out. Mako hurries after her and you follow them.

Out in the yard, your landlady is hastily tying a Zambia wrap around her waist as she advances round the side of her house.

She, you, Bertha, and Mako gather and look out over the ragged grass. In the middle of this effort at lawn, in a dusty patch, the new woman struggles with her clothing.

She wears a pale shirt with a billowing frill down the front, as though she is dressed for dinner. Slim dark pants complete her outfit.

She fumbles first at the buttons on her shirt and then at the ones of her trousers. Horrified, you watch her claw at her zipper.

"See," the woman screams.

"Now, see me. I'm going to take off my clothes, Shine, I'm going to do it. And I want to see what you'll do."

"Kachasu," says Bertha. "Or Zed. I've never seen a woman who can take that moonshine hard stuff."

Your eyes water as you watch. The woman's frenzy mirrors the panic you endured a few hours ago when Shine stood at your door. What if you were younger? What would you have done if a man like Shine, an accountant with a job, paid you attention? Bertha's words sound harsh in your ears. Your stomach tightens as you recall Gertrude and the stone in your hand. You sidle away from Bertha and your memories, closer to Mai Manyanga.

The woman peels off her shirt and flings it away. The garment hooks on a clump of spiky pampas grass. Her hands creep across her shoulders to slide away her bra straps. Again and again her fingers fumble. By the time she manages to work on her zip, not even Bertha snorts because the woman's rage billows out from her until, like smoke, it suffocates everything.

Your landlady breaks the spell by inhaling deeply in irritation. She glances at Shine's room where the lights are out, then once more at the enraged woman.

"Shine's gone now. About time!" smirks Bertha.

You and Mako agree, at which Bertha adds, "I've been waiting quietly all this time. There's someone I want to bring in here from my workplace."

Widow Manyanga whispers crossly, "What is that little thing doing there?"

Your landlady uses the prefix *ka* to describe Shine's woman, calling her a small, foolish object unworthy of attention.

"Who told her," your landlady cries, "that this is where to come to do things like that? Where did she hear it? That what I do here is run a brothel?"

Bertha snorts in a way that implies many answers to the widow's question. You keep still and Mako is trembling.

The half-naked woman continues shouting. In a moment she triumphs over her zip. She pushes her trousers down over her buttocks, wiggling and hopping like a dancing girl in a chart-topping rumba troupe.

Bertha laughs, cutting your landlady off in the middle of great indignation. Using the interruption to sift through her options, the widow hitches up her Zambia cloth, throws her shoulders back, and inflates her chest.

"Maria!" Mai Manyanga opens her lungs and throws up her right hand. This gesture comforts you so that you are glad you are standing close to her.

"Maria na Marita vakataura naIshe," the widow bawls, releasing her voice for the first time since her recent period of silence in a roar of righteous indignation.

Aghast at the evening's events, you raise your right hand also. Then you lift both arms and wave them in time to the widow's rhythm.

"Vakataura naIshe, dai magara pano, Lazaro haaifa," Mai Manyanga rumbles. "If you had stayed, Lord, Lazarus would not have died."

Your landlady, both hands above her head, palms to the woman stripping on the lawn, sways in ecstasy.

Mako bows her head and clasps her hands together, lips moving. You start to hum.

Bertha walks away to fish the blouse off the pampas grass. Having retrieved it, she wades a little way onto the lawn.

"Get dressed," Bertha says, as she throws the garment at the woman. "You're putting us all to shame here."

Your landlady finishes her hymn.

"Yes, cover it up," she says, having cooled her own temper with her chorus. "And then get away!"

Shine's woman stands with her trousers around her ankles, eyeing the shirt at her feet, not knowing what to do.

"Foolish girls," your landlady scoffs. "What can that boy give them?

A pair of shoes? They should look at us," the widow goes on. "They must learn from their elder sisters. Because getting a man to marry isn't a game. It's as bad as war, and you have to know how to fight that one."

You continue to hum, with arms raised, palms fluttering to support your landlady.

This backing appears to inspire her.

"So why lie down?" she shrugs, turning her back on Shine's woman. "Why, if you're not going to get anything?"

Thinking twice of leaving, the widow stops beside you.

"Keep on standing, that's what I say," she admonishes. "And keep things together. So these men keep everything where everything should be kept. Isn't that right, vasikana?"

Tired now, your arms fall to your sides. Reading your exhaustion as a signal, Mai Manyanga turns toward her cottage declaring, "We'll bring the fire of the Holy Spirit down against whatever brought that silly thing to my garden. We'll pray for forgiveness for her. Remember, girls, the kingdom of God is taken with violence. Let us be violent tonight, in praying for forgiveness."

"We are sleepy," Bertha objects. "Besides, that one back there needs watching," she hurries on, to stop Mai Manyanga's protest. "She just might start again, shouting up a curse for everyone since that's what she came for. Mako and I will watch her carefully through our curtains."

"Let's get down on our knees," your landlady suggests to you. "You and I together, Tambudzai. We'll pray for this woman."

Seized by the need for prayer, she glances at the gravel but decides not to fall onto it. Instead, Widow Manyanga fills her lungs and once more belts out her chorus.

"Did anyone say I am going anywhere?" Shine's woman shouts. Her voice keeps rising until it hangs in the night like a querulous star. "Well, watch this space. Just keep tuned. You've got the right address. I'm not going anywhere."

Christine has been sitting beneath the jacaranda tree by the gate, so silent and still that neither you nor your companions have noticed her.

"Now, sister, what's up?" the landlady's niece calls.

Mai Manyanga stiffens. Ignoring her niece, she puts her mouth close to your ear and says, "Tambudzai, aren't you coming?" With that, she stalks away.

You hurry after her, glad to be leaving the scene.

"Go and tell Christine to get that woman out of this yard," your landlady says. "And then tell her to lock the gate. That one must not bring any demons back inside here."

"Coming here to do that!" the widow mutters as she proceeds. "Do I have a shebeen? In VaManyanga's house! Tss, why does she think she can do what she wants at VaManyanga's?"

Christine is already on the lawn, urging the woman back into her clothes, when you return to carry out Mai Manyanga's instruction. Shine's woman allows herself to be pacified and soon the three of you pass through the gate.

"Here." Christine holds a pair of shoes out and leans against the gatepost, watching Shine's woman step into them.

"Now go, and don't come back," Christine says when the woman finishes dressing.

Shine's woman hesitates.

"Away," Christine urges.

Christine stands silent guard as Shine's woman dwindles to a dark dot, moving against silver washes of moonlight that flood the potholed road. You subside onto a granite boulder beneath the gnarled tree, at odds with yourself once more, not knowing why, fighting back tears.

CHAPTER 7

A jacaranda blossom swirls to the ground, its gentle purple now a pale metallic hue. The moon shadows have edges sharp as knives.

You are still under the big tree by the gate, sitting on a boulder. Christine does not sit next to you. She stands arms crossed, fists balled into armpits, staring into the night as though she is examining a spectacle she has seen too many times before.

You are about to return to Mai Manyanga and prayers when Kiri turns to you.

"Let's run," she breathes.

The change is disconcerting. One minute she is absent, the next she is with you, a woman wide enough, compelling enough to jump from there to here in a moment by the power of her will.

She gazes toward the house where Mai Manyanga is waiting for you. In the pause between Christine's suggestion and your ability to respond, the widow gives up, sweeping off to her cottage. You do not say anything now that it is just the two of you. You want to put your head on Christine's chest and weep.

"Let's run," Christine says again.

You realize she does not want this, the weeping.

You agree with her silently, as you are always doing, agreeing with people greater than you. This evening you concede that there shall be no weeping.

"Run," you echo. You hear yourself and you are angry with yourself because the word is a lie, standing in for the truth that you wish to lay your head on her chest and let the water dammed inside you pour out.

Christine raises her upper lip, drawing down a trace of something amused or disgusted into the space between you. You welcome this admission, however veiled, of how the woman sees you. Perhaps this is the moment of hope when you can announce, "I am so sick of being sick of myself. I think you can. Kiri, would you help me?" But her lips seal together again before you speak.

"Just talking," she shrugs, allowing her voice to waft away like smoke into the night air.

"Anyone can see you're not the kind," she resumes after a while. "What did that to you, cutting off your legs like someone who has been to war, so that you couldn't even come and get your parcel?"

"Your aunt's calling," you say, to stop the ridicule. You stand with what you believe is firm purpose, pushing back against being taunted by this woman from the village.

"It was not just your mother," Christine resumes. "It was Netsai, too. Only your father did not do anything. Your sister helped your mother carry the mealie, hobbled all the way, although you know how she goes hopla-hopla on that only leg of hers. She also sent her greetings. I am as good as your younger mother. I know your aunt Lucia very well. We went to war and came back from it together."

You had seen it coming. The only reason for Christine's closeness to your family while being a stranger to you was that their bond was formed during the war when you were absent from the village. That period of strife was the one in which the gap between you and the homestead widened. Since home was unsafe, you spent term time at the Young Ladies' College of the Sacred Heart and holidays at your uncle's mission.

"We were taught not to be selfish during the war," continues Christine, who up until this evening had not displayed much interest in conversation. "Because then everyone dies. There was a boy I liked. They kept on sending him up to the front until he was killed. I thought even then, that's selfishness. In spite of what they taught us. Even though we fought the war, it was full of liars."

It is now too late to begin the conversation you should have had weeks ago, when Christine came, concerning your family and their need and your inability to do anything about those needs because of your city poverty. Christine has that layer under her skin that cuts off her outside from her inside and allows no communication between the person she once believed she could be and the person she has in fact become. The one does not acknowledge the other's existence. The women from war are like that, a new kind of being that no one knew before, not exactly male but no longer female. It is rumoured the blood stopped flowing to their wombs the first time they killed a person. People whisper that the unspeakable acts were even more iniquitous when performed by women, so that the ancestors tied up the nation's prosperity in repugnance at the awfulness of it, just as they had done to the women's wombs. It occurs to you that you are more like Christine than you are like Mai Manyanga: Christine with her fruitless war that brought nothing but false hope and a fresh, more complete variety of discouragement. You with your worthless education intensifying your beggary, making it all the more ludicrous.

Christine starts to run. Phrases from the widow's choruses float down on the quiet night air. You jog after her, not for her company but to put distance between yourself and the singing. After a few metres, your eyes glaze with effort. When you focus outward once more, you see only the night. Christine jumps out from behind a tree. You almost bump into her.

"That is what we learnt," she says. "Running is easy. Everyone can do it. If you don't, you don't live. What were you doing, if it wasn't running that you pretended you couldn't?"

"After all that," you gasp, in reluctant admiration. "All day. In her garden!"

"I don't sweat," she says. "I run to town, three nights at least in a week."

She appears to like the fact that you are impressed by her endurance since she goes on, "I have to. It's the only way. Because of all the things that never stop. Just like tonight in that garden."

She turns away, only to resume again after a little pause, "That's the good thing about what the war taught us. There's only one kind of blood, not many like some like to say. We saw it seep from every wound. And even those who couldn't run knew how, after they saw it. It's true, Tambudzai. If you've seen blood, you know about running."

Christine jumps like an athlete preparing for a race before she continues, "If I have the same choice, I will never repeat it. I learnt you run away from blood. You don't run to it, pretending it is water. That you can pour wherever and drink, a river flowing to quench your thirst, lying that it's water."

Her shadow is brutish as she leaps. You lean against the tree trunk. Your breath, which had begun to calm, rushes into your lungs uncomfortably shallow.

"Why aren't you answering anything?" says Christine, a rough disappointment invading her voice.

You want her to run again, away, without you, so that you can stay in this in-between place not in the city and not at the widow's. You did not find the words to speak of Mai Manyanga's sling when you saw it, nor do you want to this evening.

"You are saying you did not see the blood in Mai Manyanga's living room?" Christine persists. "That although you were in the house, you didn't hear anything?"

Now that she has spoken of it, you want to move again, to dart away from the scene you witnessed many weeks ago, before Christine came, in Mai Manyanga's living room. You want to leave Christine's truth, that once you have seen blood you are covered by it, behind in the heart of this war-woman. Yet you are beginning to realize blood does not only speak, it follows. You saw the blood spurt from your sister's leg during the war, just after you had graduated from your uncle's mission, and you fled from then on. You kept on fleeing from the sight all through your years at the Young Ladies' College of the Sacred Heart.

"No one heard anything," you murmur in self-defence.

You want to sit down, but there is only a fence.

"Is anyone thinking anything about any of it?" asks Christine.

"O Mwariwe tiitire nyasha. Oh great God, have mercy on us."

The anguish Widow Manyanga had not mustered for Shine's woman slithers through her window into the night, a distant wretchedness.

"M-hm," says Christine. "Once you have seen it, it is difficult forever after. The first time, if you are that kind of person whose heart is weak, blood can be like a trap. It fastens. Either you want it all the time, or you are afraid of it until the end of your days."

Your breathing remains shallow and difficult. Pain heaves beneath your breath, gripping your throat so that you cannot speak. You know, although you have said little about that evening, that you have already said too much and you must not dare to deliver another sentence or else you will drown in a pit of disgrace.

"Don't worry," Christine says. "It isn't your fault. It isn't the fault of anyone in the house. Everyone told my auntie over there. But she just doesn't listen to anyone."

"Vanamai, uyai ticheme. Women, let us wail together," the widow moans her chorus. "Kuna Mwari ati itire nyasha. To God, to beg His mercy."

"The family sent people to tell her. But all she did was boast to them. Saying she was carrying out VaManyanga's wishes so nobody could tell her anything. Since she was the last to see him and so she knows what her husband wanted."

"O Mwari we, tiitire nyasha," Mai Manyanga wails, her voice thinned by the distance.

"One day I will tell you about that," Christine says. Her promise sounds like a threat.

The singing grows louder as Mai Manyanga returns down the drive.

"I'm the one she's looking for," you say. "I said I was going to pray with her."

"Let's go," says Christine. "We can catch a ride to town."

"I'll get a dollar," you say, changing your mind, even though you do not want to spend any money on the trip to town and back.

You wait until Mai Manyanga returns to the cottage before hurrying back down the road. Once in your room, you contemplate crawling into bed, but Mai Manyanga starts wailing again. You pull a dollar from its hiding place in a drawer and quickly change your top and shoes.

Outside once more, you walk beside Christine, staring at your moon shadow. It is bigger than you. It moves parts of its body that you do not. It runs when you are walking.

"My aunt is bleeding," Christine says. "She is not well. Her sons are frightened."

You want her to be quiet, but she goes on, "They are all pretending they don't know who did it, but it was Larky that evening. Do those boys ever do anything quietly? So why are all of you in the house lying that you didn't hear anything? Are you going to tell me something, Tambudzai? Why keep quiet? Are you a Manyanga? My aunt won't live long but we in her family, we didn't want to wait and see if her sons managed to kill her first. That's why it was decided for me to come here and make sure those boys keep order."

You sniff the air. Smoke. Spices. One of the residents on the road has been, or perhaps is still, braaing.

Your nose remembers that evening some months ago. The smell of marinating meat was thick in the main house.

You never do find out whether it's the actual date or not. It is the day the widow and her sons choose to celebrate Ignore's, the youngest one's, birthday.

The widow begins preparing the day before. She departs twice in the Nissan that has just come back from the mechanic so that the garage finally holds a car. However, each time she pumps petrol into the carburetor, the exhaust pipe spits out dark fumes as though it has indigestion.

You go into the kitchen at midmorning that day, hoping everyone else has left. You want to simmer your porridge, but you abandon your task the minute you walk in. Bertha and Mako are ensconced in chairs. It is a month-end week-end and they have orange juice, margarine, and jam spread out on the little table. They have toast and scrambled eggs with slivers of bacon. You look at their food dully, your mouth not taking the trouble to water.

With a guffaw, Bertha proposes a wager: Will the widow's double cab make it back from the outing, or will it break down so that Mai Manyanga has to call the mechanic again? Mako takes on the bet. Giving another great laugh, Bertha opts for the widow's ruin. When

Bertha finally quiets down, Mako insists that God, who is great and merciful, will favour the widow.

In the evening, the Manyanga sons arrive on time. They are equipped with cooler boxes and ice cubes and women who agree to congregate in Praise's car with six packs of Castle and a bottle of Mukuyu wine. Envy blossoms in your heart, for at this point, in spite of your inaction, you still entertain a desire not for marriage itself but for the security the state of being married brings. You do not direct your grudge against the wives you have not seen, but against these vain, vacant-eyed, plastic-nailed creatures who are enjoying a life of security and ease, the kind of living you had envisioned for yourself and up until that calamitous day at the agency had worked for so diligently. Like the widow who takes no stand against her son's entanglements, you forgive the Manyanga men their dalliances and fantasize desperately about encountering one of them in the hall.

The family living room is unlocked for the occasion. Once the men are settled with their drinks, your landlady sings, "Mwakanaka, Mambo Jesu." The men join in, tunefully, if lacking the widow's fervour. The hymn done, Mai Manyanga conducts a prayer. After this the sons return to their snacks. From time to time one of them carries a dish of roasted peanuts or chicken wings to the women in the car, who grow raucous whenever their refreshments need replenishing. Mai Manyanga enjoys her sons' presence, and is not in the least put out by these arrangements. You suspect the Manyanga looseness will be a challenge once you have made your move, but you tell yourself you will cross that bridge when you have to.

The murmur of voices changes to the clink, at rich intervals, of glass and china as the Manyangas mould sadza into balls, dip them in gravy, and chew at fragrant meat. The family's conversation dwindles to a distant hum.

You fall asleep lightly, unable to find a place of deep rest with the smell of food tantalizing your stomach. Not much time passes before the ripples of the family's speech swell. Sentences reach you in waves of sound that grow until it seems they smash at the bed, pound at the wall, and toss the floor hither and thither. The air itself seems to quiver and tremble. The darkness of the night shudders to the rhythm of an old, half-forgotten music that you last heard many years ago on the homestead and a swift copper note vibrates from one corner of the room to the other. Shine adds a dark bass line to this melody, while the voice of the woman he is with crescendos shrilly.

You open anxious eyes to the sound of distressed cries.

"Yowe! Yowe! Yowe!"

As you surface from your half dream, you realize the voice is Mako's.

"Vasikana, Shine," your housemate continues. "Vanhu kani, come and look. Come and see what happened."

You do not move, only sliding out of bed after Bertha's door opens.

Mako is hunched over in the middle of the hall between kitchen and living room. She props herself up against a wall as well as she can. She is shaking.

Swathes of scarlet thicken and congeal on the floor. The clots in the family room extend all the way back to the dining table. Drops crust and flake on the grandfather clock, the cabinet, carpet, and occasional tables. The beer mugs that toasted the family's celebrations are strewn in jagged pieces across the floor. On the wooden shelves, shards from family photographs glint on taut stiff pools. Mrs. Manyanga and her husband are spattered but upright and stare out with the same pride as ever.

You want to remain suspended between one breath and another but after you exhale, you creep forward behind Bertha and Mako, to see your landlady seated at the dining room table. The remains of dinner lie caked on the plates scattered before her. The widow's colourful doek is by her chair. Her ogbada of the same bright print is slit from shoulder to breast as though a drunken surgeon had attempted reconstructive surgery.

She smiles and says in a flat yet triumphant tone like a hostess resuming the conversation, "I saved him. I protected my Igi from both of them. Go, Bertha, Tambu, Mako. Go all of you and find him. And when you have found him, I want you to look after my Igi. Make sure that no harm comes to him."

Mechanically, you kneel in the blood. The smell makes you gag.

You take your landlady's hand to knead forth a response, but Widow Manyanga repeats in the same voice, "Go, vasikana, to my Igi. I want you to look after him."

Blood is on your knees. Standing, you reach for a paper napkin and wipe it off, feeling as though the snakes of your womb have opened their jaws and everything is plummeting out of you to the ground.

"This is what happens when you give birth," the widow says.

Bertha, who alone can act, goes out. She returns a few minutes later carrying a cup of steaming tea.

"Is there anyone here with any Panadol?" she asks.

Everyone is quiet. No one has any medication.

"I know Larky wants to kill Igi," your landlady resumes in a moan. "Because this house is Igi's birthday present. Larky wants to kill him because my son Igi is the only one who is fighting for me. Yes, Larky and Praise. The two want to kill me." She smiles dully before she continues, "If it were not for the last one that came out, I would be like a stray, an unloved dog kicked about by everyone because of those two who came first. Yes, this house is a present for Igi's birthday. My Igi. When my Igi has my things I am keeping them and not throwing them somewhere to another woman."

"Shame. Too bad," says Bertha, speaking more quietly than she has ever done before. "You, are you sure there's no one with a Panadol?"

Walking carefully down the hall, Shine's woman, a new, unfamiliar face, stops at the living room door, observing. No one pays her any attention. Tense in her desire not to be noticed, she steals on tiptoe out through the verandah.

You and your housemates do not look at each other. You draw in a series of deep breaths and let them out in a shudder, feeling how you are the world and it is hollow and the three of you are falling through it.

"Then she started singing that song again," you say to Christine. "The one she always sings about King Jesus."

"You were and you are still lying," Christine says softly. "When things like that happen there's a lot of noise."

You pass under a row of jacarandas. The moon is higher, the soft wind cooler. Christine pulls you off the gravel, where your feet are crunching, onto the grass. The streetlights on the main road to town glow up ahead.

"I know why you don't want to say you knew something," she resumes. "Because it's too much. You say how can a woman be like that? You cannot answer, so you say no she isn't." She sighs loudly and continues with venom, "Ignore! His mother did the same, ignoring what he was doing. Even now, my aunt is also ignoring the sickness in her womb that is eating her away from the inside," she remarks with annoyance.

Your own blood runs cold as you wonder where you will live if Mai Manyanga should die before you find alternative accommodation.

"Fear," your companion continues. "It's caught hold of them. Now Ignore has stolen the inheritance from the rest. So when he boasted about his birthday present, Larky went and punched him. And then my aunt jumped up. Saying to Larky, if you are going to kill anyone, kill me and not my son. That is when Larky's door burst open and his memory of himself flew out of it. He grabbed the meat knife and jumped at Ignore. So Ignore ran behind his mother."

You turn into Lomagundi Road, glad you will soon be in a combi where it is impossible to continue such conversations.

"We saw such things," your companion says. "During the liberation struggle. Then it was in the bush, but now it is in the home. And still no one talks. They just say it happened, or they even say it didn't happen, and then ignore it."

"Anyhow, that's how I came here," Christine proceeds quietly. "When I was back home, just being there, pretending it's life, like everyone else, they called me and said, 'Go and see what is happening with your aunt. Those young men know what kind of a woman you are.'" She splutters between a laugh and a cough. "That fighting was just like a madness. Maybe they thought because I'd seen so much of it, I was the best one to deal with what's happening here in Harare."

You come to a bus stop and sit on the bench. You start trembling. You stand up again because sitting is heavier than standing.

"I didn't want to come," says Christine, "because I don't want to get mixed up in it. My aunt married her husband when she was a young woman. And this is what it has now come to. With us it looks like there's always blood. I don't know if it's just my family."

The first combis that pass by, long intervals between them so late in the night, are crammed with people. When you return to a place beside her on the bench, Christine relates in a scornful voice the matters you should not be mixed up in.

Your landlady's husband moved up to Harare from Masvingo. Before the move, VaManyanga was employed as an attendant at a fuel station by a white man named Peacock. At Independence, this Peacock left the country for New Zealand, bequeathing to VaManyanga the fuel station and all its movable property. In a murky arrangement with the nation's long-distance bus company involving fuel discounts, shares, and severance packages, a junior manager was fired. VaManyanga applied for the position and was successful, while running his business on the side. By similar means, within a few years, he obtained the position of CEO with the Zimbabwe People's National Buses. Transferred to the parastatal's head office in the capital, VaManyanga disposed of the service station and snapped up a property in the southern suburbs. Christine's voice drips with disdain as she describes this violation of what she had fought for, while you are so excited by the knowledge that your very being emits a low hum of admiration for the man who promoted himself so astutely.

Christine flags down another combi. It stops, although it is already packed with more people than are allowed. Then, because you are late-night travellers who are at his mercy, the conductor charges double and you part with an entire dollar, leaving no fare for getting back at the end of your outing. The other passengers rumble with discontent but pull out dirty wads of low-denomination notes, or handfuls of change. You feel you are dissolving through the seat onto the tarmac where wheels will churn you to invisibility.

You climb out after Christine when the combi stops at Copacabana. She steers you eastward over a cavernous pavement in silence for the first couple of hundred metres.

"He became quite rich," she says in the end, as an afterthought. "It turns out he was good at what they called doing business. That's what they called it after Independence. You know," she observes, "it is better to call it April 18. What do we really know about independence? Maybe that it was just for people like my uncle." Her voice is sad now, rather than scornful, as she divulges how VaManyanga soon purchased a new dwelling in an area further to the city's north, from another white person who was also departing to New Zealand, where there was not, nor could ever be—since all the earlier nations had been eradicated—any talk of indigenizing anything. It turns out that, just like you, everyone had applauded VaManyanga's achievements. No one queried anything. Relatives and colleagues alike praised the way the newly independent businessman had turned his inheritance into hard currency and deposited it safely in a bank on the Isle of Man.

"What did they want? Of course, to borrow my uncle's money from him," Christine snorts. You shake your head and suck your teeth, genuinely outraged on behalf of your companion's uncle.

"He was too shrewd. I admit he was clever," shrugs your companion. "So hardly anybody got anything. So what did they start saying? That all that money he made could never just come from hard work, but that he had some wicked, blood-drinking goblins. So some of them started trying to find out what muti my uncle was using. Some wanted to neutralize it with stronger medicine, others wanted to use it themselves. More than one mouth said his charms contained pieces of kidnapped children's bodies." As she mentions this, Christine confirms her uncle was the sort of man who might well have gone so far as taking the children's parts to South Africa for sale or for imbuing with magical properties, or that he could very well have buried the organs in places where he wanted to establish further ZPNB depots.

VaManyanga, though, you find out to your satisfaction, did not let rumours derail his upward mobility. He soon purchased more properties and moved out of his second home to enjoy a grander lifestyle. Visits to the village where their niece lived became less frequent. Christine tells you she was comfortable with that, as she had ceased to either like or respect her relatives.

Understanding with some impatience that Christine is speaking not only about the Manyangas, but about all people who harbour the same intense cravings for advancement, "This came with the war," you say. "All of it. Nobody ever did things like that before you people went to Mozambique and went about doing what you know you did."

"There is nothing any freedom fighter did," your companion says, "that people didn't do in the villages. You know they started doing those things themselves very easily. And all of them are carrying on. Me, when the war ended, I swore I would find something to do with my own hands. I pledged I won't do that kind of thing anymore. No matter what happens."

With this Christine walks ahead briskly, bringing you soon to the disco, whose vibrations curtail further talking. She talks her way past the outsize bouncers at the club door, who look you over, objecting with pointed questions to two women entering the club unaccompanied. Down in the basement with the strobe going too fast and the music pumping a hallucinogenic rhythm, your companion surveys the room, weaves through dancers and tables to prop her elbows on the bar. She gives the solitary man beside her a sidelong glance, demonstrating how to extract all the booze you want from men without having any parts of your body grabbed. You discover you are good at it. It is marvellous to be good at something. You haven't been good at much in a long time. Even the things you were good at, your education, your copywriting at the advertising agency—in fact one and the same thing—have in the end conspired against you, handing out a sentence of isolation.

Soon you are too drunk to think of anything but downing more.

While you drain glass after glass of vodka, Christine starts taking liquor with every second or third glass of Mazoe.

You lurch into a woman on your way back from the toilet. The woman has spiky hair. Her skin is white.

"Mind!" she says, setting her drink on a table, wiping dripping fingers on the back of her jeans.

You stare at her, your eyes attempting to focus. When the image is as clear as it is going to get: "Tracey!" you bellow.

"Excuse me?" says the white woman, giving you a tolerant smile.

"I know you," you tell her. "I used to work for you. And we went to school together. "Are you going to pretend?" you crescendo. "You know you know me."

Even as you speak, you are aware this person is not that particular white woman, the executive from the advertising agency who schemed with her fellow white people to steal the ideas you sweated over and produced for copy. With this knowledge, the hole in the universe yawns wide in front of you again and the woman who knows better than the one you hear roaring disappears into its depths. Making yourself as large as you can, you scream, "Don't pretend with me, Tracey!"

"Katrin," the woman responds, backing away. "Katrin."

"Both," you insist. "I mean, you're my boss. From the advertising."

The woman takes a deep breath. "Not me," she says, exhaling sharply.

"Liar!"

She moves away onto the dance floor, joining a multiracial pocket of people, complexions ranging from ebony to pale marble. You follow her. She ignores you. You hear someone talking loudly, telling you she is not the woman who employed you at the advertising agency. You know this sensible voice is located in your brain. You don't listen to it. "You are lying. That's what you are doing," you keep shouting. As you shout you lunge. The white woman sees you coming. She dodges round you and you fall into a trio of dancers. Bracing themselves on their platform shoes, tossing their weaves, "Get away," they shout, shoving you from one to the other.

The men from the door surge onto the dance floor. They clamp the flesh of your upper arm in their fingers, asking which you prefer, calming down and being reasonable or being prohibited. They have, however, reckoned without Christine. Your companion plants her fists on her hips and informs the bouncers she is an Independence struggle ex-combatant, Moscow trained, and she can see half a dozen others still in fighting form around the bar; nor does it matter if some are not actually Soviet alumni but were trained in China, they are all comrades and fighters.

In spite of Christine's intervention, the bouncers keep holding on to your arm, saying they are hired to end things; that when out-of-control women start beginning their messes with peaceful dancers, that is what they are ending. So Christine tells them you are under control and heaves you up the stairs and out onto the street. You refuse to walk. Christine drags you away from the club. You shout more and more loudly for her to release you. When she doesn't, you scream that you will be damned if you ever go anywhere with her again. While you fling abuse at her, Christine manoeuvres you to the nearest bus stop. She props you up on the termite-eaten bench, pushes a dollar note into your jeans pocket, and tells you to take the first combi travelling toward Mai Manyanga's.

CHAPTER 8

"What happened?"

Your eyelids slither apart. The earth spins. You slit your eyes against a brilliant dawn. You are lying on the pavement at the bus stop.

Looking down at you are two elderly men. They wear khaki suits and little caps: cooks, on their way to work in the northern suburbs.

"Who knows with these ones? It could be anything," says one, after a moment's reflection.

"Now what? What can be done?" the other asks.

"With women," says the first. "When it's like this, you know what it is. It's their ancestors tying them up." He straightens and his shadow lifts from over you.

"Love potion experts, these are the ones. Busy rotting their husbands' guts and killing them one after the other. Don't touch her. Otherwise you'll be in for something. Absolute witches."

Sweat, paraffin, and a long lack of washing. The smell rolls over you.

"I said don't touch her. She'll take what should be yours and it won't come back to you."

The odour recedes.

"Do you see anyone touching anything?" says the man who was warned to leave you alone.

There is rustling.

"Ah, what's this? Wasting money," says the first speaker.

"Since she is here, not yet dead," says the other. "I'll say it's not wasting."

A fifty-cent coin is pressed into your palm. You drift away as footsteps recede.

Later, you open your eyes again and lean over to vomit. The mess fills the cracks in the pavement. Ants and tiny spiders scurry around in indignation. You heave yourself up, clutching the fifty-cent piece, the evening's booty. Ants and spiders trek over your body.

Regiments of them defy the city's low pressure in the widow's shower. You are thinking, as you attack both them and your skin with your washcloth, "I am the kind of person two cooks give a coin to. No, I am not that person. I am. I am not. Would I know it if I am that person?"

When you were young and in fighting spirit, growing mealie cobs in the family field and selling them to raise money for your school fees, you were not this person that you have become. When and how did it happen? When you were amongst the brightest, in spite of running kilometres to school and studying beside a sooty candle? No, it couldn't have been then either. Nor was it in the days that followed at middle school at your uncle's mission, where you remained focused on a better life and so continued to excel. This leaves only your secondary school, the Young Ladies' College of the Sacred Heart. It must have been there that your metamorphosis took place. Yet how awful it is to admit that closeness to white people at the convent had ruined your heart, had caused your womb, from which you reproduced yourself before you gave birth to anything else, to shrink between your hip bones.

You give up the struggle against your knowledge and concede at last a fiendish truth that you first encountered at the university. In an interview, a Ghanaian writer called Ama Ata Aidoo declared at first she had not known she was the colour she eventually learned she was, that the term *black* held no meaning for her until she found herself amongst white people. You laughed then as you read it, thinking, *Oh, as though they dip you in paint.* Now, the ants crawling over you as frenzied as ever in the drizzle of tepid water from the clogged-up showerhead, you know much better. The Ghanaian woman's story calls to mind that aspect of your cousin Nyasha that you had disliked but were obliged to endure when you shared a room with her at the mission.

There was frequently something dismissive, close to sneering, yet at the same time hinting at hurt in her words when she spoke about white people. It frightened you, in those days, to hear how hostile your cousin was toward the Europeans. Now, labouring to define the onset of your fading, the notion of one group of people disparaging another so malignantly once more dismays you.

Christine has taken to whistling. This morning she is caught up in the tune that everyone sang when it was said the war was over and everything that needed to be conquered had been. "Big Brother has come with high morale. Big Brother has come with happiness." She allows a sad lilt to permeate her breath under the pulse of celebration. You decide you will go into the garden to do whatever she is doing beside her, whether it is weeding, or hoeing, or watering. And you will sing, putting the words to the tune.

A few minutes later, while you dry your arms and legs, you discard the urge to join your companion from the night before, since to do so would be a foolish step away from steering your circumstances back onto a proper course. Christine has shown she cannot contribute to any progress in your life. You leave the bathroom, resolving now to keep your distance from the ex-combatant as your next step toward advancement. Your feet make wet marks on the parquet flooring. You forgot your flip-flops and dirty your feet with walking.

The ants file with you, past you, and into you as you open your door. You panic at this symptom that persists into relative sobriety. You feel you are creeping up over the edge of a precipice and that this cliff beckons you; worse, that you have a secret desire to fall over its edge into oblivion and that there is no way to stop that fall because you are the precipice.

In dread you traverse your room. Even as you lower yourself onto your bed, you know it is not your intention to engage with the things that must be faced. The insects advance up the bed's legs and into the covers the moment you thud onto the mattress. You close your eyes while your mind whirls on the problem of how to escape from your predicament. Piece by piece you devise a plan. You will go somewhere where there are no people like the landlady's niece, who constantly hark back to the days of war and injustice. At the same time, you must insulate yourself from the shocks that result from engaging too much with white people. Exhaustion propels you over the border of wakefulness into a sleep from which you half hope you will not wake.

An orange sun flames angrily in the west when you next open your eyes. The ants troop up the walls. They have grown as big as wasps. The widow sings a strange hymn in her cottage. Treble shines ivory and the bass gleams like ebony. Note by note, the melody trembles to the ceiling. You blink the music and the insects away, afraid to think of anything while equally frightened of emptying your mind in case the space is occupied by something more horrible.

The only objects you possess that point to the human being you were meant to be are your academic certificates. Getting up, you drag them out of the plastic bag in which you wrapped them against dampness and silverfish, sneezing as the must tickles the hairs in your nostrils.

In the ensuing days you steal out, when no one is about, to buy the newspaper at the corner. You spread it out on the bed on your return and run a finger down the tiny print, embarking once again on the old routine of searching the smalls. Every time you send off an application you command yourself neither to wait for nor to expect a response. Of course you do precisely this, spending many hours looking through the window for the postman.

You are overjoyed the first few times you are invited to an interview, dressing carefully on each occasion in your Lady Dis and suit that now hangs encouragingly loose. The young men interviewing you invariably grin absentmindedly, twiddle pens between their fingers, and call you Auntie. Once it is a young woman. You want to strike twenty years off your age, to shout, "Here I am, I'm new, remade; look at me, I'm just beginning!" For in many ways you feel you are starting everything afresh after resolving to make things work. Telling yourself you must be thick skinned and persevere, you nevertheless pore with growing alarm over reports appearing in the media more and more frequently of people with degrees like yours, obtained more recently, leaving the country for work in South Africa, Namibia, and even Mozambique and Zambia. You have never been attracted to teaching as more than a temporary interlude, but, lowering your expectations several notches, you stumble one morning up thirteen flights of stairs at the Ministry of Education. Searching through narrow dark corridors, nose wrinkled against fumes seeping out of the lavatories, you eventually locate the door you require.

The official at the broken desk is overjoyed to see you. You are the first, you learn, in all his years as a public servant, to return willingly to teaching.

Giving you this information, the gaunt little man pokes a finger out from a frayed cuff and runs it over pages in a rumpled ledger. After a few minutes' examination he offers you a post as a biology teacher.

"I am not qualified," you object. "Have you looked at the certificates carefully? My degree is in sociology."

The official pushes his cuffs up his arms. He rocks his chair's legs back and forth, smiling like a senior pupil coaching a backward junior.

"These are your transcripts," he says, patting the sheets on the desk. You nod.

"We recognize this degree, of course. It is from our own university."

Having settled every objection with this observation, the officer dials a number. He argues over the phone with the receptionist at the school he has in mind. Finely phrased insults slither back and forth, until he hints he can have the girl removed whenever he wishes. After some minutes of this, he places the receiver gently in its cradle, but once it is there he presses down on it until tendons ridge from his wrist to his fingers.

"She won't see you now," he says, distressed. "What I wanted was this morning. Now. For the headmistress to meet you. Or this afternoon. At any rate today. To make sure the thing with this position is finished. Her name is Mrs. Samaita. She is a very good woman."

He scribbles a number on a scrap of newsprint and pushes it across the desk, instructing, "In two days. She says she has time for you the day after tomorrow."

Mrs. Samaita, the headmistress, turns out to be a tough, large soul who uses her charisma to run her school efficiently according to her own standards of correctness.

"You have a degree. That is good," she says when you meet, smoothing out your certificates and transcripts.

Her desk is small and lopsided. The rest of the room is as devoid of elegance, reminding you of your seedy quarters at Widow Manyanga's. However, you ignore these indications that you are but buying time, have still far to go on your way up in the world. Instead you bask in the warmth of the headmistress's approbation, promising yourself that with this foothold, you will work your way forward, avoiding the mistakes that have so far interrupted your progress.

"With this solid second-class degree of yours," the headmistress continues, "it is good you are still here and not in South Africa or Europe. Or even Botswana. Imagine," she says, "now Zimbabweans are going to that little place and other little places like Zambia. Some are even opting for Mozambique and Malawi. All of it is happening within living memory, a couple of decades after our independence. I am one, Miss Sigauke, who is not afraid to say we did not set the right goals when we should have done so. I insist on setting them here at Northlea High School. You are welcome to the team if you will help me."

Not sure what particular misgivings the headmistress has about independence, nor what she means by the right goals, you smile blandly. When you do not respond, she looks you over carefully and muses, "Are we to commend your patriotism or deplore a certain lack of initiative?"

Your smile spreads over your face more affably.

"Still," the headmistress continues, pressing her thumbs against her lips as she makes her decision. "I am not going to chase you away with pessimism. Under the school's circumstances, I am looking at the degree, not the subject. Although it would have been much better if you had managed biology at A level."

Next, in spite of her brave words, the headmistress sighs. Her plywood desk wobbles against her midriff, almost upsetting a display cabinet next to it that is crammed with an assortment of trophies.

"But we have a good library with all the textbooks," she nods. "I will show you where it is. The librarian will explain how the system works."

She concludes with the hope that you have enrolled for the National Certificate in Education as you do not have a professional qualification and she has a strict policy on teachers' credentials at her establishment.

The headmistress does you the courtesy of guiding you to the library herself instead of calling a junior. From the librarian in her cramped cubbyhole you fetch syllabuses and past examination papers. Several texts are missing and the librarian tells you with resignation that the students throw them out of the windows at examination time in order to retrieve them from the grounds outside. You take all this as a welcome challenge after so long without any responsibilities, determining not only to teach your students biology, but also to relay to them the standards you had learnt first at your uncle's Methodist mission and subsequently at the Catholic convent. Setting your priorities high, you visit your alma mater, the University of Zimbabwe, for supplementary material. You spend hours in the old familiar library devising lessons you yourself find fascinating.

Your pupils are all born frees, or as nearly so as to make no difference; the oldest amongst them were toddlers at Independence. They bear no resemblance to your adolescent self. The energy in their bearing as they walk across the lawns, clatter down the red tile corridors, or charge around the playing fields tells you these young women see their future stretch into glittering horizons. Their forthright manner of meeting your gaze, even the least intelligent, indicates they expect more of the world than you ever dreamed the planet contained. You discover this is true even for those not city-born, who moved in from the villages to live with relatives. Unaccustomed to such young people, with every class you stand in a room of strangers. The situation ignites a smouldering resentment, a kind of grudge, which has you imagining it would be therapeutic for the young ladies to endure, before their characters are fully formed, the same rigours as you did. All this interferes badly with your attempt to reinvent yourself as a model teacher.

You are particularly wary of one Esmeralda, a young woman with artificial nails several millimetres longer than the regulations allow, who, through means at her disposal that the other girls do not command, regularly coaxes the prefects into abandoning their duty. One morning, in your early days, you catch her sticking an artificial nail back on with art stock glue. As you confiscate the nail so that she has to walk around with one spoilt finger, you realize this is a beginning, not an end. Next you surprise her several times as she brushes on lip gloss behind a textbook and are convinced that your pupil is out to get you. Finally, when you come upon her writing, not notes on waterborne diseases, but a message to a male person in the bad grammar of cell phone texts, on a bulky gadget she has sneaked into your lesson, you discern that sooner or later there will be trouble.

Although a ringleader, Esmeralda is not the only girl who engages in scandalous behaviour. Many pierce multiple holes in their ears and other parts of their bodies. Green-skirted, beige-bloused, increasing numbers of them stop walking down the corridors and take to swaggering. They emphasize the *r*'s at the ends of words, and the boldest attempt to roll them. They stop opening their mouths, so that their vowels rise into their noses, in an effort to sound American. Most appallingly, neither lectures nor diagrams of fast-mutating viruses nor anything else you draw attention to blunts your charges' appetite for experimentation. Your first strategy is to ignore them. Good teaching contracts into pages of dictated notes and putting up of exercises on the chalkboard. Then, after a few weeks, you are placed on the roster for outdoor supervision.

Doing rounds, your preferred strategy is to shout a greeting at a groundsman or sing the chorus of a hymn to signal to the young ladies that authority approaches. When you do detect a group hunched over a bottle or a cigarette, you expect them to hide the contraband and stub out whatever they are smoking. Instead, they regard you brazenly or collapse in giggles. You dismiss immediately a wild notion that emanates from a feeble place in your heart, that your charges are gravely confused, in need of rescue. You perceive the unwavering eyes as mockery, the laughter as scoffing at everything you have become. Crushing sympathy, convinced that their freedom-filled, post-Independence up-bringing is vastly more advantageous than yours was, you buy a large black log book in whose pages you record names, classes, and offences. You send off your lists, along with the girls caught, to the headmistress.

It does not take your students long to realize there is little to recommend you. Halfway through the second term, they retaliate, baptizing you Tambudzai the Grief, TTG for short. During periods when you confiscate numerous cell phones and send many girls to detention, this escalates to MG—Mega-Grief. Esmeralda openly snorts, "Ah, Mega!" when you pass.

The most serious crime a girl can commit is climbing into a car driven by an unaccompanied man who is not a certified relation. Your staff handbook expounds over several paragraphs the heinousness of this misdeed and lists a dozen remedies that range from sessions with guardians to expulsion. In spite of this, there appears to be rough competition amongst certain pupils to see who flouts the rule most spectacularly by occupying the most expensive vehicle.

Mrs. Samaita is impassive when you approach her about the matter over tea in the staff room.

"I have looked at the lists you gave me," she says. "Generally it has not affected results. A number of those girls obtain top marks, so the school record remains commendable."

You are immediately outraged.

"But the form threes," you insist, less scandalized on behalf of your students' prospects than by your headmistress's invalidation of all your efforts. "I have put the names down. Some of those girls in those cars are even in form two."

"Live and let live," the headmistress says. "Let sleeping dogs lie. Focus on what is necessary. It would be different," she proceeds with a shrug, "if we could prove something like statutory rape. Since this is hardly possible, it becomes another problem."

Energized by your discontent, one afternoon after lessons you take a trip to the police station, which in any case is at the shopping centre through which you pass on your way to and from school. There, sitting in the queue on the shaky wooden bench, your black book with students' names, the registration numbers of the vehicles they sat in as well as descriptions of the middle-aged gentlemen who drove them neatly entered, you remember your headmistress's words, rise, and continue on your way to your lodgings. Your distress deepens as you walk through the common, taking a shortcut to the road along which combis to Mai Manyanga's run. Attempting distraction, you apply yourself to imagining what you will buy with the twenty dollars you lay away each month by walking this part of your route, but prices are increasing, as are your needs, so you are not consoled.

The grass is tall. At night, snakes and criminals slide around in it. Your stomach tenses fearfully, as it does whenever you take this path. Some months ago, there had been a meeting in the school hall that you did not attend, at which parents threatened to go out in force to cut the common grass themselves as it was a threat to their daughters. Upon contacting the city council to inform them of the resolution, the parents were warned that regardless of any action the council did or did not take, only the council had authority to remove any material or growth from the common. The stink of decomposition seeps skyward, flowing into your lungs. Then your eyes water and your nose and throat begin to pour, preventing you from smelling anything. Sneezing to the combi stop and through the rest of the journey, you are almost relieved to turn into the widow's drive.

Inside, Bertha's open doorway gapes into the corridor. The bed is stripped, her belongings cleared. The colleague she had once alluded to did not appear. Now you and Mako are left to endure the consequences of Shine's uncontrolled sexual appetites on your own. Then Shine himself departs the following month. Mako starts telling you she is thinking of leaving too, of escaping the tension and gloom that continue to build up over Mai Manyanga's, intensified by visits from her resentful-looking sons who these days stop by individually, never in pairs or all together.

You are too tired to lie to Mako, yourself, or your colleagues at work that you will shortly depart as well. You acknowledge that you are a woman without options. To divert yourself from this truth, you spend hours every night and weekend preparing more and more detailed lessons and increasing their complexity until you can scarcely comprehend what you have written yourself.

The students become so obstreperous that you speculate they will, at the end of the year, return nothing but failures. You double efforts at lesson planning, special reading, and drilling. When something inside you says enough is enough, you do not want to hear it. You begin taking a glass of wine at night as you pore over the girls' exercise books. This escalates to two and then three. When you retire, moments after you lay your head on the pillow, you fall away into a void that you had before been wary of, but for which you are now grateful. In the morning you have difficulty waking.

On receiving your salary at the end of the month, you catch a combi to town. It is an odd, not entirely pleasant, sensation to walk down First Street Mall after so many years, toward Edgars. Inside, you revel in the colours, textures, and cuts of the newest fashions. As you hold up one garment and struggle into another, the changing room mirror hints that not all is lost as you approach middle age. Walking and regular feeding, plus, you suppose, your families' genes, have rescued you from the signs of getting on. All but trembling with excitement over spending so much money on goods that are not actually necessary but merely desired, you pay for a trouser suit and coordinating blouse in bottle green. Leaving the store, an impulse takes you into a hairdresser's salon. You emerge with your hair neatly plaited, regretting only that you did not have enough cash on you to obtain a manicure, as so many of your older students have.

One morning, you rise later than usual. You intend to move quickly with your breakfast and toilet, but every limb drags. It takes you longer than normal to walk to the combi stop and then through the common. The assembly bell rings as you tramp up the school drive. Such tardiness is an offence for which you have punished scores of students. Having the privilege, as you think of it, of correcting means you are yourself to set a proper example. This you have striven to do since you took up employment at Northlea High some eight months earlier. Now, though, as has been the case all your adult life, you are failing dismally.

"What's wrong with you? Knocking over everyone you meet. Is that why you wait until the bell's gone?"

Out of your mouth you fling your fear of another defeat, directed at a group of first formers whom you almost bump into as they scurry from the classrooms to the hall on the other side of the school grounds.

"We are sorry, Miss Sigauke," they breathe, bobbing respectful curtsies. Fright illuminates their eyes. "We are hurrying to get there in time."

Mollified by the impact of your intervention, you unlock your office in a calmer state of mind. Following assembly, you spend the early part of the morning grading examination papers. It is an enjoyable task as you feel you exhibit considerable benevolence in allocating your students their grades. Completing the work well before tea time, you enjoy a sense of control.

At break time in the staff room, Mr. Chauke, A-level maths, and Mr. Tiza, O-level physical science, who call each other Brains One and Brains Two, push ahead of you into the queue for the hot water urn. They murmur, "Sorry, sorry, Miss Sigauke!" holding their cups under the spout. You hurry away from this annoyance.

Mrs. Samaita waves you over to her table.

After accepting a cupcake from First Year Shona Attachment, whose name you do not remember, the headmistress pushes some newspaper clippings at you.

"Have you seen these?" she asks. "Have you had the form threes yet?"

Each article depicts a gentleman, short, lean, and tautly muscled, who strikes you as being outrageously pleased with himself as he stands in front of a long, low Mercedes. Your mouth tastes of bitter gravel as you recognize the vehicle. ADF 3ZW, you recite to yourself the registration number recorded several times in your log book. The car's bonnet, against which the man's buttocks are propped, bears giant packs of brightly coloured cordials, jars of jam, blocks of laundry soap, packets of crisps, and jumbo-size packages of assorted fruit drops. More provisions spill out of the back windows. Blue-smocked staff dance in front of the vehicle. Some have pulled on over their uniforms baggy T-shirts on which the man's face is printed. Other assistants cavort around the man and his automobile. In a passenger seat, half concealed by the chauffeur and packages, sits your third form pupil Esmeralda.

"All the girls are going wild about this," sighs Mrs. Samaita. "They're treating that Esmeralda like a queen. I will have to make an announcement about it tomorrow at assembly. Why on earth is she wearing her school uniform? I hope no one at the ministry's seen it."

"Head teacher," says Chauke, sauntering by. "He is the business face of the chairperson of the Mining Council. Now that the country has discovered all these diamonds and platinum and oil, please let us be advised no one will touch him. Or anything he wants. In that position, he can't be touched by anything."

"Show him the picture and ask him for a donation," says Tiza.

You join the rest of the teachers in clicking teeth, shaking heads, and placing teacups back on saucers.

"Let us hope," Mrs. Samaita says, "that this Esmeralda does not end up like some of the girls we have had. Coming back to school after two weeks, with a doctor's report saying something about her womb, looking as thin as a coat hanger."

"That will serve her right," breathes Ms. Moyo, Fashion and Fabrics. "If she can't comport herself as we all try to teach them. Doesn't everyone know the wires in that girl's head are broken?"

You all give grunts of agreement. Your smile attaches itself to your face more tenaciously as your anxiety increases. Nothing can touch *him*, but this impunity does not apply to people like you. Men like the one in the photograph always find out. He can obtain staff reports, with your list of names and registration numbers. You might have been seen at the police station. You whisper a little prayer of thanksgiving that you were too cowardly to make a statement. Like all the others in the staff room, you know Esmeralda's reputation and so, weighing the risks, favour no engagement although the law is being broken. You sense you are smiling too broadly, showing too many teeth. You press your lips together.

When it is time for the form three biology lesson, you discover Esmeralda has smuggled in several copies of the publication that carries the largest, most detailed photograph.

She is perched on her desk, twisting a gold watch around her wrist, evoking fascinated glances from her classmates and accepting homage like a goddess.

"MG's here. Already," Esmeralda says as you enter.

You breathe quickly in irritation. You swallow it down. You advance to your table.

"Your latest offerings," you begin, meeting eyes glazed with fear or amusement or boredom.

Your pupil opens her desk and slides in several newspapers.

"From your latest offerings," you repeat. You observe with surprised interest, very much as though examining another person, that in spite of swallowing and holding deep breaths, your breathing is growing more rapid.

"From the work you submitted, clearly we shall have to return to the first principles of diffusion," you say. "We shall have, once more, to apply these principles at length and in detail to the case of human respiration that you are required to know for your O-level syllabus."

Your pupil accepts a newspaper from the girl beside her and slides this one into her desk also.

"Diffusion. A definition, please," you demand.

No one answers.

"I shall walk round the class and count to five," you say.

One.

You pick up your T square and take a few steps.

Moving slowly, you approach Elizabeth. Like Esmeralda, this pupil Elizabeth is Rhodes scholar material. However, she is a meek girl. This morning she has the sense not to look at you as you approach her.

Two!

Your class holds its breath.

Three! Four!

You reach Elizabeth and raise the T square.

Five.

Your chest rises and falls. Sweat runs down your face. It slithers into your eyes. It gushes out of your armpits mingled with antiperspirant. You have seen how they do not want a qualification in biology, you say;

in which case your pupils will receive a qualification in violence. Two or three young women pull at you. This has no effect. Instead, you escape yourself into an unbearable radiance.

The young goddess slips out and runs into the next classroom.

Ms. Rusike, returning with Esmeralda, takes a quiet look and disappears to inform Mrs. Samaita.

Someone laughs. She bites her lip until it bleeds when you glare at her. Exhilarated by her fear, you return your attention to Elizabeth. Seconds later, your headmistress enters the classroom. She expects you to stop but you do not. The headmistress touches you gently on the shoulder. You throw the T square at the chalkboard. You twine your arms around your head. You howl a long rising note that shudders through the room.

Eventually you follow the headmistress to her office. She offers you a cup of tea, which you refuse. With no questions, pitching her voice low, speaking calmly and slowly, the headmistress gives you several days off to recover. Telling everyone you have received bad news concerning a close relative, she escorts you to her car and drives you to the widow's.

That weekend you are more frightened than you have ever been, besieged by a great terror that leaves no space for remorse. Your only concern is to keep your job, not least so that you can continue to pay your rent. Christine, who has moved into Bertha's old room, waylays you in front of her door and invites you inside. "You can come and get the mealie meal," she reminds you. You make an excuse about visiting her the following day. On Sunday you cannot face her, believing she will see how the radiance that you escaped into in the classroom has dimmed to a pulsing purple sphere that sucks out all your energy, so that each word you utter is an intolerable effort. You sit in your room and remain silent when she knocks at your door.

The next day, Monday, you peer round your door tentatively, expecting her to have deposited the sack of mealie meal from your mother. You sigh in relief on seeing nothing obstructing the doorway. At school once more, you are restless as you sit in your office, but when there is no mention of the incident by lunchtime, you feel a surge of hope light up deep within you where it had almost been extinguished.

The gleam of it attracts a timid little junior who offers to carry your bag as you return from the staff room.

When you unlock your office, the child carries it to your desk, taking three skipping steps to each of yours. Reaching her destination, the girl sets your bag soundlessly on the floor.

"What class are you in?" you ask, impressed by this deference.

"One Muuyu," is the answer. "I mean One Muuyu, ma'am," she corrects herself, twisting her fingers together at her mistake.

"All right," you dismiss her. "Make sure you stay like that and do what your teachers tell you. If you do, we'll meet in form three."

She scampers off in delight, and you take out your register to draft remarks for your class reports.

"Chinembiri, Elizabeth," the name soon confronts you. Gracious with new power, you draft several flattering comments.

As you are so engaged, a knock sounds at the door.

"Enter," you call out.

The door opens and First Form Shona Attachment stands doubtfully in the entrance.

"Miss Sigauke, the head teacher wants you to join her. In her office," she says.

You do not like to be disturbed at your pleasurable task, but must oblige.

Three people are seated in the head teacher's small room. When you become the fourth, the room is much too full.

You take the single vacant chair beside the coffee table. Mrs. Samaita nods at a couple seated on the sofa pressed up against the far wall.

The woman covers her eyes when she sees you. She gulps several times but is unable to swallow down what she must. She gasps and then sobs gently. The man beside her touches her elbow and tells her to hush. His voice carries only half a heart, as though he is glad his companion's wretchedness pushes at everything anyone can see and breathe and touch.

"Mr. and Mrs. Chinembiri. Elizabeth's parents," your headmistress says.

The woman uncovers her eyes. She points a finger in your direction. You are astonished when the quivering digit lets out a thin, high scream. There is no respite when it falls silent again: it elongates dangerously in your direction.

"Hi-i-i, hi-i-i," the woman grieves, her voice dry and fragile as a drought-stricken leaf.

"Surely, who would have thought anybody would live to see such days?" the man says. Tears fill his eyes as he regards his wife. "These days we see now cut a mother up into pieces."

Your headmistress picks up a ballpoint pen. Grasping it between her finger and thumb, round and round she twists it.

"Hasn't everybody suffered? Suffered enough to satisfy anyone?" your pupil's mother demands. "Who? Who wants people to suffer more? It's you, teacher. You are saying suffer more. You want to show my daughter and me the meaning of agony by killing the child. Nhai, tell me, my daughter's teacher, are you like maize in a field of manure? Is that how it is here, where we send our children every day, that you grow on the dung of the way we are hurt?"

"Mrs. Chinembiri," says Mrs. Samaita in order to prevent the woman speaking further and so growing still more tormented, "is Elizabeth's mother, Miss Sigauke. And Mr. Chinembiri here is the father. I had asked them to come and discuss other things," your headmistress continues. "Before . . . before this . . . this later matter happened."

"Yes," Mr. Chinembiri says in a low voice. "We know we have not yet paid school fees. It's because we are struggling with the rent."

"And then this new thing happened," Mrs. Samaita concludes. "When they were coming anyway."

Your headmistress puts down the pen and informs the couple, "Amai and Baba Chinembiri, this is the teacher, Miss Sigauke."

"We just wanted to see her," your pupil's father says. "Maybe Elizabeth did something bad, but her injuries are so big we wanted to see the teacher. I am the driver. This one beside me is the cook. We must get back quickly to our Europeans over there in Kamfinsa."

Mai Chinembiri pitches over but comes to immediately and places the sign of the cross between herself and you. Softly she begins to keen again. The sound oppresses you. You clamp your hand over her mouth. Your pupil's father does not dare touch you. Mrs. Samaita reaches for the phone, scattering copper trophies over her desk. Some girls in the corridor who are changing classes let out peals of laughter bright as the sun. You listen to the girls. Then you laugh with them. You hear her but you cannot see this laughing woman. You keep listening to her gurgling like a hyena high at the back of her throat.

PART 2
SUSPENDED

CHAPTER 9

Now you understand. You arrived on the back of a hyena. The treacherous creature dropped you from far above onto a desert floor. There is nothing here except, at the floor's limits, infinite walls.

You are an ill-made person. You are being unmade. The hyena laughhowls at your destruction. It screams like a demented spirit and the floor dissolves beneath you.

"Good evening," the hyena says.

You are petrified: will the floor disappear altogether? You make an effort to keep every muscle frozen.

"Good evening," the hyena says again.

You are silent. You do not trust.

At once you realize you should have made another response. For halfway through your silence the softness opens its jaws and swallows you.

You curl your arms around your head. Your knees touch your chin. Even like this you are not big enough. The softness is bigger. You allow yourself to be swallowed.

"How are you feeling, Tambudzai?" the hyena goes on.

You are not there. You are not anywhere.

"Tambudzai," the voice says. "You should be feeling better now. After so much sleep, you should be able to talk. Come on, Tambudzai, you must be much better."

You try not to return. The voice keeps talking.

"You even slept when we moved you. But now it's evening. The others are already on their way. Aren't you hungry after such long sleeping?"

You rock your head to and fro. You do not know what to do now. Perhaps you should be grateful to the hyena for its words? You try to open your eyes but succeed only in rolling your eyeballs. You try to smile. Your tongue lolls, your mouth dribbles. Saliva trickles toward your ear.

"What's your name?" the voice asks.

You breathe in slowly, concentrating.

"Name," you exhale.

"Yours. You don't have to repeat. This is not grade one. I want your name." The hyena voice cracks. It conceals the crevice.

"Answer," it says more gently.

"Answer," you echo. You are proud of yourself. Once more you have brought out your voice. Yours.

"Not that."

The voice breaks more impatiently, too much to hide.

"What are you called? What do people say when they call you?"

What does your mother call you? And your father? Your mother said something when you were on her knees. She called you Trouble. "Tambudzai," you say softly, pleased you have come to this knowledge.

"OK," the speaker says. Her voice does not listen. "Now tell me your surname. And today's date."

"March . . . March . . ." you begin with an effort.

"Confusion. Of surname with date," the speaker says slowly, scratching with a cylinder at a pale rectangle suspended in the air.

"Oh!" you say, unhappy to have failed again after such effort.

The woman breathes in sharply and gives your knee a shove. "OK. About the name. That's enough," she says without interest.

Your eyes fasten on a fuzz of shades and colours. You struggle with swirls and dabs that move, giving the impression of an attempt at something that will never be completed.

In the middle is a long dark oval. There is dark and light.

"You do not know it?" the oval asks. "That is not right. That date is wrong."

"Wrong?" you repeat.

"Tss!" The speaking oval is exasperated. "Yes. The date."

"What date?" you inquire.

102

"If this goes on I will bring you a calendar," she says. "That could help. But better for you to manage without it."

"Calendar?"

The oval snorts and stands and turns into a woman.

Far away in the new space, pale green undulates like a serpent, like the veil your mother ties to her head. It shrinks and yawns between two walls. It is a curtain.

"What about washing?" says the woman. "The bathroom, it's over there." She thrusts a hanging chin over a shoulder attached to nothing. "That way."

"No," you say. You do not want to go away.

"Do you know where you are?" she asks, watching you curl up once more.

You put your arms over your head for answer.

"Eh-eh, don't go sleeping again, like you're a woman in labour," she says, trying to hide her hiss in a whisper.

She moves away to sit on a mattress that floats high in the air.

"Hospital!" you exclaim, both question and answer.

"Already one day," she says. "It was yesterday when you came."

She is eager about what she is saying. Her words blunder forth quickly.

"You're lucky you're out already. When you came they put you in restraining. Now that you are quiet it seems impossible that you were shouting like that, as if someone was murdering you."

She returns and bends over you, murmuring. "You have been sedated. Your doctor's orders. Are you comfortable? Or should we give you some more medication?"

"Doctor?"

You connect the word with hospital. You smile.

"M-hm," she smiles back. "You have already been seen."

"Seen? Why do they want to see me?"

The woman bursts out laughing. She glances around. Her eyes flash like sharpened kitchen knives.

"You don't really know where you are, I can see that," she breathes. "What time is it? Can you tell me?"

Your eyes close to get away from her. She presses closer.

"It is OK," she says. "I am a nurse. I want to ask you some questions, please."

She moves closer still. You start screaming.

You do not know it, but it is later.

"She doesn't look as though she's going to do anything. Let's bring her back like that," someone says.

"You think that is best?" someone else responds. "Mm, maybe not. From what they said, she might start more trouble."

A hand grips your arm. You struggle with limbs of cotton wool and the hyena is at the bottom of the purple pond of your fear, laughing.

Your pants are pulled down and a needle burns into your buttocks.

You fight to pull your fingers out of the pool whose cracks are hardening like the lava from a volcano.

Feet pad forward. Knees creak as their owner squats before you.

It is the Voice.

"Hello. What's your name?" the Voice begins again.

You like this. You are good at this.

"Name!" you agree, at ease in a gentle current of repetition.

You are lifted. Metal scrapes. Rubber whines.

Eyelids crawl apart. You cannot focus.

The woman draws pale green curtains against the afternoon glare.

Her nurse's cap is a jagged dark outline against the sunlight.

"I am a student," she says, twisting her fingers. Anxiety shreds her speech.

"Student," you say. A shrill note of horror swells in your head. It pierces too far to endure. The purple hyena opens its jaws and all sensation vanishes.

The student nurse does not see the scavenger. She does not believe that you have vanished.

"I have to go," she says. "I will see you another time. Then we can talk."

"Take your blerry hands awf'a me!" a voice blares around you.

A pink oval is leading you through a room. There is light on one side.

The light is windows. A world stares in on the other side. The world is a wall. In between drift shadows that believe they are people.

"Didn't you hear me?" this new person screams.

You are afraid. You stop. You touch your mouth. It is closed.

"Just move," the aide says, and brushes your shoulder.

You move on, feeling better.

"I said take your blerry hands awf'a me!" the new creature rages.

You walk down a corridor beyond which, you later learn, is the geriatric ward whose inmates share a day and dining room with your wing. Fingers of light leak round burglar bars that throttle high narrow windows. Dust dances in the columns of watery light. Iron doors gape like condemned eyes in the whitewashed walls.

"Isolation rooms," the oval says cheerfully. "That's where you were. Aren't you glad they let you out?"

You come to a door.

"Dr. Winton," your guide announces, having knocked on it. "Your patient." She touches your shoulder again to guide you forward.

You take a seat. The chair is hardboard on a metal frame, like the one in the classroom. You do not want to sit on it. Dr. Winton looks at you refusing. Something tells you you cannot keep refusing while the white woman looks at you, so you sit.

The doctor leans over her plywood desk and peels off a strip of varnish. She rolls it between finger and thumb, drops the fragment on the desk, and puts out a hand.

You do not take it.

She sits down again and asks you questions. Where were you born?

Umtali, you tell her.

"Umtali?" she says.

Mutare, you correct yourself, after a pause. You are confused. What is the difference between Mutare and Umtali? You know there is a difference between them, but you do not know what it is or what it means.

Where did you go to school?

Your mind slides around, sluggishly working out what to say because you are too tired and drugged to prevent yourself hearing the words you say and so telling her means confessing to yourself, a thing you do not want to do.

Birth into a poor family, you say. Struggle to achieve your education, planting a field of green mealies and selling them to keep yourself in school when your mother refuses to vend at the market for you as she had done for your brother. This you do not say, because who can speak ill of a mother? To do so will increase the crime of being born who you are and where it happened, justifying all the calamity that befalls you. It is better to concentrate on the positive things that happened. Your uncle, Babamukuru, your father's elder brother and the head of the clan, returned from England to take up a position as headmaster not far from your home. After your brother dies he brings you to his mission for a superior education.

"Aha," says the doctor who knows nothing. "Guilt. Following an event seen as a sacrifice. You feel guilty about the death of your brother."

You divert her probing by launching into the story of your cousin Nyasha, your uncle's daughter.

"A companion, a sister," the doctor says.

"Someone I could look up to," you say. "Who could explain things to me. Until she got sick. Then I knew she didn't know anything. I didn't need a sister. I had lots of them."

"How did she recover?" the doctor asks after you tell her of your cousin's attempt at suicide from an eating disorder.

You shrug. You don't know how your cousin recovered as the odds were so completely against her. In any case you feel the doctor is going off track. Her concern should be with your recovery, not your cousin's.

"Nyasha always manages," you tell her. "She always wins and gets the best of everything. Even her birth."

"You think so?" the doctor says, raising an eyebrow. "Even after she engaged with the outcomes of her own birth in a difficult manner?"

You cause another distraction by telling Dr. Winton that in any case you did not see much of your cousin's illness as you moved from your uncle's mission after winning a scholarship to a prestigious multiracial college in Umtali, the Young Ladies' College of the Sacred Heart.

Dr. Winton cannot conceal a frown as you continue to narrate how well you did there, to the extent of achieving the best O-level results in the school.

"What happened?" she asks quietly when you fall silent again.

You cannot tell her that things keep repeating, that this time too it was as with your mother, and that you were not recognized because it was necessary to prefer another, your white classmate. You talk about the war instead, how it ruined everyone's nerves and many bodies, about how twins at your school lost their parents, your sister her leg, and Babamukuru his walking. You tell yourself you will not cry and you do not.

The doctor insists, carefully, that she wants to know what you have done in the meanwhile that might have led to you sitting in her office. You relate episodes from Steers et al. where you worked. You want to explain what it really did to you. The words crawl slowly into your throat, for the hurts of adulthood have not assailed you as violently as those of childhood. Nevertheless this lesser assault is too much and again you cannot speak of Tracey Stevenson, the eternal favourite at school, who, you discovered with dull resignation, was your boss at the advertising agency.

"I saw a woman at a disco who looked like Tracey. You know, Tracey that girl at school," you say, in the end, judging you have offered just enough to throw dust in the doctor's eyes. You go on evenly to see what the doctor will do, "I wanted to beat her up."

"It seems to me that you don't like white people," the doctor says.

"Of course I do," you respond. "Anyway, it's neither here nor there," you continue with one of your shrugs. "They never see me. It doesn't make any difference who they are. Nobody sees me."

You stand up. When you are at the door you think of the corridor outside.

Dr. Winton watches you carefully.

"I wonder what would happen," she says, "if you stopped hiding behind the door to the world that you have closed. If you stepped out. For some reality testing?"

"I'm not," you say.

She keeps quiet.

"Hiding," you say.

"Does this make you frightening to yourself, Tambudzai? Being cooped up behind the door with all these fears?"

The hyena is tired. It does not laugh. It does not leap. All it does is lie there. The doctor looks at her watch and informs you that you still have fifteen minutes.

"People who fear greatly can sometimes substitute themselves for the thing they fear," says Dr. Winton, looking at you in a way that makes you uncomfortable.

"I am ashamed," you say.

"Of what?" the doctor asks.

"I don't have the things that make me better. I want to be better. I want the things that make me."

You circle round this matter for several minutes until Dr. Winton pulls your file forward. She scribbles on a sheet of austerity-quality duplicating paper, which kind of paper had been introduced during the war and retained after Independence. She purses her lips as though she is satisfied with the session. She books you in for another period.

"Do you want some?"

There is a woman behind the door. She talks to you when you return to the dayroom. She is shaped like a pear, with a shiny doek of black hair on her head. She is holding a breast out over the neck of her chiffon nightgown.

"Cecilia, stop that!" Student Nurse shouts at the pear-shaped person.

The woman tucks her breast back inside.

"Tie it up," Student Nurse orders in a voice that makes you glad the nurse ignores you.

Cecilia pulls a face. She ties up the gown.

As soon as Student Nurse looks away, she pulls her breast out again.

"Have some," she coaxes. "It will make you feel better."

"Mrs. Flower!" Student Nurse shouts in exasperation as you back away into a sofa.

Mrs. Flower settles in a corner, turns her breast up, and sucks it. She looks over her shoulder, grins like a baby, and continues drinking.

"That's enough," orders Student Nurse. She kicks the brakes on the wheelchair she is pushing to locked.

"Get your blerry hands awf'a me, you great black whore," wheezes the tiny old man in the wheelchair.

"Iwe, Mr. Porter," Student Nurse snaps. "Don't give me some more trouble!"

"Are you all right, Mrs. Flower?" Student Nurse asks, quietly re-arranging her features. "Come, I will show you this."

Student Nurse leads Mrs. Flower to the coffee table and puts a magazine in the woman's hands. Mrs. Flower flicks through ragged, beverage-stained pages. One article describes how to knit a baby's lay-ette. Mrs. Flower bursts into tears.

Student Nurse shrugs her shoulders. She rounds on the cursing old grandfather in the wheelchair, whose insults she has been absorbing.

"Ed Porter, what have you done?" she scolds. "Did something scare you shitless? Is that why it's happened again already!"

She grips the wheelchair's handles and swings it toward the door through which you have just entered.

"You, oh yer black devil, didn't yer hear me? Let go there," the chair's occupant yells and wheezes.

"Keep still," Student Nurse says through gritted teeth. "You'll dirty everything with your number two."

Mr. Porter raises the cane he carries across his lap and endeavours to hook the crook around his assailant's neck.

"Yer blerry black whore," he howls at the woman who wheels him away. He pants as though his lungs, like his knuckles, are gnarled with arthritis.

Up the furious old man arcs his cane. Down it thwacks on Student Nurse's shoulder.

The chair rolls toward you. Ed Porter manages to turn a wheel and stop it. Student Nurse revolves round the chair like a satellite, trying to find a way to her quarry.

"Mr. Porter, I'm sorry," she finally says from a safe distance. "Don't pretend you don't know what you've done. All I want is to do my work."

She approaches the chair to pry her patient's hands from the stick. But Ed whirls his cane and clobbers her over her back, shouting, "Black whore! You filthy bitch!"

"Orderly," Student Nurse yells at the assistant who escorted you. "Come over here. Help me get him!"

The orderly, who is chatting at the station, glances round and shrugs, saying she is going for lunch.

"Don't you dare touch me," yells Ed, triumphantly waving his stick.

The meal bell rings. You start moving with the rest of the patients.

"Mr. Porter! I'm not going to take you to your table as you are. If you get hungry later on, don't think I am going to do anything to help."

The old man's hands grab at the chair's rubber wheels. His bulbous fingers slip over the metal frame.

"Oi, give us a hand here, mate." Pain and mortification pinch his face.

A tall young man whose forehead delves into blue caves where his eyes once looked out turns, too uncertainly and too slowly. The young man stops. One knee is bent, the foot is in the air. Just as slowly, a thought crawls into his mind until it lights up his eyes. Time is magnified endlessly for this youngster, Rudolph. He dreams his way over to Mr. Porter.

Mr. Porter glares viciously at Student Nurse and swings his cane as Rudolph pushes him to a table. Grinning, Student Nurse sidesteps neatly.

"Iwe! You, Mr. Porter," she laughs. "What can I do if you want to eat like that? When you've finished, and maybe you've done some more, what then? I'll still come and change you."

"And a good afternoon to yer," Ed puts his tormenter down superbly.

You drift past Ed in search of a seat in a current of shadows shuffling to their places.

"Are you in for drugs?" Rudolph says as he wafts away on his own search.

You shake your head.

"Have you?" Rudolph's voice floats out, the way mist settles on mountains.

The boy's sadness stops you in your tracks and you stare.

"I told you, didn't I?" he asks.

"You, Rudolph, go and eat. You too, Tambudzai," shouts Student Nurse.

"They . . . they put holes in it," Rudolph says with regret. "With the . . . the smoke. So a wind whipped through . . . through it. That's what they wanted, hey! So that it all comes out." With a look of satisfaction he drifts further away.

You find a vacant seat opposite Mr. and Mrs. van Byl. She wears a pink bow in her hair, he a suit and tie. Both have real, different names, but they explain to each and every available ear that they are married. They hold hands and try to eat linked to each other until Student Nurse asks them to mind their table manners.

When you sit down you see Rudolph pause again in midstep. It takes him a long time to put his foot down.

Beside you, around the corner of the table, a woman's head is bent low. Wisps of white, soft hair surround your companion's head like a halo.

"Hello, dear," she says, raising her head when you sit. Her face is all translucent skin, fragile as eggshells, rippling over brittle cheekbones when she smiles. Her joy over your taking a seat beside her collapses her mouth over her gums.

She picks up in her feeble fingers the spoon she dropped when she greeted you and proceeds to do her best with the soup, leaving her false teeth by her plate. "Do you think I should put them back in, dear?" she asks, trying to chew soft bits of vegetable. "I really don't know whether or not I ought to."

She sets her spoon down again and looks at you, expecting an answer.

"It depends," you mutter.

"Well, that's what I thought," she says, revealing her gums once more in agreement. She picks up her dentures. "And I thought, I wonder if I'll get on any better having them in or out."

With a sigh she settles the dentures back in, takes a test mouthful, and stops to wiggle them into position.

"But I do like it here," she goes on. "I do like this house better than the other one. It's so much safer here and everyone's very nice. I never felt safe in the other house after I lost my husband. Did I tell you that I lost my husband, dear? It was during the war."

You prevent yourself remembering something you do not want to recall. The effort plays havoc with your appetite. At one moment you do not want the slightest taste of anything; the next you are ravenous and gulp down every morsel.

"Who are you then, dear?" the old woman inquires when her own bowl is almost empty and you have been waiting for the main course for several minutes.

"Tambudzai," you answer. The information leaves you reluctantly.

"I'm Mabel," she replies and takes a long while spooning up a last mouthful with uncertain fingers. "My Frank always called me Mabs, but did I tell you I lost him during the war? Those people came and took him. In the night. They poked a gun in his ribs, just as if he was a piece of meat, and they took him away. I had a good woman who looked after me, but I don't know what happened to my dog, Fido. Have you seen Fido by any chance?" she asks in her thin voice and peers around. "What did you say your name was, dear? Did you say it's Edie?" she encourages you when you do not answer. "Is that what you said? I'm sure you did. Yes, Edie used to come and sit with me. I'm sure you're my daughter Edie."

Recognition lumbers up from the purple pool, like an ancient, clumsy animal.

"Borrowdale." You shake your head at the mammoth in your memory. "I know your house. I saw you there, in Borrowdale."

"I knew it." Your companion beams with the low-wattage glow of elderly people. "What did they do with Fido, dear? Did they shoot him too when I left? I knew you're my daughter Edie."

Your companion fumbles at the edge of her plate and picks up a forkful of potato from the dish that has just been set in front of her.

A cruel smile hovers above your lips at the widow's fall in the world that has made you and her and all the other white people in the establishment equal.

"I'm not your daughter," you tell her. "My name is Tambudzai." You pause. "Tambudzai Sigauke."

"Are you sure?" the widow inquires after several seconds. "Aren't you, dear? You're not her? Well, that's very strange. You're the spitting image of my daughter Edie."

You shake your head again. A vine unfurls deep within you. The spiteful grin cannot sit on its leaves.

"Well, if you're not, that's very kind," the widow says. "It's very kind of you to come down like this to see me."

Drops brim in your eyes, plop into your gravy. You have no will to stop them.

"I want to give you something, dear," the widow says. "It's awfully kind of you to come all this way. I was so afraid before, I didn't talk to anybody."

Your companion puts down her knife and fork to pull at a large ring of gold and amber, repeating, as she struggles with it, that you are the spitting image of her daughter Edie.

"I can give you a bigger dose," the nurse says when she comes to give you your injection. "To make the effect stronger. And work faster."

Observing the flow of tears that began at lunchtime, she leans in closer and continues, "I want to ask you some questions. I need your help. I am doing my degree. There is a dissertation. I must have an interesting subject. You know, talking to me is good for you. We are the same, you and I! We are not like these European doctors. You know, so you mustn't worry about anything, my sister, Tambu. You can just answer what I am asking."

She inquires in a low, furtive voice, whether you are satisfied with your partner, how often you have sexual relations with him, and whether you feel that this part of your life has any bearing on your situation. As she puts these questions to you, she stares as though you are a book in which she has marked the most important chapter.

"Do you mind if I write the answers down?" she asks, more at ease now that the interview has begun.

You do not have the strength to do anything but gaze at this student nurse, the front of your linen robe wet with tears. At first her expression is expectant. It transforms to a disappointed glare. Eventually she slips her pen and small notebook into her uniform pocket as she walks away, leaving you once again feeling ashamed for reasons you cannot fathom.

CHAPTER 10

You discover you are the pool. The shadows in the dayroom are ponds. Together you form the ocean. This ocean pours from your eyes without end.

"Still like that?" snaps Student Nurse. "Do you want us to feel sorry for you? We haven't heard that someone has died or anything."

Cecilia Flower passes you over when she wanders round the dayroom offering her breast to people, as though the pool is poisonous. Ed Porter keeps abusing the student nurse. His shouting reaches you distantly. Mabs Riley, introducing herself again at every encounter, says she is astonished at how kind you are. She attempts to pull the ring off her finger, but fails each time. Bones shrink when people die, she says, or else they will use soap and then you will inherit it.

Although the old one is unaware of it, her spells of innocent generosity bequeath you an effective legacy, their repetition gradually persuading you that abandoned in your interior is a kernel of value. Efforts to disinter this more estimable remnant of your personality, though, are sabotaged by some wretched fragment, emptier than you dare remember, that can be loosened only by fresh torrents flowing over your cheeks. You exasperate the orderlies, who compel you to change your smock often. Finally they insist you carry a towel, which you forget to pick up when you change location so that they are obliged to assist you.

One day, when you have graduated out of the hospital gown into your own clothes, there are two people sitting beside you.

"It's us. How are you, Tambudzai? Don't you remember?" one of them asks sternly. In spite the gruff tone, you sense her anxiety.

There is a pause during which low, synchronized sighs tell you they have glanced at each other.

"Try," she says. "Think! It's me, your aunt Lucia. Here is Kiri with me."

Thinking being the last thing you want to do, you resent these visitors with their masked voices asking troubling questions you neither can nor wish to grapple with. Discouraged and apprehensive at your silence, after the first few times they go away shaking their heads. Finally, when your state has confounded them on several further occasions, they begin to make jokes.

The afternoon that they resort to this tactic, Student Nurse has seated you next to Widow Riley in the garden. The woman has taken to pairing the two of you up, to calling you "murungu" when she orders you around since you are now a white woman's daughter; and she laughs cadaverously at Widow Riley's befuddlement. This treatment from Student Nurse of course causes your tears to cascade, which in turn prompts her to inquire roughly why you carry on like that before turning away with barely restrained mirth.

"It's us again!" the woman with the louder voice begins at visiting hours this afternoon. "Don't tell me you haven't eaten or slept, Tambudzai. It looks like you've been sitting there since we last left you."

Metal scrapes on the stone paving when they move their garden chairs closer. Their body heat radiates about you as they press forward and peer. It is stronger than before with a new pulse that is as captivating as a dance or song. A third presence accompanies them.

"What now? Shall we go again?" says the loud woman as softly as she is able. "Just wait a few more days?"

"Can this be sleep?" her companion wonders. "That never ends. With the eyes wide open like that? I've seen many things, but mmm, this, I've never seen it."

The new woman catches her breath. "She's dead," she says, breaking the silent probing she has undertaken. "I mean dying!"

"If you're dying you don't cry like that," says the first. "Your spirit is busy with other things and you use all your strength for departing.

Anyway, this is the first time you've seen her. She's been like this every time we've come. If she's going home, she's taking her time about it."

Metal scratches again on the paving stones. "Call the nurse," the third insists loudly. "Nurse, nurse, Tambudzai's not moving."

"Sit down, Nyasha," says the second woman, "don't embarrass everybody. Dying doesn't look like that. Didn't you hear your aunt Lucia?"

"Is there something wrong with her?" Widow Riley asks. "I didn't think there was anything wrong with my Edie. She sits there all day, nice and quiet. She's such a good girl to come here to see me."

There is a thud as Nyasha drops back into her chair, soothing the old woman with a murmur. A moment later, tissues dab your face.

"Lucia, when was it?" Christine says, to take the conversation in another direction. "When did you see eyes staring like that for the first time? Wasn't it when everything was smashed and torn and red was white and white was red and floating in a river that was running out, that should have kept on running inside our sister's body?"

Your tears flow faster. The woman wiping your tears replaces the wet tissue with a dry one.

"Right, Kiri," relents your aunt Lucia, a relative of the womb, being your mother's younger sister. "Yes, we did see our sisters looking back like that, as though they were dead, although still living."

Christine grunts a hoarse laugh. "So, little sister Nyasha, the next time you see a corpse that cries, call me to examine it again. If there is one thing that me and my sister Lucia here have our PhDs in, it's in knowing whether a body is dead or living."

They have landed in territory they seldom speak of with this discussion. It takes them a moment or two of silence to leave plains ankle deep in men burnt crisp, black and small as babies, infants who throb red blood from every orifice, the faeces of men who watch their daughters cut off their husbands' genitals, and pieces of women, scarlet decorations, that bob on the branches of forests. You hear the click of the padlock, the distant splash of a small object in a wide sea. They say to each other without talking, knowing they lie, "Now we won't find those keys anymore. M-m, never."

With a rare show of discomfort, Widow Riley heaves herself up.

Heading for the dayroom, she bumps into the glass door that should be open but is not and falls. Student Nurse and Nyasha hurry from different directions to lift her.

"Watch where you're going. Why don't you see?" says Student Nurse, while Widow Riley apologizes for the trouble.

"'Let's go," says Aunt Lucia, speaking of leaving many places at once. "I have work to do, Nyasha, not time for sitting here. Leave her now. Maybe she does not want us here. She'll wake up when she's so wet it makes her uncomfortable."

"It's very kind of you to help me along," Widow Riley says, as Student Nurse leads her into the dayroom. "Where are you taking me, dear?'"

Your cousin has no more tissues. Her palms move over your face. You feel the faint motion of air as she withdraws them. The hyena stops laughing. You blink and rise through a purple lake.

"You see, she could hear us all the time," Christine says caustically. She nods at your chest. "At least you have changed shirts. I saw you needed clothes and so I brought everything over. When you were in bed over there and behaving as though there was not a person."

You do not thank your visitor; nevertheless, at this moment she becomes not a far-off, suspicious ex-combatant, but a friendly companion.

Nyasha goes out to the loo and returns with a handful of toilet paper.

"Svina! Wring it!" Student Nurse laughs when you contemplate the tissue in your hands. "Ha-ha, I meant your shirt, you, not those bits of paper."

"Kiri's the one who found me the very day that you were taken from your headmistress's office," your aunt Lucia explains.

"I phoned back to the village as soon as Mrs. Samaita told us," says Kiri. "It was God who saw to it that your niece Freedom had just left the Council Houses when I got through. They sent someone to call her back. She was the one who said immediately that I should contact Lucia in Harare. That girl has already grown up."

"It is good you found me after we lost touch," nods Mainini Lucia.

"Tambudzai," says Cousin Nyasha softly, "how are you feeling?"

Tears well up in your eyes again.

Nyasha nods and says, "I see."

"What is there to see?" says Mainini. "She's got to stop this soon, isn't it?"

"Lucia sent the message via the Council Houses. To your mother," says Christine more gently.

"My sister is always busy with many things," says Lucia. "Doing everything to keep that home together. But I told her, come to Harare, you are the one your daughter needs to see, isn't it? I am expecting her any time. If she has not come yet, it is only because something must have stopped her."

"When Lucia was busy, I took over," explains Christine. "Sending our little Freedom back and forth with messages. She ran up and down, even though she said she doesn't know you, Tambudzai. How can you not know your niece? I couldn't believe it when I heard you haven't been home. Not even to celebrate when your sister returned from war! Or to greet the nieces she brought with her. Poor Netsai," says Christine with a shake of her head. "Hers is a hard situation. I don't know why so many of us who were involved in the fighting have ended up like this. I do not know what I would have done if it weren't for meeting my companion, Lucia, here when I had to get the news to your family, Tambudzai."

"Let's leave that for now," Lucia snaps. "All I want Tambudzai to know is that Freedom left a message saying your mother is coming."

Following that first conversation, your relatives visit you a number of times. Sometimes they are together. More often Nyasha appears on her own. Before she comes you always remind yourself to thank her for the Lady Dis, but you never remember. Your mother sends messages about arranging the journey for the following week, after that the following week and then the following. You learn Mainini Lucia and Christine are working hard at something, that this something is very successful so that Mainini Lucia can pay your treatment costs with only a little help from Nyasha. Your cousin appears to need the company. She chatters on about the courses she studied, the degrees she earned, and the

119

places she obtained them in England and Europe. You do not ask and she does not talk of what she is doing now that she is back in the country. You cling to her words of being somewhere else, infinitely distant from where you are. Assuming she will not approve of this, you do not tell her. Her visits are like it was when you were growing up—Nyasha talking and giving of her energy, while you listen and take in silence. Degree by degree, your cousin's visits being something to look forward to, you feel better. Due to your new progress, Dr. Winton changes your medication from injections to a mixture of tablets.

Eventually talk during these meetings turns to the matter that weighs on everyone's mind: what will happen to you when you are discharged? Your visitors do their best to be delicate about not immediately offering accommodation.

"When you are out of here you will have to go down there," begins your aunt on a day the three visit together. "To the homestead." She nods at your cousin. "Nyasha will take you. So it won't be said you did not have a home to go to. And that you couldn't find a way to get there."

"If you want to drive down with me," your cousin says. "I don't think a matter like this should be taken for granted."

"My aunt Manyanga told me she has been praying for you from the very first day," says Christine. "'She's also praying for that girl you nearly murdered. She wanted me to let you know that particularly.'"

A girl was nearly murdered? By you? You smile, refusing to take it in. Having no intention to believe such a thing, you fight and win against the perils of contemplation.

"I think," Christine goes on, "that she is happy to pray for you. There is somebody in your room. This one is paying double the rent. I have put your other things under my bed."

Nyasha pushes herself out of her chair. "I must go now," she says. "To pick up the children. Since I took the car." Aunt Lucia pulls Nyasha back. For five minutes, she says. Nyasha allows herself to be seated.

Then Mainini Lucia explains about her house for the next half hour. It is in Kuwadzana, one of the townships. She doesn't expect you to like it, nor, she implies, does she expect to like you in it.

Your aunt looks you over, churning options around in her head.

"I am too busy," she makes up her mind. "You will need some help and attention, at least in the beginning. If there is somewhere else you are thinking about, like Nyasha says, maybe you can ask your cousin and maybe she can do some looking."

Energy draining from you, you regard your hands curled in your lap, without saying anything.

Your cousin pushes her lower lip over the top one and wonders whether there might possibly be another option.

"Which one?" snaps Mainini, who used up her last store of patience during the liberation struggle.

Student Nurse rings a bell. Your aunt and Kiri stand up. You walk them to the door, giving a wide berth to Cecilia Flower, who is taking a teacup out of Widow Riley's hand and offering the old lady her weeping breast in its place. Student Nurse dodges Ed Porter's cane and Mrs. Riley exclaims, "Thank you very much for coming down to see me and Edie."

After a few more such sessions it is settled that you will live with your cousin.

Nyasha is punctual the day you leave, hurries in and bustles out of the ward with your bags. She dumps them on top of the rest of your luggage, which she retrieved earlier from Widow Manyanga's.

You kneel beside Widow Riley to say goodbye. She asks who you are. You tell her and she says she could have sworn you were her daughter.

Ed swings his stick and hollers obscenities at the staff as you go by, while Student Nurse almost imperceptibly lifts a corner of her mouth and allows her gaze to sear across your back.

"That woman," you tell your cousin, compassion thickening your voice. "Her husband was killed in the war."

"That nurse doesn't seem very happy about things either," your cousin says.

Outside the tarmac glitters like a serpent in the afternoon sun. Either the world has fooled you, or you are foolish. You shake an incredulous head as you take in evidence that your cousin is just like you. It all seems disconcerting and palpably wrong. You no longer ignore the

121

signs that are all about her, as you did while you were in the ward. To fetch you she has thrown on a faded T-shirt and jeans disfigured by a cluster of old, frayed holes in the middle of the thigh, not ripped at the knee as fashion dictated. Her car keys poke from another tear in her back pocket. You grow puzzled about the Lady Dis. Although you now understand why all that arrived from Nyasha during her years in the West was a single package containing the shoes, you find no way of explaining to yourself why she presented the beautiful footwear to you, while she was herself in a difficult plight; nor do you comprehend how this is possible: to have a degree in England and Europe and still wrestle with adverse prospects. It is an effort to hold yourself together when you cross the tarmac and see her car. Your mood plummets as you realize you will gain little from living with your cousin, who has turned out not much better than yourself in spite of all her childhood advantages.

"So we are going," you murmur as you survey the vehicle for the sake of saying something. Appalled by the scratched and dented tiny contraption, you promise yourself that somehow, even though it is late for you, you will develop VaManyanga's touch for upward mobility.

"Matchsticks," Nyasha replies. "Remember. I pulled the short one."

She ignores your attempt at laughter.

"The children wanted to come too," Nyasha tells you, fumbling in her bag. "It's better they didn't but they can't wait to see you. They're so excited. Their father's an only child. You know what happened to us as a family. With my brother disappearing off the radar somewhere in the United States. So they never imagined having an aunt."

She discovers the car keys poking through the hole in her pocket and pulls them out, causing more ripping.

"Shit. This is just about the last pair," she says, causing your heart to fall further.

She rattles the driver's door open, climbs in, and turns the key in the ignition impatiently. The car's insides scrape, as though it was meant to be pedalled rather than powered by fuel.

"They haven't talked about anything else since I told them," she says, and carries on without pause, in the same conversational manner, "Come on, Gloria. It's Cousin Tambudzai. You've got to start."

Down by the Research Institute, a group of gardeners attends to beds of pink and yellow roses. Student Nurse is a silhouette behind the green curtains in the ward. As though it is not bad enough that so many people have seen your cousin's battered vehicle, it squawks like a distressed peacock each time Nyasha tries the ignition.

After a few attempts, Nyasha lets out the hand brake and throws her door open again. She grips the steering wheel in one hand and heaves against the chassis with her chest. Your mouth drops open, dismay rises as you watch your cousin *push the car herself.* The vehicle rolls. Nyasha jumps back in. Her feet balance the clutch and accelerator. The engine revs. The gardeners by the institute straighten up and clap. Mortified, you look away, only to see Student Nurse's shadowy form disappear toward the dayroom.

"Children?" you prompt, once you have obeyed your cousin's gesture to jump in, in order to cover up with civility your growing dissatisfaction with your position. For the first time since the night with Christine, you think of the Manyanga sons.

"Anesu and Panashe," your cousin gushes, but cuts the conversation short to keep her vehicle chugging at a give-way sign. The car bounds over potholes the size of continents, and through trenches that work gangs have left open like expectant graves. A quarter of an hour later, it turns into a miniature jungle. Bamboo poles run north, east, and southward. Barbed wire sags from them in rusted dejection. Your cousin jumps out and engages a tarnished padlock. The poles sway but hold their ground. Nyasha gives a violent twist, grins, and holds the lock with its chain aloft, like a champion. Embarrassed by her lunacy, you promptly start plotting escape.

You judder through brambles encroaching on the track, over disintegrating lumps of tarmac lurking beneath withering grass, and finally over a once fine brick drive in grey and black, which now resembles a maize cob from a year of miserable harvest. Patches of parched lawn poke up through the rubble. Thorn bushes tear at the car's cracked paint. Your cousin begins to hum, with the air of an empress returning to her fort after battle.

Gas gurgles out of the exhaust as Nyasha manoeuvres into the garage. She jumps out and gives the car a pat, grinning, "Atta girl, Gloria! There's my engine!"

Next she whirls round, all earlier irritation forgotten. Arms stretched out, she beams, "Welcome. It's all over. Don't worry. You're home now, Tambu!"

You were never one for chaos, least of all now, and there is decidedly too much of it. Paper sacks spill cement over old children's toys and abandoned bicycles. Grocery boxes of mouldy cardboard split under mountains of South African wine bottles. Thin white grubs wriggle in and out of termite-infested wicker baskets.

"Mama! Mama's home!" a child yells.

The kitchen stable door scrapes open. A slat falls off. A pale hand reaches out, picks up the plank, and rams it back into place. When the hand disappears, a girl of seven or eight, whose skin is lighter than you expected your niece's complexion to be, bounds out. You suspect many reasons, most of them stemming from disregard, for Nyasha not telling you that she has married a white man. Concealing your vexed apprehension, you arrange your face in a smile.

A boy, younger than the girl, emerges holding on to his father's hand. Once inside the garage, he quickly joins his sister in prodding and pulling at your luggage.

"Let Auntie Tambu do that," Nyasha suggests. She unfolds determined fingers from handles and fasteners. Your cousin encircles her daughter in the crook of her arm and holds her son against her stomach. Your Cousin-Brother-in-Law kisses you on both cheeks, which you are not prepared for, then his wife on the lips, which you are not prepared for either. The four crowd together to examine you.

"This," Nyasha informs the children formally, "is your aunt Tambudzai."

"Her?" your niece asks doubtfully.

"You can call her Maiguru," her mother replies.

While your niece compares the word with the person, the household help, clothed in a geometric patterned uniform, hurries forward.

"Give us a hand, Leon," Nyasha says to her husband, as she heaves a bag onto her shoulder.

Leon grabs a couple of pieces. You start after them to the house, leaving the maid to bring in the rest.

"Thank you, Mai T," Nyasha says, stopping.

The maid insists on heaving up another carryall.

"Thank you, Mai Taka," your cousin repeats. "This is Maiguru Tambudzai. We are sisters. We are helping to carry her luggage."

At this, Mai Taka grabs a small parcel and places it in your nephew's hands. She gives another to your niece, then leads the children away. Nyasha gives you a look. Confused, you pick up two of the remaining pieces.

"Occupational therapy," your cousin grins, "is good for you."

You are immediately resentful, judging that this is no way to treat a convalescent, that living in Europe has not improved your cousin at all; if anything, it has made her more ill-mannered. You continue to smile with all of your face. Inside, your head shakes angrily.

In the kitchen, oily puddles slick over the floor in front of the sink. Shiny black worms wriggle in the thick water. The edges of the draining board look soft and rotten. A sour smell seeps up. Your fingers itch for a mop and brush at so much dampness and neglect, just as they had done, fruitlessly, at Widow Manyanga's house. Your cousin doesn't seem to mind. She stands with her back to the muck as she inquires about the day's events.

"Everything's fine, Mha-mha," Mai Taka assures her.

"No problems?" Nyasha follows up. "Not with anything?"

"The only problem is that there is no problem, Mai Anesu," answers Mai Taka with an attempt at grumbling.

"Those participant people at the workshop ate everything! That's the trouble," she carries on with pride. "What do they think? That this place is a hotel? They say they come here to learn something, isn't that what they say? Something that you want to teach them. Not to eat like politicians and the people who vote for them at a rally. One day I want to cook something bad so they don't just eat and eat. But they always like my cooking. When a person eats like that, I don't think a person has come to learn anything."

"Oh, they'll learn yet," chuckles Nyasha, pleased that the people she left behind to fetch you have been fed. She continues, throwing a glance in your direction, "That's why Mai Taka's given name is Wonderful."

"Mai Taka, I have to ask you again," she says, casting a thoughtful eye over the help's petite, round figure. "Are you sure you're not carrying anything in there?"

"Haven't I got Taka already?" says the help. "Why should I get pregnant, Mha-mha? When there's so much you need me to do?"

"What's not really wonderful is that the plumbers were meant to come in," Nyasha explains as though she has given up on service delivery. Thus changing the subject, she beckons you into the living room. "It sits in the cracks, the water, I mean, and then when the hard board is waterlogged it drips, no matter how well you dry it. Anyway," your cousin laughs as though she is coughing. "That's proof. I always suspected kitchens aren't what they're made out to be. Poor Mai Taka! It shouldn't be a prison sentence. No woman should have to go in them unless she's willing. And me, I'm the luckiest woman on earth to have someone who lives in to do my cooking."

"Yes," smiles Cousin-Brother-in-Law, speaking with a slight, unfamiliar accent. "What we need to see is that men also are made to be more willing. So, my best wife of all, will you tell me what you want me to prepare for dinner?"

Nyasha orders chops and wonders how many participants there are so that she can, if necessary, include them.

Cousin-Brother-in-Law says he will walk down and find out before he goes into the kitchen.

The children cluster round her again and Nyasha drops onto a sofa.

"Anesu, say hello to your auntie Tambu. Maiguru Tambudzai," she instructs. "You, too, Panashe. When we are here, children, we say welcome outside, then we say hello inside the house. We clap the way I showed you. You have to ask how everyone is."

"Nyama chirombowe, Maiguru." Leon, who has not yet gone out, begins the ritual. His nicely domed hands produce a soft, warm resonance.

The children copy their father.

"You say nyama shewe, because you are a girl," Nyasha instructs Anesu, giving you a glance of consternation.

"Why?" Anesu asks, and when she does not receive an answer repeats, "Nyama chirombowe."

"Why do girls have to say that? Why do girls have to clap different?" persists the child.

Nyasha considers this for a while before she replies, "You know what, there isn't any sensible answer to that. So the best thing is, you make up your own mind."

"I did!" Anesu says.

"Then you'll have to see what happens," Nyasha says.

"I did," Anesu says again. "I did and nothing happened."

"How are you, Banamunini?" you ask, as you are a few months older than Nyasha. You inquire where he is from and compliment him on his Shona accent.

"It is because of Nyasha's father," Cousin-Brother-in-Law says.

Reviving, Nyasha nods with satisfaction. "German speakers have this unusual ability to get their tongues around our language's more challenging consonant constellations."

"My father-in-law's the only one who listens to my Shona," Leon continues in such a way that you cannot tell whether he is angry with everyone else who does not attend to him, or pleased with his father-in-law who does.

"Also when I am at the homestead," Cousin-Brother-in-Law concludes, "even though my Shona is better than their English, everyone speaks to me in the colonial language."

"You have been there!" you exclaim. "Babamunini, you were there, all the way down in the village?"

"My father-in-law is a very wise man," Cousin-Brother-in-Law says. "He insisted that was where he wanted to receive Nyasha's lobola."

Your cousin puts an arm around her daughter's neck. "Do you know how much my dad asked for?" she asks with a careless laugh. "I grant you it's difficult to know what's best. And he always said he couldn't charge any lobola for me in case he had to give it back. So he asked for a symbolic one hundred deutschmarks."

You swallow a wince at the mention of this lowly sum, while Nyasha says bitterly, "Yes, so you can imagine what they think of me. And then of course they laugh at Leon too, saying he's murungu asina mari. To them, if you're white there's something wrong with you if you're not wealthy."

Cousin-Brother-in-Law stretches his arm across the back of his chair. The two hold hands.

"Yes," says Cousin-Brother-in-Law. "People here think too much about money. But what does it mean to be without money? Nyasha and I are happy."

"I preferred all or nothing," says Nyasha, stroking the back of her husband's hand with her thumb. "Which meant nothing, because going all means reducing everything to a payment."

Cousin-Brother-in-Law grips Nyasha's hand more firmly.

"I could not disappoint my father-in-law and I didn't want to disappoint my new family." Cousin-Brother-in-Law flashes an imploring look at his wife. "That's why we agreed on a token. Every culture has them, such tokens. And it was good for us to follow the culture in any way we can. That's where I learnt the clapping."

"And some other cultural practices," says Nyasha drily. "He even had to skin a goat."

"It was awful. I felt sick every minute. But I wanted to do everything properly for the family," Cousin-Brother-in-Law smiles. "And in any case, I enjoy the meat. I also wear shoes of leather. So I could see there is not really much difference."

Cousin-Brother-in-Law believes his ability with the Shona language is not due simply to being the German brand of European. He informs you his good accent is the result of having once spent several months hiking through Kenya where the sounds of the language are similar to Shona.

"As well," Cousin-Brother-in-Law concludes this new drift, "I had a Kenyan girlfriend also at that time. So my father-in-law's place was for me not very unusual."

"That's good you chose Zimbabwe from all that way, Mwaramu!"

you encourage your new relative. "It means you like us better than you like those Kenyans, those Kikuyus and Masais."

Nyasha stares at you for a few seconds. "Gikuyus," she says finally. Then she jumps up to crane her head around sun-filter drapes that hang over the large window. Broad ladders run up and down the fabric. Mai Taka has attempted to stitch them, for they are torn in many places. Nyasha appears oblivious to this as she stares into the garden.

Beyond the window, about a dozen young women pore over papers and folders. Two huge ancient computers stand on the wooden trestle table they surround. As she stands there, viewing her work, your cousin inhales, exhales, and relaxes. She turns back to announce she is returning to her workshop. The children skip away after their mother.

When you are left alone, Leon ventures into small talk, telling you of the work he is doing at the National Archives, concerning the representation of groups of people in main news bulletins, especially their deaths, across different demographic categories, and how this evolves over time. He asks your opinion on this. You smile, as you do not have an opinion on the topic. Next he outlines briefly how the purpose of Nyasha's workshop is to give not only a voice, but an analytical one, to the youth, and he offers to introduce you to some of your cousin's young women.

CHAPTER 11

You have entered a new realm of impossibility, worse even than the discovery that your cousin had been placed on the slide to impoverishment, in spite of her degrees, in Europe. You had not believed there was such a thing on this earth as a European without means or money. Now, in her reckless manner, Nyasha has married one. She has made him your relative. Starting out on your road to permanent recovery, this is something you will first have to live down and then deal with. How your cousin, who identified herself when she first came to visit at the hospital by the affectionate radiance that you remember her for, could show such poor judgement is perfectly baffling. You want one or the other, a powerful radiance or obvious failure, not this liminal complexity. In the old days at the mission when you shared a room, you perceived that Nyasha was always ahead of you, seeing things by a different light than that which illuminated your senses, hearing in a different register sounds that fell on both your ears. Her worldview told you there were different ways of being human and yours had nothing to do with hers, leaving you with the distinct belief that hers was the preferable manner. You feel she has let you down immensely without herself being disappointed. A battalion of ants creeps round the back of your neck as you sit in Nyasha's living room. You pretend to yawn and turn an involuntary gesture to brush them off into a polite pat of your mouth.

Deliberately, you turn your mind from the impasse your cousin represents, grateful to the elders who say too much thought wears a mind down like the grating of one grindstone against another. You comfort yourself with the idea that although your relative's residence is in as dismal a state of repair as the Manyangas', Cousin-Brother-in-Law's poverty is less ruinous than your own, for he has at least provided Nyasha with a home. There must therefore be more to Leon than is at first apparent, which means that the house's decline can only be due to your cousin's housewifely negligence. Your in-law must himself be a victim of Nyasha's incorrigible temperament.

When Nyasha does not return, in his too-familiar-for-comfort European way, Cousin-Brother-in-Law Leon shows you to your room. He runs up and down the stairs several times, bringing up your bags. You grip the balustrade for steadiness as you follow, since you still feel a degree of weakness after almost three months in hospital, particularly now, in response to the anxieties your cousin's home has called forth. The railing shudders and shakes at your grasp. Cousin-Brother-in-Law places a hand on your shoulder. "Careful," he warns as you sway.

The walls are splashed with little handprints in chocolate, mud, paint, and tomato sauce. Piles of ancient computers loom like a row of mountains on the landing. Behind them are cartons of outgrown children's clothes and garbage bags full of old curtain material. This confirms what you had supposed: your cousin has given in to chaos, is wildly wasting her entire upbringing and her immeasurable advantages. The disorder emphasizes to you that well-being demands choices more astute than Nyasha's.

"My wife wanted to show you this herself," Leon says, throwing open the door to a north-facing room. "She calls it the beauty spot. Her philosophy is that every woman must have one. At a minimum."

He laughs shortly and disappears to bring up more luggage.

Left alone, you sit on the large four-poster bed to test it for comfort. A door leads off to the left. Opening it, you discover a yellow and amber bathroom. You run water, throwing in your cousin's bath salts and oils.

Cousin-Brother-in-Law has gathered your belongings on the landing. He kicks and drags them in. Ignoring the running bath, he stalks over to the French window, opens the red amber curtains, and steps out onto a narrow balcony.

"She says you can do things with space," Leon says. "That here she has enough room to make a difference. Her philosophy is that space promotes co-operation, lack of it, fighting."

"How big is this plot?" you ask.

"Two and a half acres," Cousin-Brother-in-Law replies. A distressed smile slips over his face.

"How far are you with your doctorate?"

You continue to make conversation, wondering again how to excavate the submerged portion of Cousin-Brother-in-Law.

"Well, it's happening," Cousin-Brother-in-Law responds to your inquiry with indifference. "Look, your bath's full," he changes the subject. "I'll turn it off for you."

The water stops and Cousin-Brother-in-Law comes out humming a seventies Nigerian Afrobeat hit about women who try to turn themselves into ladies by invariably seizing the biggest piece of meat at every opportunity. He mouths the words softly as he walks back onto the balcony.

"I know that one," you say. "'Lady.' Fela Kuti."

"She says she wants to build a place where women can study women's issues with modern technology. I ask her who she thinks is interested in women's issues. And I try to tell her nobody here is interested in any of these things that she thinks are important, not even the women. I explain to her, least of all the women."

You are inclined to agree. You cannot think of anyone who is interested in women's issues, apart from the woman who has issues, but you are concerned that Cousin-Brother-in-Law will repeat this to Nyasha, which will result in trouble. All the same, you are glad that you and Cousin-Brother-in-Law both understand the prerequisites of self-preservation.

"I'm thinking of changing my thesis to something else," Leon says.

"Can you help me get a place at your university?" you ask.

"I have changed my mind about some things that I thought about your country," Cousin-Brother-in-Law goes on. "It is true, there is too much that is wrong. At the same time too many are too happy to keep saying what is wrong. Not enough see what is right also. I am thinking I will look at the imagery in Zimbabwean stone sculpture instead of images of death. Do you know that five of the top ten stone sculptors in the world are Zimbabwean?"

"Where is it?" you ask.

"Haven't you seen any of it?" says Leon. His forehead wrinkles in incomprehension. "You must have. It's all everywhere! Really. All over the world."

"Your university," you say. "Where do you study? In which city?"

"Berlin," Cousin-Brother-in-Law answers. "We met when we were both flying there. From Nairobi. I saw her at the airport. She didn't speak German then and immigration in Frankfurt was giving her a hard time. So I said we were travelling together."

"How long does it take to learn German?"

"It is a difficult language," says Cousin-Brother-in-Law. As though he does not like having to contemplate his mother tongue and its difficulties, he leaves the verandah.

At the door he asks whether he can bring you a sundowner.

You decline. When he has gone, you walk over to the French window.

Down on the lawn, Nyasha and the domestic help carry trays heaped with food and drinks. Arriving at the worktable, they set the refreshments down. Nyasha pulls a garden chair over and seats herself amidst the workshop participants. The pale gold of midafternoon shimmers through the open space, carrying the warm blossom-sweetened scent of early November. Excited laughter peals. Nyasha leans forward, her elbows on the wooden table. She talks intently and nobody reaches for scones or biscuits. The participants gaze at your cousin, they take notes. And then they are all laughing again. They are jumping up, shuffling their papers into heaps, and pushing them into rucksacks. They fling their arms here and there, and around each other, and Nyasha is lost in the heart of it.

Turning back into the room, amber, orange, yellow, ochre flow into each other, as though in the first movement of swirling on and away. The room is three times as big as your old place at Mai Manyanga's, rekindling in you a tenacious conviction that for all your misgivings, your cousin is your crossing place, your stepping-stone to becoming the remarkable, well-to-do person you wish to be. Fortified by this notion, you drag clothes out of bags. The naturally stained saligna wardrobe gleams with such a sophisticated lustre that you are almost afraid to touch it. Refusing to be bullied by the furniture, you grasp the cool brass handles. Your composure regained, you revel in the metal's smooth, cold beauty. Yes, you insist to yourself as you fold your clothes and lay them away, these are the things that you were made for.

There is a desk by the window. It is the desk your uncle, Nyasha's father, used in his study at his mission home. He stopped doing so at the time your extended family resolved to send your brother from the village to live with the head of the clan, since, when this decision was implemented, your cousin Chido moved from the bedroom he shared with Nyasha into the study with your brother. You arrange your magazines from the agency and other papers on your uncle's desk with an air of ownership. Babamukuru only started using the room and the desk again when Chido went to America to university. Second born, to an older brother, Nyasha has nevertheless managed to coax the fine piece of furniture from her father. Stacking letters and periodicals, you struggle to fathom why Nyasha's peculiarities do not prevent her from achieving, whereas yours, although you are a second-born girl like she is, ensure your ruin. An ant scurries along the grain of the wood. You regard it, suspicious that it has crawled out of your imagination. Its antennae wave. You close your eyes. When you open them it is still there, on urgent business, perhaps rushing toward a prize such as a hidden sugar crystal. You will be like the ant, you decide. You do not yet know how, but come what may, you will focus on the prize until you possess it. As you enjoy your cousin's bath, you construct a fabulous vision of your relatives visiting you in your own spectacularly superior dwelling.

The little family is milling here and there, around the little table that stands in the middle of the good-sized dining room and in and out of the spacious kitchen, when you go down to dinner. The meal cannot progress until a particular serving scoop required for the sauce is found. There is also a sizeable list of other items that Mai Taka has not attended to in the whirlwind of busyness resulting from Nyasha's workshop. Your niece and nephew scuttle with whoops and wails from their bedrooms, and through the hall to search in various drawers for favourite forks and spoons that should have, but have not since the last meal, been either washed up or—as the help confirms—seen. Everyone is touching everyone else and speaking all at once as they investigate the spaces behind cupboard doors and consult each other with varying degrees of restraint.

"Where's my knife, Mama?" wails Panashe in despair. Your nephew follows this more hopefully with, "I haven't got my knife! Mama, can I have red sauce?"

"Thank goodness there's no one here from the workshop," says Nyasha. "It's potatoes. No spaghetti, no red sauce," she says, pulling her son against her stomach. "That would have been just too much."

"Dum-di-du-u-um. Dum-di-dum, la la la-la-la," Cousin-Brother-in-Law hums Fela Kuti's hit at Nyasha's mention of the workshop participants. "That means the big pieces of meat are safe," he cannot resist adding. "Maybe I can have one."

"Tomato sauce," Anesu tells her brother.

"Tomato sauce," agrees Panashe. "Tomato sauce. Red sauce."

When they finally subside, you see chops steaming on a silver serving platter and a dish of pommes frites crisp with flavour on the table. Leon excuses the fact that there is not any rosemary and white wine sauce since he did not attend to it himself but asked Mai Taka to do so after he had spent time getting to know you.

"I was clear," he says rather sheepishly. "I explained the ingredients. And showed them to her. It's the language problem."

Your cousin nods.

"She said yes all the time," observes Cousin-Brother-in-Law with an expression of complete incomprehension.

Nyasha nods more calmly.

Cousin-Brother-in-Law leaps up, saying he will now attend to the matter as it was his responsibility.

"I don't understand. She was very emphatic." He shakes his head as he pushes aside his chair. "About managing everything. But as you can see, she understood very little."

"That can happen," your cousin says.

"Why yes is said when it is meant no? This is something that it is always difficult for me to understand," says Leon.

"That kind of thing can be difficult," says Nyasha.

"But here it is done constantly!" Cousin-Brother-in-Law exclaims before he goes out to the kitchen.

Popping a bottle of sparkling wine, your cousin pours a glass for herself and her husband.

"It's not the best way to celebrate your homecoming, Tambu, but really, I got this for myself," she admits. "You've no idea how I missed you. Over all these years. It could have been a more auspicious reunion. But what will you have, not to destroy the equilibrium that's just been given back to you? Especially since you've already tippled. Leon said he was getting you a sundowner."

You opt for a sip, explaining that no alcohol passed your lips, that all you did was enjoy a refreshing bath.

"Take your time about getting back on your feet," Nyasha says kindly. "Take it from me. Relax as much as you can."

You sip your drinks until Leon returns with the sauce. Over the meal, Nyasha talks about her travels, how having completed her A levels she had yearned to return to England but had found the country in which she had spent much of her childhood disappointing and so had opted for continental Europe.

When you are all done with the meat and potatoes and your cousin is stacking the plates, "Dessert, Mama! We didn't have it!" Anesu cries.

"Mama says we can have dessert every time when we have a very special visitor," your niece explains affably enough, although she looks accusingly in your direction. "Even in the week. When there aren't any visitors like that, Mama says we can only have dessert at weekends."

Hopeful and preoccupied at the same time, the young lady demands, "Auntie Tambudzai, are you special?"

"Oh, yes, I am," you reassure your niece. "I'm so special I'm in the beauty spot."

"That's Mama's!" the girl exclaims as though talking to an uncomprehending schoolchild. She grows cross-eyed with concentration as she examines you.

"No, Mama," she decides at last, turning to Nyasha. "Auntie Tambudzai isn't special. She's just . . . just . . . she's just . . ." your niece says as though being "just" is an act as perfidious as sedition.

"Just human capital," supplies Cousin-Brother-in-Law with a snort.

Nyasha stands up and fetches the dessert along with another bottle of wine.

"Enough, Leon!" she says, popping the latter open. "Capital is an object. Even if it's a concept. Created by humans. Certain ones. For their own benefit."

Your cousin turns to her daughter, suggesting that if the child hugged you, you would cease being "just," and metamorphose into "special."

Your niece hugs you. You endure the closeness, overcoming a desire to pull away from the warm, round body.

The moment your niece's arms fall, "Now can I have the ice cream, Mama?" she asks.

Nyasha scoops a spoon into the plastic carton of Devonshire, declaring it is just as well human beings grow out of cupboard love, while Leon starts fretting about the biggest-piece-of-meat syndrome Fela Kuti sings about spreading to his daughter.

"We should have stayed in Germany. We should teach the children all guests are equal," he says, pouring honey over his ice cream. "I do not like this 'special' affair. In Germany we do not have this kind of thing. You have it here from the British. From them because they have a class system which is terrible. And their administration system is worse than ours as Germans."

Nyasha thinks Leon should give girl children a break, instead of comparing them to man-made abstract nouns or countries.

"But look at your students," Cousin-Brother-in-Law says, filling his glass. "The way they behave begins somewhere. It begins when they are children, here in this country. And most of them have not been to foreign lands, where they can see another way of living that can change their thinking. The way they are begins in this place, in this time of history. That is why they are human capital and nothing more. Value has been added to them, but it is not their value for themselves that has been added. That is why you can do nothing with them, Nyasha. It is only value for someone else, for the person who has added it to them."

"Yum!" Anesu exclaims, rubbing her stomach with her left hand and running the right around her dessert bowl's creamy rim.

"Pana," she says. "One hand goes on your tummy. See? The other has to go round and round your bowl. Like this, see? Can you?"

"Oh!" says Panashe, distressed. "I can't. Ane, I can't do it!"

"Finger first," demonstrates Anesu. "That's more difficult. On the bowl."

The boy's plastic bowl spins off the table. Nyasha catches it, reflexes intact even after several glasses of wine.

"Here, Panashe, this is how," Nyasha says. Standing behind her son, she puts her hands over his until he catches the rhythm. Nyasha grins and tells Panashe he is wonderful.

"Story time," Leon booms, looking at his watch. "You two, what do you want me to read for you today?"

The children kiss their mother good night, hug you, and Leon leads them away, Panashe demanding *Die kleine Raupe Nimmersatt* and Anesu insisting on *Das doppelte Lottchen*.

"I should read to them in English," Nyasha nods to herself, picking up the wine bottle. "But I don't. And I ought to read to them in Shona. How can I, when I'm still paying for that damn English upbringing? Maybe that's something you could do, Tambu, when you feel a little better? This is only going to last as long as Leon has his grant. Then I don't know. I have to find a way to earn something."

She does not allow herself to be drawn when you inquire about the workshops, beyond saying she is teaching theory and practice of narrative. She tips the wine bottle up again. It is empty. She departs to make a pot of rooibos tea.

"Do you ever think of the classes you taught at that school?" she asks on her return.

Her countenance is shining again, not with the damp glow of alcohol, but in a serene way that emanates from her centre, a place that you do not know whether you possess and believe that if you did, you would find nothing resembling light in it. You fight an impulse to get up and slap your cousin. You become absorbed in sugaring your tea so as not to answer.

She would like to know about Northlea, she continues, approaching the matter softly-softly as she sips the red-bush infusion. "I have my issues too with some of my young people. It's not as if issues and young people are altogether unheard of."

"Northlea?" you exclaim. "No, I wasn't there long enough. I didn't get involved. Things happen everywhere, but no, I didn't take part in any of that issues stuff. For me it was just the usual duties."

"I haven't told anybody here, I mean Leon, anything about why, well, let's say the details about, well, your experience," your cousin says. "I was going to. But then I just told him Mainini Lucia had contacted me, after a friend had contacted her. I couldn't. Not everything."

"OK," you nod.

"I just said something about a fight. That got out of hand."

"OK," you say again. You settle back in your seat in relief.

"You could go and visit the girl," Nyasha suggests. "Kiri never found out what she's called. What was her name?"

"Oh, you! You're still thinking about that thing," you reply. Your throat is tight but you give a laugh. "That thing about the newspapers. And you're calling it an issue? Wasn't it just people? These things happen!"

"Issues need to be explored," your cousin says. "Clarified."

You try to laugh again. Your mouth hangs open for a second. You close it because no sound emerges.

"How about forgetting?" you say. "Sometimes forgetting is better than remembering when nothing can be done."

"Forgetting is harder than you think," says Nyasha. "Especially when something can be done. And ought to be. It's a question of choices."

"They want to forget, too," you say. "Because what can they do? Forgetting. That is what they have been doing already for a quarter of a year. If I go, they'll see me again. They'll remember all the things they thought then. For their revenge. They might find someone to do something."

"Do it," persists Nyasha. "For your own good. Sometimes your own good is the common good. We are wired for the right act to benefit everyone."

Your laugh is a wry guffaw that you break off as, distantly, you hear the hyena cackle. You request another glass of wine. Nyasha brings in another bottle, pops it open, and says it's the last. Leon returns from reading to the children. He reassures Nyasha that they are asleep. Nyasha puts an arm around his waist and leans against him. You excuse yourself as soon as you have drained your glass and climb back up the stairs. As you get ready for bed you kick a soft mass by the bedside table. It gives to the touch of your foot, emitting a stale, musty odour. It is the bag of mealie meal Christine brought from the village. Your cousin has rescued it from Widow Manyanga's. You throw it into the back of the closet. Your hand rests on the brass handles again as you figure out a way to rid yourself of the bag the next morning, without anyone noticing.

CHAPTER 12

You wake up early, still influenced by ward routine in which an orderly would roll the medication trolley by at dawn. Stretching luxuriously in your three-quarter bed, you listen to kingfishers rattle out their sharp twitters and starlings chatter anxiously. You mull over the previous night's conversation. What was your cousin's point in suggesting you apologize for that sad, mad, and foolish incident concerning your pupil? Seeing no sense in revisiting such an unthinkable aberration, you have put it firmly behind you.

You strive—you believe earnestly—to understand your cousin. First you mull over Nyasha's initial hesitation to share her house with you. Disappointed by that, you weigh up her reluctance to condemn for you the people whose actions brought you down. She barely suppresses a yawn when you talk about the board women at the hostel whose policies had caused Mrs. May to send you to Widow Riley where you encountered a bad-tempered maid. Her reminiscing about old mission adventures when you find fault with the Manyangas, who wasted all their opportunities, making it impossible for you to continue to lodge with them, magnifies your discouragement. "I wish I could help" is all she says when you fret that before all this were Tracey Stevenson and her staff at Steers et al. Advertising Agency who paid you miserly wages for copy white men put their names to. You observe her all but biting her tongue on several occasions so as not to exclaim impetuously about something or other that you have done or omitted.

A new idea unfurls within you. For the first time since meeting

Nyasha decades ago, you begin to suspect that your cousin does not like you. You are convinced there can be no other reason for her suggesting such a thing as engaging with the Chinembiris on the very same day she brought you into her home. The idea slips under the light duvet and lies down with you when you go to bed; it rises with you each morning.

To fortify yourself against it all, you remind yourself you have already decided to escape Nyasha's negligence. You vow to succeed more than anyone in your family has managed, including your uncle and aunt at the mission and your cousin, but you will only depart for this major move when you are ready. After all, you have a right to live in her house as she is not only your cousin, but someone you grew up with as a sister. More importantly, Mainini Lucia, who stands *in loco maternis* since both your mothers are absent, has ordered the two of you to cohabit.

You spend a lot of time contemplating how you will launch your next sortie into life when you are well enough. You lie in late enjoying the room, planning the incredible life you have contracted yourself to build. You descend to the kitchen after the family has eaten and left. Nyasha has instructed Mai Taka to engage herself thoroughly in your convalescence. When you appear the help cheerfully prepares for you scrambled eggs, toast, and coffee.

Your relatives eat early because of the children's school timetable. One morning, however, a few weeks after your arrival, you roll out of the comfort of bed, put on the dressing gown your cousin first lent then gave you, and go down to find Leon and Nyasha at the table. It is well past the time for all of them to be away at their different tasks. You hesitate in the doorway, assessing the situation, whether it is good or bad and whether, should it be the latter, you want to be part of it. You are about to close the door and retreat softly up the stairs when Nyasha, without looking up, says, "Good morning, Tambu. It's all right. Come on in if you want to."

Retreat being impossible, you return the greeting and proceed.

Your cousin is slumped forward, her chin in her hands. A bowl of homemade mulberry yogurt, Leon's speciality, sits ignored in front of her. She usually seats herself so as to avoid viewing the glistening anne-lids. At this morning's angle, although she can see them clearly, she does not give the wiggling forms a glance.

Cousin-Brother-in-Law is leaning back in his chair. His arms are folded over his chest with a touch of defiance. His expression alternates between I-told-you-so and the beginnings of disenchantment.

Mai Taka turns round as you enter, her weight on one leg. She crushes several worms as she does so. She stares from you to your cousin.

Resenting Mai Taka's soundless plea to intervene, you sit down in your usual seat.

"Good morning, Maiguru. What can I make for you?" Mai Taka says dutifully, turning back to the sink.

"Scrambled," you reply.

You wait. Mai Taka rearranges some dishes in the sink, draws breath sharply, and begins a long, slow limp to the pantry where the tray of eggs is kept.

Nyasha and Leon look at each other. There is no shine about your cousin today. She looks as though all her energy is being drained away from her to sustain a far-off, raging furnace.

"You hope for the best. You believe," says Nyasha, in such a faint voice it is practically a whisper. "But it's all talk, talk, talk. There can't be a country that hates women as much as this one."

"Yemen," nods Leon. "Pakistan. Saudi Arabia."

Mai Taka returns with two eggs in a bowl. She breaks them and dips in a fork.

"Go down. Have a rest," Nyasha says to the help.

Mai Taka keeps beating the eggs, her face set like clotting blood.

Nyasha goes over and takes the fork from the woman's hand.

"If you get better later on, and you are able, please come back," she says, holding the fork as if she wants nothing but to return it to the woman.

"Go on. It's all right," she encourages, in a voice that says a day with-out backup is more than she wishes to deal with.

Refusing to move, "No, no, it is OK, Mha-mha," Mai Taka says.

"Go!" Nyasha repeats, unscrewing a bottle of cooking oil. She pours a thin short stream into a frying pan.

"You can give it to me," Mai Taka says without enthusiasm.

Fat starts to smoke in the frying pan.

You observe all this, watching in the way you do when you do not want to be involved, mentally placing wagers with yourself concerning what will happen, weighing the consequences of each possible outcome against your wish, which at this moment is breakfast.

As unobtrusively as possible, you pour cereal into your bowl.

Mai Taka, her injury much more pronounced now, hobbles back to the sink and recommences cleaning the dishes.

"Shall I drive you down, Mai Taka, if it's too difficult for you to walk?" says Leon.

"Fine, sir, Ba'Anesu, I'm going now," Mai Taka agrees meekly, having interpreted the offer as an order. "I can manage. See, it is not all that bad!"

She limps out through the stable door. Her scarfed head bobs past the kitchen window as she shuffles down to the servants' quarters.

"There have to be alternatives," says Nyasha.

Pressing her lips together, she gives the scrambled eggs a hefty stir.

You spoon up the last of the cereal from your bowl and hold up your breakfast plate.

"Sometimes I think if I had known, I wouldn't have come back here!"

Nyasha tips the rest of your breakfast into your plate, then sinks back into her seat and rests her chin upon the heels of her hands once more.

"We can go back to Germany. If I do not find a job. There we can at least live on social security," says Cousin-Brother-in-Law.

"Not coming back is one thing," says Nyasha through fingers that hide her face. "Giving up and going back is another."

"What will you do with the children?" asks Leon. "Do you think I will leave them here? Where I come from the state pays you to look after your little ones. That is the one good achievement of capital!"

"Whatever," says Nyasha, refusing to engage.

"So that's it," says Leon. His voice is calm but his face changes colour the way the faces of white people do when they grow angry.

You commiserate with Cousin-Brother-in-Law, confident Nyasha must have dragged him to your hopeless country in the first place. Aversion to your cousin's stubbornness grows. You chew your eggs, the longing you quietly harbour to leave the house, the country, the continent burgeoning in your heart as you suspect it does also in Cousin-Brother-in-Law's. You want to be part of a stable, prosperous nation like his. Each mouthful of breakfast takes too long to chew, because you do not have enough saliva.

"You want to be away from your children. This makes it all convenient," Leon says softly. "You will let me go, so you do not have them. Pretending that you are doing something here with this nothing, these workshops and these egotistical young women."

Nyasha takes her hands away from her eyes. She looks as though she is going to cry as a result of her old, youthful rage coming back or, if not that, because the last of her energy has been devoured and she is broken.

"Capital is about scale," goes on Cousin-Brother-in-Law. "Women like you just haven't got it. Scale. Because no one wants you to have it. They have to make sure you never do! They don't want women like that. They want women the way they are now, just something with a shelf life, that ages. Can't you see there's nothing about women to interest any kind of capital unless it's solutions for aging? Botox, liposuction. That's at one end of the scale. At the other end, all they have to do is keep you being women. Like Mai Taka. The scale of the billionaire or the scale of numbers. Not the scale of Nyasha or Tambudzai," Cousin-Brother-in-Law says coldly.

There is a blade-toothed rodent gnawing in your stomach. It is the hunger you used to suffer when you ate ice cream cones from the vendor at the park gate across from the hostel. It digs on and on, making a hole that, like the animal's teeth, grows bigger and bigger. Because of it, suddenly you are ravenously hungry again.

"Whatever they are telling you now, capital is never human, it's only numbers. Capital's just like your politicians. It knows those women out there are nothing but quantities! Think about your aunt at the home-stead, Nyasha! She's a bit in a calculation. A vote here, a price there for a dose of something. The people out here are just translated into ballots and markets for GMOs, Depo-Provera, and fertilizer."

You blob chilli sauce onto your eggs, wondering why everything, especially when white people say it, must come back to the village and your mother. You add two more spoons of sugar to your coffee and find a clean spoon to scoop the cream off the milk in its carton.

"That is what I want to hear. Absolutely right now," Nyasha says to Leon.

"If you wanted to make it alone," Leon continues, "then maybe you'd have a chance. Maybe someone would listen to you, without feeling threatened. But you want to do it with others. Can you think what it does to them, thinking of dozens and dozens of little Nyashas? All acting together."

Nyasha wipes her eyes, although no tears have fallen.

"As I said, it is the question of proportion," says Leon, reverting to impersonal phrases. "In your case the proportion is . . . it is . . ."

"Small?" suggests Nyasha. She stands up to clear the table. "Insignificant? Irrelevant?"

Leon jumps up to help because he always helps his wife with the housework. He spills milk and rattles dishes as he lifts them.

There is a cold piece of toast in the wicker basket on the table. You take it and pile on Cousin-Brother-in-Law's homemade peach jam made of fruit harvested from your cousin's trees.

"Go-go-go," a voice calls as you stir the last of the sugar in the bottom of your teacup.

"Hello, hello!" Nyasha and Leon welcome the visitors as one voice.

"Child! Yes, child of mine, carry on like that. Tomorrow and tomorrow and tomorrow," Mainini Lucia calls as she enters. "That's what a child of mine does. She keeps on going, isn't it?"

Nyasha twines her arms around Mainini's neck, as though she will never let go. Mainini stands rather stiffly, as all war veterans do when faced with close physical contact. Nyasha uncoils her arms from her aunt to put a hand on Christine's shoulder. Leon advances with a brilliant smile and kisses both ex-combatants on both cheeks. They stand and take it. You hurry to embrace your mother's sister and Christine, who has become an aunt by association. Having finished the greetings, Aunt Lucia bustles forward with Christine behind her. The scale of everything increases.

"Kiri, oh, this is wonderful. I am so glad you came," Nyasha cries. She grips Mainini's arm with both hands.

"Did you ever call us and not get an answer when it was possible for us to give one, Nyasha?" Mainini grins.

"We are one less today," says Nyasha, folding her arms and leaning against the sink in dejection. "Mai Taka isn't well."

"It doesn't matter," says Mainini Lucia. "When you have two women who know what has to be done like Kiri and me, it is like you have ten. Didn't we say we will always support you? And it's better to support a woman who is supporting other women, isn't it? Let us start now, so we finish quickly. And," Mainini goes on with a laugh that sounds like Student Nurse's, "here is Tambudzai. We are not three. We are already four!"

Christine hands Leon the cardboard box she is holding. Cousin-Brother-in-Law balances it on some plates stacked beside the sink. He disappears into the pantry and Nyasha takes the box from the draining board. Leon returns carrying bags of tomatoes and onions, ginger and garlic, while Nyasha clears a space on the table in which she deposits the container.

"That box," Cousin-Brother-in-Law begins, holding the vegetables and looking at the sink. "Where is it?"

"Here, Babamunini," you say, coming to his assistance.

Your cousin disappears into the scullery before any more conversation can develop to delay her work further. You take the vegetables from Cousin-Brother-in-Law and find somewhere to put them.

"Tell us about this new workshop, Nyasha," Mainini says when Nyasha returns, three maid's smocks draped over her arm. Mainini accepts a garment and lays it over the back of a chair.

"One day I will send someone from my company to these courses

147

that you do, daughter," she muses as she unbuckles the belt of the grey uniform she wears. "Are you going to show them how to make a film this time?"

"I wish," sighs Nyasha sadly. "I'm glad anything's happening at all. You know me, Mainini. I had these huge hopes and ambitions. For all sorts of things. I wanted to start us telling different stories. Stuff that's uplifting. Not just the nonsense on television. Not all that tragedy, either, as though that's the only story there is. I've been dreaming of stories of things and people we can admire that in the long run make us better than we've managed to be so far."

"Let your participants sit in front of the camera," says Leon. "Let them tell their own stories. That's something they'd like and admire. I mean, Nyasha, why think of other things, big things, when you can think of your little self?"

"Maybe it would be better if you taught them something useful," Mainini suggests. "Like how to make advertisements. Then Tambudzai can help. I hope she hasn't forgotten everything she learned at that advertising agency."

"You're right, both of you," Nyasha says in a conciliatory tone. "I just thought they could find value in telling someone else's story too, looking outside of themselves," she continues, pulling her smock over her head and closing the buttons.

"You hope," says Cousin-Brother-in-Law. His eyebrows twitch with the effort of maintaining a straight face. "How about going for the Oscars? With a comedy. Or a drama. Or a tragicomedy. Let us make a new hybrid, for example, *The Great African Dictatress*."

Nyasha ignores him.

Cousin-Brother-in-Law hums the Nigerian song about women and big pieces of meat as he leaves the kitchen.

"Men," says Nyasha. "They don't want the biggest piece, right? They just want a piece of meat, that's all."

"Du-du-du," Kiri hums the infectious melody under her breath.

"Sometimes you can listen to Babamunini, even though he is a white person," recommends Aunt Lucia. "Sometimes there is nothing you can do to change anything. Remember Kiri and I went to war. If you see us who went to fight not trying to do anything about this country of ours, you should understand there is a reason."

"He says he wants to go back to Germany," Nyasha confides. "As soon as he's finished his doctorate," she goes on, as though both completion of his research and departure are imminent. You realize she does not know Cousin-Brother-in-Law is mulling another thesis because he is no longer interested in his subject. You are surprised your in-law is behaving in the way you expect your own black men to do, first of all by being so indecisive and then by not telling his wife. You begin to suspect that Cousin-Brother-in-Law and Nyasha are not being honest, that they found each other because neither possesses the hardiness success requires, so they have dressed discouragement up in the glamour of intellect.

"The task I gave the girls was to research a great African woman. It was their workshop preparation," says Nyasha. "Only three understood what it was about. And what did all the others do? Can you believe it, seventeen of my participants wrote only about themselves."

Christine laughs and says, "Zimbabwe! So, Nyasha, Mukwasha Leon has already seen something of us."

"I'll get to them," promises Nyasha. "It's just that no one has taken the trouble. Not seriously. They see what they see, right? And no one has taught those poor young people anything different."

You grow increasingly galled by your cousin and her assumption that everyone has the luxury she has of surviving without being obsessed with one's own person. All three of them think that now she has taken you out of the institution into her care, everything is wonderful for you. They do not know what it is to struggle with the prospect that the hyena is you, nor how this combat marshals in the task of finishing the brutish animal off, while ensuring you remain alive yourself. You squash an ant scuttling over the table and raise your finger to inspect its crushed black body, but your finger is clean.

"You help too, Tambudzai," Mainini says.

Increasingly uneasy in this sphere where the three women have found their place, you contemplate following Cousin-Brother-in-Law. Added to everything else, you have no intention of cooking for a gang of young women whom only Nyasha truly thinks are worth the effort. After all, you came to your cousin's not to be a chef but to continue your recovery.

"Begin by washing those breakfast dishes, Tambu!" commands Mainini Lucia. "When you have finished, tell your cousin, and she will find you something else to take things forward."

Nyasha turns her head to hide a smile.

"Look at this," Mainini Lucia orders, putting her hand to her breast pocket. "Tambudzai, read what is written on it."

Your aunt does not give you the chance to comply. "AK Security," she pronounces.

She pulls the maid's smock over her head and smooths it down. The grey uniform she is removing falls around her ankles.

"Mine," Mainini boasts as her head erupts through the neck hole. "I designed it myself. Logo, uniform, everything. For my own company."

Mainini steps out of the circle the charcoal-coloured uniform makes around her feet and holds the dress out to you. You examine it closely, finding the red and white *A* and *K* intertwined on the logo's dark grey background impressive.

"What people want. Already. That is what they'll let you do," says Nyasha. "Service. What they won't let you do is allow you to create something yourself that they might end up wanting."

"AK Security," nods Christine. "That is where I work now. Didn't I tell you, Tambudzai, that when it is time, I will move from my aunt Manyanga's."

"Congratulations, Mainini," you say. Your respect for your aunt Lucia swells tremendously. You are glad that you have listened to her and honoured her as your mother. "And you, also Kiri, congratulations," you smile. "Even though you came back from war it is like you didn't go. Now you are just like everybody else who is advancing."

Christine turns away from you as she does up her smock buttons. You start washing up with a new energy, hope spreading throughout your person. Mainini Lucia was always a woman able to do what others of her sex couldn't. Christine, though, has shaken off the habit of failure that made her scorn VaManyanga's journey to prosperity, and has taken a step toward her own profit. These examples give you confidence, reassuring you that when the time comes, you will accomplish fine things too.

"Even going to war has its uses. Only you don't always know what will be useful and how it will be when it's happening," Mainini says with conviction, as though she had once been ashamed of being a woman who had seen too much blood. "Yes, sometimes we wondered why we went to war when we came back and everyone was shocked and began to hate us. And the war had swallowed up too much, even the things that came out of the womb that strengthened the heart." Mainini pauses, remembering her little son whom she had left to fight in the conviction that her risk was the down payment on a better life for both of them. You heard the story once in the early days after the war, how, when the Rhodesian soldiers came, the young boy ran back to the kraal at the homestead to let out the cattle as he had been told he must in order to prevent the Rhodesians butchering the entire herd. Instead, the soldiers drove bullets through the boy's back as he lifted the logs that closed the cattle pen. The force of the bullets leaving his body ripped his stomach open and spread his intestines on the sand that was mixed with cow dung. Your mother scooped her sister's child's intestines back into his little body. It was in the days before Babamukuru was paralysed. Your uncle drove the boy to the General Hospital in Umtali, where he died.

"It was so difficult when everybody was afraid and started saying that we who fought were going naked at night, drinking blood and flying with evil spirits," Mainini Lucia says in that voice of the former freedom fighter that cuts dangerously even when quiet. "Ignoring them all, I said to myself, look, I can face any tsotsi in any corner, even if that robber is holding a gun. He won't know what hit him when I get him. China trained. We are fighters with Kiri here, even if she was trained in Moscow! I said that is something that you were given: yourself and other women like you—you can begin with that."

"She has made a place for us veterans!" exclaims Christine.

"My child, Tambu" says Mainini. "War just shrinks in peacetime, isn't it? That's what I saw. I just went into that little space that is still there. So how can Kiri and I be useless?"

Nyasha picks up a knife. You do not have a smock, but when you have finished the dishes, you start peeling and dicing vegetables, while Nyasha apologizes again that the crew is one short because of Mai Taka's injury. She shakes her head, admitting that each encounter with such abuse depresses her.

"I still think, though, every time I do a workshop with the young women, it makes a difference," she says fiercely. "It changes something. I make myself think it. I have to. But really, it's only my hope."

You smile along with Mainini and Christine, although you allow more irony into your expression than they do.

By midday curries and stews to be frozen for the next workshop are simmering on the stove. You all turn to baking cakes, scones, and biscuits for the workshop participants' teas.

Leon brings the children back from school in Gloria. Your niece and nephew demand to scrape the bowls after the batter is poured into moulds. You can see your cousin's hairs standing up on her arms. You offer to help by taking the children to buy ice cream, and you look forward to the treat yourself.

Your offer does not turn out well, for Nyasha throws you a savage look as she strides off to fetch her purse. Carefully she counts out cents, looking at every coin twice to make sure she has the correct value. You wish, as you accept the fistful of change, that Mainini had moved from Kuwadzana to a reasonable area like the northern suburbs. Then you would find a way to make her invite you to live with her, and offer you a job, as she has offered Christine.

"Be good," your cousin orders her children. "If you are, we'll have a treat," she promises with a show of her old recklessness. "We'll all go out to the cinema at the weekend."

"Ten days, twice a day, that's twenty teas for fifteen people," your cousin goes on, not waiting for her brain to switch from one task to the other, letting everything stream in parallel.

"Stop at Mai Taka's on your way," she calls as you walk out. "And find out how she's doing."

CHAPTER 13

Mai Taka's leg is better. Her weekend begins with Saturday afternoon off. Nevertheless, she assures Nyasha she will work all day as she was absent the previous day of the great workshop cooking. As the family has planned an outing, by two o'clock she is dressed up in a turquoise tight-topped, loose-skirted dress. Excited about the trip to the cinema, her eyes shine with the prospect of folding the story away in her mind and undoing the bundle of it when she returns, to reproduce the wonder for her own little Taka, for his father has forbidden the boy to tag along when his mother is busy working for their common employers. You deck yourself out in the bottle-green trouser suit you bought with your teacher's salary. On your feet are the Lady Dis. You remind yourself finally to thank your cousin, but immediately you forget.

Cousin-Brother-in-Law unlocks the vehicle. Your niece and nephew shout and jump up and down, reciting a catechism of ice creams.

"Chocolate!"

"Cherry . . . cherry . . . ripple!"

"Vanilla!"

"The yellow one. It tastes like cream!"

"Oh, you mean Devonshire."

Panashe nods at his elder sister.

"Then say what you mean," Anesu returns tersely, sounding much like her mother.

"Def . . . Defsha," repeats Panashe triumphantly.

"Devonshire, OK. Listen! De . . . von . . . shire," corrects the sister.

"Dev'shire," your nephew finally manages. Your niece nods approval. The little boy grows more confident.

"But rum and raisins," he admits, happily shaking his head. "M-m, I hate rum and raisins."

"Rum and *raisin*," Anesu corrects her brother once again. "Children aren't meant to like it because it's got alcohol in it. Pana, you know what alcohol is, don't you?"

Panashe nods. "It's the wine Mama likes."

"Jah, that's one kind," Anesu sniffs, unimpressed by her brother's powers of observation. "That's it. That's why children don't like it," she goes on primly.

Chuckling happily, Panashe scrambles into Gloria. Mai Taka scoops your nephew onto her lap. Cousin-Brother-in-Law pats the boy's head and says, "You can have rum and raisin today if you want to. The rum taste is only flavouring."

"But he said he doesn't like it," points out Anesu. Panashe nods agreement.

In the ensuing silence, you all realize that you have finished organizing the children, that you are suspended in a state of waiting for Nyasha.

A screech like the cry of a furious banshee crashes through the garage. Leon's fist is balled the hooter.

"Papa!"

Anesu wrinkles her forehead and covers her ears with her hands. Panashe does the same.

Mai Taka ducks her head beneath Panashe's shoulder as the blare continues.

In the upstairs room next to the beauty spot a window opens. Everyone waits for Nyasha to poke out her head. She does not. The window closes again, just as slowly as it opened, annoying you with your cousin's game-playing. You hate such stages of waiting because you prefer to be moving, to have started without the anxiety embedded in arrival.

Finally the window opens all the way. Nyasha pops her head out and shouts down that she will leave the office in two minutes: she has almost finished the new concept for the next workshop in which the young women discover their own greatness, not in the cinema or in a boyfriend, but buried in themselves by means of telling their own stories.

Leon gives an I-told-you-so grunt, accompanied by a small, tight smile.

Missing this, Mai Taka straightens her neck and relaxes.

"Toda kuona Mary, Mary, Mary-wo," she sings a nursery rhyme. "We want to see Mary, Mary, Mary-wo."

Your niece and nephew do not know the chorus. Two minutes pass rapidly while they learn. Leon climbs out of the car and paces about the garage.

"How many times? How many times have I told you?" Cousin-Brother-in-Law grumbles when Nyasha finally appears.

"We are your family, Nyasha! You chose to have us. You chose to have me and both children. I would have been happy with you or just one child. We all suffered when you were pregnant. Even the one in your stomach. I am not. And your children are not participants in your workshop!" he shouts.

The children from next door crowd at the fence beyond the garage. They stick their noses and mouths through the wire mesh. Taka has gone over to play with them. His eyes large, he waves slowly at his mother.

"A mother is what they want," Cousin-Brother-in-Law insists. "They do not want a workshop facilitator."

"For God's sake," Nyasha says. "Whether they like it or not, I trained to be other things besides a female parent. So right now I am a workshop facilitator. Get over it!"

"Mary, Mary-wo," Mai Taka sings in a louder voice. The children join her.

You remember feet planted in circles, the sand white and the girl in the middle going round and round, singing in a high piercing voice about how she wanted to see Mary; and if any boys were brave enough to join the circle the girl might approach one and kneel down in front of him, miming with a hand on her head or back the ailment Mary suffered from, and the brave boy found an ailment no one had sung of and became Mary himself. Shocked and disappointed at Cousin-Brother-in-Law's outburst, which is not the superior conduct you expect of a European, you hold on to the memory, slipping away from a developing argument into dusty recall. If you are disillusioned by Cousin-Brother-in-Law, however, your anger is aimed at Nyasha, who cannot be grateful for the fact that, though her husband might be unpleasant on occasion, she never experiences the abuse that Mai Taka routinely endures.

You hum and then sing along to take your mind off the thickening atmosphere, deriving a new comfort from this unexpected childhood joy.

Climbing into the car again, Leon pushes the key into the ignition.

Nyasha sets her jaw. A moment later, she opens her mouth as though to let out something enormous and dangerously alive. Finally she inhales, breathing in without stopping as though she is pulling the sky down through her body into the ground. A moment later, she opens her door.

"Yay!" yell Panashe and Anesu.

"Mama's coming!" your niece and nephew shout. "Yes, yay, Mama!"

Nyasha brushes her lips to her husband's cheek. Cousin-Brother-in-Law's blue-knuckled fingers clench the steering wheel, but he does not start the motor until Nyasha is settled and has buckled her seat belt. For your part, you are relieved the fracas has ended peacefully, yet this only increases your rancour at your personal concerns, which exhibit no such easy resolution.

After you have jostled a few metres over the gap-toothed, mealie-cob drive, Nyasha starts on "Ten Green Bottles."

She sings too loudly, with dreadful discord, the result of trying too hard when she is too tired. "And if one green bottle should accidentally fall," the chorus echoes.

The children join in first, then everyone else, so that by the time Gloria rattles to a stop in front of the sagging gate you are all yelling at the top of your voices.

Cousin-Brother-in-Law, comforted by the repair of his relationship, leaves the car to deal with the security lock.

Silence, the guard who is Mai Taka's husband, appears noiselessly from the bushes.

"He is waiting for me," Mai Taka breathes, stiffening. "He said so: If you go with them you will see me. Now he is doing it."

"You, Wonderful! Mai Taka!" the night guard calls his wife.

"My God, my father, oh my mother," whispers Mai Taka. She turns a frozen gaze on her husband.

"I am getting out," she decides after a tense moment, her hand on the door handle.

"Stay there," Nyasha breathes, without moving her eyes or changing her tone, as though no one has approached and she has not seen anything.

Leon pushes the gate open while the security guard watches.

"I should not have come." Mai Taka shakes her head over the seat rest at your cousin. "I must go if I do not want someone to kick me tonight like I am that someone's football!"

Mai Taka lifts Panashe from her lap.

"Don't you dare open that door," your cousin hisses.

"It might be all right for her to go, Nyasha. Just let her get out nicely," you tell your cousin, alarmed at Nyasha's foolishness in treating Mai Taka as though she were a workshop participant.

"Mai Taka, can't you hear me?" Silence calls. He makes sure his tone is mild because Cousin-Brother-in-Law is approaching. Mai Taka sits petrified between the two authorities.

"What is the matter?" Cousin-Brother-in-Law asks, raising a hand to greet the night watchman.

"Afternoon, sir!" Silence nods. He rubs his palms together.

"Please, madam," Mai Taka begs, her breath so shallow and quick that she can scarcely form the words.

"Please, Mai Anesu, let me go. Otherwise I do not know what is going to happen. He is smiling, but when you know him, you will know why he smiles like that when he is angriest!"

157

"Angry?" your cousin says quietly. "We'll see about anger!"

"Silence! Baba Taka!" she calls winding down her window.

"Make space, everyone. Go on!" she orders you. "Let's get someone else in here."

Silence takes several steps forward. "Yes, madam?"

"Do you want transport to go somewhere?" asks Nyasha.

"No, madam," the guard replies. "I had made my plan where to go on my off this weekend. That one," he points his forehead toward his wife. His voice glitters and slithers like snakeskin. "That one knows it."

Cousin-Brother-in-Law finishes opening the gate and returns to the vehicle. Mai Taka chews her lips and bends her neck. In this position she decides the damage is already irreversible.

"Yes, I know it," Mai Taka storms at her husband. She straightens up and juts her chin. "And if you are going where you want on your off, Baba waTaka, I can go where I want too on mine. Today I know where I am going on my off. I am going to see the movie!"

"Be quiet, Mai Taka," Nyasha hisses again. "Thank you, BabawaTaka," she calls more loudly.

"You are going, madam?" Silence, whose presence curdles the blood of the most merciless of thieves, strolls forward. Taking a couple of strides, he plants himself in front of the vehicle.

"We are going," Nyasha confirms.

"All right," Silence nods steadily. "Then, may I speak to the boss?"

Leon, who is tapping his fingers on the steering wheel and does not speak Shona well enough to understand, wants to know what is going on.

"He wants to talk to you," says Nyasha.

"Yes, BabawaTaka, what is it?" begins Leon, looking out.

"Boss," says Silence.

"Is there a problem?" Leon says. "I am sure we can sort it out."

"I don't know if it is a problem," replies Silence. "I just want to know, is it good for my wife to think she belongs to another family? A family that is not mine? Even if it is the family of her Europeans?"

Nyasha rolls her eyes. You let the fifth green bottle fall. Then you cannot hold any bottles at all. One after another they plunge. You pray Mai Taka will disembark.

Leon pauses to reflect.

"Yes," he responds finally. "I see it is a good thing. A very good thing for one afternoon, Baba waTaka, if the family sees it like that also, and has asked her and they have agreed about what they are doing."

"But it is her afternoon off," Silence insists. "I know that work is work. I never question her or stop her when she comes to work. Her afternoon off is not time for working!"

"It is work," your cousin interjects icily. "As you see, Panashe is on her lap. That's why we need her."

"Boss," Silence goes on, ignoring your cousin, "I am saying, if it is work, no one can say anything against that. Mai Taka did not tell me about work. That is why when it is off, it is better to ask the husband."

"I think Mai Anesu has told you what is happening," Leon says, starting the car.

Silence raises his chin. His eyelids draw together until all that is visible is a bright darkness glistening through narrow slits.

"If she is working, she should have said," he nods quietly. "You see, my wife just lies to me. She said she just wanted to see this film at the shopping centre. She said it is what she wants. That is why she is not wearing her uniform."

"Are you the one who tells me to wear a uniform, Silence?" Mai Taka flares up. "No, it's not you who has to tell me!"

Silence shines the cold light of his eyes on his wife.

"Mai Taka," he warns. "Someone taught you to lie to me. I told you leave that one, that dress you are wearing. I told you put on your uniform. It is all right now. Go, I will see you when you come back."

"Ah, so why doesn't he move?" mutters Leon.

"You will tell me what I ask," Silence promises Mai Taka. He turns to Nyasha.

"Mai Anesu," the guard inquires, picking now at his fingernails. "If I work for you and you give me a house on your property, that house is for me and my family, is it not?"

"It is," says Nyasha. "As long as you are employed here."

"See!" Silence moves round to grasp the car bonnet on either side of his wife's window. He lowers his head between his arms so he can speak to her directly. "You have heard it for yourself. I want to hear what you say this evening when you return. When you are on my property."

You cannot stand the tension anymore. You lean across the children and the help and open the door. Silence pulls it wide. Mai Taka leans over and drags it closed.

Astonished, you all stare at Mai Taka, who defiantly presses down the lock.

"Mai Anesu, you said she is working, is that not so?" Silence begins again.

"Yes, Baba Taka," agrees his employer. "That is what I said."

"If it is work, it is overtime. Mai Anesu, she must be paid," says Silence, raising his chin.

"She will be paid," confirms Nyasha coldly. She turns to her husband with an intense look. After a minute Leon nods and Nyasha relaxes.

"All right? She will be paid," Cousin-Brother-in-Law says.

"Thank you, boss," Silence replies. He steps back and waves.

"Please, Mai Taka," Nyasha warns as you set off. "Please, be careful how you deal with your husband when you get back."

"Let's go," Mai Taka replies with determination.

"Yes," says Nyasha, sounding even more exhausted. "Let's."

You are wearied too by what has just passed. Only Mai Taka sits upright, her energy crackling around her.

"Nothing that happens now will stop anything anymore," Mai Taka shrugs. "In fact, from the time I went down yesterday, everything was already going to happen. Remember, Mai Anesu, I said, no, it's better for me not to go. He had already kicked my leg that morning. So what is going to happen today will happen when I have seen the film and not when I haven't seen it. Mai Anesu, now don't think of anything."

Anesu buries her face in the back of her mother's seat. Nyasha twists round to stroke her daughter's head. Leon rolls the car through the gate. Silence pulls on a listing pole to close it.

You look out of the window, your face pressed so close to the pane that the glass mists.

Your cousin has tracked down a new, able mechanic. So the car rumbles on as you ascend the little hill near Kamfinsa Shopping Centre and as Leon dodges potholes on Churchill Avenue.

Women who seem stunned by the fact of their existence trudge along the verges, babies on their backs, bags of seed and fertilizer on their heads, or else they simply stand, waiting for combis. Cousin-Brother-in-Law shakes his head as Gloria eases through the traffic lights, which are working.

"So here we are!" Your cousin forces gaiety into her voice when you finally turn in to the car park at Avondale Shopping Centre. "Now we can do what we've been meaning to do for ages. Have some fun."

Cousin-Brother-in-Law starts glowering again, as you walk through rows of four-wheel drives, most of them with white number plates, BMWs, and Mercedes-Benzes. Imagining dismal endings to the afternoon, you fear that fun is the last thing he is capable of having.

"That's your bourgeoisie," Leon mutters.

"A-nnn-na-nn-si," spells out Anesu, half-reading each letter, as they are taught in the new phonetic system. "A-na-n-si," the little girl repeats more fluently.

Anesu looks at her mother. Nyasha nods a smile. "Look, Panashe," she says. "It says what Anansi is, can you see?"

The sun flames off the tarmac. Panashe lifts his face and squints.

"No, no oranges, thanks," your cousin smiles at a fruit vendor who steps out from under the shade of a tree and accosts Leon, calling him "baas."

The vendor pleads. Nyasha rummages in her bag and makes a face when she finds no small change, only the note for the cinema tickets. The man's face cracks into a smile of hope.

"When I come out," your cousin says.

"They'll want muzungu prices," mutters Leon forlornly. So saying, he strides off toward the cinema.

"Mama!" warns Anesu, but it is too late.

Panashe works out the answer to his mother's question. "S-s-pa-ih-da-e-r . . . spider," he triumphs. "It says, Anansi, the spider."

Your nephew's face crumbles.

"I don't like spiders," quavers your nephew. "I don't want to see the spider!"

"Shit!" swears Nyasha under her breath.

"Go to the supermarket for the fruit and veg," says Leon when you catch up with him at the box office.

"Panashe doesn't want to see the spider film," sighs Nyasha.

"I don't like them! I don't want to see them!" the boy wails.

"Spiders with popcorn?" your cousin encourages hopefully. "And chocolate," she adds tentatively, as though her son were a little experiment.

Panashe starts crying.

Leon picks his son up, which makes your nephew pump his lungs full and howl at the top of his voice. People turn to see what the tall white man is doing to the little brown person.

"Incy wincy spider," chants Mai Taka, hooking her thumbs about each other and waving her fingers in Panashe's face. Her smile looms behind her waggling digits. In a few minutes Panashe is convinced the spider went up the wall only to be washed down the drain, and it is evident your nephew is not afraid as long as he keeps his arms around Mai Taka's legs.

"Four for Anansi. Two for *Pretty Woman*," orders Nyasha, rebelling at the counter.

Cousin-Brother-in-Law looks down his nose at her.

"Oh, all right, six for Anansi," says Nyasha.

When you emerge from the Elite 100 an hour and a half later, Anesu and Panashe chase each other around the foyer.

"Those ones! Ah, the West Africans. Those Nigerians," laughs Mai Taka.

"Ghanaians," corrects Leon.

"Oh, those Ghananians," Mai Taka bubbles with enjoyment. "I am so glad I saw it, Mai Anesu! And Panashe was enjoying it all the time.

I-ih, Mha-mha, when will we be able to do things like that? Like those from West Africa?"

Nyasha winces and Leon changes the conversation by saying he would like pineapple for the next day's breakfast. Nyasha pulls a list out of her bag and gives it to you with the change from the tickets, saying, "If you don't mind, Tambu."

The others saunter off to wait for you in the car, the children demanding a second ice cream.

In the supermarket next to the cinema, you prod thirsty-looking pineapples to discover a fresh one. This causes their leaves to fall off them. A woman comes up to examine the paw-paws. Your shoulders bump. She turns to look at you, and gasps, "Tambu!"

You recognize her immediately: Tracey Stevenson, your boss at Steers, D'Arcy and MacPedius, and, before that, your most dangerous rival for the class prize at the Young Ladies' College of the Sacred Heart. She stands before you grinning and holding out her hand. Your mouth dries as the evening at the nightclub with Christine laughs at you from a cave at the bottom of your heart. A handful of ants troop over your neck as you fight to dispel the notion that your former classmate can hear what you are thinking. The most recent memory overcome, you tremble as others crowd back. You are at the convent on your first day, and your uncle is already disappointed that you are not allocated rooms on the same basis as white girls are. Your lavatory is flooded because you are not allowed to use the white girls' toilets where the incinerators stand and, without an incinerator of your own, you and your roommates have thrown your pads into the toilet bowl. The headmistress makes a public announcement at assembly concerning the "African girls," their dirtiness, and their cost to the school. Then, as the war intensifies, she calls you to her office to reassure you, joking that no one will be cut in half to meet government quotas for African students. In spite of this, the only one from your dormitory, you take the school bus to the town hall on Friday evenings to knit woollens for the Rhodesian soldiers. Deep down, as you hunker in your seat, looking out of the window to repel conversation, you know that things are meant to be different. In the hall, clicking knitting needles chatter, "Mistake! Illogical!" There comes a time when you can no longer smile. No, you tell that other memory, the one that includes Tracey and trophies and the college moving goalposts; no, I will not think this.

Tracey pushes her trolley beside yours, commenting on the price of produce in relation to its quality, which she judges is on the verge of extortion, entirely fuelled by unrestrained corruption. You change the subject, asking about girls you both knew who were in your class. Tracey is still in touch with a few and gives you scraps of news. Neither of you has much shopping to do and you agree to catch up.

After delivering Leon's pineapple and Nyasha's groceries, you join Tracey for drinks at the Mediterranean Bakery next to the cinema. It is her treat. You marvel at the grace and ease with which your companion obtains his attention and extracts a menu from the waiter. She pores over the café's offerings for a few minutes, after which she declares she is uninterested in the burgers with chips, the chicken with chips, the pork chop with chips. The quiche is an option, but in the end she decides against it. You agree that you are not interested either. In the end your decision is not to eat, but only to drink.

"I remember what yours is," Tracey smiles. There is a patina of nostalgia in her voice as she orders two double gin and tonics. At the same moment, without a word, you both burst out laughing, recalling Steers, D'Arcy and MacPedius Advertising Agency happy hour on Friday evenings.

"You look as though you got through everything in one piece, though," Tracey says, squeezing citrus into her glass in an old habit. "And you've lost weight. That's great. I'm really glad. You're looking magnificent."

You nod. "I'm doing all right. You don't look so bad yourself."

"I've been looking out for you for a while now," Tracey says. "This place is a dorp. I thought I'd bump into you at some point. Well, it's happened, although it took a while."

She gazes at you directly and says, "You're not married, are you?"

When you do not answer, she lets the moment pass. You speak about school again, how you would have liked to keep in touch with more old classmates, and then turn to conversation concerning how the country is going to the dogs. You keep the waiter busy. You giggle. The sun goes down.

Hours later you sway on rolling paving stones, making too much noise and patting the black velvet of night, in an effort to say goodbye. Tracey finds everything bloody hilarious too and guides you by the elbow to her red Pajero after you accept her offer of a ride home.

She stops at a traffic light, telling you it got so bloody unbearable at the agency she had to leave after you did. At the corner of Churchill Avenue, the robot's red light flickers and goes out, leaving you in darkness. Across the intersection, three or four streetlights in a row are burnt out, then comes one that glows. In the dark spaces between the puddles of weak yellow light, flying insects whirl and hurl themselves against the windscreen, following their instincts for brighter places.

Krr-rr-rr, krr-rr-rr, the crickets shriek when the SUV pulls up at Nyasha's gate. Silence does not appear to unlock the padlock. You climb over the sagging barbed wire and careen up the cratered mealie-cob drive toward your cousin's house.

CHAPTER 14

For the first time since you left the hostel, or rather since you left the advertising agency on the pretence of marriage, your heart beats calmly in your chest. After your period of troubles, events are finally conspiring for you and not against you. This development that you desired so strongly is due, of all things, to your meeting with Tracey Stevenson. Scarcely allowing hope, you had prepared yourself as well as you were able for a much longer delay, only to have your wait shortened by your former colleague. Promising to keep in touch, she wrote down your number and gave you hers. You are satisfied that, concurring affably with everything she mentioned, displaying neither rudeness nor resentment, you played your part in reordering your affairs. You credit your first meal in the dayroom at the hospital for this beneficial improvement in your disposition. It was there that Widow Riley, confused as she was, revealed to you how perceptions, including of one such as you, do shift. This opened a crack in your estimation of yourself, through which you began a lethargic climb away from the lowliness to which you considered both born and condemned. Alone in your room, you laugh softly at the way the old woman took you for her daughter Edie. At your cousin's, your new cheerfulness is further encouraged by your growing relationship with your white, German relative.

You are, you observe with satisfaction, the only member of the household who enjoys such contentment. Mai Taka enters the kitchen on Monday making an effort to appear grateful for the excursion. The poor performance is easy to see through and Nyasha soon extracts from the help the news that, yes, she did sit down with little Taka on the evening of the outing to charm her boy with Anansi's antics. Silence, however, had barged in and forbidden Mai Taka to fill the boy's head with foreign nonsense. The next day he took Taka away with him. Mai Taka had not seen either of them since and would have been at her wit's end had she not received a message from her sister-in-law, whose son worked a few roads down, that Silence had deposited the boy with his grandmother, but that since he had not left any money for the boy's upkeep, Mai Taka should forward enough for the school levy, as well as Taka's birth certificate if she wanted the boy to continue with his education. Silence himself did not come home, so that she suspects he had spent the rest of the time in the arms of his fourteen-year-old lover. Mai Taka announces that she is relieved to have been spared a beating and observes it is like a blessing in disguise that her husband seems to have absconded. In conclusion she declares her only regret is not having taken her son to her own mother, but she philosophizes there is not much she can do about it, as a child, when the father is known, belongs to the paternal family. Concern over Mai Taka adds to Nyasha's worries over her workshops and her family.

For your part, uplifted by inner serenity, you surge with energy. There is not much into which you can channel your new vitality. You take to stargazing at night when the family has retired. You consult a children's encyclopedia that Nyasha and Leon have bought your niece and nephew, hoping for useful diagrams, but it is in German and concerned exclusively with the Northern Hemisphere. When Cousin-Brother-in-Law learns of this, he remembers an old *Birds of Africa* he purchased while in Kenya. It takes him several days to find it, but when he does, you spend long stretches with Cousin-Brother-in-Law's book and binoculars sitting on your little balcony, ticking off in pencil against their photographs the species that visit your relative's garden. Each morning you wake much earlier than has been your habit to hum softly if shrilly the birdsong of a turquoise-breasted starling that sits in one of the custard apple trees by the garage and chatters. You pop into the garden to see whether you can identify any other avian company and when this is done, you return to make yourself a cup of coffee.

"Mangwanani, Maiguru! Marara here?" Anesu and Panashe chorus as you enter one morning soon after the outing to the cinema.

You step over the glistening annelids on the floor and pick up a bottle of filtered water, which you empty into the kettle.

"Panashe, for goodness' sake, get on with it." Nyasha scowls at her son, appearing not to have heard your murmured greeting. Your nephew stares back at his mother, who, day by day, is growing more frazzled.

Anesu swallows a mouthful of porridge, wearing a contemplative expression.

"You sometimes have a tummy ache, right?" she asks her brother eventually.

Your niece keeps examining her brother. A drop balances on the rim of his eye, then splashes out.

"You have one now, don't you?" Anesu demands. "It's hurting, isn't it?"

A flood of tears soaks Panashe's face.

Anesu turns to her mother and says in an accusing voice, "You see, it's when you shout at him in the morning. That's why. It makes his tummy hurt."

"I didn't shout," says Nyasha curtly. She slits open a packet of red sausages that she intends to pack for her children's snacks.

"You did, Mama," an adamant Anesu points out. "That's why he hasn't done his shoelaces."

"You, young lady, and you too, Panashe, get on with it," Nyasha orders. "I'll do the shoelaces when he's finished eating. He's got to get some breakfast inside him."

Anesu balances her spoon on the edge of her plate. "It's only because he's frightened," she says.

She takes another mouthful of porridge before she continues, "He's done them before. He just doesn't want to go to school today. That's why he can't remember how to do it. He doesn't want his tummy to ache. Mama, his teacher makes his tummy ache too because she always hits the children."

Your cousin dabs a red sausage with kitchen paper, packs it in cling wrap, as though she has been concentrating on the task too intently to hear. A moment later, she puts the food down in shock.

"Hits? The little ones?"

"In Germany it is illegal," says Cousin-Brother-in-Law.

Your cousin looks as though she is about to sob, once again situating herself beyond your understanding. Weeping alongside a first grader— even nearly doing so—is a nauseating act of ghastly femininity. You have no desire to expend energy on sympathy for a minor matter of corporal punishment. Women in Zimbabwe are undaunted by such things. Your cousin, on the other hand, has been enfeebled by her so-journs first in England then in Europe. Acquiring a degree in political science at London School of Economics, another in filmmaking in Hamburg, and coming back to Zimbabwe where no one wants her to have either has caused her disposition to grow yet more fanciful. Zimbabwean women, you remind yourself, know how to order things to go away. They shriek with grief and throw themselves around. They go to war. They drug patients in order to get ahead. They get on with it. If one thing doesn't turn out, a Zimbabwean woman simply turns to another. Your head overflowing with such thoughts, you are pleased that your meeting with Tracey and your subsequent peace of mind over it prove that you are a true Zimbabwean woman. You suppress a shudder of pity for your cousin, who, notwithstanding her education and ideals, will never amount to anything. Nyasha does not belong. Like her husband, she is a kindly import. For the first time in your life you feel significantly superior.

Nyasha walks across to Panashe and pulls his head to her stomach as though she believes that the other side of it is the only place the little boy will be safe. Since he is sitting at the breakfast table, this is uncomfortable for your nephew, but he endures.

"Because of our past, we are people who understand how instincts can easily become brutal," says Cousin-Brother-in-Law. "We know such a thing must be stopped before it begins. We do not allow teachers to beat other people's children. Nobody is allowed to beat children."

"How are the children taught?" you ask. "How do they learn anything?"

Your cousin, who as a teenager was herself brutally beaten by her father, closes her eyes.

"Are you afraid of your teacher?" she asks her son when she looks about the kitchen again.

The boy shakes his head. A tear caught on his eyelash splashes to his lip.

"Yes, you are," Anesu insists, scooping honey into her milk. "You cried on the cricket pitch on Tuesday."

Panashe's tears drip faster.

"Tell Mama!" orders Anesu. "Tell Mama and Papa why you don't like your teacher."

Nyasha and Leon exchange glances.

"Tambudzai, what kind of society do you have here?" asks Cousin-Brother-in-Law. "What kind of country do you build when children are raised in fear?"

"People aren't afraid," you say. "What we are is disciplined. We know how to behave properly most of the time. We know how to teach people to do it."

"She scolds me," Panashe says to his mother. More tears roll down his cheeks. "If I don't understand, she says, you silly boy, why don't you understand. And she beats all the children."

"Does she beat you?" asks your cousin. "And the correct information is," she goes on, turning to her husband, "there's a law against it here too."

"Well, if there is a law, it doesn't seem to make it illegal," Leon smirks. He drums his fingers on the table to the rhythm of his favourite Fela.

"Once she did. She did once," Anesu reveals calmly. "Once she hit him."

"A boy did toilet in his pants, Mama," your nephew gulps. "The teacher hit him. With a hosepipe. Colin did toilet. It smelt bad. The teacher hit him and Colin did toilet because the teacher hit!"

Now tears roll quietly down Nyasha's cheeks. "This is a peace-loving country," she grunts.

You nod at Cousin-Brother-in-Law.

"Full of peace-loving people," Nyasha goes on, either ignoring you or not having seen you. "You read it every day in the newspapers. I hate to think what people do to their children in one that isn't."

You pour your coffee, finding that this little family is too emotional about everything, takes Western values about many matters too seriously, and this is—well, somewhat primitive.

"Skin them as soon as they do anything wrong," says Leon. "And make designer handbags out of them for the generals' wives. That is what they will do with them when they stop being peaceful."

Nyasha gives Leon a look, and he says, "Yes, I am telling it. I have to tell this because, as a German, I know. This kind of thing has been done."

"He didn't mean it, Panashe," Anesu bursts out after there is a pause. She leans over to her distraught brother. "He was only joking, weren't you, Papa? Nobody makes things out of children's skins."

"Don't worry." Nyasha dribbles honey into Panashe's cup of warm milk. She holds it to his mouth. The boy pushes his lips together fiercely.

"Panashe, I'm going to tell the head teacher a thing or two," Nyasha declares. She wipes away the boy's tears with the back of her hand. "That woman belongs in jail."

"Don't go," your nephew cries. "Mama, please don't go and tell the headmaster. He will . . . he will . . . *skin* me!"

"He will not put her in jail," says Leon. "You know, Nyasha, here no one ends up in jail if that is the place they should be."

Cousin-Brother-in-Law pulls his son onto his lap.

"Don't worry about that teacher anymore, Panashe," he says. "I will go with your mother to talk to the headmaster. Your shoes, your breakfast, anything at all, don't let the teacher or the headmaster or anyone at all stop you doing anything," he says. "No matter what."

Leon scoops up porridge from the spoon Nyasha has discarded. Slowly Panashe opens his mouth.

You concentrate on your cup to avoid taking part in the conversation. You are stirring sugar into your coffee, in preparation for leaving the kitchen as soon as possible, regretting having been drawn into the family's conversation, when the telephone rings.

"For you," Mai Taka calls.

Gratefully heading out of the kitchen with your mug, you take the receiver from her hand.

"Hi, Tahm-boo," the voice says. "It's Tracey Stevenson."

You set your cup down on the telephone stand slowly, so as not to be overwhelmed by what you have wished for and waited for. You are still all but stunned that your patience has paid off.

Tracey is very gracious. Without mentioning either your leaving the advertising agency or your meeting at the supermarket, she informs you she has contacted you to make you an offer. You ask for a moment to fetch pen and paper.

On your return, having rushed up to your room, you take down the organization's name: Green Jacaranda Getaway Safaris. No, you do not have an email address. Although it is still early days of the Internet, and not even Nyasha has it, you are ashamed. Tracey suggests a meeting in which she will give you more details of the post she has for you. Your fingers quiver. You still them, forcing yourself to forget the past and concentrate on the present moment. You record the place and time of the appointment. Tracey Stevenson was your boss. She is to be again. Beyond those two facts, your future beckons. You must hold on to your tomorrow at all costs.

Cousin-Brother-in-Law will not hear of you travelling to your appointment at another café in Avondale by combi and insists on driving you himself. You do not learn as much as you would like about Green Jacaranda beyond that it is a start-up dealing in environmentally friendly entrepreneurship solutions over a range of programmes. Your work in administration will include project management. Besides a salary that you are sure is several times what your cousin makes with her training, the deal includes accommodation, which, Tracey explains to you, is not an expression of the goodness of her heart, but a business decision that enables her to obtain appreciable tax benefits. Tracey asks you to report at the office on the first day of the following month. Auspiciously, in the last year of the millennium, you return to the ranks of the employed and see your prospects stretch out before you.

The day that Tracey requested you move is the last day of Nyasha's new workshop. Your cousin is tired. By the time you are to leave, Mai Taka has not come up from the servants' quarters.

"They'll be well occupied for a couple of hours," Nyasha says with grim satisfaction. "Now that they can't figure out what to write sensibly about themselves."

Your clothes are packed in the new suitcase your relatives bought for you. You do not know what to make of this, whether they are so unsophisticated as to spend the little they have on you and thus have less themselves, or whether it is their way of hurrying you away. You decide not to be concerned. The outcome of their gift is that you will make a better impression on Tracey than arriving with clothes in crumpled plastic bags and threadbare backpacks, and this is good. You thank them for the lovely suitcase for the hundredth time as you all troop down the stairs. They urge you not to mention it.

You have stashed the bag of mealie meal Kiri brought up to Harare from your mother in a corner of the wardrobe you have cleared of your belongings. You wish you had actually removed it as you intended. But there is so much clutter everywhere in the house, you are positive it will not be discovered for months. By that time it will no longer be edible and nobody will associate you with it. Abandoning the gift is an act as significant as digging up your umbilical cord and carrying it away from where it was buried. You feel greatly relieved as you enter the garage.

All the family are present to send you off. Leon arranges your belongings in Gloria's boot. Panashe holds a boxful of shoes out to his father and chatters on about a girl at school who habitually slew giants on Fridays.

"How does she slay them?" his mother asks.

"She ties them up with string," Panashe explains as you set off. "Then she puts lots and lots of candy-floss in his mouth. Lots and lots of candy-floss."

Anesu, who has grown quieter since her brother's crisis, listens while your nephew carefully explains the giant's torture. As the car shudders across the drive, a workshop participant races across the lawn.

"Slow down," Nyasha says.

The car stops.

"I am not going to write about me," the young woman says. She looks down at her stomach and says, "Can I write about my mother? She was shot. The person who shot her is free. Because of the pardon. The president's."

"Yes, write that," Nyasha says.

"Maybe it is about me, anyway," the girl says softly. "Since because of that man I am an orphan." Shoulders drooping lower, she starts back to the group.

"She is one of the three. Who got it the first time," Nyasha says.

Leon has his hands on the steering wheel, but has not remembered to drive.

"Let's go," Nyasha says.

Cousin-Brother-in-Law opens his mouth, then eases his foot off the brake without a word.

Down by the gate, down behind the bushes, the staff quarters' door flies off its hinges. Mai Taka rolls down the stone steps in front of the dirty-walled building. She lands in a heap in the sandy clearing at the foot of the steps. A shadowy figure hovers behind her. It leaps down the steps in one jump, swinging a bicycle chain round, like a propeller.

Mai Taka wears her nightdress. The chain cuts through the cloth. She scrambles up.

Nyasha turns Panashe's head away, then leaps out of the car, shouting at Leon to follow.

"Mai Taka! Mai Taka!" screams Anesu.

Mai Taka trips over bushes. A length of the cloth she holds to her chest catches in branches. Mai Taka rakes at the bush and shakes it. Silence stands outside the quarters. The chain dangles beside his feet in the sand.

"Come and help us, Silence, come and help us," Leon calls, approaching the help.

"Leon!" Nyasha cautions.

Cousin-Brother-in-Law drags his gaze from Silence to Mai Taka. His face pales with understanding. Nyasha wedges an arm under Mai Taka's shoulder, Cousin-Brother-in-Law pushes his under the other. They drag Mai Taka between them.

"You'll have to get out," Nyasha says when the three reach the car, because you are sitting there, watching.

She adds, "With the children."

Mai Taka's eyes swivel back in their orbits. The car smells like a rotten wound after you vacate it and the help climbs in.

Nyasha walks back to pick up out of the bush the cloth Mai Taka dropped. She stands motionless for many seconds before bending down. When she straightens up, she arranges the thing she has retrieved into a bundle.

"I didn't know," Nyasha whispers, returning to the car. "Mai Taka, I didn't know. I should have followed that gut suspicion I had, when I asked."

Mai Taka hugs the bundle and whimpers.

Mai Taka refuses to lie down on Anesu's bed or to recline in the living room on the sofa. Nyasha pushes a chair for the woman between the wall and the kitchen table. Mai Taka slumps forward. Leon and Nyasha discuss what to do with the injured patient, who needs to be treated, and with the bundle that must be incinerated.

"He will kill her," Nyasha says. "I've been doing my research. Doctors here don't like to talk, but when they do, they say they sew patients together a few times. Then the next time they see them, they open them up for the postmortem."

Mai Taka opens her eyes and asks, "Mai Anesu, where is my baby?"

"It is in the garage," Nyasha says. "I have put your fetus in a bucket with the towels you wrapped it in."

Mai Taka tries to stand up. Holding first on to the table and then on to the sink, she half crawls and half walks toward the garage.

"Leon, come," says Nyasha. "We'll take her to the hospital."

You remain with the children, who are upset by what they have seen. Once the three of you are alone, however, Panashe crawls onto your lap. Anesu goes through the bookshelf in her room and then you sit in Panashe's room, while your niece reads from *Die kleine Raupe Nimmersatt*. Trying to dismiss but not succeeding in pushing your delayed move from your cousin's house to the back of your mind, you pay no attention to the unfamiliar language.

When Nyasha and Leon return with Mai Taka, both children are asleep. Meeting the three in the kitchen, the first thing you notice is that the bundle is gone. Mai Taka, unsteady on her feet, is led to her kitchen chair. Her eyes keep opening and closing, showing too much white. Once the woman is settled, Leon leaves once more for the chemist's. They had tried several on the way but had not found one with a stock of the required medication.

"Something to eat now, Mai Taka?" Nyasha soothes the woman, holding her hand.

Mai Taka's eyes are closed. She shivers.

"Tea. Something little," Nyasha says. "Porridge. Sadza. There's lots of gravy. You must eat something for the medicine, even if it's little-little."

They have returned from Parirenyatwa Hospital with a list of charitable mission hospitals within a hundred-kilometre radius that offer immediate, affordable, and tolerable services, for though your relatives are covered by Leon's medical aid, the house help is not. Your cousin sits on the floor in the hall by the telephone and calls the first one on the list. The out-of-town lines are bad. Nyasha dials the same number again and again.

Leon returns three-quarters of an hour later with strong antibiotics and barbiturates.

"We have to go to St. Andrew's now," Nyasha says, coming back into the kitchen. "They'll take her and do it today, if we get there before four o'clock."

"That's a trip," says Leon. "I'll walk over and talk to Matthew, next door. Maybe he can lend us some money for the petrol."

You take Nyasha aside and negotiate to call Tracey to pick you up from your cousin's house. Nyasha has coaxed Mai Taka to lie down in Anesu's bed by the time you leave, having first told the little girl she would spend the night with her brother. Leon has not been able to borrow the money from the neighbour and is busy trying German colleagues.

PART 3
ARRIVING

CHAPTER 15

On the way to your new home, you remember how, in all the commotion surrounding Mai Taka and Silence, you have forgotten to thank your cousin suitably for the time you spent at her house. You had expected to do so in the car, once safely on your way, as premature gratitude could easily have eddied through the air to covetous spirits, giving them time to sabotage your happiness from envy. Resolving to call her as soon as you have settled in, when she has had time to manage the matter with Mai Taka, you decide to use part of your first salary to purchase Nyasha a thank-you present. This settled, you respond more freely to Tracey's small talk.

In Avondale West, not far from the Mediterranean Bakery, Tracey turns into a close. Each of half a dozen gateways arranged in a semicircle around the road leads to a quarter-acre plot. These pieces of land were dissected out of a sprawling farm decades ago as news of sunny Rhodesia—called "God's own country"—was circulated to attract dissatisfied Europeans from the north of the world. The former farmhouse, situated at the centre of the U, its grounds spreading out on either side, is still the largest, most imposing building. Smaller lots run up the sides of the road.

You had hoped, the day Tracey brought you to view your new home two weeks ago, that the former farmhouse would be yours. It was not too difficult, though, to swallow disappointment when the Pajero stopped halfway down the close, in front of the smallest building. You comforted yourself by observing how the outside of the house was newly renovated and neat, the terms reassuringly good: a modest amount deducted from your salary with an option within five years to exchange the lease for an agreement of sale. Restless to leave Nyasha's household, your savings from your period at the advertising agency, meagerly supplemented by your months of teaching, dangerously low, you quickly signed.

This afternoon, you are even more eager to recommence earning a living than you were a fortnight ago, when you first visited your new residence. The abject scene of Mai Taka and the impossibility of ferrying her to hospital, even though white Cousin-Brother-in-Law was involved, reminded you fearfully that the hardship of your village origins could pursue you in the city as well.

Tracey cuts the engine. The remote control does not work: there is no power at the moment. The gardener slides the gate open. The vehicle rolls toward a large bungalow behind which are staff quarters. The buildings are painted a dusky peach that glows warmly, like sunset, and there is a margin of brown along the bottom to prevent the walls being spoilt by splashes of dirt. You nod, giving a contented smile. You see yourself working hard from here until you make your way up as far as Borrowdale.

Behind a rainbow from a borehole-fed water sprinkler, the front garden and vegetable patch thrive like a Ministry of Agriculture model garden. There is only a hint of history, nothing unpleasant, in the ancient paving stones that lead to the house. When Tracey and you have grown used to each other, your boss tells you she employed an artist friend who did the props for the advertisements to age the new ones down. The gardener pushes the gate closed and stands to attention next to the Pajero.

"How are you, madam?" he salutes. His overalls are clean and tidy if old, his gumboots glossy at the top although the base is muddy. Mouth smiling, he raises his chin. His eyes gleam as he examines you.

"Remember, you're perfectly safe, Tambu," Tracey says as you climb out. She pronounces your name with a better accent, as though she has been practising since the weekend you met. "No one will get over that!" she exclaims with satisfaction, pointing at the redbrick back wall. "I asked them to put an extra metre on top above the standard, just to make sure," she continues. "No point in leaving anything to chance when in principle you can do something about it. And there's a boom at the top of the close that's manned every night. All the householders chip in. No one's going to mug you, or anything like that. So you don't need your own night watchman. Alfred can enjoy his sleep except on the nights he mans the boom."

The housekeeper, the gardener's wife, emerges from under a trellis covered with grapevine. As they were both off the day you visited, they are meeting you for the first time. After scrutinizing you for a few seconds, the man cups his hand over his heart. The woman curtseys. She claps twice after you shake hands.

"Where are you from, Mai?" you enquire politely as the couple haul loads of your luggage into their arms. "You are mai who?"

"Ma'Tabitha. I am from the Save River. But I married. To a man from afar, Phiri, from Malawi."

"VaPhiri, how are you?" you say to the gardener. You relax as he has done and raise your hands in a soundless clap. It is good to have someone around from closer to your home than Harare. You chat briefly about the river the woman mentioned, since you once spent several days' holiday there with Babamukuru and his family a quarter of a century ago.

"They were with the property before I bought it," says Tracey, "which makes everything much easier. It's as if they own the place and you're the odd one out. Very convenient for a working woman."

Once more you refuse to harbour anything like resentment or jealousy concerning Tracey's diverse advantages, such as the salary she had earned at the advertising agency that was many times yours by virtue of her being an advertising executive while you were a mere copywriter, although your qualifications were similar, and were obtained from the same institutions—first the Young Ladies' College of the Sacred Heart, and then the university in Harare. You swallow the past of your common school days and remind yourself that Tracey had a year more work experience than you do, as you had repeated your A levels at which second chance you scored only average marks, whereas she had excelled at her first attempt. Your smile, like Ba' and Ma'Tabitha's, etches deeper into your face. Like them you cannot indulge yourself in any discontent. You must be happy with what you have and how much better it is than where you have been. The long trek from the hostel has ended. You possess the contract to a wonderful bungalow that after five years will become your property. You cannot allow anything else to matter.

Tracey has Ba' and Ma'Tabitha go on ahead, stopping under the grapevine that leads to the back entrance to admire the glitterstone swimming pool on the northern side of the building.

"You don't swim, do you?" she asks. "Unless you've learnt in between. They say glitterstone's cold," she cautions. "But your favourite place at school was behind the hall with your books and that blanket of yours. Not the swimming pool, really."

You laugh and move on. When Nyasha comes, Panashe and Anesu will splash in that pool. So will Leon.

"I love these black granite surfaces," says Tracey as you enter the kitchen. She runs a finger over the speckled countertops.

You imitate the gesture, enjoying the smoothness.

"I did tell you it's all local, didn't I?" she goes on. "Do you know, five of the ten best stone sculptors in the world are Zimbabwean?"

"Yes," you tell her, grateful for your lesson from Cousin-Brother-in-Law. "I'd love to see their pieces."

Your smile expanding on your face, you compare the stone colours to Mai Manyanga's ochre. You are overwhelmed. Your good fortune all but brings you to tears as you stand next to your boss, digesting how you have earned your own kitchen without having to marry any of the Manyanga brothers.

"That history of ours in stone goes back centuries. To the dzimbahwe and the Zimbabwe birds," your boss muses. "I've got to find a way to put that into the Green Jacaranda itinerary. I haven't been able to so far as, well, the stone quarrying isn't exactly green. Still," she goes on, leading the way, "in principle, there's got to be a solution! After all, we do try to make it sustainable."

You follow your boss to the living room, a wide airy space that opens through French windows onto the front garden. You run your palm over a black granite coffee table framed in wood from a historical railway sleeper. Next you drop onto an ivory-coloured leather sofa.

"Nice, isn't it?" Tracey nods with a grin that acknowledges your appreciation. "It's so obvious, you'd think it would occur to more people to add value to our heritage," she continues, making you think of your cousin Nyasha, whose mind, like your boss's, does not leave a matter once it decides to settle. You smile again, at Tracey's enthusiasm.

"Not very likely, though," she proceeds with some disappointment. "Not with the guys we have in government. We've got a good fair trade deal with the suppliers down in Mutoko. So we hope it's just vicious rumours about the government nationalizing everything. This indigenization thing. What d'you think they're doing, Tambu?"

Smile steady, you raise your shoulders and shake your head.

Tracey cocks hers to the side in scarcely disguised surprise. "You must have an opinion," she says, settling on the sofa arm, which indents under her weight. "Everyone does. No one can't. Especially not these days."

"I don't believe in politics," you say, hoping the answer is acceptable, and wondering, if it is not, what answer would be preferable.

"Of course you do." Tracey says. "Otherwise there's no way you'd have moved out from that cushy job at the agency. And there was that note you wrote, with that rot about getting married. I thought, hmm, there's more than meets the eye here. Quite the politician. Well, that makes two of us who realized we had to get out," she goes on, crossing the room to an armchair. "In principle three," she adds in afterthought as she leans back. "With Pedzi. Although that's not quite the same as I headhunted her before she left on her own the way we did."

You are startled to hear Tracey call a job that had been so grossly unfair that it had exhausted your long patience "cushy." At the same time, you had never in your life been concerned with politics. You understand that people like you, who are clawing their way forward, do not have time for it. Most recently you have been so concerned with your personal predicament that you have not thought much about the subject at all, leaving such to Nyasha and Leon. Struck by Tracey's assumption that you would have considered such matters, caught unaware by her probing, which forebodes unanticipated, sensitive angles to your job, you ignore the jolt you suffer on hearing of Pedzi.

"Shall we leave them here?" Ma'Tabitha calls from the hall. She indicates the pile of baggage she and Ba'Tabitha have brought in and stacked.

Tracey stands up, saying she will leave you to settle in. You are about to ask Ma'Tabitha to take the bags to the bedroom when you remember your arrival on the other side of town in Gloria.

"Bring the rest," you say when you have picked up as much as you can carry.

"It is no problem, madam! I will carry them!" Ma'Tabitha smiles and insists you relinquish your load.

Pedzi, who had been the receptionist at the agency, is the receptionist-cum-typist-cum-project-officer at Green Jacaranda Safaris. She comes round the receptionist's desk to give you a hug on the day you begin. She is genuinely pleased to see you and confides she cannot keep up with the workload as the organization expands. You hug her back. After this moment of intimacy, you stand apart, look each other up and down, and declare how well and beautiful and marvellously styled the other looks. You disclaim the compliment, while Pedzi, on the other hand, pleased, says, "Thank you!" After this moment of reunion, she motions you to a minimalist, post-colonial Zimbo-chic wrought iron and leather chair. Asking you, with professional politeness, to wait so that Tracey can show you around, she speaks softly into the intercom, in a low-pitched business voice. You remember how none of the clients at Steers et al. ever forgot that voice and sometimes called the agency just in order to hear her speak.

Tracey comes through immediately. Laying an arm round your shoulders, she asks whether you have settled in over the weekend, then begins a tour of the premises.

"It came to me while I was at the agency," she confides, leading you into the interior. "I was in this terrible place where I couldn't reconcile what I was doing with what I believed in. Making more money for people with so much they didn't need more at one point stopped being all that fulfilling. Honey Valley, Blue Train," she says, ticking off the accounts she worked on. "Afro Sheen. That one did it. It was like getting people to pay for something instead of getting something from the product. But I loved what I was doing, the variety, the people, the buzz, everything. So I started reading around and thinking about it, and that's when I came up with ecotourism!"

Your boss holds the swing door from the reception into the business area open for you.

"This way we can sensitize people to and advocate against climate change at the same time as we're doing business," Tracey explains, brimming with the enthusiasm with which she did everything, from sending electric shocks up frogs' legs in the biology lab at Sacred Heart to sitting in on a campaign recording. Your boss's excitement ignites your own dormant appetite for adventure. Savouring a sense that this office is the perfect place for you, you are confident you will achieve more success than you did at the convent and advertising agency. It is small and safe, a sheltered community in which you will garner recognition for work well done, and with this acknowledgement will finally come the upward mobility you are so hungry for.

"We can actually show our clients what the change in the weather is doing to the most vulnerable while they enjoy a normal safari. Green Jacaranda Safaris is the first NGO to come up with the concept," continues Tracey proudly, leading you up a narrow hall that has no window. You are disappointed that your new workplace is not as lavish as the advertising offices had been. You are, however, pleased to be part of a proper establishment and not obliged to improvise in a run-down house like your cousin must.

"Our edge is that we're forward looking, visionary. We don't bring people in from Europe to workshop our locals. We've got a unique product, maximizing what we've got on the ground. It's like adding value to our weather. Everyone loves it. Zimbabwe's always going to be here. People are always going to want great weather. In principle, it's our one definitely sustainable resource. Climate tourism is the next big thing. There'll be dozens of ventures like ours in five years' time, but we'll have this country, and if things go the way I intend, even all of southern Africa, covered."

Your boss indicates a room to the right with a nod. Remarking, "That's the boardroom," she opens the door.

The longish, rather narrow space faces Jason Moyo Avenue to the north. The city council has made an effort to keep this part of the Central Business District, which everyone calls the CBD, presentable, since the old five-star Thomas Hotel, visible from the boardroom's far window, stands in the next block. The central park, renamed Africa Unity Square from Cecil Square soon after Independence, with its paths arranged in the pattern of the British flag, which is green and clean enough for people to lounge on the grass, lies across the way from the hotel. Looking out at this view, you enjoy a welcome sense of security.

Tracey leans against a windowsill. "The rents down here aren't what they used to be. That's good," she says. "We had to soundproof it. Now we've done that, it's fine for our purposes."

On your way out, your heart sinks as you catch sight through the other window of another Zimbabwe, whose heart is the Fourth Street Bus Terminus. People are moving in from the rural areas. The migration is swelling the terminus, distending it toward your offices. The city council, skilfully deploying avoidance strategies in preference to planning, is issuing transport licences to numerous combi owners in an attempt, it is said, to prevent the snaking queues of people becoming so desperate for transport that they riot. With the increase in travellers, in the terminus, and the roads around it are developing into markets. Women and adolescent boys sell airtime, vegetables, mazhanje and matohwe fruit, which are not stocked in supermarkets, and cheap Chinese biscuits, almost to the Green Jacaranda block doorstep. The city council has abandoned cleaning in favour of other pursuits. A pall of decaying leaves, pods, plastic wrappers, and peels is heaped at every corner. Tracey tells you she pays one of the vagrants twice a week to pile rubbish from the overflowing bins in the nearby sanitary lane and burn it. Turning your back to the view, you admire the dining suite, which is of the same post-colonial Zimbo-chic design as in the reception, that serves as boardroom furniture.

"We'll move one day," grins Tracey. "For the moment, this place serves its purpose. Our corporate values are investment, building the future, not wasting it. I get to put funds into the programme instead of paying those guys who've taken over the upmarket buildings. If I were a donor, Tambu, I wouldn't put a cent into today's development aid bling!" She looks proudly at the table and chairs. "Everything's one hundred percent local. The proper boardroom fixtures will be too, when we get them."

You walk back into the hall. Tracey gestures at a door and tells you, "That will be your office."

"Space to swing the proverbial cat," you say with a chuckle, peering inside.

Tracey gives you a look and says, "That's the idea."

The room is separated from the boardroom by a tiny space, which turns out to be an extremely orderly stationery cupboard.

"Loos," Tracey waves at two doors on the left. "Did you read that article about the city's water reticulation system in last week's *Clarion*? Apparently Harare doesn't have a reticulation system anymore because the old one rusted away. That's what's causing the water problems. At least partly. You know, like the cholera Pedzi said they had in Mabvuku. And goodness knows where else they're not telling us about. Chitungwiza, I bet! We're going backward, Tambu. Peasants, serfs, warlords, running sewage. It's so Middle Ages! So I put in a shower as well, for all those low-pressure days. It makes everyone feel a little more comfortable. So, in principle it's a good investment."

Forecasting that the politicians will keep the water supply to the Central Business District functioning in order not to jeopardize their own affairs, Tracey asks what you think about the disintegrating service delivery in the city. You respond that with the rate of change being so fast, it is difficult to form an opinion. To your relief, Tracey lets this go and proceeds down the passage to a nook at the end where a sink, hot plate, fridge, and cupboard have been installed to make a kitchen.

"And this," she smiles proudly, turning from the alcove after she has pointed out all the appliances, and returning to a door she had passed, "is where I do the things that are important for my soul."

Inside, your boss settles behind a mukwa desk and gestures for you to take a seat on a chair done up in leather upholstery that softens a frame of the same softly glowing wood.

"Welcome, Tambu, to Green Jacaranda Getaway Safaris, the only exclusive ecotourism service on the whole continent. Which we happen to have thought up right here. There's so much we could do for this country. In this country." She shakes her head. "I don't know if we ever will. The odds seem so much against everything. You know what, Tambu? You and I will have to make a plan."

Skirting this invitation to engage, you tell your boss how delighted you are to have an opportunity to serve her pioneering establishment.

When you have finished, she says, "Here," and passes a brochure across the desk.

"This time I want an answer. Tell me truly what you think."

Your boss's demand for another opinion so soon is frustrating; it is absurd even that Tracey should ask for truth now, so early, when you have not had time to weigh anything.

"Think of it like bouncing ideas around," Tracey smiles. "The way we used to do at the advertising agency."

"I see there is a website," you say, endeavouring to appear familiar with the technology and hoping you sound professional. "I would like to have a look at it first. To connect everything I've seen and that I will be observing and learning in the next few days."

"We don't have the billboards here," your boss tells you. "Our agents distribute those overseas. We haven't started offering the tours locally yet. Everyone has a kumusha, although, in principle, you never know—the townspeople—I've been thinking of doing something for children. One day maybe. But our clients are from Sweden, Denmark, some from Germany. Places like that. Some Spanish and Italians. The government's working on the Chinese, which promises to be a great market, but, it's all bilateral with the Asians, you know. Looking east. Surely you've heard and can tell me the implications of that?"

You nod noncommittally, trying to recall the phrases in the newspapers you browsed through occasionally at your cousin's.

"The Chinese are interested in governments, not people," continues Tracey. "That being the case, we can't get to them, especially given our funding sources. So in principle it's your Europeans. That's an established market so, for the time being, we can't change our continent's 'single singular thought.' Nature, which naturally also means weather. Sun. As time goes on and things get worse or better, we'll strategize for the next phase."

You hand the brochure back.

"The thing is to consolidate. I want us to get to the point where we're running along sustainably. Then we can start shifting the paradigm."

Tracey turns the flyer over in her fingers.

Four women laugh up at her as a moment ago they beamed up at you. The bodies beneath the faces are wrapped in brightly patterned Zambia cloths. One woman kneels on the ground behind a clay water pot. Another stands beside the first, carrying her jar in her arms. The third one still has her vessel positioned on her head upon a head pad. She is not using her hands but balances it perfectly. The fourth has her bum out, arms spread, and one leg raised in some kind of dance. Behind them is a semicircle of pole and dagga huts.

"The world's finest organic game," the tagline reads. "Eat only what you dare to pick, kill, or catch . . . The ultimate eco—in African." You know there is no such language as African, but you kept your expression constant as you read and continue to do so now.

Your boss gazes at each of the women in turn. "We didn't want to use head pads," she sighs, remembering the photo shoot. "But our kind of hair's so slippery we had to go with it. You need good hair to work properly with those things. So"—she is apologetic—"these models are . . . well, since they in principle are our market, we just had to go with the pads."

You nod and tell your boss that she had made the correct decision.

CHAPTER 16

You put a certain nagging wretchedness down to how much has slipped away from throughout your life. You are unable to stifle a recurrent anxiety that exasperates during your early days of employment at Green Jacaranda. Concerned not to let your newest opportunity float away, you are constantly on the lookout for handholds, like low-lying branches above a raging river, which you can grasp first to balance yourself and, subsequently, to heave yourself upward, which in this case means northward to the affluent suburbs that signal undeniable success. The environment in the building, however, depresses you, holding out not much promise that you are on track to meet the future you are chasing.

The only exception to the general air of discouragement that rests over the building comes from the shopfront enterprise on—surprisingly enough—the eastern, bus terminal side, which is run by a woman called Mai Moetsabi. You are amazed to discover that although she is not Zimbabwean, she presides over her establishment, the Queen of Africa Boutique, with admirable work habits. You arrive for duty at half past seven every morning to find Mai Moetsabi's boutique doors already open. In the first part of the morning, she waves a welcome to staff arriving for work and later nods at all who go into the building on business. Her desk faces the entrance to her shop, allowing her to greet everyone entering throughout the many hours she is present. Displayed in flamboyant constellations throughout her store, Mai Moetsabi's garments are of best Ghanaian wax print and Nigerian lace, offset by satins, shiny as the recently discovered diamonds of the eastern regions. She books seats on the new Air Zimbabwe flight to Beijing via Singapore in search of silks and trinkets. Shoppers are still going in and out with appreciative murmurs when you leave at five in the evening. The woman reassures you, for her success, although she looks sufficiently like you to pass as a woman from your village, is indisputable. Her achievement nods, yes, women like you can flourish. By the time you arrive at Green Jacaranda, Mai Moetsabi's well-to-do, competent, and yet gregarious air has earned her, with grudging recognition that is not quite respect, with an inflection that stops short of affection, the same name she gave to her shop, the Queen of Africa.

Past Queen Moetsabi's boutique, your office building veers into a passage. Down one side of this entrance loom unlit booths, where every individual's ambition is partitioned into half a square metre. In these stands are desperately stocked, though seldom bought, phone cards, plastic jewellery, and traditional cures with added value in the form of plastic wrapping and shipping costs from East Asia.

Opposite the cramped stalls is a space that the mysterious proprietor of your building, who is whispered to be a serving cabinet minister, calls a studio. Here three aspiring young seamstresses—diplomas in dressmaking from the People's College of Zimbabwe hung on the wall—bicker and scowl at each other. Sharing half a dozen tailors and two sewing machines to produce workmen's overalls, layettes, and orderlies' dustcoats in poly-cotton, their squabbling escalates into threats whenever a customer approaches and they tussle for business. You rarely see the same face in the studio twice. Visitors on tailoring errands, who always receive a gracious nod from Mai Moetsabi, are normally first-time customers, or people returning items they bought with complaints that the cut is asymmetrical or that seams are crooked. A shouting match generally erupts when this happens, for, rather than admit their mistakes, the young graduates search for segments of perfectly straight stitches on the returned garments, after which they fling insults at their clients.

The only other affluent-looking location in the building is the street front opposite Queen Moetsabi's. You never venture into it, for its air is as grim and repelling as the Queen of Africa's is inviting. There, under the impassive eye of a woman known to all merely as Sister Mai Gamu, two nervous copy typists committed, when you first arrived, hand-written CVs to two-page memory stores on secondhand electrical typewriters. "Is it on now?" "It isn't!" "It is!" "It's gone!" the overwrought young women call to each other as the power supply surges and wanes, shouting so loudly in their frustration that people pursuing their affairs in the entrance hall laugh at them.

You learn, before your first month at Green Jacaranda is over, to keep clear of Sister Mai Gamu, and to pity the young women she employs when you catch a glimpse of them through the large glass windows, their faces to the wall, waggling plugs this way and that to coax their defective machines into working. One eye stone blue with cataract although she has not yet reached forty, Mai Gamu writes up larger orders and does the cash box. It is rumoured she is an incognito politician's wife, at fifth or sixth far down the matrimonial ladder, hence her permanent expression of intent to commit grievous assault. To prevent such a scandal, the politician bought the building that Green Jacaranda Safaris is housed in and gave his wife the western shop front.

You meet the women who make up your office building's community as you enter the building, in the lift and on the staircase when the lift is broken. From bits and pieces, spoken kindly enough not to raise any alarm in your mind at first, you discover Mai Moetsabi, whose commercial shrewdness you so admire, left her home in Botswana a few years after your own country's independence in search of a freedom fighter her church in Francistown had sheltered in the nineteen seventies. Several of the women working in the building being single mothers and disappointed, a joke went round that the short foreign woman only smiled like that and was successful because she never found him. Rumours or none, the garments in the Queen of Africa Boutique shimmer and glitter like good omens of the new abundant life you have recently begun and are determined—at any cost—to hold on to.

In the second or third, in any case, no later than the fourth month after you commence employment at Green Jacaranda, there is a commotion on Jason Moyo Avenue below your offices. Mai Moetsabi had worked late the night before, not only creating a fetching new display in the storefront window, but also developing the theme in appealing ways throughout her shop floor. By midmorning of the following day, a group of youths had gathered on the pavement outside her shop. They are enthusiastic and keen, pointing out particular garments to each other, pressing their faces close to the windows and staring as though they are guests at a Paris catwalk. The one or two who have cell phones and money in them, SMS their "maFace." The crowd keeps growing hour by hour. By lunchtime the window Pedzi opens to cool the reception lets a buzzing commotion from the street into the room.

"What's bringing them here?" Pedzi murmurs as you squeeze through the press of bodies on your way to buy lunch at the Eastside Arcade since the samoosa man you usually purchase from has not appeared. "Just because of that woman from Botswana down there, who says she's the queen of Africa?"

At the food stall, you choose coleslaw and a hamburger from a menu that includes smoked sausages, curry with chips or rice, as well as two kinds of sadza accompanied by pigs' trotters or goulash. Crossing back to the office, you meet the samoosa man for whom you had waited in vain. He lifts an anxious hand, muttering, "Ah, I came and saw it wasn't a place to come. Aiwa, it's like that! I'll see if I can come and serve you, my customers, tomorrow."

Turning the corner onto Jason Moyo, you jar to a halt, seeing that the crowd has grown thicker. Assessing the situation to be not significantly threatening, you thread your way through the churning bodies that block the entrance. Pedzi's shoulders bump into yours. A couple of bona fide clients clutch their wallets as they push by. You make it to the lift and jab the button, grateful that your lunch pack is intact.

"Hey! Hey!" a high, timid voice calls.

You turn around. You cannot see who is speaking. Pedzi stands on tiptoe to assess what is going on, although this only adds one or two centimetres to her height as she is already wearing heels.

"Are you listening to me?" The voice rises more shrilly.

"She's come out of Queen Moetsabi's. It's one of the girls," Pedzi reports to you, chewing a chip and looking down for a brief moment before she turns back to the tumult. Her fingers extract chips from their oily bag and raise them to her mouth automatically.

"Hey, imi!" the voice quivers on. "I've been sent to tell you not to block everywhere like that. To let through the people with money."

"Ha-a-a," a rough voice answers. "Who are you to tell us where to stand?"

"Yes, that boss of yours should come out if she wants to speak to us, and not send us little children."

"Tell me, my young sister," a young man says. "Can it be that you have grown your own testicles?"

In the hilarity that follows, someone else bawls, "We can't be sure what medicine these foreigners are bringing here, that can cause a sex change in little females."

The lift does not arrive. You press the button again and stare up at the blinking light that tells you it is stuck on the fourth floor.

"I'm sure I've seen that one. The one who began talking about Mai Moetsabi. He's always in Sister Mai Gamu's shop," Pedzi whispers. "The man and woman he's with, too. The three of them spend the day in there often."

"If that woman doesn't want us to see what she's doing, why did she come here all the way from Botswana in the first place?" yet another voice roars.

"Haa-a, then she should just go back. Because this is Zimbabwe!"

A patter of song comes from the pavement.

"Mbuya Nehanda kufa wachitaura, shuwa," a sharp tenor leads. "Mbuya Nehanda died with these words on her lips."

"Kuti tino tora sei mabasa?" singers respond, adapting the old war anthem about how to take back the country to the more current concern of procuring jobs. "Tora gidi uzvitonge. Take a gun and rule yourself."

There is a small explosion, followed by the sound of glass splintering on concrete.

"Brothers, sisters," a calm voice calls. It is the queen of Africa. "Relatives, don't be angry, please."

The singing grows more ferocious. "Tino tora sei mabasa? How can we take jobs?"

"Up the stairs," says Pedzi, kicking off her high heels. Living in Mabvuku, she is quick to react at the first signs of any mob violence. Pausing only to gather up her shoes, she shouts at you to follow.

You do not flee immediately, transfixed by the queen of Africa, whose voice grows gentler and firmer.

"It is just this young lady. We are sorry! Please forgive her if she doesn't know how to talk to you. That is why I have come out now. To talk to you properly. We are very sorry!"

The crowd gradually quiets down. Your foot on the bottom stair, you are astonished at Mai Moetsabi's bravery.

"Say sorry," the queen orders.

"Sorry," the little girl squeaks.

"Louder!" a male voice calls from the crowd.

"Sorry!" the young woman shrieks.

A murmur of amusement ripples through the throng.

"No, it's not about treating each other badly," says Mai Moetsabi in even tones that carry not a hint of indignation. "I only wanted her to thank you for your interest and to ask anyone who wants to buy anything or see anything more to come into the shop. I will show you everything, but let us make a way to walk," says the queen.

The trio of two men and a young woman gives a victory laugh and detaches itself from the crowd.

The rumours start up the very same week that the near-riot happens.

"With all that fat, it's a pity she got there so quickly to sort the boys out. As if she's even black. She's only yellow, like all those BaTswana," says a woman who runs a spa on the second floor.

"She says she keeps going back to build some classrooms and a hall at the school she went to in that little dry country of theirs," the hairdresser, who runs the second spa on that floor, rasps. "Ha! That's what they say. Don't we know people like that only travel to get muti for their business? Parts of twins and albinos."

197

There is some talk of how the medicine must be working well because politicians have been seen amongst Mai Moetsabi's clients. Further whispers link the unruly afternoon mob to Sister Mai Gamu, arguing that the politician's wife wants the Queen of Africa Boutique for herself because she thinks the medicine charm will still be potent.

The rumours escalate into discontent.

"Ask me if she will last to the end of the year."

"Don't worry. She can't. No one can do anything if that wife of someone is against you."

The atmosphere in the building worsens.

The women's expressions grow satisfied as Mai Moetsabi appears to be losing the battle that her fine performance precipitated. Prior to the upheaval, there had been on occasion, particularly on May 25, Africa Day, photographs in the *Clarion* and other newspapers of some of the country's dignitaries wearing African attire, said to be purchased from the Queen of Africa. You and Pedzi occasionally played a game called "spot the Queen of Africa garment on the national leader." In the weeks after the disturbance in front of Mai Moetsabi's the photographs undergo a transformation as the leaders and their wives replace kente and ankara with Chanel, Pierre Cardin, and Gucci. Whether due to this new preference amongst the elite, or because of other causes, Queen Moetsabi's business soon falls into decline. There is snickering in the lift and corridors over this development. For your part, you are alarmed to see Mai Moetsabi, whom you so respected, descend too into a state you recognize with foreboding: one in which success is impossible.

However, the queen surprises you and everybody else by rallying. She adds nail polish, lipstick, and manicure sets to her displays. Slowly she phases out the West African fabrics. She contracts a young woman with qualifications from the polytechnic to sit with cuticle cutters, nail buffs, and razor blades at a folding table set in a corner of the shop.

At this enterprise, which you find so thrilling, the spa women's complexions grow duller. Life seeps out of their eyes. In the end they are replaced by two inspired young women who encroach on Sister Mai Gamu's territory with a couple of computers discarded by a local businessman. Observing the Queen of Africa, where business is different but as brisk as usual, with resentful admiration, the seamstresses on the ground floor predict that the new typists will not last until Easter. The comments are particularly sarcastic concerning Ms. Ngwenya, who comes from Bulawayo.

These events raise your anxiety levels once again. The question of who can and who cannot, who does and who does not succeed, returns to echo ominously, bringing bitterness back into your soul. You doubt that, were you put to such a test, you would find the inner resources to triumph as Mai Moetsabi has. You are discouraged by thoughts that it is only a matter of time until your work tosses further trials your way, even though your energy is still depleted by the events that took you to Nyasha's. Once more, you hear the hyena laughing as you drift off to sleep. In a final effort to remain focused on your ambitions, undistracted by your own misgivings or the society around you, you set out to emulate Queen Moetsabi. You take to braving combi queues half a kilometre long early in the morning in order to arrive at work by seven o'clock. Your tensions are exacerbated by unexpected hikes in fares after you have calculated your monthly budget. Gritting your teeth, you add a frightening 10 percent to your transport allocation. Practically your only encouragement comes from submitting your reports ahead of schedule, despite increasingly frequent random power outages.

At the office you speak regularly with hotel owners in Harare and airline chief executives to ensure the best service for Green Jacaranda customers. You administer evaluation questionnaires to the company's clients on their last night in the country. Tracey entrusts the statistical analysis to you from the beginning. After some time you take on the task of developing the company's shorter questionnaires for the different sites that the tourists stay at, although Tracey continues to generate the main one that assesses the overall tour.

During this interval, Pedzi becomes secretive. Your colleague takes to arriving at work earlier than either you or the queen of Africa. She spends less time in banter and chatter with you and the other women in the building. She sits in thrall in front of her computer at lunchtime. When the office is not busy, she makes surreptitious phone calls.

One day, after a month of her solitary pursuits, Pedzi arrives at the usual time carrying two files she has just photocopied at Ms. Ngwenya's. The receptionist hands the documents to Tracey. Her eyes sparkle with anticipation as she requests the boss to read them at once, and launches into a two-minute pitch concerning low-budget excursions into high-density suburbs. Tracey raises her eyebrows in interest and explains how she enjoys having ideas suggested to her by her employees provided it leads to progress. She promises to examine Pedzi's proposal after she has completed her morning round of phone calls and emails.

True to her word, Tracey calls Pedzi into her office after mid-morning tea. The door closes. They do not emerge until the man who sells samoosas comes by to ask if they want any. You knock on the door. They are sitting on the mukwa and leather chairs, opposite each other, bent over the small table between them on which Pedzi's files lie open. Tracey's short spiky hair mixes with Pedzi's purple weave. You are asked to deliver the usual order of coleslaw (large) and two samoosas each. As you depart, Tracey calls you back and asks you to make them some tea.

You do as requested, feeling like a kettle that takes too long to boil: people might well lose interest in tea and go on to something stronger. You ponder, as you serve the receptionist and boss lunch, how young Pedzi, for all her belly piercing and fake fingernails, has shown herself more proficient than you where it matters—in giving birth to ideas. You realize Pedzi's new ability is far superior to your copywriting expertise, which you displayed so skilfully while she, Tracey, and you worked at the advertising agency. There you were fed figures, positioning statements, and articles from trade magazines. Here Pedzi, as astonishingly as Mai Moetsabi, has created a fine potential out of nothing. As everything was created once already, in her act of presenting her documents, Pedzi has fashioned herself ahead of you into a co- or at the very least into a quasi creator. Your stomach tightens bitterly as you close the door on the intently concentrating pair. They do not even take the time to say thank you. As your fear deepens, you focus it and nourish it on Pedzi.

A few days later, you are called into the boss's office along with Pedzi for the decision. Tracey's verdict is that your colleague's programme is not original. Tracey has downloaded several files from the Internet that show there is competition from several countries in the area of high-density suburb tourism. One file outlines plans to do the same in some New York ghettos and send the money raised over to your region. Another shows how a concern in South Africa has removed all the risk by constructing the ghetto in an upmarket area. Your hopes rise at these revelations, only to be dashed when, after a ten-minute presentation, Tracey concludes that the receptionist's proposal is nevertheless sound and marketable. Since it is a novelty in the country, she and Pedzi will prepare it for pitching to potential investors and Pedzi herself shall occupy the position of project manager. Tracey starts a brainstorming session to find a suitable title for the new initiative. You find yourself unable to contribute. Pedzi drops phrases like "Coolest Cruisings" and "There. Where? Mabvuku!" chanting the name of her high-density township to a hip-hop beat. Tracey says that while it sounds good, it will not work on paper. The debate goes on for the best part of an hour. Disbelief stuns you when the two women agree on "Postmodern Neo-Urban High-Density Networking in Climatically Vulnerable Digitally Disadvantaged Sectors." You place mental bets on the possibility of Pedzi being successful, at the same time entertaining horrible visions of the erstwhile receptionist becoming a codirector with Tracey and firing you.

What does in fact transpire is that Pedzi continues with co- or quasi creating her project. You observe her elevating herself, finding yourself incapable of devising any action that will give you your own advantage, or of blocking the former receptionist who, since you are also a project manager, has raised herself to become formally your equal.

Bearing in mind that the boss will not move Green Jacaranda Safaris to new premises and needing an office in which she can attend to her creation, Pedzi grasps her aspiration in both hands and goes off to speak to Sister Mai Gamu. When the women in the building find out, the rumours boil over. Everyone predicts your colleague will have to leave within six months since Mai Gamu cannot stomach anyone but herself aspiring to anything, as was quite clearly shown during the drama with the queen of Africa. Contrary to everyone's forecasts, however, within a few weeks of Pedzi's presentation to Tracey, the politician allocates Green Jacaranda an additional cubbyhole of office space. The area is narrow and dark, lit only by a small window high in the wall that opens onto the dim sanitary lane at the back of the block. The three-plate stove and small fridge have to be manoeuvred into new positions to access the door to the extra office. With Tracey and Pedzi, you spend the best part of a morning doing this.

A small desk and chair arrive, as well as a couple of shelves, all in your offices' post-colonial Zimbo-chic. Realizing there is no alternative, you hug Pedzi, tell her how pleased you are for her, and offer her any help she might need. Considering a comment about swinging a cat, possibly by its tail, you think better of it.

The women in the other storeys, though, have much to say about the latest developments at Green Jacaranda. After you have congratulated Pedzi, you take to going down at the end of the day to join the irate gossip. The main object of discussion is how the allocation of Green Jacaranda's extra office has nothing at all to do with Pedzi, how Tracey had in fact had a secret meeting with Mai Gamu, at which she, Tracey, shouted a whole lot of ruling party slogans, which only went to show that you truly could never trust white people. During one gossip session, one or two of the women start toyi-toying and raising clenched fists. There is some brandy in someone's handbag. Sipping and dancing, the women end up threatening to take the lift to Green Jacaranda to show your European boss she will never be able to chant party slogans better than they can, not even if she lives for a thousand years. To prevent chaos, two women stand up to restrain the war dancers, and after this you realize you must have nothing more to do with these people.

CHAPTER 17

Your niece and nephew visit you in your new home perhaps twice a month. They enjoy your pool. Ba'Tabitha shows Leon how to work the pump against the time when he and Nyasha will have their own. You treat your cousin and her family to sumptuous braais when they agree to stay for a meal. This is not often. On the occasions they do, Ba'Tabitha gets the fire going and Ma'Tabitha marinates the beef, chicken, pork and kudu, buffalo, or ostrich with chilli and coriander from the garden. Cousin-Brother-in-Law indulges in the game meat that you order from a wholesaler at a massive discount, courtesy of working at Green Jacaranda. Your in-law says he loves his shift at the grill and keeps turning the meat cuts, so they take longer than envisaged to brown. Nyasha says she uses the time to gather herself. You leave her "gathering herself" beside the pool or in the white leather chairs in the living room as you huddle with Ma'Tabitha over sauces and salads. You smile down and pat heads when your niece and nephew run into the kitchen demanding ice cream. Anesu remembers fondly the time that you took them to the ice cream man when their mother was cooking.

Inwardly, however, your dread looms in shuffling shadows. The malevolent voices of the women in your building crescendo above you in your sleep. A horrible atmosphere of repressed violence descends over the Green Jacaranda building. It settles round you as though it is your aura. You discern its presence engulfing you distinctly. You grow increasingly petrified that others too must perceive it. You labour under a sense that something unspeakable is about to occur, or that you will execute this abominable happening. Many times you come to believe you *are* the unutterable occurrence.

You become so agitated you cannot sleep in spite of the antidepressants Dr. Winton prescribed. Your concentration falters. You make mistakes in your analyses and send hotels the wrong questionnaires. Pedzi looms as an increasing threat, and your fear of what all this forebodes causes further deterioration. It does not help that Green Jacaranda pays for driving school as Tracey, maybe sensing your disarray, decides you should, in due course, leave the office to supervise tours in the field. You are so distraught over the statistics that you fail the written test several times. Your attempts at the road test edge toward double figures.

Beside yourself with apprehension, when your relatives are not visiting, you spend more and more of your free time curled up on your leather sofa in front of your television. Their visits in turn become less frequent. As the weather is warm, you often doze off and wake up on the couch in the early morning. You rise, struggling to summon back to mind the matters you must remember without recalling the ghastliness that haunts you.

You arrive home late one night after having remained at the office for several hours to read all the information on competitors you can find, as well as Asian and Latin American sites in order to identify new activities for the approaching group of tourists. Unable to think of a single innovation, your confidence in being able to manage the tours not only adequately but excellently, the latest condition for keeping pace with your colleagues, deserts you. The hyena laughs as you enter the gate. It has slunk once more as close to you as your skin, ready to drag away the last scraps of certainty you have preserved the moment you falter.

Even though everything is already impossible, it all grows worse when you enter the kitchen. A small sack sits on the table. It is the bag of mealie meal that Christine brought to the city from your mother.

"It was left here by Mai Anesu," says Ma'Tabitha, who is waiting up for you, although you have told her not to.

Silently you curse yourself for not having hidden the bag well enough and when you have done with yourself, you swear at your cousin. You refuse the dinner that Ma'Tabitha offers and pace from living room to bedroom, unable to settle. When she finally leaves, you stand by the kitchen table staring at the small sack of meal, which is by now covered in weevil webs and emits a stronger, staler must than ever. You should have eaten it, you reprimand yourself, cooked your mother's love while at Mai Manyanga's and taken it into your body. In this way you would have made a home wherever you were. At these thoughts, anger overcomes you. You drag the sack off the table and push it into the dustbin. You fetch a bottle of wine from the pantry, switch on the TV, and force yourself to be engrossed in an Australian soap that is showing on the satellite channel. You fill the long advertisement pauses with lengthy draughts from your glass and are quite surprised to find a few hours later that you have drunk all three of the bottles you had stored. Vaguely you smile, for the horror that lurks at the back of your mind has dissolved into a blur of dim purple fur. The TV drones, your head whooshes. You doze off without realizing it. You wake frantically brushing away a column of ants that troops over your stomach.

You open your eyes. They march on. You close your eyes. The insects continue parading. Staring at them the thing you promised yourself you will never recall pops back into memory. She is a corpse, long dead, lying by a bus shelter, dined on by creeping things, gnawed at by scavengers.

You rush away from her into the kitchen. Once and for all, you must bury this woman. You rip the lid from the rubbish bin and heave up the bag of mealie meal. You scatter its contents across the floor and over the furniture. While rage flays at you like a whip, you scoop the meal up again and run out into the garden. There, you drag the hoe from the garage. You dig a hole deep as a grave and pour in the gift from your mother.

Dogs bark far away. To your ears, they are drawing closer, as to hunted quarry. Unnerved, you lumber to your room, pulling off your blouse as you stumble. You want your head concealed beneath the bed covers, your body on the mattress curled into a ball like a fetus. Stretching forward to search for pyjamas, you sway back from the bed, stricken. You switch off the light. You flick it on again. This makes no difference.

Growing as does your horror, a head lies on your pillow. You plunge the room into darkness once more then flood it with light again. Features and proportions change as the head mutates into a small, misshapen person.

The legs convulse and shatter into an army of students in the green and beige of Northlea uniform. Rushing forward with a scream, you grip one between finger and thumb to flow her away. Her teeth fasten on the flesh of your thumb. You realize it is your mother. You shake your hand. She holds on. Banging your wrist against its rim you succeed finally in throwing her into the wastepaper bin by the door.

"A womb," she sobs. "One just like mine. You want to drown me in it!"

The basket is of woven sisal. Your mother grabs at the threads, struggling, yet unable, to haul herself out. You surge back across the room, grasping for the next diminutive apparition that has also metamorphosed into your mother.

"A womb! Oh no, how can it be! How can a womb tell me what is what? Baba wanguwe, oh my father! You elders, how can it happen?" your mother screams as you dispose of the next one beside her. Both of them strive to climb out, tearing and groping at each other until they lose hold and slither back down.

You spend the rest of the night picking up the creatures in uniform who are your mother and interring them in the wastepaper bin, lobbing them in and pulling your dressing gown over the top to prevent their escape while you trap the remainder.

When you wake, you are in bed. Your dressing gown still covers the bin. You pick up your slippers, as you had grasped a stone at the market more than two years ago, with the intention of hurling them, this time at your wastepaper bin, but you do not throw as you become aware that someone is howling. A scream wails about the room, making the windowpanes shudder. You clamp your teeth. The cry continues. It is the howl you had wished that girl Elizabeth to utter. It was meant to be her, so that you would not have to scream it.

For many days thereafter you go to work without having closed your eyes, propped up on your bed with a book that you pretend to read.

You dare doze off only in your office where you are surrounded by people. When you wake, you fret, worried that your colleagues might catch you napping. You take more time to complete your tasks and make more mistakes. It is an increasing effort to correct them. You recognize you have taken a certain path, arrived at a place you had not known was your journey's destination and locked yourself in. Sorrow and shame prevent you from divulging your torment and confusion to anyone. As the days pass and each night crawls by, you repeat to yourself the conversations you had with Nyasha the evening you arrived at your cousin's. Finally, after many such episodes, you resolve to launch a search for your freedom.

At first you intend to use the telephone. In the end, you get out of bed in the middle of a wakeful night to write a letter. You sit with pen in hand, struggling to bring your heart round to finish what is necessary. When you do begin to set phrases down, you spend hours in anguished composition; for though it seemed acceptable—even glorious—to you at the time, you find now no cause compelling enough to justify such brutality as you wrought upon a young person whose education had been handed over to you. With every word you inscribe on your paper, scratch out, and rewrite, you understand that in addition to her skin, you shattered a young girl's trust.

You think to find out where Elizabeth lives and send her money, to put bills in an envelope and hand it to someone outside her house. But then you speculate that she is writing her final examinations by now and waiting to attend university, so that the sum you can spare will be of little account, will serve only to make her and her family angrier than ever at futile dollars flung in their faces without consultation. How you regret now, in the solitude of night, scorning the opportunity you had in Mrs. Samaita's office when reparation could have been made for at least part of what you had committed.

"Go-go-go, madam!"

Someone is tapping at the window. It is Ma'Tabitha. Your first impulse is to ignore the noise but you are afraid of more loneliness so that it is good to see another human being.

"What is it?" you ask.

She cannot hear you. You open your curtain and point to the front door.

Ma'Tabitha's face looms out of the night. She steps forward, barely dressed in a night dress, a Zambia cloth, and a pair of flip-flops.

You open the window.

"The light? I saw it," she whispers anxiously. "I always see it. Only today it was too much."

Flying ants raised by a brief storm flutter around the porch lamp.

"Come in," you return. "It's just that? You don't want anything?"

"When the light stayed on all the time and then the big one went on, I wondered," Ma'Tabitha's whisper continues. "I said so to Ba'Tabitha. I said to my husband, can everything be all right when the light in madam's is on all the time? He said, go and check."

You wait. She does not move.

"I see," you nod.

"Are you all right, madam?"

You pull yourself together and reply that you are meditating on a business matter and have been doing so for a number of nights.

"I am sorry, madam. I did not want to disturb you," Ma'Tabitha apologizes. "Ba'Tabitha and I thought maybe something has happened."

"Thank you, Ma'Tabitha, everything is all right!" You force a smile and add, "Please, do not call me madam." You pause and take a deep breath before you continue. "Ms. It is Ms. Sigauke."

"Good night, madam."

You hold her gaze with yours.

"Good night, Madam Ms. Sigauke," Ma'Tabitha says.

You listen to the sound of her flip-flops, the slap of rubber on her sole followed by the softer thump of her foot striking the ground. When you cannot hear her anymore, leaving the window open on a sudden fancy, you return to your letter and rethink the course you must take. What will happen if you discover the Chinembiris' address? Will they laugh at your coming, after all this time, to say you are sorry: If you were woman enough to thrash their daughter as you did, what has happened to develop in you the weakness of contrition? Should they smell feebleness, what will they do? How large is Elizabeth's family and who are they? What number of young uncles, cousin- and womb-brothers will there be, if they decide on retribution?

Having considered all, you compose two lines asking Mrs. Samaita for a meeting. You carry the envelope to work and put it in the out tray for Pedzi, who still does the reception work in spite of being promoted to project manager.

Mrs. Samaita's office phones a few days later, and on the very next afternoon you take a seat in the wobbly wooden chair in front of the desk where you sat for your interview on the day you met her. You gaze wistfully past the headmistress at the cupboard full of trophies.

Mrs. Samaita is distressed when you tell her you must, without delay, apologize to Elizabeth and her family. You are given to understand that the young woman is now permanently deaf in one ear and that she missed several months of school for rehabilitation so that she is now a year behind. The headmistress suggests you speak to Elizabeth there and then with no further undertaking. Relief rises in your chest at this mention of an easier option. Could this be a way out? you wonder. In the end you remain adamant, for now that you have brought yourself to it, you are single-minded about your repentance. In the end Elizabeth is called in. She pretends she does not see you apart from responding to your "Mhoro, hello, Elizabeth!" She will not tell you herself, but agrees that the headmistress may give you her home address.

Your former pupil lives in Highfields, in the area of housing where rent had been two pounds during the colonial days, but the government at Independence transformed much of the settlement into a home-ownership area. Many people owned their houses now and the Chinembiris too had worked their way into this situation, so that, without a landlord to evict anyone, many of the clan had migrated from various farms and communal lands to the little building.

When you arrive, Mai Chinembiri is bent over the small hump of verge that marks the limit of the road and the beginning of her property. She has built up, running parallel to the street, a ridge of earth and is putting in some sweet potato seedlings. A band of young men— whom you take to be various of Elizabeth's relatives—are smoking by the gate, while another group of older men lounge on the steps to the little house drinking Shake-Shake from cardboard cartons.

You are respectful. You introduce yourself as Ms. Tambudzai Sigauke.

"Oh, so you are the one who goes round killing other people's children," Elizabeth's elder brother says when the introductions are finished. He squints down his cigarette. "And breaking their ears, haikona!"

You bend your head. Tears fall out of your eyes of their own accord. You clench your jaw so that they will not see this weakness.

"Look at her! Ha, maybe something was wrong. See how sorry she is," a voice calls slowly from the porch. You feel the speaker's eyes taking you in.

"Wouldn't you be sorry," his neighbour, who, unlike the others, is sipping from a Scud, begins dryly. "You would, wouldn't you, if someone was about to do to you exactly what you did to another, and you knew the very thing you had done to this other person?"

"You never know," the elder brother agrees with the last Chinembiri. "Maybe she only wants to look down on us some more. When do people like her ever see us?"

"If she was a politician, I'd say on voting day," the Scud drinker suggests. "Maybe that's what she's practising for, don't you think?"

Some of the young men smile, but the curve in their lips is tense, their eyes hard.

"Auntie, leave now. We've seen you. Tomorrow, we will know who you are. But if you go now, quietly without causing any trouble with anyone here, we will just say it is finished," decides the elder brother.

The atmosphere lightens a fraction.

"Do what he says," the second youth says. "He's holding himself in, but we are the ones who know this person. You don't. When he bursts out nothing can hold him."

Mai Chinembiri cleans her hands on her Zambia wrap.

"I have heard everything and I do not know why you are still standing there," she says to you quietly. Your ex-pupil's mother lifts her chin. "Why are you not moving? Why? It is not your ear that is now not hearing."

When you remain standing, the woman first narrows then closes her eyes. The young men wait. Mai Chinembiri looks at the youths. Finally she moves forward, an arm extended.

You take her hand. You want to hold it, but she pulls away at first contact.

"This way," she nods. You follow her to the back porch. You walk round the side of the house, for each of her three rooms is packed with mattresses, blankets, and clothes stacked in cardboard boxes.

At the back, you sit on a wooden stool. Mai Chinembiri takes a seat on the bottom step. You sit in silence for a long time.

"I have come," you begin at last.

"As I see," Elizabeth's mother says. "Her father is not here. That is good. He said this second time he does not want to see you."

You nod. "Where is she? Can I ask you to forgive me?"

"Her heart is like her father's," Mai Chinembiri responds. "I spoke to her quite a few times before you came. She behaved as though I did not say anything."

"Shall I wait?"

"Perhaps another time if you and I speak well together. But it is hard for him. You know now his daughter can no longer hear everything. As for her!" Mai Chinembiri gulps, her voice wet with tears that course down her face. "As for her, when I speak to her, I have told you, it is as though she cannot hear anything. She says I did not protect her."

"Don't do that, Mai," you whisper, taking her hand.

This time the mother does not have the strength to shake you off. Grief flows to and fro through your intertwined fingers, and the tears from your two faces mingle so that it is as though you are washing your hands. Ah, how you wish the tears would cleanse away everything the four hands hold.

After a little while Mai Chinembiri pulls away. She wipes the back of her hand across her eyes. The wetness smears over her face.

"It is done," she says. "Whether you come or you do not there is no longer any difference. Perhaps we could have saved that ear if we could have paid for the hospital."

The woman regards you accusingly. "The money came from the school after two weeks. Her class, they did that for Elizabeth but then it was too late for the ear to keep on hearing."

Your regret tastes foul in your mouth. You know you have prescribed for yourself a life sentence. You repeat your request for forgiveness anyway. Mai Chinembiri remains silent. As there is nothing more you can do, you repeat softly your apology and prepare to leave, saying you will do what you can for Elizabeth if the family finds a specialist. The mother agrees, although you both know it is too far for Mrs. Chinembiri to heave herself over the ridge of sweet potatoes beside the road, in search of an ENT surgeon.

"We had planned something for you," the elder brother says, as you walk past the front of the building. "I hope we never see you again, because that will make things better for all of us."

You watch the road furtively as you walk, hardly daring to raise your head, hoping to see Elizabeth's green skirt approach down the narrow road from the combi rank, but only the young men's silence thickens behind you, and then the silence is taken and tossed away by the shouts, the curses, the laughter of neighbourhood life.

CHAPTER 18

The money you had imagined you might spend on Elizabeth you end up spending on yourself. You have a weekly appointment with the hairdresser, instead of once a month as recommended. You order the most expensive hot oil and sulphur treatments each time and experiment lavishly with Indian, Brazilian, and Korean weaves. You indulge yourself with diverse manicures and pedicures. You graduate rapidly to Thai foot massages. On the masseur's mattress you prefer the Swedish. Eyebrows are plucked, hairs are electrocuted, you are wrapped in mud, and pores are shocked into closure. Your skin grows soft and smooth. Your clothes account at Jason Moyo department stores edges toward the sum in your bank account. The rigours of the past years having whittled your body down, young men glance at you twice, while young women assume grudging "if only I could be like her" expressions. You do not see anything these days, when you look into the mirror, except the reflection of your bedroom and imported satin sheets, your two cell phones, and far beyond that a shadowy outline mocked up with blush, lipstick, and eyebrow pencil that you do not examine in any way for substance.

Leaving the office on weekdays, you turn not toward the Fourth Street bus terminus but walk down to the cinema complex on Robert Mugabe Avenue. There, after haggling with the attendant who wishes you to sit through one screening and then return to the foyer to purchase another ticket, you savour victory when you are permitted to pay up front for both the evening sessions. You sit until the very last note of music has vibrated away over the end credits, not once weeping, never brightened by gladness. After the cinema, you take a solitary dinner in a nearby restaurant, this being preferable to a lonely repast at home that relaxes too much, enabling the unease that wafts beneath your polished exterior to leak through your depleted defences. Once the waiter has brought your order, feeling neither hunger nor satiation nor enjoyment, you clear your plate. After that you trek through a number of night-clubs, picking up cacophonous company on the way, yet always avoiding the Island in case you bump into Christine.

At weekends, you sit in Harare Gardens. You watch couples cuddling on the lawn and taking wedding photos with their arms around each other. At these times, regret over not moving in on the Manyanga brothers ripples through the hollowness in your chest. You hold an image of Larkey in your mind for some seconds, then you breathe in deeply, clench your jaw, and force the vain pining from your mind.

You decide to inquire about an experienced nganga. This solution turns out to be impossible, like all else you have tried. You cannot ask Baba and Ma'Tabitha. Seeking solace and such personal advice from your domestics is unthinkable. Tracey has no idea of those things and Pedzi is a high-swag city girl who would enjoy a laugh at your predicament. Auntie Marsha does the horoscope in the *Clarion*. She is too foolish to attend to. Instead you visit the Queen Victoria Library on Saturday mornings before you take up position in the park, looking for information on occult and spiritual divining.

At work you revert to the old pattern from the advertising agency, in which you deliver admirably to order, but cannot begin anything without instruction. All the same, you are a model of decorum, showing impeccable deference to everybody you meet in your building's community. You take to greeting Sister Mai Gamu as affably as you wave at the queen of Africa. You nod cordially to the politician's wife's typists and, on the few mornings that you feel exceptionally courteous, you extend the pleasantries to asking how supplies of paper and ink cartridges are, under the prevailing difficult circumstances in the country. You buy a couple of quarter-litre bottles of brandy, which you tuck away in your handbag, against the Gossip Club accosting you on the stairs or in the lift, but although you see them through the windows in the office doors, they no longer summon you to enter.

In the office, you take care to solicit, every day, lunch requests from Pedzi and Tracey. This you do in order to preempt them with volition before they order your service, thereby reminding you again of your position relative to theirs, your built-in inadequacy that prevents you engaging with their exuberant sorority. Later, you knock, then carefully set down their orders, which they now thank you for, as they are no longer in the first throes of creating their new product. You smile and express your willingness to see to it immediately, if they require any further attention. All the while you simmer internally with resentment.

The one upward current in your situation is that after six months of failing, you finally obtain your driver's licence. This accomplishment coincides with the inauguration of Pedzi's project. You realize you have taken too many attempts to succeed at the road test when Tracey looks at your certification with a quiet nod of her head and instructs Pedzi to buy a Highway Code booklet and make an appointment for her provisional licence. Comparing yourself to Pedzi, as always, considering that Pedzi will probably obtain her road licence the first time she attempts it, dulls your pleasure in your achievement. Your dissatisfaction increases whenever you enter your car and head for the office or home. Then the purple Mazda SUV that Green Jacaranda purchased for you swerves perilously through amber traffic lights and in and out of queues of cars. Furious, you honk twice as loudly back at anyone who sounds a hooter in displeasure.

At the premises, while Tracey works on new signings, sponsors, and programmes, and attends to the eco-spin-offs that include the granite miners, you dream of being out in the savannah or climbing mountains as you busy yourself with the overseas agents and their holidaymaker clients, as well as with your principal responsibilities of bookings and statistical analysis. Your boss has built up her ecotourism enterprise in the northwest of the county on her brother's, Nils Stevenson's, farm. This you learn several weeks after your final road test, being then called into Tracey's office and offered a seat, as at your first day. As discreetly as possible, while still allowing you to feel like a valued member of the organization, Tracey reveals how she settled for the arrangement with her brother when old Mrs. Stevenson died first, followed in one year to the week by the departure of her husband. As stubbornly as the family had resisted putting an *e* into Nils's name in order to celebrate their Viking origins, Nils resisted his sister's claim to any part of the family property. On leaving Steers, D'Arcy and MacPedius Advertising Agency, your boss threatened her brother with the law. The outcome was an out-of-court settlement sanctioned by the Zimbabwe Tourism Authority that allowed her to build a village on several acres of the ranch. The agreement stated the land was to be sectioned within five years of the date of signature. However, as Tracey became much too busy with the success of her venture, greatly due to the location of her project next to a water hole, the subdivision did not take place.

After accepting formal congratulations for acquiring your driving licence, you receive the news you have been longing to hear. In addition to the statistical analysis and bookings, now, finally, you will accompany the company's clients as tour supervisor. According to this plan, you are to bring a much-needed capacity into the organization that has so far been outsourced at unjustifiable expense in the opinion of Green Jacaranda and its donors, as Green Jacaranda already employs three full-time staff. Tracey's eyes are bright but noncommittal as she relays this. Your success at your rationalizing task will upgrade your position from project manager to that of tour manager in due course, if all goes well. Tracey wishes you good luck and lets you know you are under a three-month probation period.

You surrender to this new task, as though your job is the God whom you met for the first time decades before when you arrived at your uncle's Methodist mission. You enjoyed many trips around all parts of the country when you lived with your relatives, for your uncle put into practice during the holidays his belief that seeing was part of education. He always included a lecture during the family outings: Mr. Smith's Kariba hydroelectricity plant and the sunken Tonga village whose outraged spirits stirred the river snake god to eat up several Italian engineers, to say nothing of their workers. Then Rhodes's grave up in the Matopo Hills overlooking Bulawayo, which had once been the most potent shrine of Mwari, the God of all people from Zambia through your own country and into South Africa, where freedom fighters under cover of night held sacred cleansing rituals during the war, and which, you had discovered as you researched for advertising campaigns, young male Zimbabweans now marked their property with urine. The magic of these sites was strong and real to your teenage person. It hovered over the crumbling location that you visited as Zimbabwe Ruins, that you encountered again at Steers, D'Arcy and MacPedius Advertising Agency, rehabilitated and renamed Great Zimbabwe. Your promotion is like an opening up of time that allows you to recharge your middle-aged soul with your determined young self. There was generosity in that earlier person, flowing from delight at those years' exuberance, when the journeys undertaken with Babamukuru and his family induced a conviction that you were a person amongst people, like all others, part of a marvellous world. You welcome the rebirth of your youthful exhilaration and are eager to pass on your excitement to your clients during visits to the sites you have not visited for decades.

The watering hole Tracey chose as the site of Green Jacaranda Safaris does not shrink at the same pace as other well-frequented water sources in the parched, sandy plains of the northwest. By the time you arrive with your contingent of tourists, it has withdrawn a mere half metre or so from where its bank emerged when the Stevensons acquired it; but the elephants still wade to the middle to siphon water up into their trunks and out onto their backs. Buffalo still wallow in muddy satisfaction at the pool's edges. You are soon accustomed to seeing a full five Xs against the items on big game viewing each time you gather the client satisfaction questionnaires.

It is immensely beautiful up on the Stevensons' property. Every morning, recalling at this serene moment during the tour your upbringing first at the mission and then at the convent, you murmur a short prayer, giving thanks for being surprised by such happiness when you believed you had lost all capacity for revival or betterment. There is exquisite delight in the ripple of pale gold grass over the plain. Immeasurable peace abides in a giraffe's neck curving brown and deep gold against the sky that shines too blue to look at, as in the animal's velvet plucking of foliage. The rumble of a lion's purr, the arc of the tusk of an elephant bull, the calculated flick of a predator bird's wing rekindle awe at the fact that you are part of such existence. In the evenings, long drinks anticipate freshly caught fish grilled on an open fire by the chef with a marinade of mazhanje juice or marula liqueur. There are madora and matemba, and sorghum beer for those who dare later in the night, when dancers entertain the guests in the establishment's central clearing. In the cold season, when even the sun is white, grass stalks sway gently in the breeze and your visitors catch their breath. The smell of smoke from the estate hands' cooking lingers over the safari lands, and, on some evenings, a rim of red glows in the distance like a full moon rising, over in the villages where people reside, their untended fires crackling and smoking with destruction. On those nights, the sky smells like home. Your brochure reads, and you advise your group, that the settlers, in awe, named the sprawling veld God's Own Country. The clients exclaim and question each other over every animal track encountered, dung beetle chuckled over, and pool that looked refreshing but might harbour bilharzia. Following discussion amongst themselves, they are interested in your opinion.

Thus the patina of what your mother, with stinging distaste, labelled "the Englishness," which you acquired at the Young Ladies' College of the Sacred Heart, at last turns into a grand advantage. How restoring it is, even as you plod toward middle age, to reap a positive outcome from the convent that, while it educated you, rendered you "them," "they," "the Africans." As tour supervisor at Green Jacaranda, you are still Zimbabwean enough, which is to say African enough, to be interesting to the tourists, but not so strange as to be threatening. They communicate comfortably with your anglicized accent, and you reproduce it assiduously, although you still mutilate some of the diphthongs. The person you have become at the end of a long, twisting route is fascinatingly enigmatic, yet at the same time endearingly familiar to the clients. Not in a place that you can call home, but itinerant, away from the homestead and from the office on Jason Moyo, you become a star.

You spend time with the older women in the groups. They bring small gifts with which to appreciate various people they encounter. You are presented with chocolates, long, narrow chiffon scarves, and perfume samples. Frau Bachmann, who travels regularly with her husband, is particularly generous bringing in addition little German Christmas cakes, which she urges you to keep to share with your family. "Charming!" is their enthusiastic comment—"Entzückend!" from Frau Bachmann— as you explain how in earlier times possessing a sacred totem animal that was cared for and not eaten ensured conservation. If the totem animal was eaten, one's teeth invariably fell out, you continue, laughing. These days, however, people find herbalists who give them medicine so they can eat whatever they like. You explain the phrase for incest translates literally to "eating totem." "Amazing!" your clients nod as you conclude. For your part, you file away German words in order to test them on Cousin-Brother-in-Law.

In season, the tourists take out their cameras and run reels of film when you show them the tree the eco-safaris are named for. Here is your boss in so many photographs, the kindly yet wily Zimbabwean of Scandinavian extraction. You too are in many frames on the opposite shores of seas and oceans. You stand smiling somewhat stiffly, under the purple canopy of the jacaranda tree, or beneath the shade of an acacia in the vastness of the savannah. So will you be remembered.

Returning to the office from your seventh, particularly satisfying, safari, when you are expecting your promotion to the position of tour manager, you notice a change has come over Tracey. She leaves the premises to meet government officials in their offices more frequently. Taciturn after such appointments, she utters short and abrupt sentences. She rarely speaks of principles. You persuade yourself at first that the change in your boss's demeanour is due to strain between her and her newly appointed project manager, exacerbated by your absence. Hoping this is the case, you keep a sharp if covert eye open for signs of this dissent. As it turns out, after a few days in which you pore over statistics from the questionnaires and write extensive reports on each aspect of the excursion—this last an additional task that you have now been distinguished with—you are obliged to concede that your success is not the cause of the new tension in the office. Your boss and the former receptionist continue to be an admirable team. To make matters worse, the results of a pre-survey indicate Pedzi's ghetto arrivals and satisfaction scores will be at least as high as yours.

Its official name being unspeakable, Pedzi's project is branded the Green Jacaranda Ghetto Getaway on all publicity material. Having developed into a practically no-cost option for clients to incorporate into the usual Green Jacaranda safari a modified high-density community experience, it consists of a tour, one night in a home, breakfast the following day, and a choice of activities before resuming the standard programme.

Pedzi is aware of the dangers of too much success and acts diligently to circumvent them. She does not, in the beginning, raise a single hair of her plucked eyebrows at you when you return with many tales of satisfied clients. She navigates the rivalry between the office building's occupants by keeping the glass foyer doors open when she is working at reception, even though this is against the boss's advice and company policy, in order to disarm each woman who passes with a smile, even those whom she now, in her new role as businesswoman, finds frustrating. She even grins at the youths who congregate for pickings around the city council's overflowing rubbish bins. So intent on her advancement is she that Pedzi dashes them a couple of local dollars to remove the refuse outside of Tracey's schedule.

Little by little, however, Pedzi is eventually overcome by the brightness of her prospects. She promises the seamstresses several times a week that she will soon have an outfit made. When she does not turn up for measurements and they inquire she tells them she has changed her mind, that the outfit will be made for her sister. Eventually she is promising everybody on all the floors everything and delivering nothing. Nevertheless, Pedzi is proof that a girl from the high-density areas can become a successful businesswoman. She remains immensely popular. Tracey frets about the donors appearing at short notice to find women from the lower levels drinking instant coffee and eating samoosas at the donors' expense. For their part, the co-tenants begin to ask when they go out for lunch whether they may bring first Pedzi, and gradually all three of you, coleslaw and samoosas or sadza and stew when they return.

"Hey, anyone? Hamburgers? Salad? Samoosas?" Pedzi calls calmly through the office at the request of her newfound sisters who either come up to take the order or use the telephone.

As the launch of the Ghetto Getaway approaches, Pedzi relays information throughout the Green Jacaranda building concerning her soon-to-be improved finances, and reminds everybody that they all stand to benefit as, in principle, they had all been party to her breakthrough as part of her work community.

This is when Sister Mai Gamu makes it known that she is a baker of eight-tier wedding cakes, and reveals she also possesses a bridal boutique in a more affluent section of Harare's avenues. Her grey eye staring dully, she entreats Pedzi to advertise the ghetto as an original wedding venue for Green Jacaranda clients and other Europeans. She confides her secret yearning that a wedding party will include a best man and she will become a German citizen, thus getting her own back on her spouse. Pedzi accepts a business card without commitment, promising vaguely to pass on the information; but when she discusses matters with the younger seamstresses, she vows she will never take Mai Gamu's card, a politician's inferior common-law wife, out of her pocket when her clients land at Harare Airport.

As the Ghetto Getaway momentum grows, half a dozen businesswomen on the floors above and below express their willingness to take in as many as three Ghetto Getaway clients a night. Pedzi's sister, in preparation, evicts half a dozen lodgers from her backyard shacks.

Everyone is so satisfied with your colleague's skills and character that the little beautician at the Queen of Africa Boutique and other young women begin to inquire tentatively how much it costs to go on holiday on the Stevensons' farm. Pedzi promises to speak to Tracey about a Christmas special, when clientele from the north is slow, so that this season is tailor-made for the locals.

"Hey, Pedzi!" your boss grins one day when the office lunch of samoosas and coleslaw, plus the sadza and stew that Pedzi has now taken to eating, are arranged on the small kitchen counter and you are offering each other portions.

"You know what?" your boss promises. "As soon as you hit your thousandth client, you'll get a raise. When you get your ten thousandth, we'll see about that mortgage."

You become more restless and ponder how you too can bring in thousands of clients. With this on your mind, you take several more groups of tourists on tour. The year closes and another opens.

"Everything's bho! Everything's bho!" Pedzi sings at the top of her voice one morning. You have returned from the Green Jacaranda camp and have not as yet discovered any additional idea for your own department.

"It's not *bho*," you snap. "It's *beau*. French."

The young men studying at your uncle's mission used to speak French to each other both in delight and in order to show off their erudition, before the government declared that such erudition, and the Pan-African interaction it engendered, was unnecessary for natives and banished the language from their classrooms.

You have become accustomed to mentioning fairly random facts to colleagues outside the tours because you wish, like the young Sister Mai Gamu, you have a secret. You wish, like the young men at the mission, to parade your learning. Now you mention how the mission education was damaged to Pedzi.

"We have to go into the boardroom," the young woman responds, her eyes glinting expectantly, unimpressed by your story.

"It's the Ghetto Getaway proposal's first anniversary," she goes on. "It's amazing! What won't I do next? Become the president of this country. The queen of England. Or the pope. We have to wait there for Ms. Stevenson. Everything's bho! Everything's bho!" she goes out singing.

In the boardroom you bang your knees on the wrought iron. A speck of blood dots your skirt.

Pedzi sits opposite, her eyes growing calmer and more inscrutable.

The boss enters some minutes later.

"I'm glad you're already here," she says. Delving into the bag she sets on the table, Tracey pulls out a carton of orange juice and a bottle of sparkling wine.

"We're toasting Pedzi," Tracey says after she has placed the goods on the tabletop. With that, she sets about removing the gold foil from the wine bottle.

You nod, aware of a sensation you last had many months ago, an emptying in the area of your womb.

Pedzi goes out to the kitchen nook. She returns moments later with a tray of cups, glasses, and half a dozen Mediterranean Bakery chocolate croissants, cold from the fridge.

"Thanks, Pedzi!"

Tracey arranges the glasses on the table and pours. Her lips are pursed; there are little indentations, like cellulite, on her chin. Around her mouth a white line of tension creases.

Pedzi maintains her position behind the boss.

"What about my raise, ma'am?" she inquires, pretending the query is a joke.

"Ah, yes," recalls Tracey. She remains bent over the glasses. Wine froths out of one and drips onto the table. The tips of the boss's ears redden. Finally she straightens up. "One thousand. When did he check in?"

"She. Three weeks ago," answers Pedzi.

"A testament," says your boss. She raises her glass. A gleam of satisfaction lights up her eyes as she surveys you and your companion before continuing, "to the fact that anyone can achieve anything, in principle, if they want it badly enough. To Pedzi! The queen of the Ghetto Getaway."

"To the queen of the ghetto! And the Ghetto Getaway," you toast sarcastically. Between the words and your frustration, wine bubbles up and dribbles from your nostrils. You gasp and choke.

Tracey's smile slips into a smirk, then steadies.

Pedzi distributes paper napkins.

"Bho," she repeats, bowing. "Are you going to say anything about Her Majesty's reward?"

"That will be discussed separately," Tracey promises. "Don't worry, I've already done the paperwork. I'm onto everything we agreed."

You lean back in your chair estimating percentages and calculating monthlies, speculating whether Pedzi's earnings will now outstrip your income.

Tracey pushes her glass away and sits up meaningfully.

"Everything's better than you think," she says in a voice that carries too much conviction. As a result, her words fill you with dread.

"It's times like this when you have to keep your eye on the ball. This is when there're opportunities everywhere. Tambu," she goes on, facing you squarely. She doesn't blink, while her voice keeps weighing you down. "Pedzi's shown us the way," Tracey nods. "That's the direction we've got to go in."

Pedzi imitates Tracey's nod.

"She's thinking outside the paradigm," your boss explains. "That's what we all have to do if we're going to manage this time in this country."

She pauses and looks at you a little sadly.

"You've had a great deal of time to come up with something," she proceeds. "We have to add value to our programme. So I ended up thinking, building on what Pedzi's done. I thought it would be a good idea for you to have your own brand as well, Tambu."

You nod cautiously.

"Queen Tambu," says Pedzi, crossing one arm across her chest, trapping the hand in her armpit, rapping the fingers of the other on the table. "Hmm! D'you think so? Anyway, of what?"

"That's what we're here for," says Tracey.

You clasp your fingers together in your lap. Your armpits sweat. Your heart beats so loudly you can hardly hear anything. You dare not breathe in or out.

"Actually, Pedzi, more like very different from what you've done, really," your boss is explaining in a placatory manner when you succeed in making out the conversation again.

"Any competition with the Ghetto Getaway is a nonstarter. I'm thinking out of town. Like the farm, but not the farm. Celebrating roots. Where people come from. I was thinking, out in the village," your boss goes on.

"Queen of the village," says Pedzi. She pushes her chair back and laughs. Her navel ring jigs up and down under her T-shirt.

Tracey takes a deep breath and tries to smile.

Into the silence, as the thought comes to her, Pedzi exclaims, "Hey, but we don't have a village. Why are you talking about a village for her, when there's nothing like that?"

Tracey's hands curl into fists. She unclenches them with an effort. A moment later she clasps them together upon the table.

"What's the matter, Tracey?" Pedzi grumbles. "We have a farm. That's where she takes the clients. It looked as if they all enjoyed it."

Tracey's face blanches.

"She's been going all the time," Pedzi shrugs. "That's nothing new. How she can be queen of your farm?"

"Green Jacaranda does not have a farm," your boss says finally, her voice even.

Involuntarily you and Pedzi glance at each other. Neither of you acknowledges the gesture. Turning away from each other, you both stare at the table.

"We can't go through this situation any other way." Tracey pushes her chin forward. "Pedzi, basically, the farm isn't mine. That's the trouble with inheritance laws in this country. It's all there on paper, in principle. But it can just be too bloody difficult!"

"The clients went there. Just a month ago," Pedzi protests.

You remain quiet, anticipating imminent advancement.

"I can't go into details," Tracey says, crumbling her croissant. "The farm is . . . well . . . Green Jacaranda does not own any of it. Nils . . . my brother and I had an agreement. Jah, what good is any agreement these days?"

The boss raises her glass to her lips, does not drink, reaches for a carton, and mixes the wine with orange juice.

"Well, there's been trouble. Some of those . . . thugs . . . skellems who call themselves ex-combatants, or war vets . . . they've occupied the rondavels. They're hunting the game. And they're camping in our tourists' village! It's not like we're not the only ones. There's a whole lot of these . . . these invasions. I've been thinking how we can go on. Just the other day I realized, we're safest in a real village. If we can get one." Your boss grunts despondently. "That was their philosophy during the war too, wasn't it? Being part of the village. For a safety strategy."

You swallow without answering. Your mouth dries, then bitter saliva floods your tongue. As an urbanite, Pedzi does not know the horrors each person lived through at your homestead during the war, the kind of violence that not even Mainini Lucia and Kiri have succeeded in running from, that leaps from their bowels onto their tongues again and again. You observe a leg spinning against the blue of the sky. A woman is falling onto sand and spiky grass. It is your sister who is injured. No, it is you.

Tracey and Pedzi are discussing Green Jacaranda's situation calmly, as your mind returns to the boardroom. You realize that although a hyena is laughing, the sound is only in your head.

"Are you all right, Tambu?" Tracey asks.

"Have those people done anything?" you whisper, trying to keep your voice even. Your skin tautens as though it will fall off your bones, but you are only smiling. "Has the army been called?"

"Take it easy, Tahm-boo," your boss says, her Rhodesian accent returning inexplicably. She lays a hand on your arm. "No, it's unlikely they'll be calling the army. After all, they're all the same lot. Along with the guys I've been seeing about my permit. Still, it's pretty all right, all things considered. Nils!" she sighs with some venom. "He's finally got it into his head how things work here. He's talking to them, not waving his rifle. Thank God he's done with the Stevenson heroics."

Tracey pauses to put her thoughts in order.

"And it seems they've asked around in the building," she goes on. "About who we are and what we're doing. Some people say that Lindiwe Ngwenya is their woman here. Or else the Moetsabi woman. You know how it is. People will say anything! But there's no point in panicking. Everything's fine so far. Basically, what we had wasn't the best arrangement. We didn't have the real control we need. It's just that people like my brother don't know how to talk to people. If I'd been there I'd have sorted it all out."

"You can't. You can't talk once they've decided what they want to do and they're doing it," you say listlessly, remembering too much that you do not wish to. You believe Tracey can do many things and she has proved this again and again, yet you know she cannot get the better of liberation war fighters when they say yes, we are coming.

"Can't what?" asks Pedzi, folding her arms more tightly and pressing her lips together, for this is in the days before war camps come to the city. "What d'you mean, can't?"

"Negotiate," snaps Tracey. "Talk. Obviously that's what she means. Taahmboodzahee, you've got to stop this. Pedzi's right. In a way, you're beginning to sound like my brother."

The boss steadies herself before she continues brusquely, "If Nils has enough sense to play his cards right, it might not come to the worst. I'm talking about the farm. But that's got nothing to do with us now. The part that does affect us is that we have to find a new place. Quickly. In time for the next group of clients."

Pedzi puts her head in her hands, understanding before you do.

"It's fine," says Tracey. "I've already discussed everything with the donors and they like what I'm suggesting. You have a rural background, Tambu. You embody it. That's how you can, if you're up to it, take on the brand we created up on the farm. This time in a village."

"Queen of the village!" snorts Pedzi.

Tracey picks up her champagne glass in a toast to Green Jacaranda.

"Green Jacaranda. Always green. Whatever happens!"

"Green Jacaranda," you answer.

"And to the queen of the village," says Pedzi.

The meeting ends soon after this. While you all clear the things away, you screw up the nerve to tell your boss you cannot answer her at once. You inform her you need time to consider taking on this new responsibility. Tracey nods more emphatically than usual. There is relief in her voice when she cautions you that your contemplation should not take too long. When the boardroom is tidy, Tracey calls Pedzi into her office. Pedzi emerges looking smug. The expression on her face prods you toward your decision.

The boss requests your presence as soon as Pedzi has left. She tells you that she hopes you have had sufficient time to consider and asks whether you have come to a decision.

You do not answer.

Your boss sighs impatiently.

"I take it that means agreement," she says.

"We've got to find a name," she presses on. "Open air, safari, land. That's all the same. Be that as it may, though, the village isn't going to be like the farm. Less glamour. We have to find a substitute pulling factor. This name's got to be something . . . it's got to sound like a move to more authenticity. Something to tell the clients they're going deeper into Africa, into everything, but just as safely."

"Green," you breathe.

Your boss looks annoyed.

You hardly notice. A moment later, your mind whizzing, you add, "Eco."

"*Green* and *eco* are tautological," Tracey reprimands. "Anyway, we've got that already, everywhere. Everything's Green Jacaranda eco! And you can't say village," she says. "That kind of promise doesn't work these days either. It's got to sound like fun, not under development, soil erosion and microfinance. That's your assignment, then, Tambudzai," she concludes, her accent improving. "You were always good at literature. No wonder you were the whiz kid copywriter."

You promise to present an idea by the next morning.

"Good," says Tracey. She picks up a folder.

"This is the concept. I typed it up when I couldn't get back to sleep last night. Go through it and we'll discuss it. If you have any initial questions, ask now. Share your thoughts with me on your way out this evening."

"After lunch," you promise, still nervous but determined to grasp tightly at this new possibility of victory.

"Fine," the boss nods. "We have to set it up for the next quarter."

You skim over the pages as you walk to the door. Entirely on its own initiative, as though it has a life of its own, a phrase forms in your mind. You consider it for three steps.

"Transit," you say at the door.

"What?" your boss asks absentmindedly, opening her appointments diary.

"Ah, *transit*," she repeats, looking up for a moment. "Yes, *transit*. That sounds like what we're looking for."

"Green Jacaranda Getaways, as usual. We'll keep that bit for the branding," you plunge on, growing more excited. "But this will be the Village Eco Transit! Chimanimani, Pungwe Falls, Honde Valley— the fruit, they'll love it. And V-E-T, that's too good! 'Take all your pets to the VET!' Imagine it on the brochures."

"Except it'll be in German. Swedish. Danish and Italian," your boss says. She considers the matter for a second before deciding, "Well, we can always keep the tagline in English."

The boss pages through her diary and switches the telephone to loudspeaker. You leave, overwhelmed by an emotion you have missed for too long, the astonishing joy of knowing you are good at the task before you.

CHAPTER 19

A few days later you sit in your purple double cab, which you are entitled—according to your organization's regulation—to buy at 10 percent of its current value in three years' time. You relish the fact that with your promotion to village tour manager, Pedzi is now no longer your equal at number two in the company. Better still, it is you and not the former receptionist—as you still think of her privately—who has been given the vehicle.

You admire yourself in the rearview mirror, looking forward to the splendid entrance you will make in the village. You belt along Samora Machel Avenue enjoying the looks on pedestrians' faces, and the expressions of drivers below you in their third- and fourth-hand vehicles. It is a time when everything is on the move, from ex-combatants to capital, when momentum is dignity, when cars such as yours have automatic right of way over all creation except a more powerful, superior engine. Smaller vehicles, cyclists, and people scurry from the danger of your advance. Your heart smiles in a hard sort of way before you press your foot down, feeding the engine petrol.

A trio of schoolchildren pull each other out of your path. They fling their hands to their mouths and hold them there. A man by the roadside steps from the pavement onto the roadside gravel. He stretches out too late and grasps nothing but air. The old woman he wishes to save is already leaping to safety. She springs up and down in the isle in the middle of the road, like a competitor warming up for an elderly citizens' world championship contest. At the sound of your hooter, she hugs a traffic light post. Shaking your head at her stupidity, you hurtle over her headscarf, which had fallen onto the tarmac.

Streams of traffic trickle off down side roads. The arm of your speedometer bobs across the dial. The Mutare road narrows into a single lane. Swaths of farmland sweep out toward the horizon. Anticipation drives your foot hard upon the accelerator with the abandon of an incautious new driver. You are in a race with your very existence. An hour later mountains heap up on both sides. In two instead of the usual three hours, you grind over the rocks and ruts that are the road to your homestead.

On one side miserable wraiths, which are in fact maize plants, poke up from the earth. In front and behind you the soil glitters like pop stars' bling with mica, silicon, and crystals. The nearby mountains have, in the years since you last visited, grown as bald as underfed grandfathers. Further away the grey granite of the Nyanga range lowers like a ridge of frowning eyebrows. You catch your breath as you greet these sentinels to your past, suppressing every twinge of regret at the events that brought you here or at the deed you are doing. You twist the steering wheel to avoid a ditch and compel yourself to focus. Provisions packed in the back of the SUV slide up and down. Enjoying beforehand the impact you will make with these gifts, you compose yourself for the meeting ahead.

There are more homesteads in the village than you remember. Gobnosed children scramble from patches of groundnuts and scrawny pumpkins as you drive by. They cheer, kicking up calloused soles as they chase in your wake.

"Mauya, Mauya! Mauya ne-Ma-zi-da!" they chorus. "You have come! Welcome, you have come in a Mazda."

The sun beats down on the short tufts of their hair. The youngsters dance, legs turning grey in the dust that washes from your vehicle's wheels. It floats with a shimmer above the soil and around the children's feet. Their fingers flutter. Their hands twirl. Their small feet pound after you.

Closer to the homestead, at a communal tap beside a family's well, other youngsters bash at each other with cooking oil tins and pesticide pails and grind their elbows into each other's soft tissue. Past this fray your Mazda rumbles.

"Who is that one?" a girl shouts, distracted from her battle.

"That's a murungu," answers another.

"No it's not. That's a person," the girl says, turning to keep the car in sight. "And, hey, can you see, it's also a woman."

"That doesn't matter. Money, money, give us money!" a skinny boy screams, throwing his water pail down and dashing into the road. His gangmates join him, swelling your retinue of children.

Often you dreamt of this moment. You are prepared. A megapack of mixed sweets lies on the passenger seat beside you. You have eaten one or two to keep yourself going on the drive. Now you grab a handful. Toffees, chocolate eclairs, and fruit drops fly through the window, and the fight breaks out again behind your vehicle.

A couple of dogs are asleep inside your family's homestead. Their bloated tongues spill onto the earth. They pant with shallow breaths, ribs expanding like the hoods of cobras, which gentle motion nevertheless does not disturb the flies that buzz about the animals' sores. Neither animal barks at the Mazda's wheels, nor bays to alert a family member. Your vehicle stops under the old mango tree, gnarled and drooping now, that had stood guard over the family members' arrivals and departures for decades.

One animal opens an eye briefly as the car door thuds. It quivers an ear, thumps its tail in the sand once or twice, and lapses back into languor. When no one appears, you open the door again and press the horn. At this the dogs lope up and sniff at the Mazda's wheels.

At last a woman cranes her neck around the granary.

"Ewo! Svikai!" she invites without a sign of recognition.

You blink hard.

"Mai," you say in such shock that you forget to move toward her.

She is several times smaller than you remember, and her skin seems to have shrunk with her, while somehow retaining its overall mass so that where it does not hang, it has thickened like that of a pachyderm.

"Mai," you repeat.

You sense criticism in her lack of recognition. You move forward swiftly to forestall any disapproval about anything.

"Mai, I am back. I have come."

So saying, you drop to your knees beside her.

She is rubbing maize kernels off the cob in preparation for milling. Only one or two cobs are clean of seeds. The one in her hand is full, except for a few bare rows. The plastic sheeting beside her is heaped with untouched cobs. The wicker tray on her lap is all but empty. She is thinking of other things, not of what she is doing. You help her set the tray on the ground. Your gesture is unnecessary but she allows you to assist her and lays her head heavily against your neck for a moment. When she straightens up she once again is the woman who raised you.

"Ewo, Tambu," she greets you. "You of the years. Isn't that right, so many years? If this womb agreed, this mouth would say you are one from afar, nothing but a foreigner visiting. Only the womb knows better."

You swallow frustration, smile, and embrace her again. Patience is both weapon and victory. How much of it have you deployed in your life? Come what may, and soon at that, whether the people here know it or not, you will be queen of the village.

"Let us go in, my child," your mother softens, sensing the sharpness in her words. She turns gingerly onto her knees, balancing on her palms. Her fingers scrape the earth like claws. The joints are thick as bulbs ready for planting. Your mother winces as she rests her hands on a granary plank and heaves herself upward.

"There is no one to help you, Mai?" you inquire, holding her by the shoulder.

"Help? Aren't you someone?" she snaps.

You slide your hand beneath her armpit. Her weight descends.

"Anyway, cooking sadza, it can be done," Mai relents when the worst pain is out of her joints. "It's these things like the maize and the milking that are painful. And the garden. So I thank God your sister Netsai gave me her two girls. They cook and keep the place clean. They fetch water from the pump down the road, and they do the washing in the river."

"Concept, Freedom," she raises her voice as two girls come into the yard, large, awkward bundles of twigs balanced on their heads.

The girls throw their bundles down on the rack by the kitchen. Looking you over while pretending not to, they approach, linking their little fingers together and bumping against each other.

"What does walking like that mean?" scolds Mai. "You should be running. This is your mother. The one with two legs, that kept her in Harare so long we thought something destroyed her. This is your maiguru, Tambudzai, the one who comes before your mother."

The girls giggle and accelerate. You embrace. When you step back to look at them, the family likeness jolts you, so that you want to hold them against your body and promise them many things, that their lives will never be like yours, nor will there be any need to go to war like their mother did. You do not move, knowing that only by remaining resolute in your own progress will you have any chance of turning your desires into pledges that you can fulfil. The girls smile at you shyly.

"The Mozambiquans," quips Mai disparagingly.

Your nieces hang their heads.

"We learnt that during the war," your mother goes on indifferently, "while some were fighting, some were having children. Isn't that so, you Mozambiquans?"

The girls shuffle closer together.

"Weren't you born by your mother across the border?" Mai rasps on. "At the time she was meant to be fighting? But then, fighting with one leg. What kind of fighting was she meant to do? No wonder we are still living like this since people were still doing the same old things over there in spite of what they told us."

"So we were born in Mozambique," Concept, the older girl, nods. She speaks lightly as children who have recently become teenagers do when an offensive ritual is repeated. "Speaking of it is a waste of time. People born in Mozambique are back now, like everyone else."

"If I had known," your mother threatens your country's history with vigour. "If I had known that's what was happening in Mozambique, my daughter would not have lost a leg. For what? For this? For nothing!"

"You called, Mbuya?" her granddaughter continues, softly changing the subject.

"I didn't call anyone. It's nothing," Mai shrugs and turns to the kitchen. "I'm going in. Girls, show your aunt where to go."

Her voice thins. An anxiety she cannot conceal throbs in the words.

"If there's anything to carry that's been brought, your aunt will tell you and you can take it."

So saying, your mother turns toward the kitchen.

You lead your nieces back to the twin cab and pull the tarpaulin off the back. Dust ricochets. You let it settle in your lungs. Joy has gone out of everything. The girls hoist provisions to the main house looking glum and deflated.

"So the provisions are put away?" Mai asks when you join her in the kitchen.

"Yes, Mbuya," the elder girl, Concept, nods warily, settling down on the reed mat to the left of the entrance where you, as women, cluster.

"Where is Baba? How is he?" you ask.

"He's well. The cooking oil?" says Mai.

"The cooking oil!" her grandchildren echo.

"Candles?"

"Those too," the girls confirm.

"And you carried the margarine nicely?"

When she cannot think of anything else that is necessary but may not have been provided, her eyes flare for a moment, but the light is immediately extinguished.

"Finally, Tambudzai," she sniffs softly. "Now you have stopped eating everything you get alone. You've remembered you have a family. We nearly died of hunger while we waited for that to happen."

"And Dambudzo?" you ask.

Your anger at your mother over her comment is so quiet, you yourself do not hear it and keep on smiling.

"Have you heard from your last child? Is your son sending anything home from America?"

"Ireland, he is now in Ireland," your mother says, as though that explains everything, makes it clear your brother cannot be expected to provide as the Irish are not as abundantly blessed as the Americans.

"So it is time to thank my boss," you continue, in this way opening the mouth of the subject that brought you home. "She is a good boss, the one I work for," you continue.

Mai seems not to hear.

"Concept, Freedom," she scolds. "Why are you sitting there? Isn't it time to be cooking something for the traveller? Are you thinking of eating everything all by yourselves? Go to the house and bring down something to prepare for your aunt here."

The girls scramble out to fetch rice and vegetables for a stew that is the new high-carbohydrate treat in trendy women's homesteads.

"Ms. Stevenson," you proceed quickly when your nieces have gone. "That is her name. She's the one who has put me where I am at last. After so long, Mai, I am empowered. That is why I can come now, when so much time has gone. It was not a question of not knowing the womb, but one of not knowing how to come back to it."

"So it's not true," Mai sniffs disdainfully.

"What is not true, Mai?"

"What we heard all the time is that you were not working. That's what was said, that that degree of yours was just a piece of paper sitting, silently rotting. And I just kept on thinking, that's the paper. What about that daughter of mine? Tambudzai, even when Lucia sent me worse messages about you, I just kept it in my mind, surely my daughter is not sitting there like paper that has been written on and finished. I said my daughter can't be sitting there just like that, rotting."

Concept and Freedom crouch in through the low door, holding small wicker baskets in the crooks of their arms.

"Who is that friend of your mother's?" Mai turns to the girls as they settle down to their tasks. "That woman your mother fought that war with? The one who said she was going to help your mother to find a leg? The one that then disappeared to Harare to stay with a relative who was a businessman or something? Tell me," Mai demands. "She is from some other village, otherwise I would remember. She fought that war, Concept and Freedom, with your mother and my sister Lucia."

"Oh, yes! Maiguru Kiri," Concept smiles as she pulls the skin off an onion.

Freedom moves an enamel dish of tomatoes out of the way. She slits a packet of rice open with a broken knife and pours the grain into a winnowing tray.

"Yes, Auntie Kiri," she agrees, glancing from Mai to the rice she is picking over. "Maiguru Kiri comes from Jenya, you know, just under the holy mountain. She used to come here when we were little. But not so much anymore."

"That one," says Mai. "I sent her with some mealie meal for you. But when I heard what was going on, I said, ah, now Tambu will never eat it. It's better if that Christine just goes ahead and cooks it."

You smell the wood smoke from the kitchen fire more intensely in the silence that follows. Forgotten odours that cling to the years mix with the smoke—the light must of dung from the floor, people once known, their sweat, odd bits of waste, moist onion and tomato skins charring slowly.

"Hurry up now, girls," says Mai. She ends with a wince as she pushes herself up.

"Tambudzai, you come with me. Though he never comes here anymore," she grumbles on, her face pinching once more. "Even though your uncle never comes away from that mission since his accident, he only gives us one room in the new house he built here in this home. So you will have to sleep in the old house. With your nieces."

"That's all right. By the time we are finished we will have built our own houses," you promise as you follow Mai out of the kitchen. For the first time, you believe your words.

"Are you a man?" Your mother dismisses any chance of such a thing. "Isn't it your father who should be doing that, building those houses? If he can't manage why do you think you are more than he is? Anyway," she continues in the same flat tone and without taking a breath, "let's see if there is still a mattress in the back room in that old broken-down place. You have put the provisions in the front, have you not? Who goes into that back room these days, since you left your things there? The girls sleep in the side room, so if anything happens they can call your father and me easily. Let's see if the rats have left anything."

Your mother moves slowly, which gives her more time to speak. "Who is this Stevenson?" she inquires, enjoying the shock she causes you with her alertness. "Do we know that family? Are they one of our white people who farm in our parts of the country?"

You hesitate.

Mai stands still.

"White people are a problem," she remarks. "You can only work with them if you know them. That's why we prefer to do things with our own ones. You have to know this Stevenson properly to work with her, my daughter. Play cunningly. If her family is not from these parts, how can you know her? And her, what does she want with you if she doesn't know you?"

"Mai, I wouldn't say that," you object, as your mother hauls herself up the stairs that lead to the old house. "It's not like that with all of them."

"I see," she snorts. "Out with it, get it over and done with."

"I knew her for six years," you say, judging it best to be miserly with the truth.

"Oh, she was one of those white ones at your uncle's mission," says Mai. "One of those missionaries."

"Not really," you explain. "I know her from the Young Ladies' College of the Sacred Heart. We were in a class together."

"Oh-ho," breathes Mai. "I now remember when and where I heard that name," she goes on. "So now it is as I thought. You have come down here to start your madness about white people again, Tambudzai. Isn't that why you have been nothing all this time, because of too much of those people? Leave them alone. Go and find your own thing. That is what I can tell you."

Mai picks her way through the provisions in the front room of the old house. She moves slowly, surveying the parcels with satisfaction.

The mattress in the back room is in a bearable condition, with sign of neither fleas nor maggots. When Mai is satisfied the room is habitable, she leaves, promising to send Freedom up to sweep dust from surfaces and rodent droppings from under the bedstand. She goes into the side room the girls share and returns after a moment with a blanket.

Left alone, you sit on the steel bed, gingerly at first, letting your weight down slowly. The light turns from light to dark grey. You light a flickering flame from one of the candles. A chemical in the wax is pungent and irritating, although the packet claims the candles are smokeless. In the spluttering light, the burgundy of a frayed rug that covers a pile of junk in a corner curdles and thickens in the way of an arriving spirit. Its rancid smell trickles up your nostrils relentlessly, like an unwanted memory.

The fabric feels oily between thumb and finger. Rankness, of age rather than barely washed bodies, rises from remnants the rats have spared. You are about to drop the decaying mass when a dull gleam catches your attention. The thread picks out a worn pattern in what was once bright blue embroidery. Lifting it higher, you recognize the crest on its breast pocket and a moment later your Young Ladies' College of the Sacred Heart blazer.

The garment lies over a pair of broken Sandak sandals. They are your mother's size. Almost incredulous, you remember these too: a gift sent home through a relative when you began at the advertising agency.

The hardened, splitting plastic shoes lie on your old school trunk. White paint flakes, like broken snakeskin, on battered black enamel. Bending closer, you read the words TAMBUDZAI SIGAUKE. Beneath this stands an address: Young Ladies' College of the Sacred Heart, P Bag 7765, Umtali.

Your body freezes and your mind leaps out of it. You want to run across the yard and jump into your SUV. But you have committed to going forward. It seems to you the trunk vibrates with the gravity of a black hole that pulls everything into its origin. The force of it creeps across the floor, trickles through the air and up the walls and inward so that after a moment you cannot tell whether you are the box or the box is you. It is calling you to surrender something you are sure you do not have.

239

The old locks come apart with little force. Inside the old trunk, a stringless tennis racket lies on another burgundy blazer that is in better condition than the first, and larger. Underneath this, the tongues of discoloured tennis shoes loll forward as though from a throat. Right at the bottom, neatly laid together, protected by several skirts and blouses, carefully wrapped in torn but clean old plastic bags, are a dozen or more exercise books.

You rummage in the pile, pulling out books at random and not putting them back. The pungency of past decades percolates up: girls wearing lace gloves and veils to Sunday Mass, eating at heavy wooden tables set with white cloth napkins in silver rings, the constant tension from not knowing whether or not you were as you were meant to be, the brutal fighting to answer affirmatively that question, and its damage.

When Freedom comes up, it is to call you to eat, not to clean. The girls are impatient to tuck into a meal made fragrant with treats like tomato paste and garlic. They push the water bowl across to you as soon as you enter.

You have not taken half a dozen mouthfuls when a folk song jars up from the gully.

"Chemutengure! Chemutengure!" the singer rasps.

Your mother, Concept, and Freedom ignore the noise.

"Chemutengure! Chemutengure!" the singer begins again with a determined effort.

"Baba," you breathe in despair. "It's him."

The girls look at their grandmother out of the corners of their eyes. Mai continues eating as though no one has sung or spoken, as though nothing has happened.

You cannot beak off another morsel.

"Go on. Keep eating," Mai shrugs. "That's him. Someone must have told him we have a visitor. He doesn't even know who it is. But he felt the hunger biting and knew there would be something."

A thud sounds from the yard. No one moves. You too continue eating.

"It would be good," says Mai after a while, "if this Stevenson woman you work for could help you to get a leg for your sister." She pauses to suck, with a hissing sound, a piece of gristle that has lodged between her teeth.

While Mai picks up another piece of meat, as though demonstrating what your people say, that there's no point in losing your appetite over other people's sorrows, the reminder of their mother's situation badly disturbs the girls. They sit motionless, hardly breathing, their greasy hands upturned on their thighs.

You plan to promise your mother the leg she wants for your sister as a kind of barter for the programme you have come to set up. Waiting for a chance to do so, you scoop up a handful of rice and vegetables, lower your eyes, and do your best to look as though you are enjoying the meal.

"My daughter ended up with one leg, although she started with two." Mai leans forward and rubs her own shin. "One leg and two children, Tambudzai. That mathematics does not work out. That is why these children are uneducated. It is the wrong numbers. Netsai could not work. You sent nothing. The people those girls fought the war for despised and hated these girls' mother. Wasn't she just another one of all the whores from Mozambique, who they say even drank blood and ate flesh while they were whoring? Even if the government took away the school fees, how could we buy the books and school uniforms? And now they call school fees levies, treating us like children. This is what this white woman must do. We have eaten what she sent. But we can't survive on it. She must help you get a leg for your sister."

"Where will you get the leg for my mother from, Maiguru?" asks Freedom in excitement.

"Iwe, Freedom. Mai will never get her leg back," says Concept. "Why get involved? My mother is doing well with the peg. If anyone wanted to bring her a better leg, we would have seen it already. So why is it only now people are thinking about it?" She fingers a piece of sadza but does not dab it in gravy, nor put it into her mouth.

Concept reaches for the water bowl. Running her tongue over her teeth to remove particles, she sets it down in front of Mai, who rinses her hands.

The girls empty scraps from one plate into another. When they are done, and the dishes are stacked to wash up the next morning, they kneel in the kitchen doorway and bring their hands together in a respectful, soundless clap.

"Good night, Mbuya. Good night, Maiguru Tambu. Thank you, Maiguru. We have eaten. We are full. Mbuya, shall we go and see Sekuru?"

"As you wish," shrugs Mai.

You take stock. "Ah, it is time to sleep," you say, deciding to buy time to think matters through.

After you cross the yard to the house, you stand to say good night to your nieces once more. A heap lies beside the Mazda. Ignoring it, as your nieces do, you convince yourself it is a shadow.

"I think your grandfather has gone back to where he was," you observe.

"Yes, he sometimes does that," agrees Concept softly.

After this conversation, it is better to fall asleep immediately. You do not dare to go out to clean your teeth but rinse your mouth with bottled water, which you spit out through the back window.

The three-quarter moon waxes to full brightness in the early hours of morning. Its light spills across the baskets and boxes in the spare room, twisting the shadows into the swaying serpent and creeping hyena spectres of childhood.

"Chemutengure! Chemutengure!" your father wails as though he has been moaning all night.

Only half asleep, you lie tense in bed.

"Chave chemutengure vhiri rengoro. Mukadzi wemutsvayiri hashayi dovi! It's the rolling wheel of a wagon. A driver's wife always has peanut butter!" the man roars in truculent tones, as though he carries a personal grudge against any husband who keeps his wife supplied with the spread.

"Dovi! Peanut butter!" your father yells.

Footsteps shuffle through the main room.

"I forgot to put his sadza by the bed," whispers Freedom, who, being the youngest, is supposed to remember such tasks.

"Serves you right if he beats you. You were having too much fun chewing Maiguru's meat," Concept returns softly.

"Go and talk to him. I'll do it now," Freedom hisses back.

The bolt on the front door scrapes. The hinges creak, the edge of the wood grates across the floor.

Concept laughs harshly, forgetting to whisper. "I hope you left something. Go and take it, don't worry. Tell Mbuya he's still sleeping and you just remembered. But have a look." Her voice pulses with more mirth. "Where did he want to go? He's fallen straight onto Maiguru's Mazda."

By the time you hurry out, tying your Zambia cloth around your waist and tucking in a T-shirt hastily thrown on, your father has disengaged himself from the car and is swaying under the hute tree that stands at the edge of the central clearing.

Mai hurries out, draped in her night wrap also, the Zambia cloth already around her waist above a discoloured petticoat, her night doek knotted carelessly about her head. Freedom follows at a distance, hanging her head in guilt.

"Vhi-vhi-vhiri. What did I say? Oh vhiri, I said vhiri, please, vhiri, vhiri," your father moans, his fury spent as you all gather before him.

He looks back and waves at the car. "The wife of a driver? That's wrong. No, it's not the wife. No, it's the father of a driver who never lacks peanut butter. Peanut butter! The father always has it, peanut butter."

Mai is merciless.

"Wheels," she seethes. "What vhiri are these? The only thing that's going round, you rag of a fool, is your head."

Your father staggers toward you.

"It's you, my daughter. It's you, the one who has come with those wheels."

Before he reaches you he turns and gropes his way back to the car, his arms stretched wide. Mai glowers. Baba strokes the Mazda's canopy. Mai breathes deeply and shakes her head. Baba keeps on stroking the machine's doors, bumpers, and hood. When he finishes he begins to cry.

"Oh," the words choke from his chest. "Oh, is it a daughter of mine? No, it can't be. A daughter of mine, who has achieved such things? Hi-hi-hi-hi. A daughter of mine, can it be? No, never. This can't be my daughter!"

"No, no, don't touch me," he moans although no one is moving. "Today I have seen something that sews up every seam and every hem that was ripped. Let me stay and see what this murungu has done. Let me see what my daughter has brought me."

He continues moaning as you finally grip his arms and march him to the house his brother built.

"It's me, Baba. It's Tambudzai," you say to his face. But his interest is elsewhere.

"Vhiri," your father sings softly, dreamily as you march him on. "Ha, vakomana, oh men and women, vhiri, vhiri."

His foot kicks the plates Freedom has put out as you enter his bedroom. Sadza, congealed meat, gravy, and bits of vegetables scatter.

"Vhiri, oh vhiri," Baba sighs. Without saying anything to each other, you and your nieces lay him down on his koya mattress.

Night sidles west. Grey outlines the mountain behind the homestead. You do not think of sleeping.

The chattering from the side room dies down in a little while as the girls drift back into dreams. You light a candle. Finally you pick up the exercise book you discarded earlier.

An exercise toward the end of the book is called Mantra. The title is written in the middle of the line in ornate capitals. Under it the teacher has requested in small, amused script, "Please use normal writing."

You remember composing the poem but not what it says. Curious, you read once more thoughts committed to paper by your adolescent hand.

Mantra

    I do not
    do not recall, not
    in any way remember
    the sombreness she speaks of, that
    vivid concentration of her mood as she
    so often sat
    pressing thumb against
    gap-rowed maize-cobs;

do not recall
this density of distress she considers
that is thicker
than the livid cloud
dripping red bursts of
sunset on mountain,
that is deeper
than the purple
of hute juice
of the mango tree shade rippling
over her; an umbra
she knew with fear could disintegrate
whole women
I who whole
do not
encompass either her
error or
the same of her judgement

Impatient with the cryptic phrases, you drop the book back into the trunk and begin again to contemplate options for reaching your objective. You have not come to any conclusion when your mother's voice cries out.

"Mai-we, mai-we. Yuwi, yuwi, oh Father," your mother shrills. "I am being killed. I am being put to death here. Daughter. Concept, Freedom. Everyone, it is my life that is being torn away."

You walk to the door. You wait there, head bowed. Your return to the bed, and do not go out.

"Yuwi! Yuwi! He is killing me, he is killing me," your mother wails. "Oh, my daughters and granddaughters-wé. Who will save me from this man?"

You continue to listen, until, after some time, the cries diminish. When it is quiet again, you lie on the bed and turn to the wall as though you are sleeping.

CHAPTER 20

Early in the morning, you remove a small package from your overnight case and lay it on the table amongst the provisions. It contains a blouse and skirt for your mother and a short-sleeved shirt for your father that you were to present to your parents, as a kind of "open the mouth" at your official pitching of the Village Eco Transit, since you had imagined a formal meeting. You are leaving the package in the way of insurance, an ambiguous intermediate to, as it were, keep your mother's mouth open. Clearly it is time to drive away in the Green Jacaranda Mazda, but you plan to return to further the exchange. You find a spot for the package where it will easily be found after which you pad to the front door.

"Ndiwe here, Maggie? Is that you, Maggie?"

Concept and Freedom are singing as they sweep the central clearing with brooms made of branches. "Wakatora mukunda. Who took my daughter?" Their happy voices shower music over the yard.

Your mother is washing her face. An enamel basin containing warm water is balanced on the verandah wall. A slab of green Sunlight soap lies beside it. She touches her face carefully with a threadbare, greying towel.

You remember you brought food, necessities, but no scented soap, Lux, Geisha, or Palmolive to add a trace of fragrance to your mother's ablutions.

"Good morning, Tambudzai," your mother says. She does not look at you. "I thought I should leave him alone and not wash myself where he is," she says.

You are careful to keep neutral and calm.

"Good morning, Mai," you reply. "How did you sleep?"

"As you see. And maybe heard," she replies. "And you, how was your sleep?"

You reassure her you rested well.

"That is good," your mother says. She pats her cheeks and neck dry. She knots her scarf cautiously around her head and spends a few moments pulling the front over swellings on her forehead. When that is done she pinches the headscarf further down to cover a red star that shines in the white of her eye. Then she pushes the doek up again because she cannot see anything.

"What that woman, your boss, gave, in any case, we will use it. We'll survive for a little while," your mother says. "What I am thinking is, what made her want us to survive like that? That's what I have been thinking about all these hours. Even when I had my hands up like that, as beer evaporated and his aim improved, even then, I was thinking there is something this Stevenson wants, and maybe I can do it. That is why I have decided that whatever happens, I am going to listen to whatever you came to say about your work with this . . . this . . ."

"Tracey," you supply. "Tracey Stevenson."

"Ah, Maggie, uchandiurayisa, Maggie. Ah, you will be the death of me, Maggie," your nieces sing.

"That one," Mai nods. "I am going to listen to the message you say you are bringing."

The girls have swept the yard clean. They are scooping up rubbish onto a bit of aluminium roofing on the far side of the homestead. Their voices are fainter.

Mai shouts, as loudly as she can with the bruises and contusions on her face, to her granddaughters to fetch the basin of dirty water. Passing through the door into the old house, she raises a hand for you to follow. Arranging two dusty chairs face to face amongst the provisions, she lowers herself into the first and gestures for you to take the other. She listens as you outline the plan, interrupting only occasionally for clarification.

"It is for the whole village?" Mai confirms when you are done. "Not just for here, for your own reasons that will annoy the whole area?"

"Yes! It is for everybody. It is being done properly," you assure her. "But it will be built here," you hurry on as her expression turns to doubt.

"It is easier that way," your mother agrees. "That way we can tell our mambo it is our project. If it is for the whole village, it is the mambo's project and that would not be very good. On the other hand," she reflects after weighing up the situation, "if it is only our project, that will not be good either. We will never succeed with something like that. People will kill us out of jealousy."

"It is a new life to share," you explain. "All the village will have their part. It will provide something for everyone."

"All the village? Everyone?" Your mother's expression clouds over again. "I thought you said the women are going to do the work. Everything that needs to be done? How will we manage if we have to do anything with these men interfering?"

You assure Mai that, as you are in charge, you will work closely with each and every woman in the village.

"And we will be paid? Each for doing what we do? All of us, properly?" your mother asks warily. "These white people, they say something and they do it too, but the way they do it, you just never know what it is they first said they were doing."

"I tell you, Mai, I now know them," you say. After so much tension you are unable to resist a little boasting.

"Do you forget I spent all those years at the Young Ladies' College of the Sacred Heart? I know our white people. And I have worked with her for so long, I can say I now know my boss better and I also know what she is talking about."

"It's me you should know better," says your mother. Jutting her chin she attempts a toss of her head, which ends in wincing.

"Since I passed the grade seven, the Women's Club voted me treasurer for our chapter in this village. Yes, I am very good with those numbers. So I can do this thing for you. I can talk to the Women's Club and the chairwoman will carry our words to our mambo. Now I hope you are prepared, that you come ready to finish what you started," she concludes. "He will want us to open his mouth with something.

But it is no good opening the mouth and leaving the heart. So that will be another something."

You are prepared. You open your bag.

"And they will pay us like this?" your mother verifies, examining the notes. "Money I can tie up for myself in my own headscarf?"

"It will be money anyone who works with us can tie wherever he or she wants."

Your mother smiles.

"We will eat first," she decides. "Then we will go to see the Women's Club chairwoman."

"Treasurer! Makorokoto! Congratulations, treasurer," you reply with a swell of pride.

"Now," Mai begins again, standing up. "Do as if nothing has been said, you hear, Tambudzai. Wash yourself. Make tea for your father, porridge, whatever he wants. But when you speak to him, not a word. Don't tell him what we've spoken of. Certainly, don't tell him we have spoken and gone on to reach a decision."

"I have understood, Mai," you say, heart beating as you see the distance to your next promotion rapidly decrease.

"Then I will go and get dressed," your mother says. "The time will come when you will let him think he is the first to know, and the first to take the message to our mambo," she persists, from the door.

"Mai," you call.

"What is it, child?"

Thinking of it only at that moment, you rummage in your bag once more and hold out a packet of paracetamol. Your mother takes the pills and calls for water from her grandchildren.

"And this," you remember next, picking up and handing over the little package containing the blouse and skirt.

"Keep it and give it to the chairwoman," says Mai. "She will also wish to have her mouth opened."

It turns out that the chairwoman is your family's neighbour, who lives across the gully, Mrs. Samhungu. Your mother confirms that she was democratically voted in by all the members.

When you have eaten and taken Baba his breakfast, and indicated you must leave, Mai informs him she will ride with you as far as the shops. In the car, your mother gives you more instructions. You listen and agree with everything, meaning, if Tracey objects, to change later what she would like to have altered.

"Tisvikewo! We have come with someone we didn't know any-more," your mother calls out as you climb out of your vehicle at the Samhungus' homestead.

"Enter, enter, Mai Sigauke," Mai Samhungu calls from the dimness of her kitchen. "Did you sleep well? Yes, you must have. And those you are with, because, yes, the children told us someone had come whose presence you were enjoying."

"Aiwa, we woke up with everything well at our place," your mother assures the chairwoman, bending in at the door. You take places on the reed mat to the left. Mai Samhungu offers to have one of her grand-daughters make you tea, but you decline, saying you have just drunk some.

However, the chairwoman has not had breakfast yet, so that soon you have set before you a steaming teapot of thick, milky tea with lots of sugar, and a dish of sweet potatoes. Mai Samhungu takes one from her own portion and runs her thumb over it to slip the skin off.

"There is nothing better than tea with milk and sugar and a dish of sweet potatoes," she beams. "And these are the very best. We don't put any fertilizer on these ones like they do over there in the town, so they are very good. Eat, Tambudzai," she urges. "You will enjoy them."

"They are delicious, the most delicious," Mai agrees. "Like sugar and butter."

"And when you go, my daughter," Mai Samhungu enthuses at you, "I will give you a bag of my oranges. You saw the garden, didn't you, when you came down? That green one, with lemons and oranges, and bananas, whose leaves are as broad as a mat, like the one that you sit on."

You are confused. You cannot remember seeing an orchard.

"The chairwoman is good," your mother nods, swallowing some sweet potato with appetite. "We are blessed with her because she is good at everything. We have come here because she is our chairwoman, Tambudzai. But truly, you should see her oranges. As big as a baby's head. Even on those commercial farms, with all their everything, they cannot grow oranges like our chairwoman. Do not mind her, Mai Samhungu," she says, turning to the other woman. "It is no good asking her if she saw it, because when do these people from the city see anything?"

The chairwoman puts aside the remains of her breakfast, and asks what news there is from the capital.

"Ah, news from Harare, that is why we are here," announces Mai, and goes on boasting. "You see her looking just as she always looked when she was running here and there, but this child of mine has become a someone."

"You, Mai Sigauke," the chairwoman interrupts irritably. "How? When people come from Harare, do other people stop being someone?"

Your mother merely bides her time and attempts to laugh the matter off. Nevertheless, the chairwoman makes sure Mai understands the point just made by asserting in a loud voice that she, Mrs. Samhungu, is and has always been someone; which is how she has turned her abilities to good account and bit by bit introduced new ideas, new ways, new mixtures, and new crops to the pale village soil until it gave up withholding and her garden thrived, and on account of her prowess, which everyone hoped to share, she was voted chairwoman.

You sit quietly, nodding at intervals, while Mai Samhungu lists many good qualities about herself and her ventures.

Deftly, when the Women's Club chairwoman pauses for a moment to decide which of her excellent attributes to present next, your mother intervenes.

"This somebody here, my chairwoman," begins Mai, resting her hand on your thigh for an instant. "This somebody that nobody sees is here not because of herself but because of another person."

Mai Samhungu naturally inquires who that other somebody is, and why that other somebody sent somebody else to the village.

Your mother responds that you are talking about bosses and other high people so that the best thing is to listen first and then decide what to think or do; that somebody was there because of somebody's boss, and somebody's boss was expecting somebody shortly, so that the somebody was taking quite a risk to divert from the agreement that had been taken in Harare to come and pay respects to that somebody's elders, with no urging other than the wise advice from that somebody's mother.

Mai Samhungu immediately understands everything. Without too many words she and your mother agree they will discuss the matter after you leave.

The little Samhungus congregate to stare, after lugging the promised bag of oranges into the back of your twin cab. You fling sweets at them as you drive out of the chairwoman's homestead, your hand on your hooter.

"Ba-bah-ee," shout more village children from the roadside.

At the water pump, dogs slick their tongues under the spout and on the bricks beneath the dripping tap. You follow the trickle out of the tap without much interest. The thin stream of wastewater leads down past a copse of short musasa trees to Mai Samhungu's garden. The plants are healthy and fruitful. Wondering how you missed the garden as you drove in causes a surge of guilt that refuses to abate. Thinking better of dropping the last of the sweets through the window to the delight of the children who run after the car, you eat them yourself as you drive back to the city.

You turn into Jason Moyo Avenue shortly before lunchtime, mentally writing your report. The queen of Africa smiles a greeting. You smile back without seeing her, and raise a hand absentmindedly at Sister Mai Gamu. As you wait in the grimy entrance hall for the lift, you congratulate yourself on many successful indicators:

* Your mother, a key woman in the community, is persuaded to go ahead with the project.
* Your mother is the treasurer of the Women's Club, which had not been known at the time of conceptualization so that this is an additional positive outcome that was not expected.

* The money for the mambo has been deposited in reliable hands.
* The Women's Club chairwoman, another powerful woman in the community, showed herself honoured by your visit.

You step into the lift, composing your introduction. The doors do not close. You rattle them a couple of times to no effect. You hurry up the stairs.

"She's waiting for you," Pedzi informs you when you step into the foyer. "Come this side," the Ghetto Getaway project manager beckons from the reception desk. "She asked me to sit here, so I could tell you immediately."

"Twenty minutes. To put something down," you plead, reminding yourself she is a former receptionist.

Pedzi waggles black fingernails decorated with tiny golden blossoms. She tweaks a tissue from a box on the desk.

"The lift," you say. "It never works." You hold out your hand.

Pedzi walks over to you and dabs at your hairline.

"You'll do now," she says when she is done. "She said immediately."

You enter the narrow passage and walk down. Halfway to the boss's office you stop and check your armpits. As long as the sweat patch does not spread, there will not be a problem. You reach the boss's door, knock, and are told to enter.

Your attention gravitates to Tracey's desk the moment you peer into the room. Her swivel chair is empty. Apprehensively, you sidle in.

Your boss stands in front of the window that looks down into the sanitary lane, built for the wagons carrying slops in the early days of the city. She holds a copy of the *Clarion* crumpled in her hand. Spinning round as you approach, she is about to throw the newspaper into the wastepaper bin when she realizes you have caught sight of it. She holds the pages suspended over the receptacle for a second before she changes her mind.

"This," your boss says, "is not coming into this office anymore. In principle, it's a racist publication. You can't dignify it by calling it a newspaper."

"Well," you prevaricate blandly, "you can't produce an article if you haven't got anything to write. People with anything to write wouldn't be writing for the *Clarion*."

Your remark does not calm her. Her cheeks turn red.

"It's absolutely unbelievable," Tracey says, dropping the newspaper on the table, where it unfurls, showing a photograph of several top government officials in well-cut suits beside another photograph of some bedraggled, if triumphant-looking, men and women who are roasting meat on a fire in front of a farmhouse.

"It's like the . . . the . . . bloody war," your boss says, turning the paper over so that the sports page featuring two top cricketers is visible. "They're singing. They're triumphant? They've invaded lots more places. Because the Old Fossil ordered it. It's been part of his plan all along. People used to say that at the agency, but I stood up for this country. I couldn't believe it. Can you believe they were ordered to do it, to go out and destroy honest, hardworking people's homes?"

She stands with folded arms and clenched jaw, while you think about those times at the advertising agency and the happy hour with free drinks in the company pub on a Friday evening. You do not recall occasions such as your boss speaks of. In fact, you recall the opposite, your boss leading the ceremony to give your prize to another copywriter. You feel as though your womb is flowing from between your hip bones and gathering into a pool on the floor.

"Don't worry about them. Those newspapers just write what the politicians want. There's good news," you say quietly, out of breath.

"Every five years," Tracey mutters. "We'll be endangered every five years, people like me. Have our homes razed to the ground. You know, the Roman Empire used to do that with slaves and people. Just for votes."

"I can go and write the report," you say.

"No, go ahead," she says. "Green Jacaranda's going to be fine. Just as long as we can still get to the minister of tourism."

You speak for longer than you intended.

After the first few sentences your boss gives you her attention.

"Good," says Tracey, when you are done. "You say the Women's Club chairwoman? Make sure you put that into your report, Tambu. It's a formula for impact. Win-win. Everyone knows about those women's clubs. Our donors will just love it."

Your boss requests cost estimates for your family and other villagers who wish to join the project through building rondavels for the tourists on your homestead and providing entertainment, catering as well as other services. You promise your boss she will have the report earlier than she requests, complete with recommendations, perhaps as soon as the following evening.

CHAPTER 21

You work in your office until late that night. The report is ready the following lunchtime. Tracey reads it through, gives her approval, and calls you into the boardroom where you finalize the projections down to the last bale of straw required for thatching the VET rondavels.

Two weeks later you return from a second trip to the homestead. You glow with pleasure. The queen of Africa for once is too preoccupied with customers in her shop to notice you, and Sister Mai Gamu looks more ready to commit assault and battery than ever. You press the lift buttons once and the doors open.

As soon as you arrive, Pedzi is called to the boardroom for a meeting with you and Tracey.

"I assume it all went as planned?" the boss asks, rolling a biro between finger and thumb.

"It's happening," you assure your colleagues.

"Excellent. Take us through," nods Tracey.

"Handwritten," you point out, pulling your folder from your briefcase.

There are ten pages of cursive compiled over lunch, at the Half-Way House, close to Rusape.

"What I did is," you begin, folding back a printed sheet, "I took our list of requirements down with me, and I've inserted in the list here who is doing each of the tasks, and in the third column I have indicated whether any of the providers is a member of my family. I can break down all the participants," you assure your boss. "That way I can record every action in degrees of kinship."

The boss examines the file held out to her.

"It was three large rondavels and four single, construction and rent," she itemizes from memory.

"They know that," you concur. "We're encroaching on the forest a very little bit, but when that came up, I paid the mambo a small additional, well, let's call it a 'close the mouth.'"

You chuckle appreciatively at your little joke. Nobody else laughs. Tracey rolls her pen against her palm with all four fingers.

"Also the water taps," you continue, slightly flustered. "Fed from the mountain stream as discussed, at least one between every two structures. Ablutions, male and female, with shower. Some of the clients might prefer not to go to the river."

"Will they manage to schedule?" asks your boss.

"Everything," you say. "They trust me now. My mother and the chairwoman have agreed to everything."

"Are you sure?" your boss asks.

"I am sure," you say.

"Great." Tracey stands up. "Pedzi, stay here with Tamboo-dzai. Get a sense of what catering we'll need and start ordering."

"Delivery date?" inquires Pedzi.

"Tell them it's pending," Tracey instructs.

Your boss offers her hand. As you move forward, an ember of red glows through the window that looks toward the Thomas Hotel. A young woman holds earphones to her head. She looks up as though someone beckons her, then sways away.

"I think we'll put the mambo on a retainer," Tracey deliberates slowly. "That will be the best thing."

You assure Tracey she will have all the agreements she requires in the morning, drafted and ready to be signed by the beneficiaries in the village.

"With respect to the contracts," Tracey begins very carefully. "Do you think we could do it for less than we thought, than we talked of? An opening special. Let's say, Opening Eco Special?"

You regard your boss blankly.

"I know you've started negotiations," she continues. "This feedback came just after you left. From our partners."

A plea in her gaze turns over onto its back in submission. You have not seen this before. Wondering, you meet her look squarely. Your boldness lasts a few seconds. You have not done this before, either. You look away before your boss does.

"The Amsterdam partner says it's fine in principle, but they're asking for a discount. Due to the delay. Also, they mentioned the new location. They see it as a greater risk. That's their perception. I've assured them what we have now is perfectly safe. That's when they began talking about value addition."

"Value," you repeat uncertainly. "You were right, Tracey. The village is great value. Especially now Mai is fully behind everything. She wants to meet you."

"Africa," amplifies Tracey. "How're we going to add value to a bloody continent? Oh, why did they have to go onto those farms? But let's not go into it again. It's just that they had value on the farm. They expect the village to top it."

"I'm doing that," you point out, working hard to sound calm, although your armpits are sweating. "I'm working my butt off and doing a lot that is not at all easy to make our things happen because I believe in you. You have to believe I'm giving you value, Tracey."

For a moment your boss thinks about what you have just told her. Eventually she continues, "Well, I know. You engage with your village. That's your side of it. I talk to Amsterdam. That's what I do on this side. Well, for Amsterdam, obviously the farm is the farm. The village, well that means, for them, something different, maybe not as interesting."

"Different?" you repeat. "Interesting. That's what we're working to make it."

"From our point of view, yes," Tracey assures you. "Completely. We're talking, in principle, real eco values, authenticity, like millet and thatch, milk from the udder. We haven't done that before, that's unlocked value. They're talking the rest of it, you know, all those things they say go with villages on . . . uh, on our landmass, like dancing authentically . . . minimal, like agh, loincloths, naked . . . torsos."

As you begin to understand, the air in the room floats to the floor. Outside the birds in the air fly down to roost. The leaves stop taking in carbon dioxide and producing oxygen. Naked male chests are normal in traditional dance. Tracey can only be talking about the women.

"M-m, Tracey," protests Pedzi. "All of that kind of thing is too sensitive just now. Those people on the farms. We have to do something. Everyone knows. But I think it is better if we find a way. It is better if no one exposes anything."

Blushes flush through Tracey's face. She looks neither you nor Pedzi in the eye.

"Beads," she suggests. "People always have lots of them."

Pedzi giggles and turns to you whispering, "Ewo, queen of the village."

Tracey is vexed with the queen of the ghetto. "Don't you understand?" she snaps, "This is no laughing matter, either of you. Please get this into your heads. There is no choice. We have to."

You indicate you have the point in your head and you will find a way to spin the proposal. Forbidding yourself to hyperventilate, you struggle with the changes and to keep hold of your elation.

Ba'Tabitha is waiting to open the gate and lock it behind your vehicle when you arrive home several hours later.

Ma'Tabitha is waiting in the kitchen in front of the stove.

"Ma'Tabitha," you begin, for you did not give instructions for cooking and you wish to be alone.

"There are people waiting for you," says Ma'Tabitha.

She stops stirring a saucepan, looking wary.

"People? Who?" you demand.

"They wanted to wait when I told them you had travelled to Mutare. I told them you were not here, but they said they knew. So I said, well, let me put something on the stove because I saw they were not listening to me and going." Her voice falls so low you can hardly hear her. "I know that kind of woman. So I thought these are not people who come here for me to say no, so let me cook for everybody."

"Tambudzai," an energetic voice demands from the living room. "Come in here and greet us. Why are you asking Mama there in the kitchen? If you want to know then come here."

The elation you felt while you wrote the proposal that you have kept hold of for so long seeps out of you. An ant crawls over the back of your neck. Dozens more creep across your skull. You breathe deeply, resisting brushing any of the insects away. They have visited you so often that you know they are not there. Telling Ma'Tabitha everything is all right, you steel yourself and walk into the living room.

You embrace your aunt.

"Mauya, Mainini! You are welcome, Kiri," you recite automatically. "It is so good of you to come, welcome. How is Nyasha and my Cousin-Brother-in-Law, Mainini? Kiri, how is your aunt, Mai Manyanga?"

An insect runs down your arm to dissolve in the crook of your elbow. You lower yourself into your favourite leather chair.

"Ah, you Mainini Lucia and you Mainini Kiri, I never thought this would ever happen. I never thought I would enjoy you both sitting in my living room. Truly, I never thought," you hear yourself chattering. You feel you are doing well so you urge more cheerfulness into your voice. "But now here I am and you are here. Tell me, how is everybody?"

"Offer condolences," Mainini orders.

Christine hawks phlegm up the back of her nose. After that she remains impassive.

"Too bad, too bad," you murmur. "I am sorry. What happened, vasikana?"

"My aunt. Her story is always about blood," says Christine.

"It cannot be," you exclaim. You begin to want to hear the story in order to enjoy not having married those Manyangas. "The young men. Their father's sons. Going so far, with nothing holding them back, nothing."

Lucia and Christine glance at each other.

"Ah, those boys are a story, but not the one we came about," says Christine.

"But you said blood?" you repeat, conscious that you have conquered the ants. You are tense but there is no more crawling.

Lucia says, "Tell her so we can finish it."

Christine resumes and it turns out that the blood she speaks of, which had for so long been flowing when it should not have, is indeed

Widow Manyanga's although it is not from the widow's outside but from within her.

"Remember, I said it, Tambudzai," says Kiri. "Even the first time that blood wasn't just the blood from my aunt's veins. Those boys knew it was also from her womb when they started cutting each other up with bottles."

Ma'Tabitha comes in to inquire whether she might bring the food to the table.

You ask whether the pots can sit on the stove for another ten minutes.

Generously, not calculating how long the washing up will take her beyond her hours, she agrees the meal can wait.

"That's why they were always fighting," Christine goes on, hunching her shoulders high under her ears and ramming her hands into her armpits. "They knew that with that bleeding, there was nothing of life left for my aunt.

"Ignore even pretended to be helping his mother to get the house away from the others in order to keep everything for himself. Sometimes I ask if people forgot that many people went to war. Because if they have not forgotten, these people in this country, what is going on with them? Why are they so foolish? Do they think we went for this? Tss!" she goes on bitterly, sucking her teeth. "This is not what we went for and stayed for without food and blankets, even clothes, without our parents or relatives. Some of us without legs. Yet now we are helpless and there is nothing we can do to remove the things we see that we didn't go to fight for."

Mainini sucks her own teeth in loud sympathy and purses her lips.

"Those boys, they are worse," Christine nods, treating you as though you are a relative, for such things cannot be admitted to strangers who will go away and laugh.

"Even worse than my aunt's husband. And he was just a foolish old father," she goes on grimly.

Mai Tabitha sets a dish of water on the dining table and folds a towel beside it. You calculate the time your guests will stay. But it is as though Kiri is driving a thorn into a boil.

"Those Manyangas think they are town people," snorts Christine. "They're peasants, just like their parents. Just like all of us. They're just little people who had nothing but a kind old white, who gave Manyanga a job and made him a manager."

"You're telling it. Let it be said," agrees Mainini Lucia. "It's people like Tambudzai here who should hear it."

Christine elaborates with a dour sort of relish, the story she began on the night of Shine's woman and the trip to the Island. One day, under the influence of unbridled excitement and various imported beverages, with which he had that evening celebrated his increasing success, VaManyanga hurtled into a head-on collision with a combi at the corner of Jason Moyo Avenue and Second Street. Following the accident, many of the limbs that were originally cramped in the minibus in the order the packed seats imposed were seen by shocked pedestrians and by people reclining on the green, strewn far and wide over the road and pavement beside Africa Unity Square. There was blood everywhere. VaManyanga, nevertheless, stood up from the mangled mess to put one shaky leg in front of the other. All who saw him walk away recalled he looked the picture of health, in spite of his balance being a little wobbly. His biggest blow was what happened to his BMW and his temporary relegation to a lowly Datsun Sunny. People admired the stoicism with which Manyanga put up with this.

But then his body began to swell.

It was, observers said, the dishonestly obtained wealth delivering karma, damming his waters up just as he had dammed up company funds. If not, it was the wrath of an angry soul belonging to one of the omnibus passengers or to one of his muti victims. Everyone turned against Manyanga. His friends stopped congratulating him on a speedy recovery, the elegance of his home, and the size of his cars, seeing that his increased girth was the wages not of well-being but of sin. They all agreed that they had suspected all along that he was a contemptible deceiver.

VaManyanga himself was furious with his ancestors for not exacting vengeance from the combi driver. Had he not lost a BMW as a result of the reckless public transport speeding right in the city centre?

Was he, Manyanga, now to be attacked rather than pitied? This ruminating raised his blood pressure and increased his swelling further. Then, as though all that had happened was not enough, one evening as he lay in bed, the angry spirit entered the room that became Shine's. Sitting on his chest, it refused to listen to his wife's prayers, or to the choruses she sang, and scoffing at every single one of her husband's ancestors she petitioned, it attacked him pitilessly.

Gasping, sweating, and shivering all at once, both from the need for oxygen and from fear, which exacerbated the former need even more, VaManyanga's breathing difficulties grew critical, far beyond the ability of Mai Manyanga's fanning and other ministrations to assuage. Soon Mai Manyanga was at the telephone. It was working that evening. The ambulance was also available, having returned from the workshop earlier. It wailed up the Manyanga drive in no time. The emergency staff had an oxygen mask strapped over the managing director's mouth in a matter of moments. There was oxygen in the tank, but even this admirable professionalism did not dismay the vengeful spirit. It burrowed deeper into VaManyanga's lungs and kept on squeezing. When VaManyanga stopped gasping, the ambulance men declined to take the body and informed Mai Manyanga that the proper procedure was to pay up front since VaManyanga's medical aid had expired due to the lengthy duration of his treatment.

Mai Manyanga was not able to produce the money, for she was falling down in grief. Nor could she dial 999 for the police. Her sons, more sober then than they were to be subsequently, joined forces to sort out everything. This was the last time VaManyanga, whose lifestyle had always caused such a stir when portrayed on the leisure pages, was mentioned in the *Clarion*. It was also the last time his sons worked well together.

"This is how it started and went on to become something else," Christine concludes. "Everything was wrecked and fell apart. That Ignore had taken over the house, and so my aunt died a pauper. What good do we expect out of that Ignore kind of person? Those who do, like my aunt herself, weren't they just being foolish?"

"I am sorry," you say when she has finished, standing up to shake her hand, a gesture you should have offered when you first heard of Widow Manyanga's passing. Offering your condolences with sombre propriety, you pray your display of good manners will mollify your two aunts and speed up the unwanted visit.

"Tambudzai, are you sure? Do you know what you are playing with?" Mainini bristles.

You return to your seat etching a small smile onto your face, which you hope, but doubt, conveys understanding. Far from being discouraged by the story that has just been told, you are more indignant than ever that your maininis do not admire your initiative and resourcefulness. That, you reflect, is your people's problem: they have no ambition.

"What are you thinking?" demands Christine. "First it is our fathers, our uncles, and our brothers. Then it is our little sisters and our daughters. Tambudzai, you are making some people very angry with what you are planning. You want people to throw coins at your mother, your aunt Lucia's sister here, so she is just like my own womb sibling."

You give up paying attention and listen with only half an ear, as Lucia and her companion attempt to dissuade you from the Village Eco Transit enterprise. Everybody has heard about ex-combatants setting themselves up as custodians of the nation's development, in spite of displaying no understanding of business that is not related in one way or another to combat. Yes, it was their very ignorance concerning how to move the country forward that stopped the tours on Nils Stevenson's farm. If not for those very war veterans, you would be earning your living up in the northwestern gamelands. You would not be at the homestead at all. Later, when Christine is no longer mourning, you will divulge details about the VET. Even at that future date, however, just as you are keeping the case from your mind now, you will not mention the matter of the bare torsos and beadwork.

"Do not do it, Tambudzai," Mainini warns, furious with humiliation. "This new behaviour of yours is just as bad as everything else that we have seen from you. No, it is not even as bad. It is worse, isn't it? Surely you know what you are playing with. You are the one with a sister using only one leg. You know what can be done when people are roused to fury, you know it. It is no longer explosives in the ground as it was with Netsai. These days, people's arms have become the size of their sleeves for less than this thing you are doing."

"You are opening the door," nods Christine. "My uncle opened his door and untellable things came through it. Now look at all his people who remain. You cannot say this is what you want for people at your homestead."

"I have heard what you say," you reply formally. "I thank you for coming. I know I have you, my mothers, who went to war, to protect me. Please tell them there is nothing to worry about. Tell your colleagues I will give them something. The village wants this project," you go on. "Everyone there is happy something is coming that will give them benefit."

You pull several notes out of your purse. These you offer Christine respectfully, with both hands saying, "but first let me give you my chema."

Christine does not move to accept them.

You do not know what to do, so you bend lower. Christine remains immobile. You go down on your knees.

"Give it to me," says Mainini Lucia.

You walk over to your aunt.

"Here," Mainini says to Christine. "The child says here are her tears."

"Thank you," Christine says and receives the money.

"She didn't want to come," Mainini says, as relief sinks you deep into your seat again.

"I said what for?" concurs Christine, anger rising once more. "I said to Lucia, talking to you, Tambudzai, is wasting our time."

"Mainini," you interrupt. You speak quickly so that the idea you have just come upon holds clear in your thoughts. "Mainini Lucia, I know the ex-combatants are now on the farms. But I drove from home this morning and I did not see anybody. How did you hear it?"

"Aren't there people in the village?" Mainini says. "There are people. And there are children of people."

"Netsai," you say.

Neither Mainini nor Christine responds.

"Not Netsai," you say. "The girls. It must be Concept."

"You are beginning to see." Mainini smiles slightly for the first time that evening.

"Concept," you repeat, caught off guard by the idea of your young nieces being informers. "And Freedom."

"Ms. Sigauke, madam, I'm bringing the food now," Ma'Tabitha calls patiently from the kitchen.

When the cook has set down the spaghetti bolognese with a little salad, you usher your guests to the table. Ex-combatants do not generally engage in small talk. Kiri and Mainini grunt in reply to your efforts at conversation about their work at AK Security, all other subjects being too contentious. They twist a few strands of spaghetti around their forks for form's sake and depart while there is still much food on the table.

CHAPTER 22

The buildings in the village are ready, smelling of fresh thatch, cow dung floors, and new wood, all the beams treated with boric acid and not creosote, in line with your company's corporate identity. The visas are waiting at immigration. All your preparations have been excellent. The clients have flown to Amsterdam with KLM, then on to Harare with Kenya Airways. You stand in the arrivals hall at the airport. Here you are on the linoleum floor, proud of yourself. You are standing in the same spot your brother and father stood to welcome Babamukuru from England so many years ago, when you were told you could not travel to the airport and everyone agreed you must stay in the village. In a year or two, you believe, if you manage your Village Eco Transit well, you and not Tracey will check in and travel to meet clients in Europe.

This morning, you hold a sign on a metre-long staff. It sways in the air. You slip a hand higher to support it. You enjoy this. It is like the flag of your realm, which domain you see expanding magnificently. At the top of your staff, a short white banner ripples in the slight breeze, white because this is the cheapest. On the light background stands a green and purple jacaranda. Below the tree, printed in green capitals, the banner promises: "The Most Inspiring Eco Getaway in Africa."

It is three weeks after your discussion with Christine and Lucia. You returned to the homestead twice in each of those weeks, keeping busy and pushing people ahead of schedule in your determination not to consider what your maininis told you. On several occasions, the chairwoman of the Dance Committee asked you for money for costumes.

You kept a queenly silence. In the office, on the other hand, you assured Tracey all was arranged; the dancers would perform in the required—or rather in the requisite absence of—raiment. You told yourself you believe this and now, as you wait for the first batch of Green Jacaranda clients to take the Village Eco Transit, you do believe it. Your conviction has made you immensely confident. You are perfectly convinced you deserve to be held in high esteem. After all, in addition to performing the assignment excellently you have brought jobs, activity, and innovation to your village following decades of devastating peasanthood.

Pedzi is your assistant for the launch of the Village Eco Transit. Pale tourists, tired but excited, emerge like apparitions from the heat haze that shimmers over the tarmac. Soon you and the queen of the ghetto are counting heads and checking lists. You conduct yourself as though you are holding court, taking a census on your people.

"We are back again," booms ruddy, portly Herr Bachmann. He enjoyed the original Green Jacaranda safari on Nils Stevenson's farm and, when she launched it, Pedzi's ghetto getaway so much that he visited both three years running.

"No, no!" Herr Bachmann waves a hand at a hovering porter.

"There is no need. This I can do for myself," he tells the disappointed man who wished to earn a euro or a dollar. Herr Bachmann smiles at him and the porter wafts away.

Now Herr Bachmann turns to Pedzi with his arms thrown wide.

"Pedzi," he roars jovially. Pedzi beams. Herr Bachmann wraps her in a hug.

"You are beautiful. It is always good to see you. Congratulations to you and Tambudzai!" Your client flings an arm round your shoulders and squeezes. "Yes, you always manage to find a new programme. This is what I said to Claudia."

With this Mr. Bachmann moves closer to the woman beside him.

"I said, we have already had one holiday in Zimbabwe this year, but Claudia, we have to see this!" Herr Bachmann disengages his arm from you and flings it round his wife.

"Yes," agrees Frau Bachmann. "We are so excited. Tambudzai, in the brochure it says this new programme is the Village . . .Village . . . I cannot remember. Village something."

"Village Eco Transit," says Herr Bachmann, rolling his *r*.

"Yes, Village Eco Transit," Frau Bachmann agrees again. "Tambudzai, it says that is where you live . . . oh not now, but it says that is where you were born and your family lives there."

Pedzi giggles.

"It is where I come from. I live in Avondale," you explain with a smile.

"Ah, yes, Avondale," Herr Bachmann agrees warmly. "That is where they have that wonderful restaurant, with those cakes. *Lekker*! I heard some people say that word here. I know you in Zimbabwe say also *lekker*."

You lead the tourists through the dazzle of August heat. Their faces open like flowers in the sunlight.

"And the ice cream is *lekker* too," nods Frau Bachmann. "The French . . . no, it is the Mediterranean Bakery."

"Yes, we must go there when we come back from Tambudzai's village," her husband promises her.

So saying, the stout visitor turns to welcome another couple. The two newcomers walk behind the Bachmanns, adjusting their sunglasses.

"We have brought some friends for you. Ingrid and Karl. We told them about the Ghetto Getaway. And those caterpillars, what are they, the ones that are eaten?"

"Oorgh," shivers Ingrid.

"Mopani worm," Frau Bachmann says.

"Yes, ma-dora," grins her husband, pleased to remember the local word. "And there is the other word with that sound. What is it, Pedzi?"

"Macimbi," Pedzi obliges.

She smiles at the soft *d* that Herr Bachmann's tongue struggles to but cannot implode when he says *madora*.

"Oh, I could not eat them," says Claudia. "They smelled like fish but did not look like it. I did not know what it was."

You usher the group to the waiting coach.

The bus fills up quickly with guests from half a dozen operators. For

Tracey has shrewdly offered a pickup service to a number of companies, so that you can get to know their clients and eventually poach them. Meticulously you tick each Green Jacaranda guest's name off your clipboard.

Pedzi follows Herr Bachmann's group into the bus, blocking the aisle for the other tourists even though she is in tour uniform and should be behaving more graciously.

"Vee gait us, dear?" she says.

"Wie," Herr Bachmann corrects. "Wie geht es dir."

Pedzi laughs, "Fee get us, deer?

"Excuse me, Pedzi," you call with great reluctance. You do not want any animosity in the last moments before what is essentially your coronation.

Pedzi stares at you, a spark of malice flickering. You bow your head contritely. Pedzi changes her mind about a confrontation. On the pretext of storing the Bachmanns' hand luggage in the overhead compartments, she squeezes herself flat against the seats, so that the queue flows forward. You smile, keeping your head down to make sure your colleague does not think you are triumphant. It is quite the opposite. Now that you have proved to everybody you are the person you said you were, you consider ways of working better with the former receptionist who has become a project manager, when you return from the village.

Once the register is complete, you issue the official greeting.

"Welcome to all our guests!" You love talking to your clients. Your voice glows through the intercom.

"It is my pleasure to introduce you to this fabulously beautiful country, our own Zimbabwe, a world of wonders for you to sample and of course enjoy. For you who are returning, hello again. Welcome! Mauya! Sibuyile!" you repeat in three official languages, for Tracey is concerned not to marginalize anyone and emphasizes that the Green Jacaranda greeting must align with the national language policy.

"Those of you who are with Green Jacaranda are travelling now to the most luxurious Thomas Hotel. It is round the corner from our offices so there is no danger you will get lost. I will point our offices out to you when we arrive at the Thomas Hotel. You will stay there for two nights, counting tonight. Please all stay together and meet me in the lobby for check-in immediately after we arrive, even if you are familiar with Harare and the Thomas. Is that clear?"

"Yes, of course," the excited new arrivals call, but you repeat the information anyway with great precision, and enjoy that rendition as much as the first.

"All guests of other tour operators, please meet your tour leaders at the same time in the same place," you go on. "Each tour operator will have staff available bearing signs with the operator's name and their company logo."

When you complete these instructions, you ask whether anyone has any questions. You wait for uncertain hands to rise. They do not. You signal the driver.

It is important not to overload the clients with information now when they are tired after their long flights. So you and Pedzi walk up and down the aisle, smiling and asking if everyone is all right, murmuring greetings in Shona, "Mauya, makadini? Mafamba zvakanaka here?" to those who have visited before and only commenting on a particular landmark if a new client is especially interested.

You are starting the new location with a few tourists, the Bachmanns and Ingrid and Karl, plus a pair of Danes, some Swedish women, and one Belgian. On the next day's plan is a day trip to Chinhoyi Caves to acclimate the party, after which, the following morning, everyone heads off for your village in the Eastern Highlands. The new faces turn out to belong to pleasant people, and good Mr. Bachmann always makes a situation jolly.

The trip to Chinhoyi Caves works out well. All through that day there are many kind and interested questions about your home so that you are further reassured that everything will run marvellously.

The morning of your departure for the village, everyone's spirits are bubbling. Yours, of course, are frothing. You showed up early, leaving plenty of time to gorge on the Thomas breakfast of French croissants, Danish pastries, Portuguese tarts, cold meats, and full English, with eggs done in three ways, sprinkled with parsley, and kidneys, kippers, and liver, beside bangers, bacon, and bubble and squeak. Satisfied and expectant, you are enormously proud of everything: the Thomas Hotel, Green Jacaranda Safaris, Tracey Stevenson, yourself, your village, and even Pedzi.

A few minutes later you are seeing Green Jacaranda guests out of the dining room and encouraging them not to put pressure on themselves but to remember nevertheless that the coach is leaving in forty-five minutes. A puzzled Belgian belonging to another tour approaches, for his operator has not yet arrived.

"Can you tell me where is the other breakfast?" he inquires.

"Have you had a problem?" you respond, eager to help.

The man shakes his head. "There is no table," he says, "where I can find the other food."

"The other food?" you repeat.

The man stares at you blankly.

"This is the food," you say. You wave at the buffet. "If you require anything else, you can ask the waiter."

"How can I ask the waiter," the man says, "if I do not know what I shall ask for? If I see it then I can ask him, and then I can taste it and see if the taste is good. This breakfast I can have anywhere."

The visitor glances at the buffet tables like a child whose balloon has popped. Some equally disappointed Swedish women nudge each other and nod.

"Even last night, it was this kind of meal," agrees a Swede. "Have you seen the food that is local?"

You gladly explain that in your country everyone takes pride in being as good as anywhere at anything.

"Well, I think some like it like that," the Swedish woman shrugs. After this gesture she concludes, "So I think this is why there is this option for everyone to go to the village."

Concluding their remarks about the breakfast, the tourists introduce themselves to each other and soon discover that the Swedes can speak Dutch, which the Belgian also speaks. They launch into a rapid conversation and you can no longer understand them.

Half an hour later you all congregate under the flame trees whose brilliant canopy spreads scarlet blossoms over the car park.

"Po-po-o-oh," The driver in the Coaster blares his first warning.

Herr Bachmann takes a last photograph of the scarlet blossoms. Putting his camera carefully away in the bag around his neck, he removes his luggage from the porter's hand and stows it neatly in the hold. Then he climbs into the bus, calling loudly, "Is everyone sure everyone has his . . . or her . . . luggage?"

"Yes," everyone sings.

You press the last tick onto the paper, put away your clipboard, and swing the minicoach door closed. You signal the driver. The coach eases out from under the trees and into Robert Mugabe Avenue.

You make good progress, travelling in the morning. The government is aware of your country as a tourist destination. There are more roadblocks because of disturbances on the farms and angry farmers, but the police officers are courteous, and pleased that you have all your papers.

The homestead is already packed by the time you arrive, with neighbours and relatives, including many distant ones.

Babamukuru and Maiguru are there from the mission, having been driven over by Chido, who managed to take a vacation—to coincide with the opening—from the university in the United States where he lectures in tropical agriculture, and he brought a folding, battery-powered wheelchair for Babamukuru. Babamukuru sits in it now, proudly lengthening his spine and broadening his shoulders and finding every occasion to mention the wheelchair from America in conversation with village elders.

Mainini Lucia and Kiri teamed up with Nyasha to drive down in Gloria, although Cousin-Brother-in-Law decided to remain at home with the children. Now that the event is taking place, everyone is for it, and is either wishing everyone the best or waiting to see what happens.

Concept and Freedom look on proudly at their mother, the war veteran who is your sister Netsai, who has travelled back from the cooperative she works on further to the north. Your sister is hopping around, going *hopla hopla* on her one leg, saying she doesn't care who hears her and talking loudly about the fight she is engaged in with ruling party officials to obtain a place on the party list that will result in a dark-brown leg being imported for her from Mozambique.

"As if I never went to war," your sister proclaims indignantly, to whoever listens. "Did I pull this leg off myself? This leg was blasted off because I was fighting. I was fighting for what is mine. My leg is mine, and now I want to have it."

Babamunini Thomas has come down with his family from the northeast. Distant cousin Takesure has materialized from a nearby village with a new family. A good many of the relatives who gathered those decades ago to welcome Babamukuru have gathered again, to see what his daughter, the daughter of the village who has been away so long, has brought, and to see the old man himself, remembering what a fine figure he cut before his accident.

In addition to the multitudes of relatives, all the villagers who helped with clearing veld or cutting logs or mixing mud or in any other manner at all are gathered for the welcoming feast. Those who have no claim to the homestead find vantage points on rocks and branches on the mountainside. And at magrosa Mambo Mutasa positions his bagpipers on the road in their kilts, so that you are forced to stop and be serenaded.

Tracey, who came down with Pedzi the day before in her red Pajero, welcomes the guests again. There has been a compromise to enable the project to proceed, so that two of the envisioned new buildings have been built across the gully, at Mai Samhungu's.

Everything is meticulously organized. Each round house has a number daubed on the wall in red clay above colourful Ndebele patterns. Soon the check-in is complete. Freedom, giggling, heads a band of young women who show the new arrivals to their quarters, while a group of young men transports the luggage. Concept, however, stays close to her mother.

"Do you know," Tracey says to the Bachmanns as the guests are escorted back to reed mats and low wooden stools under the mango tree to be offered sweet fizzy drinks, rich tii hobvu, a gourd of mahewu, or a glass of chilled sparkling wine.

"That woman over there," Tracey gestures up at the old house.

Your mother stands on its steps, in last-minute conversation with Mai Samhungu. "That's Tambudzai's mother on the steps," Tracey continues. "Her family has been wonderful. Even her poor uncle, the man over there with the small woman beside him. He's paralysed, injured at Independence, but people still respect him. I'm sure Tambudzai will introduce you. I'll make sure you meet her mother."

The Bachmanns smile at your mother.

"Quarter of an hour? Then we have to begin," Tracey urges you anxiously under her breath.

You assure her the grand opening is running precisely to schedule. You walk over to the old house.

Your mother and Mai Samhungu have wandered inside. You call the two women. You have decided to explain the development concerning the costumes to them and let them address the rest of the group. However, they do not hear, and when you put your head round the door to signal, everyone waves and you are obliged to enter.

Java print skirts and wraps, leg rattles, as well as hand rattles and drums are strewn about the front room. Aunts and cousins, sister-cousins-in-law and age-mates you ran to primary school with so many years ago are tying straps, adjusting headpieces, and arranging Zambia cloths. They practise songs softly under their breath as they walk in and out from the side and back rooms for more intimate changes.

You put one hand in your pocket. In the other, you carry a bag of five-dollar notes, direct from the cashier at the bank, to slip from hand to hand. You open your mouth.

It seems to you that with every movement, the women are dressing more slowly in protest. You cannot look at anyone anymore. You close your mouth.

There is a suitcase on the table. It contains extra lengths of beads and chains made from monkey bread and jacaranda fruit. They are large shells. Artfully placed they conceal much.

Far from comforting you, the suitcase and money make you feel bilious. You move away. You will leave everything to fate or chance, whatever it is when you do not have a hand in it. If Tracey wants the women bare-breasted she will have to come up here herself.

You stand at the front door. You gaze down the steps. Down, down, down, and further down. The descent to the bottom is endless. You see yourself stepping down each stair, reaching the ragged patch of grass at the bottom, descending further and further, up to your shins, up to your chest until the earth closes over you.

When you have made it to the bottom of the steps, however, you turn around, clap your hands, and shout, "Vanamai, Vasikana, excuse me!"

Women hurry out of the rooms tying on belts and headbands and leg-rattle ropes, rubbing blush obtained from red rocks into cheeks, and painting white triangles on their faces and limbs.

"Are you sure we're going to get paid?" the secretary of the Women's Club asks anxiously.

Using your head and shoulders, you give a vigorous nod.

"We trust you, Tambudzai. Don't let us down. Don't you too go and start lying."

You push your hand into the bag you hold and bring out a fistful of the five-dollar notes.

There is a cheer. "Giving birth is a good thing," the older women chant.

"Tambudzai would not lie," Nyari calls. She was your classmate at the village school from first grade. She is proud of being associated with you.

"Is everybody ready?" you say. "Is everything moving? Are we finished?"

Having seen the money, being reassured, now nobody pays any attention.

Your tongue dries out, but you have been made the queen of the village. You open your mouth once again and deliver the message concerning the women's torsos. There is an angry outcry. Your mother tells everyone to be quiet and ushers the dancers back up the stairs. You depart quickly.

The marimba youth are setting up under the trees. A male voice choir is harmonizing like a group of large cats purring.

The choir finishes, to roars and applause.

Ta-tah-tata, Ta-tah-tata the marimbas begin.

Out of the house and down the steps comes your mother. She is leading two dozen women. They congregate in a semicircle in front of the house. They swing their arms and pad their bare feet in the sand in time to the music. Young and old, all your sisters and aunts and cousins wear lengths of Zambia cloth beneath colourful blouses.

Herr Bachmann undoes the zip on his camera bag. Mai pauses and throws a beady-eyed glance at the apparatus.

"I will take one of your mother," Herr Bachmann booms in his cheerful voice. "I will call it "The Mother of the Journey." Everybody will love to see it."

Frau Bachmann taps her husband's shoulder to caution him from using too much film.

Your mother stamps her foot. Dust puffs up. She raises and lowers her elbows with the rhythm of the marimba. This way and that way Mai turns her head, first to one and then to the other shoulder.

Tracey nods to the music, looking relieved that the women have rebelled.

You do not enjoy anything, although dancing had always been your forte from the time you were little. Shame fills you. You want only to close your eyes and not open them until it is payday. It does not matter now whether the women rebel or not. Your treachery has been committed.

The singing grows louder. Marimba batons cut high into the air as players outdo themselves. Hands above drums fly faster. The young singing women open their mouths wider and wider.

The dancing women move forward. Your mother raises her hands to her chest. Her fingers hover before her heart. Then with one movement she shrugs off her blouse and dashes it into the dust. This is the sign. All the women undress.

A horrified gasp goes up from the relatives. Revellers who are not kin press forward ten deep to marvel at the naked mothers and sisters.

Pa-pa! That is the Belgian applauding doubtfully. The Swedish guest pats her fingers together.

The song ends. The village women huddle close together, instinctively hunching their shoulders over so that their neck beads and shells cover their chests.

"Thank you!" You step toward the dancers. "Thank you. Let us thank them. By giving them a big pam-pam. A good clap," you urge everyone. "Let's thank them for that one. So that they can go and have a rest."

You spread your fingers to slap your palms together in front of your nose, in the flamboyant way of a master of ceremonies.

You clap once. The women do not move. The crowd holds its breath and watches in silence.

You clap again.

The only sound is of your skin meeting skin. Lucia starts forward looking furious.

"U-u-u! U-u-u!" The sound swells. Your cousin's tongue pokes in and out of her mouth as she ululates, breaking the deepening tension.

Tata-tah-tah-ta, Tata-tah-tah-ta the marimbas begin again. A girl turns round, stamps her feet, and shakes her buttocks at the visitors. Herr Bachmann extracts his hand from his pocket and throws a ten-deutschmark note into the clearing. Guests are pleased to have something to do. Various bills of small exchangeable denominations flutter onto the sand. Mrs. Samhungu springs at a note and deftly banks it inside her wrap.

Tata-tah-tah-ta the marimbas continue.

"U-u-u! U-u-u!" your mother and the women swell Nyasha's ululation.

White dust spurts from under your mother's soles. She plants her feet in the ground like tree trunks. With each of her steps it is as though a living tree is dislodged from the earth.

So your mother dances. The tips of her toes tap down, causing more clouds of dust, and she slides her back foot forward to plant it again.

Herr Bachmann snaps several photographs and then pushes you forward.

"With your mother. With the woman who is your mother," Herr Bachmann cries, focusing the camera.

"Mother," your client continues to call. "Madam Mother, move here, please. This one, please, with your daughter."

Frau Bachmann places a friendly hand on your shoulder and nudges you forward.

Your mother does not miss a beat of planting her feet and wrenching them from the earth as she gathers her strength in her calves and thighs, measures distance with burning eyes, and approaches.

Taken by surprise, Herr Bachmann continues smiling and adjusting his focus for several seconds. Tracey blanches.

"Do this for me, Tambu, please," your boss whispers.

You take your position for the photograph. Your mother leaps at the same moment.

"I am your picture, me!" your mother shrieks, rolling the camera cord over astonished Herr Bachmann's head.

"Me, that's what you think I am. Not a someone, but that I am whatever you want to put in your picture."

By the time those who want to restrain Mai start to do so, it is too late. Those who prefer to let things be are shaking their heads and at the same time laughing. Christine, Lucia, and Netsai fold their arms and consult each other.

"Well, here I am!" exclaims Mai, "I am your picture. Just see what your picture is doing."

Round and round her head by its cord Mai twirls the equipment. With a grunt she opens her hand. Away the camera sails, with everyone looking up, following the arc and then gazing down, to see where it lands.

Herr Bachmann has too much decency to grapple a fierce and half-naked woman.

"Eh! What has my camera got to do with you?" he cries sadly.

"She's got to go," Tracey breathes into your ear. "I'm sorry, Tambu, she just has to."

Your mother gazes in exultation at the camera dangling from the mango tree.

Propelled by satisfaction at the damage she has caused, Mai jumps toward Herr and Frau Bachmann.

"How dare you," she screams, although the visitors cannot understand her. "You want to laugh at my child when you are back home because her mother is a naked old woman!"

"She's got to go," your boss repeats.

Babamukuru starts out of his wheelchair and stands teetering, holding on to the armrest. Maiguru bursts into tears, for Babamukuru has not stood up since Independence. Your father, who has not taken an interest in anything, remains seated on the stairs to Babamukuru's new house.

"Don't put her together with me. No, don't put her together with her mother," Mai wails and falls onto the sand, biting grit.

You think you are obeying your boss's instructions. You approach your mother to lead her away. When you reach her, grief wells past the banks of a pale purple pool and rushes into your throat. You will it back. It wraps around your heart and constricts to stop it. Your heart refuses to be stopped. It grows and grows. You have no strength to lift her, because your tears are falling onto your mother's skin. Your heart bursts. You burst with it and fall down next to your mother.

Herr Bachmann stares at the mango tree. The camera swings backward and forward. It drops from the slender branch where it is caught, to lodge in a fork between two others.

You land, first on your knees, then in a heap, across Mai's naked torso. You caress her cheek with the back of your hand and whisper to her that everything is all wrong but it shall soon be right, as though you are speaking to a baby. Mai does not respond. It does not matter now. You are not expecting an answer. She is the child and you are the mother.

Herr Bachmann discovers a long stick. A small boy is hoisted onto distant cousin Takesure's shoulders. With one or two pokes, the camera is retrieved and returned to its owner.

You try to gather Mai up. She resists. Mai Samhungu calls to her to get up and leave the yard. When she does not, the chairwoman orders a young woman to pick up Mai's blouse and cover Mai's shoulders with it.

"Now you have found a cloth for me, now, Tambudzai," Mai wails, when she is wrapped in the blouse. She falls back in another faint.

Tracey comes over. Anger, disappointment, and embarrassment vibrate from each of her pores.

"Sort this out, Tambudzai."

You stand up and dust off your knees.

The Women's Club, having donned green and purple blouses and wraps, swarm around your mother, pushing you out of their circle. The vice treasurer and the secretary come and help Mai to her feet. You stop hurrying over to the Bachmanns and hasten back. You stretch out your hand. You mother recoils.

"Leave her," the secretary tells you. "Wait until the shock is over and she is better."

You watch as the two women lead Mai to the old house. Mai disappears through the door. You turn back to your tasks.

You apologize to Herr Bachmann on Mai's behalf, and your own, for not warning him about the photograph. You smile as you speak, and assure the Bachmanns, who are feeling very bad, that your mother is prone to hysteria and will recover soon.

"I am sorry too. I thought it would be nice. Vhy did I not think of it? Vhy did I not think of it?" Herr Bachmann says.

Christine, Lucia, and Netsai, with the help of several of the more sober men, usher the villagers away. The Women's Club joins in. You drift on the edges of groups, keeping clear of strangers and nodding at family members, not daring to speak. Once the yard is fairly empty, Lucia has a word with Tracey. When they finish nodding their heads and shaking them and stroking their chins, they shake hands. This Lucia and Tracey follow with a joint announcement that festivities at the homestead are over for the day. However, those tourists who wish to will be transported to magrosa. Mai Samhungu has succeeded in a very short time in organizing for a ghetto blaster to be set up at the shops to play Chiwoniso Maraire and Oliver Mutukudzi. An impromptu disco is to take place while dinner is prepared.

As all these arrangements are made, Chido whisks Babamukuru away to Mutare General Hospital to determine whether the progress in the head of the Sigauke clan's legs is permanent.

Pedzi is detailed to accompany the tourists, and Tracey oversees dinner herself. You remove yourself from Green Jacaranda activities and sit in the kitchen. After two or three hours, the tourists return and are fed.

Buckets of water are carried into the newly constructed ablution shacks. Gas lamps are lit in the round houses and insecticide is sprayed. Pedzi reads the next day's options out to the visitors from a printed sheet. The guests sit around a fire in the yard and contemplate the following day's hard labour, or fun, depending on their disposition, in the fields and at the river. Lucia, Kiri, and Nyasha make themselves comfortable with the guests. Later, they send Concept to fetch you. No one refers to the matter of the camera, but by the end of the evening two days' quota of the wine stored in the provisions trailer has been consumed.

In the morning there is a meeting with Tracey in the Green Jacaranda minicoach. You promised yourself to look her in the eye, but she stares straight ahead during the entire conversation, so that you see a vein in the side of her neck pulsing.

Tracey asks many questions concerning Mai's reliability, her suitability to be the Village Eco Transit's rural hostess, and why you did not warn the organization about your mother's instability.

You listen and do not answer. When your boss is finished, you go into the old house, past the side room where your nieces sleep, and into the back. You pack your small bag.

Nyasha offers to drive you, but you prefer to walk to the bus stop at magrosa. You walk over the gully and past Mai Samhungu's residence, away from the village. Your aunts and sister watch you go in silence.

As you walk past the fields and the water pump, and Mai Samhungu's orchard, a group of young men who attended the previous day's gathering accost you. They want to find out Mai's reason for throwing away Herr Bachmann's camera, why she wanted to spoil the project, and whether you are leaving in order to make sure that the programme comes to disaster, depriving them of employment. They threaten to beat you up but they accept some five-dollar notes and allow themselves to be talked out of it. Your umbilical cord is buried on the homestead; in the empty space that widens within at every step, you feel it tugging.

Eight hours after you leave the homestead you arrive in the city. At the cottage you tell Ma'Tabitha you are leaving.

You write a letter of resignation. You deliver it in person. Tracey thanks you for your thoughtfulness and graciously waives notice. She offers you an arrangement on the cottage. You decline and find small lodgings in the Avenues.

When your shame has healed sufficiently for you to speak to people without weeping, you take a combi to Greendale to see Nyasha. Your cousin listens for the best part of an hour and then invites you to join her in her nongovernmental organization. But, she says, always truthful, she still has not found anyone to sponsor her young women's programme.

Mainini Lucia's security company, on the other hand, is doing very well, as there is more war in your country's way of peace than any of you had expected. Nyasha asks whether she should convey to Mainini Lucia that there might be somebody somewhere who is now considering joining AK Security. Humbled and expecting nothing because you know everyone has seen you at your worst, you give your cousin your consent. When you finally visit Aunt Lucia in Kuwadzana you are surprised but at the same time hopeful, since your aunt has become rather wealthy. At work she is as tough as ever. She gives you little tasks. To deliver a package or a letter, to fetch forms from the tax office—such things. Over the course of several months, she delivers several lectures when she joins you in the premises' kitchen or on occasions when she gives you a ride home in her car, concerning the unhu, the quality of being human, expected of a Zimbabwean woman and a Sigauke who has many relatives who either served or fell in the war. Soon you can do nothing but keep your head low as you listen to her and watch your tears drip onto your thumbs. After many of these sessions, Mainini relents. From being a messenger, you are promoted to office orderly. Your aunt makes you sweep the floor and brew tea for everyone, including the typists in her office and the janitors. You carry their cups to them and fetch them and do the dishes. Within two years, however, you are interviewed and selected from a strong field, on merit, your aunt says, to become assistant general manager.

Christine is well employed at AK Security. She is doing business studies and also has her eye on a managerial position. She says she does not mind being passed over for promotion this time round, since there will be other opportunities; and, she says, your education is not only in your head anymore: like hers, now your knowledge is now also in your body, every bit of it, including your heart. You frequently offer to help her with her studies. This is a small first step toward maintaining your knowledge in the location of which Christine spoke.

ACKNOWLEDGEMENTS

I am immensely thankful to Julia Mundawarara, who read an early manuscript and encouraged me to persevere. My heartfelt thanks go to Spiwe N Harper and David Mungoshi for reading early chapters and giving me invaluable advice. I would not have completed this work without unwavering support from Madeleine Thien and Reginald Gibbons, to whom I am truly beholden. I am deeply grateful to Ellah Wakatama Allfrey, whose interest in the work, followed by skilful editing, led to this volume being published. Many thanks also to Fiona McCrae and all the staff at Graywolf who believed in the story told here. I am not sure what my family went through while I wrote this novel, and they have graciously not told me. I am indebted to my husband, Olaf, and my children, Tonderai, Chadamoyo, and Masimba, for ignoring some things and supporting me in others. Particular thanks are due to Tonderai for being my first reader and providing insightful comments, to Chadamoyo for an ever-attentive ear, and to Masimba for patiently scanning hundreds of pages.

Finally, I am indebted to Teju Cole and his 2015 essay "Unmournable Bodies," which put many matters into perspective for me and inspired this novel's title.

Tsitsi Dangarembga is the author of two previous novels, including *Nervous Conditions*, winner of the Commonwealth Writers' Prize. She is also a filmmaker, playwright, and director of the Institute of Creative Arts for Progress in Africa Trust. She lives in Harare, Zimbabwe.

The text of *This Mournable Body* is set in Adobe Garamond Pro. Book design by Rachel Holscher. Composition by Bookmobile Design & Digital Publisher Services, Minneapolis, Minnesota. Manufactured by Versa Press on acid-free, 30 percent post-consumer wastepaper.